The Obsidian Pebble

Book 1 of the Artefact Series

Rhys A. Jones

SPENCER HILL PRESS

Spencer Hill Press

Please visit our website at www.spencerhillpress.com

First Edition: October 2013.
Rhys A. Jones
The Obsidian Pebble : a novel / by Rhys A. Jones – 1st ed.
p. cm.

Summary:
A young boy discovers a secret about the house he and his mother inherited from his father, and must work against a ruthless businessman to protect it.

The author acknowledges the copyrighted or trademarked status and trademark owners of the following wordmarks mentioned in this fiction: Ask, Bakelite, Bing, Coke, Costa, eBay, Google, iPod, Jaguar, Klingon, National Geographic, Post-it, Rolls Royce, Scrabble, Skype, Spider-man, Taser, Toy Story, Ugg boots, Xbox, Yahoo!

Cover design by Lisa Amowitz
Edited by Vikki Ciaffone
Interior layout by Marie Romero

ISBN   978-1-937053-74-1 (paperback)
ISBN 978-1-937053-75-8 (e-book)

Printed in the United States of America

To Rhys Albert,
who taught me how to see the funny side of life.

Obsidian Pebble Lexicon

Maths — math

Phial — vial

Pants — trousers/underwear, or a derogatory term: not good, rubbish, bad.

Bed and Breakfast — Sleeping accommodations for a night and a meal in the morning, provided in guest houses and small hotels, or an establishment that provides these facilities.

Multi-storey car park — a parking garage on several levels.

Hoovering — vacuuming

Artefacts — an object made by a human being, typically one of cultural or historical interest. Also spelled artifact

Chemist shops — drug stores.

Paper round — the route taken when delivering newspapers. The job of delivering newspapers.

Jewellery — jewelery

Pelmet — A narrow border of cloth or wood, fitted across the top of a door or window to conceal the curtain fittings · *British informal* a very short skirt.

To Twig — to understand or notice or figure out.

In two minds — to have doubts

Goalposts — the posts of a goal.

999 — UK version of 911

Invigilating —to monitor examination candidates.

A doddle — something easily accomplished.

Juddering — to shake rapidly or spasmodically; vibrate conspicuously

Blancmange — a usually sweetened and flavored dessert made from gelatinous or starchy ingredients and milk.

Nisi credideritis, non intelligetis.
You will not understand unless you will have first believed.
— St Augustine

All the best.

Rhys. A. Jones.

Chapter 1

The Halloween Feast

Oz Chambers sat in his bedroom, desperately trying to concentrate on his algebra homework and ignore the tempting bottle of blood on his desk. He dragged his eyes away from the crimson phial and struggled with two maths questions, before trying to get to grips with the essay on "Sir Gawain and the Green Knight" he'd been dabbling with all week. He liked English, and especially reading, but that didn't make the essay any easier.

Oz sighed heavily. It was no good. Today was proving to be a particularly hopeless homework day because he just couldn't settle. He was simply too excited by the prospect of what was in store that evening.

So instead of writing about chivalry and other knightly stuff, he found himself wondering what it would have been like to go to Cornwall with Ruff, or to Centre Parks with Ellie. Maybe, unlike him, they'd had a rip-roaring half term full of thrills and spills.

Yeah, right.

Oz smiled. He knew exactly what they'd say if he confessed to feeling hard done by and could just imagine their scornful expressions.

Ellie Messenger was Oz's oldest friend. But unlike Oz, who was an only child, she was always complaining that she never had any time to herself, being the middle one of five. Ruff, too, had an older brother called Gareth (Gassy Gazzer) who was always hogging the Xbox, much to Ruff's disgust. Oz knew that, given the choice, Ruff and Ellie would much rather have spent the half term holidays at Penwurt with him. They'd think him completely mad to want to be anywhere else. Not that it mattered anymore, because today was Saturday and they were both back from their family breaks and due over at Oz's in just a few hours' time. Even better, the three of them were going to be spending the whole night together on this, the last Saturday of half term.

But today was not just the last weekend of the holidays, it was also the thirty-first of October and he, Ellie and Ruff had big plans. Just thinking about it sent a ripple of eager anticipation coursing through his veins. After all, he did happen to live in the oldest house in Seabourne and rumour had it that it was well and truly haunted. And, in a moment of daredevil defiance after watching a very bad episode of *Voodoo Mansions* on TV, they'd challenged themselves to spend Halloween night sleeping in the spookiest part of Oz's old house.

He got up, opened a window and inhaled a lungful of the damp autumn air. Instantly, another goose-pimply tingle flowed over him and he smiled as he recalled the pact the three of them had made together. Because on a night like Halloween, in a house like Penwurt, he was certain of only one thing—absolutely anything could happen.

* * *

A quarter of an hour later, Oz gave up completely on the essay, grabbed the bloody phial off the table and went to the bathroom. He had a quick shower, towelled himself dry and positioned himself in front of the steamy bathroom mirror. His uncombed dark hair lay flat and damp on his head and his pale blue eyes narrowed in concentration as he opened the phial and tipped it gingerly towards his lips, letting a few droplets trickle under the corner of his mouth. The blood looked thin and watery and altogether not worth the money he'd paid for it.

Sighing, he wiped it off in disgust and opted instead for a scar under his left eye. He stuck a yellow-headed boil on the side of his nose for luck and went back to his bedroom. He dressed, tidied away his schoolbooks and then went downstairs and tried to watch some TV. By the time Ruff finally pitched up, complete with paint-flecked hair and a battered backpack, it was late afternoon.

"Good week?" Oz asked as Ruff threw himself down on the bed in the spare room.

"Terrific," Ruff said in a flat tone that implied it had been anything but. As usual, a curtain of curly brown hair hung in spirals in front of Ruff's long face and partly hid a strong nose, which was, at this moment, wrinkling in disgust. "Wasn't much of a holiday, to be honest. Dad got the job of painting the chalets at this place on the edge of a moor and it was fuh-freezing. Bet you didn't know Cornwall was in the Arctic Circle, did you?"

"It isn't," Oz said.

"Felt like it. It was buzzard cold, I tell you."

Oz grinned. Ruff was the only person he knew who used the same word to describe something as brilliant or awful. In fact, Ruff used "buzzard" to describe just about everything.

"Mum's gone bananas over the food as usual," Oz explained as they shared a piece of the chocolate Ruff

Rhys A. Jones

had brought for emergencies. "She's made mini pizzas in the shape of witch's hats, freaky finger biscuits with almonds for nails and strawberry jam filling so they look like they've been chopped off at the knuckle, and Dracula knows what else. I think she's looking forward to it more than I am."

"Buzzard," Ruff said, grinning and showing Oz his chocolate-covered teeth.

"By the way, you haven't said anything about my massive boil." Oz stuck his nose out at Ruff.

"Can't see anything different," Ruff said, and ducked as an Oz-launched cushion sailed just past his left ear.

"Come on, let's go outside and grab some atmosphere."

When they went down to the kitchen to announce that they were going out to watch the little kids trick-or-treating while they waited for Ellie, the table was already laden with platters covered by a motley selection of tea towels.

"Oz, is that you?" A disembodied voice floated out from a mudroom off the kitchen, followed a moment later by a slightly flushed face. Gwen Chambers was the prettiest woman Oz knew, even if he was very biased, and even if there were a few more lines around her eyes than there used to be. Sometimes there'd be dark smudges there, as well. But even though Oz noticed, no one else seemed to and they were appearing much less often these days. A stray blond wisp had escaped the scrunch holding her hair away from her face. It hung fetchingly over one eye. She blew it away with the corner of her mouth and smiled.

"Mum, who is going to eat all this stuff?" Oz asked, laughing.

"Oh, it'll get used up, you'll see. I've seen Ruff eat, don't forget," Mrs. Chambers said before adding, in a

4

voice just loud enough to be heard, "And that's a sight one does not forget very easily."

"Mu-um," Oz chided her.

"Just a little joke." She beamed at Ruff. "Let's just say that I'll be surprised if there's a lot left over by this time tomorrow." She fetched a spoon and started stirring a pot on the stove. "If you survive the night, that is."

Oz gave a wry little shake of his head and they left her to it and went outside to check out the trick-or-treaters. They played "spot the vampire," but gave up after counting twenty in three minutes. There was a mixture of monsters and ghouls, a couple of Frankensteins, three Spider-Men and a whole coven of witches. They saw only one house that had been egged and floured and passed two with signs on the gates that said, "No Trick or Treating here. Gone OUT."

After an hour of being pestered by three-foot-high Draculas, they got fed up and headed back to Penwurt. As they stood waiting to cross the street, Ruff frowned.

"How come none of the kids visit your place to ask for treats?"

Grinnning, Oz said, "Three guesses."

"Don't tell me they're scared?"

"Fifty points to Ruffendor," Oz replied, looking pleased with himself.

"Really?" Ruff looked up at Oz's house and cooed admiringly. "I've got to say it, your place does look buzzard wicked."

Oz followed his gaze. Much bigger than the Chambers either needed or could really afford, it was like something out of a medieval storybook, with high turrets jutting out of the walls on all four corners. His dad had called these turrets "bartizans", but despite their weird name Oz thought they were brilliant; the slits in their walls made it look like there might be archers up there on watch, guarding the place from attack.

Oz even liked its colour—red, brown and yellow sandstone blocks, some stained dark from years of car fumes and dirt, others—sheltered from the elements—a deep russet, or a mellow ochre. A low stone wall topped by black wrought-iron fencing marked the border between the house and the pavement. It added to the feeling Oz quite often had that somehow Penwurt was a fortification, a place where, once inside, you were shielded from the outside world and all its dangers.

An iron gate led to a path that crossed the drive to a huge, oak-studded front door. This was set back between two forward-jutting wings in which five large mullioned windows faced the street. Behind the U-shaped front was the oldest part of the house, a long, three-story block with crenellated parapets, three tall, spindly chimneys, and high windows. A tarmac drive ran up one side, whilst the other hid a slightly overgrown, but quite secluded, walled garden.

His dad had talked of plans to renovate the old block and maybe let it as flats, but those plans had long been shelved. Instead, his mother double-locked the inside doors to the old part of the house and checked them every night, both downstairs and up. She made a point of never going through those doors if she could help it. Unlike Oz's dad, who took every chance he had to explore and for whom the oldest part of the house was a treasure trove of secrets and delights, all it did for his mother was give her the heebie-jeebies. And although post would get to it if the letters had a simple "No 2 Magnus Street" on the envelope, everyone knew the old property by the name written in black iron letters over the front door— Penwurt.

Oz nodded and smiled at last in reply to Ruff's statement.

"Yeah," he said, "that's because it is buzzard wicked."

* * *

Ellie finally arrived just before eight, much to Oz's relief, and as soon as she had dumped her stuff in a room next to Mrs. Chambers', announced that she was "well starving." In the kitchen, there seemed to be even more food than two hours before.

"I thought you should have the pumpkin soup here, since it's hot," Mrs. Chambers said. "Then you can take the rest through."

"Thanks, Mum," Oz said as his mother ladled out the steaming broth. He watched her fussing and smiled. She was almost back to her normal, over-the-top self, and he wasn't going to complain about that.

"This is amazing," Ellie said, shutting her eyes ecstatically and breathing in the aroma.

"Buzzard," was Ruff's contribution, but it emerged through a mouthful of crusty bread and came out as "buhdduh," which made Oz giggle, but Ellie merely scowled.

Oz had never invited Ellie and Ruff over to stay at Penwurt at the same time. They had, of course, both stayed on separate occasions. Ruff two or three times, and Ellie dozens over the years, but tonight was the first time for them all to be there together, and Oz was hoping that it would work out. But if that little frown of irritation on Ellie's lips was anything to go by, it did not look all that promising.

"You know that any time you've had enough tonight, just call me and I'll come and get you," Mrs. Chambers said with feeling as she cut more bread.

"Mum, we're going to be twenty yards away." Oz had been through all this with her a hundred times. It had taken ages to convince her to let them stay the night in the old block and now was not the time for her to start having cold feet.

"I know that, but all I'm saying is…"

"We'll be fine."

"Oh-kay," Mrs. Chambers said, making her eyes wide in an "I've-got-the-message" kind of way and starting to pull the tea towels off the things she'd made. The reveal immediately triggered a series of astonished oohs and aahs from everyone.

"Is that really brain pâté?" asked Ellie, goggling at a pink mass which looked exactly like it had just come out of someone's skull. Her honey-coloured hair was tied back and her large, deep blue eyes were currently twice as big as usual from staring at the food.

"Cream cheese, mushroom soup and prawns. Bit garish looking, but it tastes fantastic, even if I say so myself," Mrs. Chambers explained.

Ruff pointed to a tray covered in golfball-sized objects. "And are those…"

"Marshmallow eyeballs." Mrs. Chambers nodded and popped one into her mouth. "Delicious."

Ruff grinned and devoured one, too. Oz watched his face dissolve in rapture.

"Mmmm, see just what you mean."

"That's awful," Ellie said, groaning.

"Eyeful, more like," Oz said, pushing away his empty soup bowl. "Come on, grab a sleeping bag and let's go through."

Oz went to a door to the left of the stone stairwell, one that was usually kept locked.

But not tonight.

They crossed a passageway to another door, which opened out into a large, shabby-looking entrance hall with a massive double staircase leading up to the floor above. The place smelled musty and unused and their voices echoed into the chilly emptiness when they spoke.

"This atrium used to be the orphanage dining room," Oz announced.

"Is this where we're having the feast?" Ellie asked, sounding impressed.

"No. I thought we'd use the old dorm. It's really spooky in there."

"I've always wanted to spend a Halloween night in a real haunted house," Ruff said, rubbing his hands together. "It's going to be so spooky."

"Don't build your hopes up," Ellie said. "Nine times out of ten these things end up being rubbish."

"Nothing like a bit of enthusiasm, is there?" Ruff tutted. "And anyway, the place is a legend. It was even in *Hidden Haunted Houses of Great Britain.*"

"I didn't know that," Oz said.

"Ye-ah, it was in the reference section in Waterstone's the other day. It said something like… 'an old orphanage on Magnus Street in Seabourne now occupies the site of the Bunthorpe Encounter. One of the most famous supernatural occurrences in the country.'"

"Cool," Oz said, pleased. "I'll Google it later."

"Looks more real in a book, though, somehow, don't you think?" Ellie said.

Oz knew what she meant. He made a mental note to look it up next time he was in the bookshop. They walked up the stairs and passed a peculiar-looking, wrought-iron chandelier bearing a huge bird of prey with wings unfurled at its centre.

"That is so weirdly mingin'," Ruff said. He kept glancing at it uneasily as he climbed and Oz resisted the urge to say "buzzard" with the utmost difficulty.

On the first floor the doors had all been boarded up except for one, which, though not boarded, was padlocked. Oz took them up one more flight to the second floor, where another stairway ran up to their left to another door.

"Where does that go?" asked Ellie.

"Fire escape," Oz explained. "Quickest way down."

"Worth knowing for when the mad axe-man calls," she said with a furtive look at Ruff, who had glanced nervously behind him on hearing the words "axe-man."

Oz walked forward a few steps along the landing and stopped before a huge oak door. He pushed it open and, as if on cue, it creaked magnificently. They stepped across the threshold into a large, dark space. Ruff tried the wall switch, but nothing happened. The only light came from thin beams of moonlight slanting through the windows on the eastern wall. Oz flicked on his torch and made his way to the centre of the dorm. He pushed a couple of plugs into extension leads and instantly the lamps he'd arranged lit up the dormitory. What was revealed was a room that spanned the length of the building. Yards of oak paneling lined the walls, upon which hung a variety of old paintings and photos. Long, dusty strings of cobweb wafted in the draughty corners, adding nicely to the room's eerie air of abandonment.

"Take a look at this," Ellie called to the other two as she peered at one of the photos. The boys joined her and stared at a faded black and white print of the very room they were standing in, but lined with twenty-two beds just like an old hospital ward. "Must be what the dorm was like."

"Wow," Ruff said. "Not exactly private, was it?"

In the centre, near the lamps, Oz had laid out three folding chairs and two foldaway tables, one bearing a flat-screen monitor and his Xbox.

"There's a toilet block at the far end," Oz explained. "The lights do work in there, just in case you were wondering."

Ruff stood surveying his surroundings, open-mouthed. "This is absolutely buzzard," he said, grinning.

"What films have you got?" Ellie asked.

"*Fangman* and *Revenge of Fangman*," Oz said.

"I brought *Toy Story*."

"*Toy Story*?" Oz laughed.

"Just in case we need cheering up," Ellie explained. "You know how nervy Ruff gets."

"Hang on, I thought you were the one that said that Halloween was a load of cobblers." Oz grinned.

"Yeah, but I suppose if anything could happen on Halloween, it'd happen in a place like this, wouldn't it?"

"Hey, look at the ceiling." Ruff craned his neck upwards and Ellie followed suit.

Richly decorated wooden beams ran from east to west, red, green and blue chevrons adorning their sides. Between, on the plaster ceiling itself, detailed paintings of birds and weird-looking buildings and symbols filled the space. The effect was striking and original.

"Yeah, downstairs is like that, too," Oz explained. "It's the sixteenth-century equivalent of wallpaper, or so my dad told me."

"It's so cool," Ellie said. "And to think it's lasted all that time."

Oz nodded.

"I wish I had a long-lost uncle who would leave me something in his will. Wouldn't it be great if it's your sixteenth birthday and a crusty old lawyer bloke turns up with a crinkly yellow envelope full of stocks and bonds and stuff worth zillions?" Ruff was looking at the ceiling, but his eyes were seeing something else altogether.

Oz didn't really know what stocks and bonds were and neither, he suspected, did Ruff. But they sounded really impressive.

"As if that would ever happen to anyone," Ellie tutted.

Ruff threw her a baleful, sulky look. "It sort of happened to Oz, didn't it? His dad, anyway."

"Yeah, well, getting something like this dropped in your lap isn't exactly like winning the lottery, you know," Oz said, not wanting to let Ruff and Ellie argue. "It costs loads to run and takes ages to clean. And even the draughts have draughts."

Ellie stared at him. "You're not thinking of leaving, are you?" she asked, horrified.

Oz grinned. "Not if I have anything to do with it." He'd hoped they'd like the place, but to see them both so impressed had made his day. "Come on, let's get the food up here."

With the heaters on, it was quite cozy within their little den. They sprayed on a few more boils and let fake blood drip off their stuck-on scars, but soon Ruff had *Fangman* up on the screen and they began tucking in to Mrs. Chambers' brilliant food. Ellie enjoyed dipping spoon-shaped bits of bread into the brain pâté more than anything else, while Oz had at least half a dozen freaky fingers. Mrs. Chambers had deliberately put some marzipan in their middles because she knew Oz couldn't resist it.

All in all, it was a brilliant night.

Ellie had them in stitches as she explained how she'd accidentally broken the nose of her taekwondo teacher the week before because he'd sneezed just as she was practising a head kick. Ruff, meanwhile, obviously deeply scarred by spending a week outdoors helping his dad paint the chalets, kept on about how cold he'd been.

"I swear I saw a penguin on the lake, and one morning there was this humongous dollop next to the perimeter fence which looked moistly fresh. I think it definitely must have been polar bear poo and not anything to do with the caretaker's Alsatian like my dad said it was."

"Ugghh," Ellie said, and quickly put down the freaky fig roll she was about to bite into. "Why do you have to be so disgusting?"

Oz didn't hear Ruff's response because he was laughing so much. He'd known Ellie since the age of four. They'd attended the same playgroup and were in the same class at Hurley Street Junior School. Gwen and Ellie's mum, Fay, were friends, so Oz and Ellie had virtually grown up together. He knew he could trust her with just about anything. Funnily enough, despite only knowing Ruff for the seven weeks he'd been at Seabourne County, Oz felt much the same way about him. He only wished that Ellie did, too. But on this Halloween night, he couldn't think of anywhere else he'd rather be, nor anyone else he'd rather be with.

They'd all seen *Fangman* half a dozen times, yet when the ghoul crept into the bedroom to steal the hero's little sister, Oz thought he saw Ellie inch her chair a little closer to his own. *Fangman Two* was almost as good and they munched on fried spiders—which were really splayed-out bits of crispy bacon—and slurped on marshmallow eyeballs until the DVD finally came to an end.

"What time is it?" said Ellie, stifling a yawn as the credits rolled on the second film.

"Fifteen minutes to the witching hour," Ruff said.

"And what's supposed to happen then?" Oz asked.

"Dunno, but that's when it all happens in the films, isn't it?"

"My mum says that the real witching hour is half past three in the morning," Ellie said knowingly.

"Buzzard," Ruff retorted, "you'd think they'd all be asleep by then."

"Tell you what," Oz suggested, "why don't we turn all the lights off and just sit by the windows? See if we can see anything outside in the moonlight."

"Yeah," Ruff agreed, hopping uncomfortably. "But first I need the loo. Oh, and we're out of Coke, by the way."

"Oh, no," Oz groaned. "I left the other bottle in the fridge."

Ruff and Ellie looked at him, grinning expectantly, as he hurried out and down the atrium stairs, muttering to himself as he went.

"And while you're at it, get *Revenge of the Gargoyle Ghoul*. I left it in your bedroom," Ruff yelled after him.

Oz ran back down the staircase, through the kitchen—where his mum had left all the lights on—and went quietly upstairs to his bedroom to fetch the DVD. Ruff's room was next to his, but on the other side was the locked door to his dad's study. Oz glanced at it wistfully. It had been like that for over two years now. Ever since his dad had died. One day, when his mother felt strong enough to open it up, he would explore that room and examine all the weird and wonderful things his dad had brought back from his travels. One day.

Back in the kitchen, Oz tried to be as quiet as he could, but he had to move some dishes in the fridge to get at the Coke and grimaced as they clinked together. As he backed up with his hands full, the door thudded shut, causing the dishes to clink alarmingly once more and a couple of fridge magnets to fall clattering to the floor. One, shaped like a pink slice of cake, was there to hold the corner of a calendar up on the fridge door. This week's page had scribbles all over it, like "order four pints milk," and "hygienist—9 o'clock." But without its magnetic support, the corner of the calendar had sagged drunkenly downwards

It wasn't the noise of the dishes, nor what was written on the calendar that made the breath suddenly catch in Oz's throat. It was what was revealed on the sheet of paper behind the calendar that suddenly drew Oz's horrified stare, made him gasp and his stomach lurch.

Once, when things had been very bad, before she'd started the medicine that had helped make her better, Oz had tried asking his mother what exactly was wrong with her. It had been a particularly bad dressing-gown day of constant crying and not eating, and Oz had felt more than usually helpless. With a huge effort she'd looked up at him, sensing for once his desperation, her face full of pleading, her voice a hollow whisper.

"Since Michael has gone, it's like there's this old black dog that keeps following me around, Oz," she said, shivering. "He's always there no matter what I do to try and shake him off. And whenever I look at him he makes me feel so sad and lonely."

Oz had gone to the window and looked outside. There'd been no sign of a dog, but when he'd finally managed to get back to Mrs. Evans' class at Hurley Street Juniors, he'd drawn an ugly old black mutt in felt pen. At the end of the year, he'd taken home all his artwork and promptly forgotten all about it until, months later when she was better, Mrs. Chambers had found the drawing and pinned it up on the fridge door; she fixed the calendar over the top of it to hide it and explained that this could be their signal. If ever she was beginning to feel sad again, she'd shift the calendar so that some of the dog was showing. And if Oz thought that she was acting strangely, he could do the same. She'd called it their early warning sign. Mostly, the calendar hung square over the picture. But sometimes Oz had come down to the kitchen in the morning and found that a bit of the dog's ear was showing, or perhaps half its head, and he'd known that he'd have to be careful and not stress his mother out too much.

He looked at the badly drawn bit of ear again now and breathed in and out to let the ripple of anxiety fade. It was just a kid's drawing under a calendar, after all, wasn't it? A calendar that was too thick to be held in place by four rubber magnets, which had a tendency to slip if you closed the fridge door too hard. It was stupid to think of the ear as an omen of any kind. After all, his mother hadn't moved the calendar for months now, and she was fine; she'd just made brain pâté, for cripes' sake. He was not going to let a little thing like that spoil the night.

He repositioned the calendar to hide the drawing completely, put the fridge magnet back in place and pushed all the business about the black dog to the back of his mind.

Through the kitchen window the night beyond looked inky and solid, the only lights coming from the backs of the smaller houses in Tottridge Street. He imagined being in one of those tiny houses on a night like this with Ellie and Ruff. Yet no matter how hard he tried, he knew it just wouldn't be the same. It wouldn't have ceilings that looked like they should be in an art gallery, or a chandelier with a hunting falcon as its centrepiece. In other words, it just wouldn't be Penwurt. He held on to that pleasant thought as he made his way back to the dorm.

* * *

He decided to set his watch alarm for half past three as he climbed up the staircase, so he put the Coke bottle down to adjust the settings. There was no sound at all in the atrium as midnight approached, but outside the wind moaned as it gusted around the stone walls and beams creaked as the old place resisted the elements. Oz finished adjusting his watch and reached down to pick up the bottle when a noise made him start.

Footsteps.

Oz looked up suddenly. Maybe Ellie wanted something else from the kitchen. More likely it would be Ruff. But there was no one there.

He started to climb the stairs again. Must have been his imag… Oz stopped and stood stock-still.

Soft and deliberate and sounding very near, the footsteps came again.

The hairs on Oz's arms stood instantly to attention. He swivelled around. The atrium was empty. Except for the faint moaning of the wind, the only other noises he could hear were the hammers of his heart pounding out a drum roll.

Then they came once more. This time they were distinctly louder.

Oz tilted his head to try and pinpoint exactly where they were coming from. Not above. Not below. Oz realised he was standing on the step below the first floor landing. Whatever was making that noise was behind the wall separating him from the rooms beyond. Someone or something was walking across the floor in one of those rooms, rooms that had been locked up for years. He craned his neck to listen. The noise had died. He took another step forward just as something tapped on the wall right next to where he was standing.

Oz jumped and almost dropped the Coke bottle. His pulse took off like an Atlas rocket and he had to stuff his fist in his mouth to stop from crying out. He leapt up the remaining stairs and through the oak door into the dorm. The shock must have shown in his face because Ruff frowned the minute he entered.

"What's wrong with you?" he asked.

Oz put his quivering fingers to his lips and tiptoed across to where Ellie and Ruff were sitting with the Xbox switched on.

"What is it?" Ellie asked.

"Turn that off and listen," Oz commanded in a whisper.

"O-oz," Ellie said with an accusatory stare.

"Shhh. This is not a wind-up, honestly," Oz whispered again. "Just wait."

They did. For a very long thirty seconds until...thud...thud...thud...thud.

Ruff's eyes became instant dinner plates. "What the buzzard...?" he whispered.

"Sugar! Are they...?" Ellie asked.

"Footsteps? Yes, they are," Oz said.

"Whose?" breathed Ellie.

"Dunno, but they're coming from downstairs. From rooms that have been locked up for as long as we've been here."

Oz, Ellie and Ruff stared at each other in speechless wonder. It was Ellie who broke the stalemate.

"Sounds like *Hidden Haunted Houses of Great Britain* got it right, then," she said in a whisper edgy with excitement.

Ruff shook his head but he, too, kept his voice low. "There's probably a perfectly normal explanation."

"Is there?" Oz asked. "Like I said, as far as I know those rooms have been boarded up for years."

"Maybe it's your mum playing a trick on us," Ruff said waveringly.

"Mum? You heard her. She was more nervous than anyone about us coming here. She's on emergency standby to come and rescue us, remember? No way is that my mother."

"Then who is it?" Ellie asked.

"Or what is it?" Ruff mumbled.

Ellie shook her head and rolled her eyes.

"Well, there's only one way to find out, isn't there?" Oz said finally.

"You're not going to go looking?" Ruff asked, horrified.

But Ellie's face lit up at the suggestion and she reached into her pocket for her mobile. "We totally should. I've got three megapixels on my camera phone. We'd make loads of money if we got a picture of it."

"Wait a minute," Ruff said. "If it isn't someone trying to scare us, then maybe it's burglars."

"What's there to burgle?" Oz said with a scornful laugh.

"Okay, but we don't know, do we?" Ruff pressed on. "I don't think it's a brilliant idea to just barge in like a cow in a crystal maze."

Ellie frowned.

Oz explained. "He means bull in a china shop."

"It could be really dangerous," Ruff went on. "In *Spirit World Three*, there's this ghoul and…"

"Xbox games again, Ruff?" Ellie said, her head tilted in a scathing glare.

"Loads of these games are based on real legends," Ruff said defensively.

"I'm sure they are," Ellie said, "just as I'm sure that you're just a *little* bit scared."

"Don't tell me you're not a bit scared, too." Ruff glared back.

Ellie just smiled at him.

Ruff shook his head. "All I'm saying is that we ought to be really careful. Maybe I should stay outside on watch, just in case."

"Okay, fair point," Oz said. "But there are three of us. What could possibly happen to the three—"

The muted thud of more footsteps filtered up from somewhere beneath them once again and Oz never finished his sentence.

"So how do we get in?" Ellie whispered, her eyes glinting with anticipation.

Oz grinned. He took a couple of steps back the way he'd come before turning back to the other two, who were staring at him questioningly. "I know where the key to the padlock is," he said. "Stay here."

Chapter 2

The Ghostly Footsteps

The key was on a key ring hanging behind the door of the cupboard under the sink in the laundry room. Oz met Ellie and Ruff on the stairs outside the padlocked door on the orphanage's first floor landing.

"So, what's the plan?" Oz whispered.

Ellie shrugged and sent Ruff a disparaging glance. "If we're doing this we're doing it together, according to him."

"But I thought—"

Ellie shook her head. "Ruff's too stubborn to stay outside even though I pointed out that I'm the one that does martial arts if anything does happen—"

"Yeah, but it was never my idea to go looking anyway—"

"Okay, okay," Oz said. "We'll all go."

As quietly as he could, Oz slid the key into the padlock and felt the mechanism click smoothly open. In seconds, he had the chain on the floor in a serpentine loop.

"This door is bound to creak," Ellie whispered a warning.

But it didn't. Instead, it opened smoothly and silently and a draft of stale, dank, freezing air wafted over their faces. It was like stepping into a cave. Four doors led off the corridor. They were all shut.

"Oh, sugar," Ellie whispered.

"Which door were the footsteps coming from?" Ruff asked, his voice a nervous hiss.

"Not sure," Oz whispered back. "Let's wait to see if we hear it again."

The door swung silently shut behind them, plunging them into darkness. But Oz didn't flick on his torch, worried in case it gave them away. In pitch-blackness and with Oz in the lead, they crept forward with Ellie clutching Oz's jumper and Ruff at the rear hanging on to hers. Nothing happened for three long minutes. Oz's mind was churning. Was what was in one of these rooms a lost soul? Or could it be that waiting for them was something dark and horrible, intent on doing them real harm, like in Ruff's *Spirit World Three*? He wanted to ask Ellie and Ruff if they were thinking the same thing, but common sense told him to keep quiet. He couldn't see anything and all he could hear was Ellie's steady breathing behind him. Finally, after what seemed like an age, he put his finger on the torch's switch and was about to flick it on when it happened. Inches away, they heard the footsteps again.

"Second door," whispered Oz urgently, and reached out his hand to feel for the handle. "Ready? On three—one, two…"

"Go," Ellie and Ruff said in high-pitched unison.

Pulse accelerating madly, Oz flicked on the torch and thrust the door open. He wasn't sure what he'd been expecting. An apparition? Something spectral and ghostly? At the very least a creeping thief in a balaclava… But what he wasn't expecting was what was revealed to the three of them as they stepped across the threshold. In the stark light of the torch beam, the room, in which seconds before they had all distinctly heard footsteps, was completely and utterly empty. Oz frowned. Behind him, he heard Ruff let out a sigh that was a mixture of relief and disappointment.

They scoured the walls, floor and ceiling in the torchlight but found no sign of any footsteps in the dust that lay thick and undisturbed on the floor. Ellie took half a dozen pictures, but all they showed was more yards of dark paneling with huge cobwebs dangling from the dusty corners like net curtains. There was no other door in or out, nor any sign of occupation. And somehow, that made it worse.

"What time is it?" asked Ellie as they stood near the window that looked out onto the garden. She shivered, but Oz wasn't sure it was entirely from the cold.

"Five past midnight," Oz said, squinting at his watch.

"Looks like we've frightened it off." Ruff shone his torch into the four corners of the room one last time. There was no denying the relief in his voice.

"It? Aren't ghosts supposed to be the spirits of people?" Ellie said.

"Yeah," Ruff said as if he was talking to a three-year-old, "but it hasn't left a name and address, has it?"

Oz breathed on a window pane and drew a ghostly shape in the misty circle. "Well, if it really was a ghost, then the answer as to who it was must be here at Penwurt somewhere."

"Okay. So where do we start?" Ruff asked.

Oz looked at Ellie and they said in unison, "The library."

They hurried out and Oz sensed that the others, like him, were glad to be away from that room. They made their way back to the main house without speaking and went straight to the spiral staircase that led upstairs. But when they got to the second floor landing, Oz put up his hand and peered upwards.

"There's a light on in Caleb's room," he whispered.

"And I can hear voices," Ellie added.

There were voices. They were low and barely audible, but the rise and fall of the intonation suggested that a discussion was taking place. Oz crept forward and called out, "Ummm, hello? Anybody there?"

The voices stopped. There was the scraping of a chair on block flooring and a voice said, "Oz, is that you?"

"Caleb?"

Caleb Jones' rooms were on the same floor of Penwurt as Oz's, but on the other side of the spiral stairwell that separated the two wings. Caleb had been renting those rooms for almost as long as the Chambers had owned the house. It was pure luck that he'd been looking for somewhere at exactly the time that Oz's mum and dad had started looking for tenants. And as a colleague of Dr. Michael Chambers in the history department of the university, he'd also been the first to hear that they were renting. But he was not alone in his sitting room that night. At the table with him, and looking her usual misery-guts self, was one of the other tenants, Lucy Bishop.

"What are you three doing wandering around at this hour?" she said frostily. She was a small, thin girl with elfin features, short dark hair and a constantly intense expression. Her clothes were shapeless and fashionably drab and she'd gone for "backwards through a hedge" as a hairstyle, with great success. Her chosen subject at the university was history of art, though Oz hadn't seen her show much interest in Penwurt at all, which to him seemed full of all sorts of interesting history as well as art.

"It is Halloween," Ellie said.

"Yeah, and we were in the orphanage and we heard this—ow!" Ruff's sharp exclamation of pain was the result of Oz's shoed foot meeting with his ankle.

"Owl," Oz said in a flash of brilliant inspiration. "Hooting, you know."

"And we were having a discussion about the house and decided to find out a bit more about it," Ellie explained, taking her lead from Oz.

Lucy Bishop stared at them blankly.

"The Bunthorpe Encounter? You must have heard of it?" Ellie added.

Caleb's eyes crinkled in an almost smile, which he disguised under a hand massaging his cheek. He was thin with longish brown hair and always looked to Oz as if he needed a shave. But even though he hardly ever smiled and had a deep furrow in his forehead that lent him a slightly fierce look, Oz still felt that there was a softer centre under the stern exterior—though it was sometimes quite hard to find.

"The old place spook you a bit, then, did it?" Caleb asked.

"Sort of," Ruff muttered through clenched teeth as he rubbed his other foot against his sore ankle.

"You two are working late," Oz said to deflect attention away from Ruff's grimacing.

"Are you sure your mother approves of you wandering about at all hours like this?" Lucy Bishop said crossly.

"It was Mrs. Chambers that made us our feast," explained Ellie.

"Kids should be in bed at this time of night."

"Hang on, this is Oz's house—" Ruff's voice rose in protest.

But Oz cut him off. "Sorry if we've interrupted something."

"You haven't," Caleb said calmly. "We were just discussing an essay that Lucy is having problems with, but we can do that another time."

Lucy Bishop pushed herself away from the table and stood. "Of course we can," she said pointedly. "No rush. No pressure. I have all the time in the world."

She didn't look at any of them as she stomped out of the room.

"Who threw her toys out of the buzzard pram?" Ruff asked after she'd gone.

"She's just a bit tired," Caleb explained. "And you three look like you've just seen a ghost."

No one answered.

Caleb studied the three of them. "Look, I'm about to turn in, but how about I make us all a hot chocolate first? Good antidote for the jitters."

"I'm in," Ruff said quickly.

No one was surprised by that.

They followed Caleb down some wooden stairs that led to the ground floor of the east wing which, in grander times, had been the servants' quarters. Three minutes later, they were sitting at the table in the kitchen Caleb shared with the other tenants, sipping hot chocolate from steaming mugs. One of Mrs. Chambers' rules was that Oz was not to bother the paying guests too much. Since Lucy Bishop wore the constant look of someone who'd just opened the door of a sewerage plant by mistake, and the third tenant was another student of about the same age as her called Tim Perkins, who seemed altogether a bit too chirpy for his own good, Oz had found it no hardship. But with Caleb, it was different. He'd known Oz's dad well and although he kept a polite distance as a lodger, Oz had always found him a brilliant source of information on just about anything.

"If it's Bunthorpe you want to know about," Caleb said, "you might try *A Short History of Seabourne's Ancient Houses*. There's a copy upstairs in the library. But to cut a long story short, in 1761, something happened in a barn on this very site. An apparition appeared out of thin air. It even spoke. Four people, respectable churchgoers, all witnessed the same thing and they claimed it was a ghost. Of course, in those days superstition was rife. But someone didn't like the thought of the barn being haunted and so it ended up being burned to the ground."

In the silence that followed, Oz could hear his own pulse thudding in his ears. "Do you think there's anything to it?" he asked eventually.

Caleb inclined his head thoughtfully. "There's no doubt that this place is a bit special."

"But do you think it's haunted?" Ellie asked, her expression intent.

"Let's put it this way—I believe that some places attract strangeness like a magnet. Perhaps it's something to do with where they're sited or something about how they were built, I don't know. But too many odd things have taken place here to be put down to sheer coincidence."

"It's not just Bunthorpe we wanted to know about, though; it's the orphanage, too," Oz said quickly.

"Ah, well." Caleb clutched his mug in both hands. "This place is old, eighteenth century. But the actual building—the orphanage as you call it, that dates back to Jacobean times—the sixteen hundreds. The original house was built by an abbot. He put it on top of an old fortification that was there long before that. Bunthorpe barn was literally next door. When it was burned to the ground, the squire bought the land and the old abbot's house. He built two new wings and joined them on to try to make it a property suitable for a squire and his family. That was finished in 1770."

"Was it him that painted the ceilings and stuff?" Ruff asked.

Caleb shook his head. "The abbot started it all, but Squire Worthy did some, too. The paintings tell stories, you know. Proverbs and life histories. Amazing, aren't they?"

"So it became an orphanage after that?" Ellie said.

"Almost a hundred years later, yes. And it stayed an orphanage until the end of the First World War. I think the last orphan left around 1920."

"And after that?" Oz probed. Caleb was better than Google.

"Then it became the property of one Daniel Morsman, who had been an orphan here himself."

"Wow," Ruff said. "Liked it so much he bought the place."

"Was he famous then?" Ellie asked.

"In his time. Bit of an explorer."

"So then came Great Aunt Bessy, and after that my dad, right?"

"Absolutely," Caleb nodded. He paused to sip his hot chocolate before asking, "I assume you all know what Penwurt means?"

Oz knew, of course, but Ellie and Ruff shook their heads.

"It's a mixture of Celtic and Old English. Pen is the Celtic for hill and Wurt comes from Old English or German. It meant fate or destiny. But weird and odd will do just as well. So, it's the hill where weird things happen, and odd things have, indeed, been happening in exactly the spot we're sitting in now for a long, long time."

Suddenly, the back door rattled and Ruff jumped off his seat with fright. Oz, too, almost spilled his hot chocolate as the door flew open and a creature wearing dirty, dust-covered clothes, its hair matted with cobwebs, face smeared with dirt and its jeans torn, shambled in.

"Oh, hi," said Tim Perkins to the startled group sitting at the table.

"What happened to you?" Ruff asked with his mouth hanging open.

"Me?" Tim asked, momentarily nonplussed. "Oh, you mean my clothes?"

"And your hair," Ellie said. "I hope you didn't tip your hairdresser."

Tim looked at his reflection in the kitchen window. "Go on, be honest, would I pass muster as one of the undead, do you think??"

"Not," Ellie muttered dubiously.

"I thought I'd done well," Tim said, sounding crestfallen, "but the others at the party said I looked like a painter and decorator that had fallen asleep in a corner for two years."

"Fancy dress?" asked Caleb.

"All I could come up with," Tim explained, and took in the hot chocolate. "You four look nice and cozy."

"The Three Musketeers here have been Halloweening in the old orphanage."

"Ah." Tim grinned. "That must have been fun."

"Buzzard," Ruff said, smiling.

Ellie shot him a disbelieving glance. Clearly, the beverage was working its magic and morphing what had been quite a scary supernatural experience into a great adventure in Ruff's hot chocolate-mellowed mind.

Tim frowned as if he'd misheard and was thinking about asking Ruff something else, but then decided against it and just stood watching them and grinning good-naturedly for several long seconds. "Right," he said finally. "I'm going to hit the shower. Oz, tell your mum that I'd be happy to have a go at that guttering for her. I've managed to borrow a long ladder, okay?"

"Fine," Oz said without the faintest idea of what he was talking about.

"He seems quite…helpful," Ellie said when Tim had gone.

"Doesn't he just," Caleb said in a way that made them all glance at him. But his face remained inscrutable.

By one o'clock, they'd finally decided that going back to the orphanage was not a great idea. They would leave attacking the library until first thing next morning and, after Ruff set up an infectious bout of yawning, they all agreed that bed was probably the best option. Twenty minutes later, Oz lay in his, duvet up under his chin, mulling over the evening's events and not feeling the least bit tired, hearing his stomach groan under the internal pressure of one too many freaky fingers.

But it wasn't indigestion that was keeping sleep away. Since the conversation with Caleb, an idea had taken root in his head and was growing with every minute. The thought that Penwurt really was haunted thrilled Oz. He'd always known that it was a different sort of place and the mysterious footsteps merely confirmed what he'd suspected. He still vividly remembered the day they'd first driven here after hearing that his dad had inherited the place. The Chambers had sat in the car outside the old house like a gang of potential burglars, looking at it in silent awe.

"It's huge," Oz had said.

"It's brilliant," replied his dad. "Just look at those bartizans and those mullioned windows and that turret at the top. I bet you can see for miles from there. And this street, can't you feel it?"

Previously, they'd lived on the outskirts of the town in a small house that had been modern and identical to a hundred others on a sprawling new estate. But in the car on that first day, Gwen Chambers went very quiet.

"I dread to think what it will cost to heat," she muttered.

Michael Chambers turned to her, his eyes shining with excitement, his grin infectious.

"We'll take in lodgers. The university is always looking for accommodation."

Mrs. Chambers had merely smiled wanly. In that smile was the knowledge that she'd lost the battle before it had even started.

So began the adventure.

And in the seven or so months before the accident, what an adventure it had been. Oz and his dad explored the house, and almost every week found something new and surprising that they could investigate and enthuse over. Great Aunt Bessy had done little in the way of decoration since the middle of the last century and much of the old house was hung with ancient photographs and portraits of stern-faced people.

Oz could still clearly remember his dad's whoops of delight whenever he came across a spectacular section of fancy Georgian tiling over an ornate washstand, or another sepia print of some Edwardian gathering, the women in long dark dresses and the men moustachioed and proud, posing with their chests out. Even now, Oz still half-expected to turn a corner and find his dad studying some antique, or stroll into the library to find him running his fingers over the oak panelling, his face full of enchantment.

"There's something about this place," he'd say, looking up at Oz and grinning. "Something strange and timeless. I can feel it in every creak of these old beams."

Memory brought with it a sudden constriction in Oz's throat and a warm wetness to his eyes. It was over two years since Michael Chambers had walked out of the door to begin one of his expeditions, never to return. That was the last time Oz had seen him alive. A freak accident as he'd travelled home from the airport had seen to that. More than anything, Oz regretted that he'd never properly said goodbye to his father. He'd been too busy doing something mindless the morning his dad had left. And since that day, Penwurt had lost some of its sparkle.

But after tonight, Oz had the strangest, most tantalising conviction that they'd inadvertently stumbled upon one of the house's secrets. Recaptured somehow that promise that had excited his dad so much. And he wasn't frightened, not in the least. In fact, quite the opposite—he felt a warm glow spread up from his toes to the top of his head just thinking about it. He basked in it, revelling in the possibilities his imagination was throwing up. Caleb had said that some places attracted strangeness like a magnet. At that moment, Oz could think of no better way to describe Penwurt.

Chapter 3

Pheeps

The next morning, both Ruff and Ellie had breakfast dressed in their football kit of maroon and blue stripes in anticipation of their game that morning. But immediately after breakfast, they headed straight for the library.

"What's the big attraction?" a suspicious Mrs. Chambers asked as they wolfed down a small hill of toast and jam.

"Uh, just want to compare my English essay with Ellie and Ruff," Oz explained, with his mouth half full of cereal.

"Schoolwork? Be still my beating heart." She made a great show of collapsing into a chair. Ruff and Ellie giggled. Oz just shook his head sadly.

Making his way up the turnpike stone staircase, Oz avoided the curved iron handrail and let his fingers trace the uneven plasterwork of the walls. Beneath his feet, the steps were worn down by centuries of use so that they dipped in the middle. This was what he so loved about Penwurt; all of it was old, but parts of it were much, much older than others. The spiral stairs continued past the second floor and opened out into the library itself. As they entered, Oz caught his breath.

It was a cold, clear morning and rays of November sunshine slanted through the glass turret at the top of the library's vaulted ceiling, turning the oak panelling into molten gold. Wheels of strange symbols were carved into two of the walls. In one corner stood a four-foot-high globe atlas in a walnut stand with an antique world map in faded colours. Oz especially liked the inked sailing ship in the Pacific, which seemed to glide majestically under its own power whenever he spun the orb from west to east.

As always, the room smelled of leather and wood and old books, and Oz drank it in. This was where Oz's dad had been happiest, where Oz still felt closest to him. The slanting rays of morning light revealed a million dancing dust motes. Oz always thought they looked just like tiny nuggets of knowledge that ebbed and flowed in and out of the books and walls, microscopic secrets that could be breathed in and absorbed. While he and Ellie searched for information, Ruff seemed more interested in the wooden panelling.

"These are so buzzard amazing," he said.

"So you keep telling us," Ellie said, reaching up for a battered-looking anthology of *The Seabourne Chronicle*.

"Look at all these symbols." Ruff let his fingers trace the carvings that covered two panelled walls. "Think it's a code?"

"I think you're spending too much time on *Labyrinth Quest* on the Xbox," Oz muttered.

Ruff looked up from his examination of the panelling. "Hey, I'm only on level four. There're six more to complete." He turned back to inspect the panels, muttering distractedly. "Think there's any hidden treasure in this old place, Oz? And if we found any, would you split it with us? Maybe I wouldn't have to help my dad paint freezing chalets if we found a hidden lost masterpiece or a medieval chalice or something. You know, I bet there are secret passages behind these walls."

"Well, I wish you'd hurry up and find them so you could get lost in one. We're supposed to be doing research here," Ellie said irritably.

"There's no need to get your pants in a tangle."

Ellie looked up. "So why aren't you helping?"

"I am. Look, I found *A Short History of Seabourne's Ancient Houses* after five minutes." Ruff picked up a mouldy-looking, leather-bound book from the desk.

Oz ignored their bickering and busied himself by thumbing through a battered photograph album of the orphanage, full of faded prints of strangely dressed children and stern-looking women in long crinoline dresses. Some of the photos had fallen out of their mountings and others had become so old they'd snapped in half. But some were intact and Oz found one from 1892 that had names printed in the legend at the bottom. He recognised one of the names underneath a happy, gap-toothed boy sitting cross-legged on the floor, smiling out from a group photo of thirty children. He had his arm around the neck of the startled boy next to him and Oz wasn't quite sure if this was through affection or if it was a malicious headlock. The name in copperplate read "Daniel Morsman."

"That's just one book, Ruff," Oz said absently as he concentrated on trying to decipher some of the other faded names.

"Yeah, but it's got all the stuff about Bunthorpe in it. Listen." He thumbed it open to a marked page and read:

On that Saturday evening, a rehearsal of bell ringing was taking place in the barn at Bunthorpe owned by one Redmayne, a horse trader. 'Twas said that during a ferocious gust of wind, the doors to the barn flew open and there was a great clap of thunder, tho the sky remained clear and the weather warm. One bell ringer, a shopkeeper of sound mind, witnessed the sudden appearance of an obsidian pebble on the floor of the barn bathed in a glow of bright light. All eight bell ringers then did swear to seeing an apparition appear glowing and a'shimmering. Some swore to hearing music of a strange melody and others to words from the mouth of the apparition that had become the shape of a girl. Naturally, the bell ringers all took fright and fled. Later that night at around midnight, a fierce fire consumed the building. A farmhand returning from a tavern persuaded Redmayne that ne'er-do-wells were seen setting the barn alight, but no one yet has been brought to account.

"You sound like a Cornish farmer," Oz said, laughing at Ruff's accent.

"It's the language," Ruff explained, grinning. "Sort of makes you speak like that if you read it out loud."

"Let's have a look," Ellie said with an irritated shake of her head. She put down the old Bible she'd found before reaching for Ruff's book and squinting at the page. "That passage is from something called the *Weekly Journal* and the date is 1761."

"What do you think an obsidian pebble is?" Ruff asked.

"Dunno," Oz said.

Ruff shrugged "Still, at least we know the Bunthorpe ghost was a girl, now."

"But there's no clue about who she was," Ellie murmured after reading on for a couple of minutes.

"And Caleb said that after the fire, some squire bloke buys the land and builds this house on it," Oz said, his eyes narrowing. "What we really need to find out about now is whether this squire saw the ghost, or if anyone else later on did, when it was an orphanage."

"What time is it?" Ellie asked, suddenly turning to Ruff.

"Almost ten," Ruff said.

"What time's your dad picking us up, eleven?"

Ruff nodded. "Kick-off's at half past."

Ellie made a face. "We really ought to get warmed up. We're playing the Skullers today and I don't want to be stiff getting out on that field."

The Skullers, Oz knew, were at top of the table in Ellie and Ruff's league and he could sense Ellie's nervousness at the thought of the coming game. Ruff, on the other hand, seemed none too bothered.

"So let's go over to the park," Oz said.

"But what about the ghost?" Ruff asked

"Didn't think we'd honestly crack that in half an hour, did you?" Oz said. "No, we need to get organised. Make a plan. Research it properly."

"Cool," Ellie said, nodding.

"Buzzard," Ruff said, grinning.

Oz grinned, too. Though Ellie and Ruff weren't exactly holding hands and singing "You've Got a Friend in Me" from *Toy Story*, the success of their Halloween night and the mystery of the footsteps had at least allowed them to put their differences aside for a while.

Ellie was making for the stairs, but then turned back and retraced her steps. "Do you think your mum would mind if I borrowed some of these books?" she asked, holding up the mouldy specimen in which Ruff had found the Bunthorpe report.

"Oh, yeah, she reads that every night in bed," Oz said with a straight face.

Luckily, Ellie held back from throwing it because it was heavy and would have undoubtedly hurt a lot if it had connected with his head.

In the park, they put down their backpacks as goals and, while Ellie and Ruff alternated between defence and attack, Oz played in goal. The ground was soft and Oz revelled in diving onto the grass whenever one of the other two sent a shot his way. After one particularly spectacular save, an out of breath Ellie stood in front of him and put both hands on her hips.

"Why don't you come and play with us, Oz?"

"Yeah," Ruff added, "you're way better than our pants goalie."

Oz threw the ball back out to them and shook his head. "Can't. Have to finish my homework. Besides, Mum wants me to go shopping."

"What about next Sunday?" Ruff persisted.

"Busy. The Fanshaws are having a party."

"The week after, then?"

"No thanks," Oz said resolutely.

"But why? You're an amazing goalie."

"Just don't fancy it. Besides, those colours don't suit me."

"O-oz," protested Ellie.

But they'd been here before. Many times, in fact. Oz had his reasons, but they weren't for sharing, even with his two best mates. Luckily for him, a white van pulled up in the car park at that moment.

"Here's your dad," Oz announced to Ruff, glad of the chance to deflect the conversation.

The other two grabbed their stuff and headed for the van.

"So, what are you doing the rest of the day, since you're too busy to play with us?" Ellie asked, still, sounding miffed by Oz's rejection of their offer.

"Maths, English essay, shopping. Buzzard, as someone might say."

"English doesn't have to be in until Wednesday," Ruff said. "I haven't even started it yet."

"Some of us managed to get it all done despite being in Centre Parks with a million cousins wanting to play Scrabble or go swimming or biking every single minute of the day," Ellie said, turning haughtily away with her nose in the air.

"Yeah, well, not everyone's perfect," Ruff said.

"So I've noticed." Ellie gave him a hundred-watt smile and ducked just in time to avoid the thrown football. They clambered into the van and Oz watched them leave.

"Best of luck," he shouted after them. "And watch out for the Skullers' dirty tricks."

"We will," Ruff yelled back, "don't you worry."

"See you tomorrow, Oz," yelled Ellie.

Oz walked back through the quiet streets with that word "tomorrow" ringing in his ears. Tomorrow meant school. Yes, he'd see Ellie and Ruff all day, but Seabourne County was pretty big and full of all kinds of people, not all of whom Oz enjoyed the company of. And then, of course, there was homework. Oz groaned inwardly. It wasn't a pleasant thought.

He exited the park and crossed a few roads and then turned a corner into Magnus Street. Fifteen yards along the pavement he passed a parked people carrier with all its windows rolled down. The four occupants, a man, a woman and two small children, had their heads poking out of the windows and were staring up at the houses, nostrils flaring.

"Say, excuse me?" said the driver as Oz walked by. "Do you live around here?"

Oz turned. "Yes, I do."

The driver wore a baseball cap and a golf shirt stretched across a chest that was very broad, but not as broad as the belly beneath it. Written on the cap was the word "Broncos."

"This is a mighty fine street, with its architecture and gardens and all. And old, I guess?"

Oz nodded. "Some of the houses are sixteenth century."

"Sixteenth century?" He turned to the woman in the passenger seat. "You hear that, Darlene? Sixteenth century. Holy moly."

Oz wasn't surprised to see them there. After all, Magnus Street was on the visitor's map under "Historic Seabourne; a grand street where years ago the Great and the Good built large impressive houses so that everyone would know how important they were."

The man in the baseball cap regarded Oz. "Guess it's seen better days, but what is it we can smell?"

"Smell?" Oz said, suppressing a smile.

"Yeah. We've driven all over Scotland and the North of England—"

"And Wales, Daddy," said a small voice from the back. "Remember, all those funny names?"

"Wales, too, but we've never come across anything like this." The man frowned and shook his head. "We've been up and down this street half a dozen times and we still can't figure it out. Fact is, it doesn't really smell of anything I can put my finger on. But it's so darned zingy, makes you just want to suck it all in and then do it over again."

"What might happen." Oz nodded and smiled. "That's what you can smell. Whole street's full of it."

He turned to walk away and left them staring after him. There was no point continuing the conversation because he'd already given them the only answer he knew. There were nicer, more colourful and brighter streets by the dozen in Seabourne, of that there was no doubt. And to the casual observer the houses on both sides did look a little run down and in need of a lick of paint.

Yet there was something about Magnus Street—some hard to define quality that no one could quite explain. It was as if the atmosphere was thick with the suggestion of things yet to be and the tantalising promise that they were just around the corner. Oz was forever seeing gawping tourists ambling about, getting frozen noses on freezing February days and drenched in December downpours. But if you really pinned them down as to why they lingered, all you ever got was a faraway look in their eyes and a shake of the head and perhaps a mumbled, "…didn't want to miss anything."

Oz started whistling as he crossed the road—not because he liked the tune particularly—it was just that turning into Magnus Street tended to make you do things like that. He strolled past number 21, which was a posh architect's office, admiring the bright blue walls and gleaming silver nameplates as he went. He lingered a bit at number 11, which was a bed and breakfast called "Sleep Easy," because it had a friendly dog that sometimes licked his fingers through the gate.

He usually returned to the even side of the street just before number 3, but today he continued past it so that he could inspect their decorations. Wispy spider's webs had been sprayed all over the front gate and on the path to the front door. Half a dozen pumpkins of various sizes sat, plump and orange, between some luridly coloured pottery toads on the porch. Above them, a joke bat with ridiculously long fangs dangled from the roof, while two large stuffed ravens stood guard on the steps over a slumped skeleton, its head resting on a gravestone with R.I.P. written shakily upon it. Oz smiled. The Fanshaw twins who lived at number 3 certainly knew how to put on a show.

Oz crossed the street, pulled open the gate and was on the point of pushing it shut when he hesitated and walked back out to look at the gatepost. He knelt and pulled aside a wisteria branch that had grown to almost cover the post completely. Beneath was an old plaque, once shiny but now green and weathered. Oz ran his fingers over the faded sign and allowed himself a smile as he read—"Colonel

Thompson's Home for Destitute Children." He wondered if any orphans had ever heard footsteps at midnight in the creaky old rooms.

* * *

After lunch, Oz went shopping with his mother for school shoes and jeans. He had tried desperately to explain that there was nothing at all wrong with his current shoes, but when his mother went to fetch them and put three fingers through the gap between the sole and the upper, he shut up. And anyway, he really did need some new jeans.

He didn't mind shopping, as long as it was for no longer than about an hour. After that, something started to happen to his brain. He found himself just saying "yes" to whatever the sales assistant suggested so as to get out of the shop as quickly as he could, and usually ended up hating whatever it was he'd bought as soon as he got home. How some people could actually enjoy the process, he had no idea.

"Just like your father," was all Mrs. Chambers ever said when Oz drifted into bored and miserable mode.

As it was, they'd got jeans within twenty minutes and the shoes had taken only another half hour, so Oz was about at his limit by the time they got to the supermarket. Still, there he could at least mess about by riding the shopping trolley and browsing the latest DVDs. But it wasn't their usual supermarket and, because it was near the middle of the town, the shop had decided to stop anyone from taking a trolley off the premises by installing special wheels that locked as soon as they crossed a magical yellow line painted on the floor. So, grumpy and laden with shopping bags, Oz trudged after his mother towards the multi-storey car park. All he wanted to do was go home and have some tea, but Mrs. Chambers wasn't quite finished yet.

"Hang on just a sec, Oz," she said as they passed another row of shops.

Oz groaned. The grocery bags were cutting into his fingers like cheese wires.

"What do you think of this one?" Mrs. Chambers asked.

Grudgingly, Oz walked over to the shop window. To his surprise, all he could see were small photographs of houses. He followed his mother's pointing finger.

"Very nice," Oz said. "If you like that sort of thing."

"Exactly. Imagine just having to look after three rooms downstairs and three up," Mrs. Chambers said with what Oz suddenly twigged was an alarming degree of longing. He glanced up at the name above the window.

Gerber and Callow, Estate Agents.

"You're not serious, are you?"

"Why not?" Mrs. Chambers said, eyes bright with excitement.

"But...Penwurt's our house and it's brilliant. It's—"

"Huge and expensive to run," interrupted Mrs. Chambers. "It needs a new roof, the council tax is enough to turn your hair white, and it needs decorating so badly, it's only at Halloween that it looks half-presentable."

"Yeah, but...I mean, it was given to Dad."

Oz saw his mother's shoulder's slump. "I know, Oz," she said awkwardly. "It's just that—"

She was cut off by a man's theatrically cheerful voice behind them.

"And what do we have here? Is it a pair of Chamber pots I see?"

Oz and Mrs. Chambers turned as one. The voice belonged to a dapper-looking man with what looked like a stiff crow on his head, but which Oz knew was his carefully coiffured hair. Lorenzo Heeps' eyebrows were as dark as the crow hair, but his moustache and beard were grey-flecked. He wore these in what his mother had described to Oz as

French beard. Oz wondered if he was trying to look a bit like Johnny Depp. If he was, then he needed to buy a new mirror. Mr. Heeps was also wearing a suit and tie under a fawn trench coat.

"Lorenzo," said Mrs. Chambers, "what a nice surprise."

"Looking to move, Gwen? Had enough of Penwurt?"

"Just testing the water," she said with a nervous glance at Oz. "Just seeing how property is doing, you know."

"Badly," Heeps said, shaking his head. "Wrong time to sell or buy. Of course, an exceptional property like yours in a desirable part of town like Magnus Street could fetch a premium at any time." He smiled and showed a row of very white, even teeth. Lorenzo Heeps worked at the university and had known Oz's dad very well.

"Yes, well…oh, hello, Phillipa," Mrs. Chambers said.

Phillipa Heeps, or Pheeps as Oz liked to call her, stood behind her father, dressed as if she'd just stepped out from one of the shop windows. Oz couldn't remember ever seeing her with a hair out of place, a shirt untucked or a smidgen of a smudge on her pressed jeans or skirt. Today, as usual, her fair hair was styled perfectly so that it hung over one hazel brown eye in a carefully combed fringe. She was, he supposed, quite pretty in the way a carefully cared-for doll might be. But it was a package spoiled by a cruel mouth that enjoyed gossip and whispers far too much. Her smile in response to Mrs. Chambers' greeting looked about as genuine as one of the Fanshaws' pottery toads.

"Hello, Mrs. Chambers. Hello, Oz," she said brightly.

Oz mumbled a grudging "Hi," which earned a frowning glance from his mother.

"It is so nice to see you," Heeps gushed as he and Mrs. Chambers walked slowly down the street. "We really ought to get together to catch up. If you ever need any advice, please don't hesitate to contact me, Gwen. I do know a little bit about the housing market, you know. In fact, I consider myself something of an expert, since I have a couple of properties of my own and I am a personal acquaintance of Mr. Gerber of Gerber and Callow, who as well as being Seabourne's most successful businessman is, as you know, a generous supporter of the university..."

Oz tuned out the one-sided conversation and shook his head. Dr. Heeps was one of those people who asked you a question but then didn't really listen to the answer. At the start, when his dad had died, Dr. Heeps had come around two or three times, but then when Oz's mum had become ill he'd dropped off the radar. But then, so had lots of other people who used to visit a lot.

Oz sighed. The weight of the groceries was proving to be just a little too much for him, and he suddenly had an urge to plonk the heavy bags down on the pavement and rub at the marks on his hand.

"Careful, you might do yourself an injury," Pheeps said in a low, mean voice meant only for Oz. "You might do yourself some real damage. Runs in the family, I hear."

She said it in such a venomous tone that Oz could only stare at her in bewilderment. In return, she simply grinned at him malevolently.

"What are you on about?" Oz asked, his brows knitting.

"Come on, you two," said Heeps from ten yards away. He lifted his eyebrows at Mrs. Chambers. "Just look at them gossiping like two old fogeys. What are they like?" His grin was snowy white. "Sure we can't offer you a coffee? There's a Costa just around the corner."

"We've got to get back," said Mrs. Chambers, much to Oz's relief. "Thanks for the offer."

"Oh, dear," Heeps said with feeling. "Next time then, eh? Come on, Phillipa, let's hit those shops. We've still to find those boots you wanted."

"We've still to find those boots you wanted," mimicked Oz as they slowly climbed the stairs in the multi-storey a few minutes later.

"Come on, Oz, they're not that bad."

"Yes, they are. You've got to admit, he is a bit smarmy."

"Because he dyes his hair and whitens his teeth, you mean?"

Oz shrugged. "And Pheeps has more clothes than the rest of year eight put together."

He wanted to tell her about Pheeps' peculiar taunting, but he had the odd feeling that it was best not to, so he bit his tongue and waited for the inevitable rebuke from his mother. He just couldn't understand why everyone seemed to think Phillipa Heeps was God's gift to Seabourne. But to his surprise, Mrs. Chambers didn't scold him. Instead, she took up from where she'd left off outside the estate agent's.

"The fact is, Oz, Lorenzo is a useful chap to know and in this case, he might just be right. Penwurt is in a prime location and it may be that we'll have to look at moving sometime. I mean, staying there forever might not be an option."

Oz's insides suddenly knotted. He didn't like this conversation. "Why not? What's wrong with living at Penwurt forever?"

Mrs. Chambers stopped on the stairs and turned her face to Oz. She looked very serious and Oz had the impression that she desperately wanted to say something. Instead, she cupped his chin in her hands and he saw her eyes soften. "Nothing," she said. "Nothing at all. Come on, let's go home. It's way past tea time and I don't know about you, but I am starving."

* * *

After tea Oz heaved a great sigh.

"Homework?" asked his mother, wrinkling her nose as she said it.

"Bit of maths."

"Oh, dear," Mrs. Chambers said.

"And King Arthur stuff for English."

"Gadzooks." She made a face.

"That one's sort of cool, though. Knights that chop people's heads off, that kind of thing."

"Lovely." Mrs. Chambers nodded. "By the way, you have a rather dashing milk moustache."

"Knew that," Oz said. "Keeping it for later."

Mrs. Chambers shook her head, ripped off a paper towel and handed it to him silently. Oz proceeded to make his lip milk-free and headed upstairs to his bedroom. The familiar sight of walls plastered with blue and white posters of Seabourne United greeted him. Next to his bed, a desk groaned under the weight of books about spies and wizards and vampires, a secondhand Xbox console he'd bought off eBay with two years' worth of birthday money and, of course, his dad's old laptop. Oz threw himself down on the bed.

Ellie, of course, was right. He'd had a whole week in which to get everything done but hadn't. The question on "Sir Gawain and the Green Knight" stared back at him from his exercise book. "Just a couple of paragraphs on your feelings about the poem," was how Miss Arkwright had put it. He'd have much preferred a proper title. As it was now, he had no idea where to start.

And then there was maths.

Oz got up determinedly, grabbed his maths books and went up to the library. He plonked himself down at the desk and opened his textbook. There were lots of a's and b's and x's and y's and a heading that said "simplifying." Might as well have said "gobbledygook." Oz felt a familiar dark hole open up in his stomach. Why did he find all this stuff so hard? But he knew the answer. It was the same one that Miss Arkwright, his form tutor at Seabourne County School, had been careful to point out to him on his very first day.

"When someone loses as much school as you have over the last couple of years, Oscar, it sometimes takes quite a while to catch up. So if you need any extra help, just let me know, okay?"

He could see Miss Arkwright in his mind's eye, smiling down at him with her well-meaning expression. Up until that point Oz hadn't really thought much about how much school he'd "lost." Mrs. Evans at Hurley Street Juniors, where he'd been up until last September, had never said anything. When he stayed away for a week or sometimes two to look after his mother, all she'd ever say when he got back was, "Mum all right, Oz?"

He'd nod and then she'd say, "And are you okay?"

And Oz would nod again and just get on with things.

But he'd lost count of the times that had happened until Miss Arkwright had brought it up. The fact was that it hadn't happened now for almost eight months, but for a long time after Oz's dad had gone it had happened quite a lot. The fact was that, when his father died, something had died in his mother as well.

Once, when things were really bad and with Mrs. Chambers desperate and miserable, paralysed by grief and confined to her room, Dr. Tarpin, the Chambers' family doctor, had sat Oz down in the kitchen. He'd explained how Mrs. Chambers was very sad and how it was quite normal to get a bit depressed after losing someone very close. But he went on to explain that in Oz's mum's case that sadness had turned into an illness that needed treatment with medication. Oz had sat quietly and listened and asked no questions. But when Dr. Tarpin had left, Oz had picked up the sheet of paper upon which the GP had written the big words.

Depression. Reactive unipolar.

The second bit didn't sound too bad when he read it back. In fact, it didn't sound like an illness at all. Unipolar sounded more like something you might use to repair a broken radio. But there was nothing easily fixable about the way his mother wouldn't eat, or didn't want to be hugged, or didn't shower, or slouched about in a dressing gown for days at a time. There was nothing he could buy from an electrical shop to stop her crying for hours on end.

But he had done as much as he could in other ways, like shopping for the two of them at Mr. Virdi's greengrocery on Tricolour Street instead of the supermarket in town, and getting eggs and potatoes and bread from the milkman. Sometimes he'd decide that it was okay to leave her for the few hours of school. Sometimes it didn't seem to matter because she'd ignore him altogether, turned towards the wall in her bed, unable even to respond to his questions.

Sometimes, though, she'd beg him not to leave her. On those days, Oz would do what she couldn't, like the washing and ironing, or hoovering their kitchen and making spaghetti. And when he got back to Hurley Street School a few days or a week or two later, Mrs. Evans seemed simply to understand. He felt a dark, cold hand suddenly close around his heart. Although his mother was much, much better, a part of him lived in constant fear of things returning to the way they were. And he had a terrible feeling that Seabourne County would not be as understanding as Hurley Street Juniors had been about the Black Dog.

He forced himself to turn to the sheet of twenty questions set by his maths teacher. He'd done almost half of them and now there was nothing for it but to wrestle with the remaining eleven. Whoever had thought up algebra should have been hung in a gibbet, like they did to people in Sir Gawain's time. He let his gaze wander to the oak panelling and the strange symbols carved in two great wheels on the oak. He had no real idea what any of them meant, other than they were something to do with astrology or astronomy or something beginning with an A. Come to think of it, they were a lot like algebra, really. And as was often the case when something in the house caught his attention, he thought of how easy it would all be if his father were there. Had things been different, he could have just nipped downstairs, knocked on the study door and simply asked, "Hey Dad, you know those really weird symbols on the panelling upstairs, what exactly do they mean? And who was the girl that appeared to the bell ringers in the Bunthorpe Encounter? Oh, and by the way, you any good at algebra?"

And Michael Chambers would take off his glasses and sit back, regarding Oz with his patient, amused smile. And Oz would listen while his dad explained, whatever the question. And ten minutes would turn into an hour in which books would be taken down from shelves and stories told of trips that his dad had made to strange, inaccessible corners of abandoned cities in countries with unpronounceable names.

But things weren't different. They were the way they were and he was in the library at Penwurt, alone on a Sunday with eleven maths questions to finish and an essay to write on Sir Gawain. And all he really wanted to do was to talk to his dad and research ghosts.

Sometimes, life just wasn't fair.

Chapter 4

Badger Breath Boggs

The following morning in room 33 at Seabourne County School, Oz's class, 1C congregated for registration. As usual the room buzzed with a dozen different conversations, some louder than others.

"I went to my brother's Halloween party," boasted Tracy Roper to a bored-looking Sandra Ojo. "Me and my friend Zoe were the only ones under fourteen with invites, and I wore this wicked costume and mask which cost loads."

"Waste of money," said Lee "Jenks" Jenkins from the back. "Take a look in the mirror, Roper. You could have gone as you are now and won best monster prize, no trouble."

The small posse of Jenks' hangers-on clustered around him all sniggered, while Tracy Roper, whose pale skin was as thick as at least two rhinoceri, made eyes to the ceiling and shook her head in exasperation. Oz, sitting with Ellie and Ruff about halfway back under a poster of a rainforest, registered Jenks' insults only vaguely because he was too busy trying to take in what had happened in Ellie and Ruff's football game.

"Five-nil," he said, aghast. "Why didn't you text me?"

"No credit on my phone," Ellie mumbled, and Ruff shrugged in agreement. The three of them knew that they could have emailed or Skyped instead, but Oz let it pass. Obviously, they'd needed to just lick their wounds.

"But what happened?"

"We were rubbish," Ellie said despondently.

"Total cow dung," Ruff said, turning a page on a well-thumbed gaming magazine someone had lent him that morning.

"And I think our goalie's got narcoepileprosy," Ruff explained, shaking his head glumly.

"What?"

"You know, that disease where people fall asleep all the time. He dived the wrong way twice and he scored an own goal when the ball came off the crossbar, hit him smack on the back of the head and went in."

Oz suppressed a laugh.

"It wasn't funny, Oz," Ellie said, clearly not amused.

Oz tried to smother his laughter. But hearing Ruff describe the incompetent goalie was almost as funny as seeing Ellie's sour expression.

"It's even worse than you think," Ellie added, looking distraught.

"Why?" Oz said.

"Jenks scored two. TWO!" she wailed before spitting out her favourite expletive. "Sugar!"

"His head's so big I'm surprised he got in through the door," Ruff muttered, drooling over screenshots of *Death Planet Hub*, which was his favourite Xbox game.

"Oh, no," Oz said, and quickly glanced at Jenks, who was small in stature but very big in the mouth department and lightning fast on the soccer field. He was obviously reliving some manoeuvre from yesterday's game and, when he caught Ellie glancing over, took great pleasure in flourishing a red card from his pocket and thrusting it up in the air.

"What's that all about?" Oz asked.

"I got sent off," Ellie said, looking suddenly very sheepish.

Oz's mouth fell open. "What?" he managed to say after a few speechless seconds.

"Bad language," Ellie said and then quickly added, "We were already four-nil down. But their centre forward is a nasty piece of work and he barged right into Niko, so I told him what I thought of him. I called him a vicious git."

"But she got the words mixed up a bit," Ruff said, stifling a grin. "I don't know what vigous means, but you can guess what the other bit sounded like."

Oz tried unsuccessfully to stifle another burst of laughter.

"He deserved it," Ellie said.

"Trouble was, she yelled it out so loudly I'm surprised you didn't hear it at yours," Ruff muttered without looking up from his screen.

But this criticism was the final straw for a clearly upset Ellie, who suddenly rounded on Ruff. "Well, at least I cared enough to give him a mouthful. The rest of you just gave up after halftime. I mean, look at you. Just look at you. You can't even be bothered to stop reading some stupid magazine to tell Oz what actually happened! I hate losing. I just hate it. Of all the teams in the league to get hammered by, the Skullers are the worst. But I honestly don't think you care. I don't think you care about anything." She turned her back on them both and buried her head in her school bag, her mouth a thin gash of anger.

Ruff looked across at Oz, his expression a mixture of confusion and irritation. It looked like he was going to say something, but Oz shook his head and waved his hand out of Ellie's view as a warning; Ellie really did hate losing more than anyone Oz knew.

He risked another glance to the back. Behind Jenks sat his faithful shadow, Kieron Skinner. Tall and bony, Skinner usually wore a vacant expression and constantly picked at his forever running nose. But this morning he was grinning like a loon and smirking worse than Jenks was.

"So, did you get all your homework done, then?" Oz asked Ruff in an attempt at steering the conversation away from football.

"No. Just about managed to finish stuff for Badger Breath Boggs, that's all."

Oz groaned. "We've got maths first lesson, haven't we?"

Ruff slumped in his chair. "Thanks a bundle. I'd almost forgotten about him."

"Wish I could," Oz said. "I just hope he doesn't pick on me today. He has it in for me, I swear."

"You and half the rest of the class."

"You mean the bottom half of the rest of the class," added Oz glumly. "It's really weird. I used to like maths when I was in junior school. I was even quite good at it."

Ellie turned back. Her face was still flushed and angry-looking, but it was obvious that she had to respond to what she was hearing. "Oz, Badger Breath doesn't have it in for you because you've suddenly become a maths idiot," she said.

"No," Ruff agreed, "he has it in for you 'cos he's a miserable gonk."

There was no time for more chat about Boggs. The door to room 33 opened and in breezed Miss Arkwright, 1C's form tutor. Oz quite liked Miss Arkwright because she was a bit different. She wore smock dresses and gladiator sandals and put "Save the Whales" and rainforest posters up all over room 33. She'd even worn a flower-print headband on a day trip to Techniquest once, and she knew absolutely loads about Xbox games. Okay, so she was a bit dizzy and sometimes forgot to take registration altogether, but 1C could put up with that, no problemo. The one thing that made Oz uncomfortable about Miss Arkwright was how earnest she was. Especially, for some reason, when it came to him.

This Monday morning, however, Miss Arkwright seemed to be on a mission. She took registration in record time—even before the bell went—and told Jenks to sit down or he'd be spending the morning outside Miss Swinson's office. That shut Jenks up as Miss Swinson, aka the Volcano, was Seabourne County's deputy headmistress, and she was not the person you wanted to meet on your first day back, or any day, come to think of it. Finally satisfied at having got everyone's attention, Miss Arkwright stood in front and smiled at them all.

"Now many of you, I'm sure, will have celebrated Halloween. But I wonder how many of you know its real meaning?"

"All Hallow's Eve, miss?" volunteered Marcus Skyrme, whose arm seemed to be permanently held up in the air whenever a teacher asked a question.

"Yes, indeed, Marcus." She wrote the word "Samhain" on the board and pointed at it with her felt pen. "Our Celtic ancestors celebrated Samhain, pronounced 'Sow-ein,' as their New Year's Eve on October 31, which was then tidied up into All Hallows' Eve by the Christian church in the eleventh century—"

Jenks' voice piped up from the back. "Do you believe in ghosts, miss?"

Miss Arkwright frowned. Jenks' sidetracking tactics were well-known to all the teachers and were usually trodden on unceremoniously, but on this occasion Miss Arkwright decided that it was a fair question.

"I believe that there are more things in the world than can be explained by our common understanding, if that's what you mean, Lee."

"Yeah, but what about actual ghosts?" Jenks said, and then added theatrically, "You know, woooooooo."

Half the class laughed. For one horrible moment, Oz wondered if Jenks knew about what had happened in the orphanage and he glanced warily over at Ellie, who was looking puzzled, too. But then Oz saw Jenks' mock innocent expression and knew he was simply winding Miss Arkwright up. She cleared her throat to ensure silence before continuing. "Well, literature gives us different interpretations. Some great writers believe that ghosts are the spirits of dead people yet to pass, spirits who are unaware of their deaths. Then there are those who favour the 'herald' theory, which suggests that ghosts most often bring messages of comfort to their loved ones to say that they are well and happy, and not to grieve for them. They visit with the express purpose of helping the living cope with their loss."

"So they're not always nasty, miss?" asked Tracy Roper.

"Not always. Unless they're poltergeists, of course. And they can be very nasty, able to move furniture and even harm the living. Because of that, poltergeists are considered by some to be demonic in nature."

The class had gone very quiet.

"So…" Miss Arkwright beamed, looking slightly alarmed at the effect her explanation was having. "Since this was your first half term with me as your form tutor, I would like you to prepare a short piece of work on what you did over the holidays."

Everyone groaned. The bell rang and several people stood to go, but Miss Arkwright was having none of it.

"Stay where you are. Just one side of A4. That's not going to kill you." Miss Arkwright put her hands on her hips. "I would like a small essay entitled 'What My Dad and I Did Over Half Term.' Maybe you went to a football match, or to the cinema. Maybe your dad dressed up as Dracula—anything that you did together. Next time it'll be you and your mum, but this time, you and your da…"

She stopped abruptly and Oz froze. She was looking right at him. He could feel himself start to redden. It took four long seconds for her to recover enough to say in a slightly faltering voice, "One side of A4, okay? Now, umm…off you go and work hard this half term."

Oz got up and grabbed his bag, but Miss Arkwright stood right in front of him with her sad, earnest expression and frizzy blond hair. "Not you, Oscar," she said softly. "Stay for a minute."

Oz sat back down again. Everyone filed out of the room and as they did, almost everyone turned back to stare at Miss Arkwright pulling up a chair.

"Oscar, I am *so* sorry," she said, her big eyes strangely moist.

"It's okay, miss, really," Oz said in a voice that he hoped was low enough for just Miss Arkwright to hear.

"I don't know what I was thinking. Someone said in the staff room that we should get all of year seven to do something constructive, and I thought this would be a good way for me to learn a little more about each of you—"

"Miss, I'm okay. It's okay."

Miss Arkwright looked as if she was about to cry. "Yes, but of all the things I could have chosen." She shook her head.

"I'll do it anyway. I know what we would have done if my dad was still here, so it won't be too difficult."

"Oh, Oscar. How long has it been now?"

"Just over two years, miss."

Miss Arkwright blew her nose. When she spoke it was muffled through folds of tissue. "You know, if you want to talk at any time, I'm here. If there's anything I can do…"

Oz thought about it for a minute. What he really wanted Miss Arkwright to do was to treat him like everyone else. To not worry about upsetting him every time she mentioned fathers. But then he stared into her solemn face and saw the look of pity that he'd seen so often in his mother's and knew he couldn't say anything—even though he desperately wanted to.

"Yes, miss, I know. I'd better go. Double Badger… maths, miss." He grabbed his bag and slid out from under Miss Arkwright's spotlight gaze.

Outside, Ellie and Ruff were waiting for him.

"What did Hippie Arkwright want?" Ruff asked.

"Worried that she'd upset me with the essay title." Oz sighed.

"Oh." Ellie frowned. "Not cool."

"So now everyone else in the class must be thinking that I have been upset by it, even though I didn't even think about it at all at the time."

"Miss Arkwright's good at that," Ellie said.

"She's just buzzard mental, like all the teachers here, if you ask me," Ruff said.

Oz looked at his friend and smiled. Ruff had a knack of summing things up in just the right way. But just as Oz had feared, Miss Arkwright's attention had not gone unnoticed.

"Oy, Chambers, what's with the cosy chit-chat?" Jenks demanded, bouncing over like an over-wound jack in the box. "What have you got that the rest of us haven't, eh?"

"Just shut up, Jenks," Ellie said.

"No one asked you, Messenger. Come on, Chambers, let us in on your little secret." Jenks had pushed himself among the three of them. He had a thin, ferret-like face, which he belligerently thrust in front of Oz's. Behind him Skinner loomed.

"Yeah, little secret," Skinner said, parrot fashion. He liked nothing better than to repeat whatever he heard Jenks say.

"Weird echo in here, have you noticed?" Ruff said, pretending to look around.

Not one person in year seven was scared of either Jenks or Skinner, but they were like a pair of maddening insects that were persistent and annoying and just wouldn't go away.

Skinner started chanting. "Secret. Secret. Secr..."

No one realised that a group of year eight pupils had joined them in the corridor until a new voice spoke. It wasn't loud, but it silenced Skinner in an instant.

"Now, now, ladies, what's all the fuss?"

Jenks swung around and Oz saw his eyes light up. "Hey, Phillipa. Wassup?"

Jenks held his hand up, waiting for a high five. It hung in the air for a long and embarrassing ten seconds until Pheeps shook her head sadly, at which point Jenks pulled the hand sharply back down to his side.

"What's all this about secrets?" asked Pheeps calmly. She looked from Jenks to Oz and then Ruff, avoiding Ellie totally.

"Chambers, here, gets special treatment from Hippie Arkwright. We were trying to find out what makes him so special." Jenks sniggered.

Pheeps smiled and the image that sprang into Oz's head was that of a wolf cornering its prey. Okay, a very tidy wolf, but a wolf nonetheless. Behind her, three Pheeps clones followed, each of them with perfect hair and uniforms that looked as if they'd been worn for the first time an hour ago. They were collectively known as Pheeps' creeps, and Oz could never remember what their real names were. But he did know that they had a reputation for being arrogantly unpleasant.

"Arkwright's got a soft spot for losers," Pheeps said. "Stray kittens and lost puppies. Which one are you, Chambers?"

"Is Chambers a dog?" Skinner asked, a finger probing his left nostril. "I fancy being a pit bull terrier, myself. That would be a way cool secret."

Jenks, Ruff and Ellie turned to look at him with expressions of varying incredulity, whilst Pheeps' creeps all regarded him as if he was something they'd just wiped off the bottoms of their shoes.

"Shut up, Skinner," Jenks hissed scathingly.

"Don't tell me you haven't told them?" Pheeps continued, turning back to Oz as a nasty smile smeared itself over her face.

"Told us what?" Jenks asked.

Oz could feel the flush spreading up from his throat but was powerless to stop it.

"About his situation," Pheeps continued, almost casually. "About him being half an orphan."

"Half an orphan?" Skinner frowned.

"Everyone knows that my dad died, if that's what you mean," Oz said through gritted teeth. In his peripheral vision he saw Ellie wince.

"That's right, 'cos Arkwright set us an essay on what we did with our dads over the hol—" A frown of realisation creased Jenks' forehead and his mouth suddenly stopped working.

"Should be a nice short one for you, then, eh, Chambers?" Pheeps grinned. "But give Hippie Arkwright some credit. Maybe she does have a reason to be extra upset. Maybe she knows something that you don't. Maybe that's why she wants to cuddle you like a stray."

"What are you talking about?" Oz asked, confused.

Pheeps would have got ten out of ten in a smirking exam at that moment. Oz wanted desperately to demand that she stop talking in riddles, but the moment passed as Badger Breath Boggs appeared behind them and unceremoniously began ushering Oz and the rest of 1C into his class. Pheeps sauntered away, still wearing an annoyingly superior smile on her face.

"I don't think she's human," Ruff said as they got their maths books out.

It seemed about the right time for Oz to tell them about bumping into Pheeps and her father in town.

"Talk about bad luck," Ellie said.

"Where was she going, charm school?" Ruff asked, the corners of his mouth curving into a wry smile.

"Shopping," Oz explained. "She was looking for boots to go with her new everything else. I tell you she's gone mental. She said to me that I should be careful not to do myself an injury. All I did was put the shopping down."

"Weird," Ellie said.

"Yeah, and it was the way she said it. She had this sort of sick smile on her face." Oz shrugged.

"Maybe she's got a soft spot for you," Ruff suggested.

"Ugh, don't even joke about that," Oz said with feeling. "Her dad and mine worked at the university together. I've seen her at parties and stuff over the years."

"That must have been a bundle of laughs," Ellie said, unzipping her pencil case.

"What was she on about anyway, Arkwright's secret?" Ruff asked.

"It's just her way of winding me up," Oz said, and realised that he was trying as much to reassure himself as he was Ruff and Ellie. "Like Ruff says, she's not human."

The other two nodded sagely, since it was a pretty accurate description.

"Thinks she's so cool just because she's got money and no one says anything to her because her mother's been ill," Oz muttered.

Ellie sighed in agreement.

But Pheeps had seemed so annoyingly confident. What could Miss Arkwright possibly know about him that he didn't know himself? It didn't make any sense.

But Badger Breath Boggs was already writing on the board and they all knew that the sooner they started the better. Badger Breath's teaching style was old-fashioned and extremely boring. The class would spend one whole lesson copying from the board and listening to Boggs' droning voice. In the other lesson of the double, they would all try to do problems set by him.

Oz was always struck at how devoid of colour Boggs was. It was as if he'd decided to live his life in monochrome. His moustache was grey-flecked, his hair (what little he had of it) was silvering, and he even had a constant smattering of grey-cigarette ash on the lapels of his charcoal herringbone jacket. His eyebrows were the only feature in an otherwise sour-looking face that gave any hint of original colouring in that they were dark and bushy. But he moved very quickly for an ancient teacher of almost fifty-eight; someone once said that Badger Breath had been a ballroom dancer in his youth. Oz would always remember that, not because he agreed, but because of what Ruff's response to that suggestion had been.

"Ballroom dancer? More likely the back end of a pantomime horse, if you ask me."

For the next ninety minutes, Oz did his best to put Pheeps and Miss Arkwright to the back of his mind and concentrated on getting through maths. For about a lesson and a half, everything went well; at least, it did from Oz's perspective. Okay, he only understood about a quarter of what was going on, but Badger Breath seemed simply to want to get on with things today and was much less sarcastic than usual. It was Jenks, inevitably, who managed to change all that. He'd been pea-shooting wet balls of spit-soaked paper at people all morning and missing. But finally he struck lucky and caught Oz on the right earlobe. It was more shock than pain that triggered Oz's instinctive reaction, which consisted of swivelling around and glaring at an insolent Jenks. Yet that small, sudden movement was all Boggs needed.

Seconds later, Oz felt himself being yanked up by his shirt collar, standing at his desk and staring at the board through a teary haze, trying to decipher the figures and letters that made up the hieroglyphics written there. He wasn't crying because of the humiliation of being singled out in class, nor because of his frustration at not being able to do the sum. No, the cause of the watering in his eyes was all to do with why Badger Breath had earned his nickname.

"Well?" snarled the maths teacher, his mouth three inches from Oz's ear. With the snarl came another waft of cheesy halitosis, and Oz felt his eyes well up even more from the stench. The figures on the board swam in front of his eyes, turning them to blurry spider writing.

"Ummm," Oz dithered.

Boggs withdrew his face, pointed towards the board and yelled, "$3y + 34 = 2y + 89$ has never, and will never, result in 'ummm' as a mathematical answer. Get that into your empty head, Chambers."

Oz heard Jenks titter and felt his cheeks burn.

Boggs turned in disgust and marched to the front of the class. When he reached the blackboard he pivoted to face the whole of 1C, wearing a sour-faced scowl.

"I've seen it all before. Cocky little first years who think they know it all, so sure that you're all going to change the world." Boggs shook his head and his face sneered into a nasty imitation of a smile. "Well, let me tell you something, my naïve little friends. The real world isn't about talent shows and people making idiots of themselves on TV for thirty seconds of fame. None of you are going to wake up with magical powers that will get you all the things you want. Life is not a fantasy film. The truth is that, from now on, it's a hard slog because bills don't pay themselves. In just a few short years, you, like everyone else, will have to sell your souls to the banks to borrow money to get a mortgage to buy a house. And that means getting up early and going to work every day even when the weather's perfect and all you really want to do is go to the beach or toboggan on Marsden Hill."

Boggs' face had gone blotchy purple, and little flecks of spit had begun to froth at the corners of his mouth, but he wasn't finished yet. "I've got two years left of my thirty years of commitment to this profession. Murderers get less than I have served here. So, I have no interest whatsoever in soft-soaping you lot, and that means that I will not put up with any nonsense from any of you."

He turned his bulging glare back on Oz. "Now, some of you may have little or no interest in mathematics, a fact that will no doubt reap huge dividends when it comes to your first examination in four days' time. But this is a maths lesson, not a zoo. Although, judging by the way some of you behave, that distinction isn't always as clear-cut as it should be."

Boggs let out a deep sigh. "Sit down, Chambers, and try and get what little grey matter there is inside that skull of yours to concentrate for more than twenty seconds at a time."

Oz sat and breathed in cheese and onion-free air, wondering for the hundredth time what it was about Boggs and maths that he found so difficult. He'd loved maths at his old school, and his teacher, Mrs. Evans, had been nice. But this was Seabourne County; here they didn't do nice. And those that did, like Hippie Arkwright, sometimes tried a bit too hard. But as for Boggs, Oz had an idea that his idea of teaching was to gallop along as fast as possible with the result that anyone who couldn't match the pace got left behind. But not everyone was a sprinter and Boggs should have known that. There was no excuse for trying to maim people with vile, stinky cheese-breath, either.

"Is the exam on everything we've done this half term, sir?" asked Marcus Skyrme, who never had any trouble with maths at all.

"Everything we've done this far, including algebraic equations. So it will be to your significant benefit to sit, listen and learn for the remainder of the lesson," Boggs said, unable to resist another sideways glance at Oz.

The next twenty minutes seemed to take forever, but finally the bell for break rang. However, Badger Breath had to have the last word.

"The exam will start at period three, ten-thirty sharp on Friday, and last one hour. Do not forget. Personally, I can't wait. Leave your homework on my desk as you exit in an orderly fashion."

"Sarcy gonk," Ruff muttered as he, Ellie and Oz filed out in an atmosphere of silent gloom.

"I think I'm going to have to strangle Jenks," Oz said.

"Join the queue," Ruff agreed.

"Forget him. He isn't worth it. By the way, that book on Seabourne's ancient houses you lent me is quite good," Ellie said.

"Really? You know who the ghost is, then?" Oz asked.

"No, but I think we need to dig a bit deeper," Ellie said.

"Okay. This weekend, then? Usual time and place?"

"Buzzard," Ruff said, shaking his hair from his eyes and giving them his usual grin.

*   *   *

That afternoon after school, Oz tried finally to get to grips with his English essay before tea. But by half past five, he was getting desperate. It was time to call in the cavalry. He pulled out his phone and sent off a text. A minute later, he got a reply.

"In library marking essays. Feel free to disturb me whenever you like. CJ"

Caleb sat at a table with a pile of papers scattered in front of him and a bottle of water at his elbow.

"So, what's all this about King Arthur?" Caleb demanded as Oz approached.

"We've just done 'Sir Gawain and the Green Knight' and I've got to do two paragraphs on it by tomorrow. I'm a bit stuck."

"Was there no title?"

"No. We can do what we want. Jenks said he was going to do 'The Green Knight and other beheadings I've enjoyed.'"

"Sounds like a winner," Caleb said, arching his eyebrows.

"Yeah, but I don't even know where to start. Miss Arkwright said for us to write about how we felt about the poem." Oz sighed.

Caleb sat back and made the fingers of both hands into a steeple. "Remind me of the story."

"Well, this weird green knight challenges the Round Table to a sort of duel and lets anyone have a free hit with an axe, so long as he can give the challenger the same blow in a year and a day. Gawain accepts and chops the Green Knight's head off. Problem is, the Green Knight picks up his head and walks away. So Gawain has a year and a day to try and sort out the riddle and find out what's going on before losing his own head."

"So, what impression did the story leave you with?" Caleb asked.

Oz thought for a minute and then said, "That Gawain was a good bloke but that it was hard being chivalrous all the time, especially with girls chasing him and headless Green Knights after his neck."

"Self-sacrifice is never an easy road." Caleb nodded. "We're all human. We're all scared of things like pain and death, even Knights of the Round Table."

Oz nodded, too. It made sense.

"So why don't you just say that?" Caleb suggested. "You could explore chivalry, and I'm sure I could dig up some stuff on knightly virtues." His eyes became thoughtful slits. "I think there were five or six. Let's see—generosity, chastity, courtesy, piety, friendship, and looking good in heavy armour."

Oz laughed. His eyes strayed to some papers, covered with sketches, on the desk. Caleb called them doodles. Oz called them absolutely brilliant because they were usually very good depictions of whatever had taken Caleb's fancy to draw.

"Wow, that's the park from the turret window," Oz said, tilting his head to see better. "And that's the panelled wall with all those weird symbols on them."

Caleb nodded. "After marking essay number five on 'Eleventh Century Scottish Highland Lore,' I was becoming comatose. Needed a distraction."

"They're amazing," Oz said. "Where did you learn to draw like that?"

"I didn't. And they're just scribbles." Caleb moved some essay papers over the sketches.

A voice drifted up the stairwell from far below. "Oz! Food."

"I think I've got some prints somewhere of Gawain's pentagonal shield and the knight picking up his lopped-off head," Caleb said. "You could do illustrated paragraphs."

"Cool," Oz said as he turned to go, but then added, "Oh, if there's any spag bol left over, I could ask mum to put some on a plate for you and leave it in your fridge."

"Barter? Now that sounds like a plan," Caleb said, and allowed his lips to curl into a rare smile.

Oz started for the stairs, but there was something niggling at the back of his mind. Something else he'd been meaning to ask Caleb that had nothing to do with green knights or round tables. He whipped around.

"By the way, something happened at school today."

Caleb looked up.

"There's this girl—you know her, actually, Dr. Heeps' daughter?"

Caleb nodded and a funny little smile flickered at the corner of his mouth. Oz knew that Lorenzo Heeps was something to do with the Dean's office at the university. He also knew that his dad had smiled indulgently just like Caleb had whenever Heeps' name was mentioned.

"Anyway," Oz went on, "I'm not exactly on her Christmas card list, but she said something today...she said that maybe Miss Arkwright, my form tutor, was being extra nice to me because she knew something about me. Some sort of secret."

"Oh?" Caleb said.

"Yeah, I just wondered if there was anything...you know, if you'd heard anything...at the university, I mean...I was wondering if it had anything to do with Dad."

"Your dad? Why your dad?"

Oz squirmed. This wasn't coming out the way he meant it to. "I don't know why," he explained weakly, "it was just the way she said it after Jenks had explained that Miss Arkwright had gone all soppy on me for setting an essay on dads."

"I see," Caleb said, and muttered, "Typical. She sounds like her father's daughter, all right."

"Pardon?"

"From what little I know of her, Phillipa Heeps is a bit too self-possessed for her own good, Oz. I wouldn't worry too much about her if I were you."

Oz nodded. It was good advice, but was that a slightly awkward look he was seeing in Caleb's face? He hesitated, and a little knot of silence grew.

"Anyway, look, I'd better get on," Caleb said, suddenly becoming very interested in his marking again.

"Okay. Well, if you hear anything…"

"I'll keep my ear to the ground, Oz." Caleb kept his eyes downcast and there was not even the fleeting ghost of a smile on his lips this time.

Oz mumbled thanks, turned and ran down the stairs, trying to work out what he'd said that had made Caleb look so uncomfortable. Was it the fact that Pheeps was Dr. Heeps' daughter and Caleb didn't like discussing colleagues? Or was there something else, something he wasn't quite getting? It troubled him only as far as the kitchen. Once there, the delicious smell of his mum's spaghetti bolognese miraculously pushed all thoughts of Pheeps and Caleb's odd reaction right out of his mind.

* * *

They stayed out of his mind for the next couple of days because there were other things to think about. He did as much research as he could in the library, but there didn't seem to be anything about female ghosts appearing to the owners of Penwurt, nor terrifying orphanage children. In between reaching up to the heavy books on the topmost shelves, Oz did his best to get to grips with algebra, but it was an uphill struggle. And when Friday came, the test was even worse than Oz had feared it would be.

The way that Badger Breath had taught them to solve equations just didn't make any sense to him, and instead of going through the paper doing what he could, he got well and truly stuck on two questions early on. Before he knew it, Badger Breath was bouncing up and down on the balls of his feet at the front of the class, announcing that there were five minutes left.

Frantically, Oz turned the page to look at the other questions, but by then his brain was frazzled. He went back to the one he was stuck on. It looked simple enough: solve the simultaneous equation $3x + 2y = 8$, $3x - y = 5$. But for the life of him he couldn't remember if you had to add the x's together or take them away or multiply everything by 2. In the end, he gave up and sat back, flushed in the cheeks from knowing that he had only attempted three questions and had at least one of those wrong.

Badger Breath came round to collect the papers. He did so in complete silence until he came to Oz, where he lingered, unable to resist turning the sparsely covered paper over in his hands and smiling vindictively.

"All that revision clearly paying off, eh, Chambers?"

Oz didn't rise to the bait. Besides, even from three feet away, fear of a waft of halitosis-laden breath ensured that Oz flinched involuntarily and went into breath-holding mode. Mistaking Oz's lack of response to his question as pure ignorance, Badger Breath shook his head and walked on.

Chapter 5

The Fanshaws

On Saturday, Oz caught the bus into town and headed for the Café Ballista to meet the others. Ruff ordered his usual hot chocolate with extra cream and Oz a vanilla latte. This was their weekly treat, despite the dent it made in their pocket money. They found their favourite table in a tiny alcove and sat in comfy, battered armchairs.

Oz had long ago decided that, other than Penwurt, the Ballista was the best place to be, ever. He loved the strangeness of the place, the warm maroons and browns of the walls and the posters of exotic places like Rio and Santiago and Caracas. No one ever seemed to mind if you stayed there all day, so long as you bought something now and again. And they played great music. Not rubbish pop or golden oldies all the time, but good stuff that Oz never heard anywhere else. It was as if they had a playlist called "stuff that Oz and Ruff and Ellie really like" and put it on whenever they were there. It was warm and pleasant and had the added bonus of free wi-fi.

Ellie was shopping with her mum for her sister Macy's forthcoming birthday, so while they waited for her, Oz and Ruff researched Colonel Thompson's orphanage on Ruff's snail-paced old laptop. But apart from one or two sightings of headless horsemen in the garden—which was quite common in olden days, apparently—there was not one reported sighting of a ghost on the stairs or in the classroom. Nor was there a report of anyone being murdered or spirits with clanking chains in the night, which would have fitted better with Miss Arkwright's poltergeist theory. But there was quite a bit about the chap who'd bought the house once the orphanage had closed.

"I reckon this bloke should have been called Indiana Morsman, by the sound of it," Ruff said as he absently took another bite from a cookie the size of a small dinner plate while he studied his laptop screen. "He went all over the place looking for artefacts, it says here." He stopped chewing and looked up quizzically. "What's an artefact?"

"Something someone's made," Oz replied as he leaned over to see what Ruff had found. "My dad was always going places to see if what people thought were Greek or Egyptian artefacts were real."

"You think the ghost is him?" Ruff asked.

The chewed fragment of cookie that was halfway down Oz's gullet suddenly began coming up the other way as his throat spasmed. Was Ruff suggesting that the ghost was his dad?

"Him?" Oz spluttered between violent coughs.

"This Morsman bloke. Killed by a bomb in the Second World War, it says."

"I suppose it could be," Oz said, recovering, although his eyes watered badly. "But the Bunthorpe Encounter happened way before that, didn't it? So it couldn't have been Morsman who frightened the bell ringers."

"Yeah," Ruff agreed, "you're right."

Suddenly Ruff looked up and groaned. "Oh, no. Look what the north wind just blew in."

Oz followed Ruff's gaze. Two boys had just banged through the door, pushing and shoving and generally trying to attract as much attention as they could.

Jenks and Skinner.

"Think they'll see us?" Ruff said.

But at that moment, Skinner poked Jenks in the ribs and pointed at a far corner before sauntering off. Oz followed their meandering path and had to push himself out of his chair to see where they were headed. But then he caught a glimpse of a blond head low down in one of the overstuffed armchairs and knew immediately where they were going. The hair belonged to a girl of about nine who was busy attacking a huge, layered cream and mocha concoction that was almost as big as her head. She didn't even look up as Jenks and Skinner slid into chairs on either side of her.

"What is it?" asked Ruff, who had also stood but couldn't quite follow Oz's eye line.

"They've just found Niko's sister," Oz said.

"That's not good," muttered Ruff as Oz pushed himself away from their table and started moving across the café.

Skinner and Jenks didn't notice their approach until they were standing right in front of their table. They were too busy taunting the girl, who was trying to hold onto her drink while Skinner, smiling a predatory smile, tried to prise it out of her fingers. It was Jenks who finally looked up.

"Well, if it isn't the Pizard of Oz and Dorothy Adams."

Oz caught the blond girl's eyes. They were big and blue. And despite being defiant, they were disturbingly wet-looking, too.

"Hi Anya. Where's Niko?" Oz said, ignoring Jenks' jibe.

"He is gone to get prescription for my little brother from chemist shop. He tell me wait here and buy me this," she nodded somberly at her drink.

Jenks sneered. "Buzz off, Chambers. We're babysitting Anya, all right?"

"You want Skinner and Jenks to stay with you, Anya?" asked Oz.

Anya shook her head. Oz saw that her lip quivered slightly.

"We're not going anywhere, Chambers," Jenks said.

"What is wrong with you two buzzards?" Ruff said.

"Anya's going to share her drink with us, aren't you, Anya?" Skinner tugged harder on the plastic cup and it wobbled precariously, but Anya didn't let go.

Oz suddenly looked up and nudged Ruff. "Isn't that Seabourne United's new striker over there? What's his name now…"

"Ustenhov?" Ruff said, sounding excited.

As Jenks and Skinner craned their necks around to stare, Oz took his chance. He nipped in and deftly picked the drink from out of Anya's and Skinner's hands.

"Oy," Skinner protested, "that's mine."

"No, it isn't. It's Anya's and she's coming over to sit with us at our table, aren't you, Anya?"

The blond girl slipped under the table and out next to Ruff before Jenks and Skinner could react. Oz gave her back her drink and watched her walk across to where Ruff's laptop still sat. But Skinner wasn't going to give up so easily.

"Who do you think you are, Chambers?"

"Someone who isn't scared of you, Skinner." Oz stood his ground. "Two blokes against a little girl. That must make you two feel really good."

"They're just Russians," Jenks said in a tone that suggested that they were, therefore, fair game.

"They're Polish, you gonk," Ruff said.

"They can hardly speak English," Jenks sneered.

"Yeah," Skinner echoed.

"You should get on with them really well, then," Oz said.

"At least we don't hang around with girls," Skinner said, his eyes alight with challenge.

"Yeah, where's Messenger? Gone off to buy you some dolls?" Jenks sniggered.

"She's buying some new boots for next week's game," Ruff said.

Oz had forgotten that the return match with the Skullers was coming up so soon.

Jenks smiled, his small eyes glinting. "She's going to need more than new boots when you play us again."

"Yeah. Girls shouldn't play football, anyway," Skinner added nastily.

"I'd like to see you two say that to her. She's better than most of the blokes in our year," Oz said.

"Most, but not all," Skinner said, a sly smile on his lips.

"Anyway, how can you say that about girls? The whole point of it is that it's a mixed league," Ruff said.

"Which we are three points clear at the top of," Jenks bragged, punching the air.

"Make the most of it. It won't last," Oz said.

"Yeah? How would you know, Chambers? You can't even play," Skinner sneered.

"Yes, he can." Ruff bristled.

"What, in the yard at break time? That's not real football, is it?"

"If it means playing against idiots like you, then I'm definitely not interested," Oz said.

"You're pathetic, Chambers," Jenks said, with such vehemence that flecks of saliva flew from his mouth onto the table.

"Yeah, and next time find your own drink to steal," Skinner whined.

Jenks shook his head, grabbed Skinner's jacket and pulled him out of the café, with Oz and Ruff riding shotgun either side of them to make sure they weren't tempted to go via Anya.

Rhys A. Jones

Back at their table, Anya was concentrating hard on devouring her frappuccino. Oz watched her, glad of the distraction, trying not to think too much about what Jenks had said and failing miserably.

Pathetic.

It was probably what everyone thought, even if they didn't say it out loud. There was one way to shut them up, of course, but that way was barred with an iron gate as far as Oz was concerned.

"Jenks and Skinner," Ruff said, blowing out air. "Talk about gonks."

"Yeah," Oz agreed. There was a tinge of anxiety in Ruff's glance and Oz got the feeling that his friend was trying to cheer him up. "Think you'll beat them next time?" he asked as Anya's straw began noisily suctioning up the cream that had drifted to the bottom.

"We've got about as much chance as a snowball in a buzzard furnace," Ruff said, sighing deeply.

Five minutes later Anya's brother, Niko Piotrowski, who was Oz and Ruff's classmate in 1C, came in searching for his sister. Oz waved him over and waited while Anya explained in Polish what had happened.

Niko nodded and looked up at Oz and Ruff. "Thank you for helping Anya."

"No problem." Oz smiled at Anya. "They're a menace. They just like showing off." She returned his smile shyly and went pink in the cheeks.

"Yeah," Ruff added breezily. "Jenks and Skinner should carry a government health warning, if you ask me."

"Skinner is pig," Anya said to her shoes with feeling.

Oz looked at Ruff and they both nodded; sounded just about right to them.

They told Ellie the same story when she eventually came back. Ruff did most of the talking, and Oz noticed that he didn't mention anything about Skinner and Jenks' jibes about Ellie, or about how he had defended her. When they'd finished, all she could say was, "Can't leave you two alone for five minutes. Now, what have you found out about Penwurt's ghost?"

They explained that Morsman was an adventurer who'd spent most of his time searching for artefacts, and that Ruff's theory that maybe he was the owner of the ghostly footsteps didn't really hold up because of the date of the Bunthorpe Encounter.

Ellie agreed. They spent another half-hour trawling for information, but came up with a blank. So that afternoon they wandered around town, looking at the new cameras and tablet PCs and the games and DVDs before meeting up with Ellie's mum, who was going to run them all home. But the footsteps were never far from their thoughts, despite their frustrating lack of progress.

"You could ask your mum about the ghost," Ellie suggested as they made their way through the late afternoon streets to the car park.

"My dad might have known," Oz said. "He knew all about the orphanage, but asking Mum is not a good idea. Like I said, I think she's looking for reasons to leave as it is. A ghost would put the icing on the cake."

Which was true, even though what Oz was really thinking about was a black dog, not estate agents.

"If your dad knew such a lot about the house, perhaps you could have a look in his study," Ellie said.

"More chance of Skinner becoming prime minister," Oz said wistfully. "Strictly off-limits."

"But what could possibly be in there that could do any harm?"

Oz shook his head and shrugged. "You tell me."

"Nah, I reckon the answer is in the orphanage, anyway," Ruff said as he demolished a twelve-inch-long baguette dripping with mayonnaise. It was, after all, at least two hours since they'd had lunch.

"Wonder what it was like living there, sleeping in those beds," Ellie said.

"Must have been hard," Oz said.

"But I think Ruff's right. I think the answer's there somewhere."

"So we just keep digging?" Oz asked.

"Hi ho," said Ruff through a mouthful of bun.

"Don't fancy a game of football tomorrow, do you?" Ellie asked airily.

"Can't. Party at the Fanshaws'."

"Great," said Ruff, his face lighting up. "You can ask the weirdo twins if they know anything. S and S are probably on first-name terms with any ghost, if there is one."

"Very funny," Oz said as Ellie caught sight of her mum and began waving frantically. They piled into Ellie's nice, warm car and Oz settled back to listen to Mrs. Messenger give them a blow by blow account of Macy's very complicated love life. But Oz tuned out quite quickly. Triggered by Ruff's teasing comment, he was already thinking about the following day's party. S and S, as Ruff affectionately called them, were Sydney and Savannah Fanshaw who, for some strange reason, seemed to like Oz quite a lot. At least, he thought they did.

That was the trouble with S and S. It was sometimes quite difficult to tell.

* * *

Sunday lunchtime, Oz locked the front door and he and his mother headed for number 3. They were almost at the gate of Penwurt before Oz saw, out of the corner of his eye, a tall ladder leaning up against the gable end. He stopped to look up at it. Tim Perkins was at the very top, scooping out some disgusting-looking muck from the guttering and throwing it down to the ground in damp, dark, splattering mounds. The noise it made as it hit the ground was gross.

"That looks like fun," Oz yelled.

Tim slowly swivelled his head to look down without relinquishing his one-handed, white-knuckled grip on the iron bracket that held the guttering firmly to the house. He did not look as if he was enjoying himself.

"Not to be recommended after a late night on the town," he shouted, and then added cheerily, "Still, someone's got to do it."

Oz saw that Tim wore a belt around his waist studded with screwdrivers, a clipped-on measuring tape and a host of other impressive-looking tools. He certainly looked like he knew what he was doing.

Outside number 3, the Halloween decorations were still up, even though the pumpkins were looking the worse for wear after last night's early frost. When Oz glanced back at Penwurt, he saw that Tim had moved around to the old block but was still up the ladder.

"Is he getting paid for doing that?" he asked his mum.

"No," she said, clearly delighted. "Fantastic, isn't it? He's so helpful. I said I'd make him a casserole this week and he seemed very happy with that."

Oz made a face. "He didn't look very happy up that ladder just now. Do you think he's all there?"

"Well, you know what they say about gift horses—you never look them in the mouth, whether they're all there or otherwise," Mrs. Chambers said without looking back. When they reached the front door of number 3, she turned to Oz. "You ready for this?"

"Yeah," Oz said, and watched his mother press the doorbell. A moment later, a man with a startlingly orange tan opened the door. His face immediately split into a broad grin and Oz quickly lost count of the number of sparkling teeth on show in his generous mouth.

"Gwen and Oscar. Welcome, welcome." Theo Fanshaw pulled Mrs. Chambers across the threshold and Oz followed in a fallout cloud of powerful aftershave. "Leticia, Gwen and Oscar are here," he yelled at no one in particular, before adding in a quieter voice, "So glad you could come. Especially you, Oscar. Sydney and Savannah have been looking forward to it all day. They're desperate for company so that they can escape from us old fogies." He snorted a laugh.

From a door in the hallway, an equally orange-complexioned woman with very thin arms appeared. She was wearing something very sparkly. Mrs. Fanshaw grabbed Mrs. Chambers and kissed the air on either side of her cheeks.

"Maavellous to see you both. Now, Gwen, some champagne with a smidgen of cassis, or would you prefer buck's fizz?"

Oz watched as his mother was led away towards a room that buzzed with conversation. She threw Oz one nervous, over-the-shoulder glance, to which he responded with a reassuring smile and a low thumbs-up. A door opened and Oz glimpsed a room full of people, including Lorenzo Heeps, who was laughing uproariously at someone's joke as he smoothed a stray, inky strand of hair back in place.

"The girls are upstairs in their suite," Mr. Fanshaw said. "They have refreshments waiting for you." He beamed and made Oz wish he'd brought his sunglasses. "You know your way, don't you?" Mr. Fanshaw walked towards the door to the party, leaving Oz alone in the hall.

As he mounted the stairs, Oz studied the interior of number 3. It was full of polished furniture, which looked old and expensive. The paint gleamed and the chandeliers glittered. The paintings on the wall all looked like someone had decided to throw loaded paintbrushes at the canvas blindfolded. If they were meant to depict something, Oz couldn't tell what it was. He concluded that they were probably what people called "abstract" and probably therefore very expensive. Oz preferred paintings where you could tell where the sky ended and the ground began, and the people didn't look like they'd been through a blender.

S and S were not pupils at Seabourne County. They attended a private school and sometimes Oz would see them arriving home in their mother's huge 4x4, dressed in grey and lilac uniforms with lilac bowler hats. He hardly ever saw them around town, unless accompanied by their parents. It was only really at Christmas and at other party times that he ever spoke to them.

Which was probably just as well.

Oz turned left at the top of the stairs where the polished wooden floor gave way to a pink carpet. He walked through a pink door and into a pink-walled apartment.

S and S liked pink. They tended to dress in identical clothes, which, given that they were scarily identical themselves, made it especially hard to tell them apart. A fact that always caused them great amusement. They both stood as he entered.

"Hello, Oz," said Sydney and Savannah in unison.

"Hi," Oz said, and walked into the twins' suite, which was furnished by a cerise sofa, a pink TV and a cherry formica-topped table laden with sandwiches and crisps.

"Want some pink lemonade?" asked one of them. Oz thought it might be Sydney.

"Yeah, great," said Oz.

The girls both had large, identically mournful brown eyes and the same long brown hair. Today, they both wore coral jeans, rose coloured T-shirts and baby-pink Ugg boots on their feet.

"Nice spread," Oz said, admiring their food. "Expecting many people?"

"Only you," Savannah giggled.

Oz almost choked on his lemonade. "Really? blimey, uh…great."

"We've got a new video game."

"We thought you'd like to see it."

"We know you like games."

"Yeah, I do," Oz said.

"We watch you play sometimes." Savannah smiled, showing a row of perfect teeth that matched her father's.

The beaker of lemonade froze an inch from Oz's mouth. "Really? You watch me play?"

"Yes. We can see into your house with the telescope Daddy bought us."

This time the lemonade exploded out of Oz's mouth in a volcanic splutter. "What?"

"Do you want to see it?" Sydney said.

Oz nodded dumbly, dabbed lemonade off his shirt and followed the girls up more stairs to the floor above and into a converted attic room. In front of a large window at the gable end sat a squat-looking telescope on a tripod. The window looked out onto Magnus Street and Oz could see Penwurt opposite quite clearly.

"It's called a hybrid spotting and astro scope. Magnifies up to a hundred times," Savannah explained. But she did so without bragging. That was one thing about the twins he liked. They had all this stuff, but didn't gloat.

"We can see everything from up here," Sydney added.

"I bet you can," Oz said.

"It's all computerised for looking at stars. You just tell it what star you want to look at and it'll find it," Savannah went on.

"But we prefer to look at things down here." Sydney grinned. She sat on a chair in front of the telescope and put her eye to the eyepiece and adjusted the telescope position. "Why is that man up a ladder measuring your house?"

"Measuring? Oh, you mean Tim; uh, he's not measuring, he's cleaning out the gutters."

"Well, he's measuring it now, look."

Sydney got up and Oz sat in the chair. An involuntary gasp escaped his lips as he looked through the telescope. There was a small red dot in the viewfinder, which helped locate whatever you wanted to look at. It was centred now on Penwurt where Tim, magnified enough to see the pimples on his nose, was up the ladder. But Sydney was right; he did have a steel measuring tape out along the length of the guttering and was scribbling something down in a book. Oz could even see the writing on the pen he was using,

"Maybe he wants to know how many yards of guttering he's cleaned. Or he's thinking of replacing some damaged bit. He's very, uh…helpful like that," he said as Tim put the tape away and got out a scoop, ready to do some more de-crudding. Oz sat back, impressed. "This is awesomely powerful."

"We see all sorts of things from up here," Savannah said, grinning. "But we don't watch you all the time."

"No, we watch other people, too," added Sydney. "Last weekend we watched you and your friend Rufus and that girl Ellie playing games."

"Oh, yeah?" Oz said airily, not knowing what else to say but making a mental note to make sure his curtains were completely closed every day. He turned again to the telescope and Sydney showed him how to change the magnification and how to use the laser sight to pan, while Oz joked about being glad this wasn't a rifle, which triggered a burst of giggling from the girls.

"We like it when you come to visit. We think you're funny," the twins sang together. But Oz only half-heard them. He'd picked up two other people on the grounds of

Penwurt. One of them was Caleb, and he seemed to be trying to reason with a very animated Lucy Bishop, who was pacing up and down and waving her arms about with a very fierce look on her face.

Savannah was saying, "There's an attachment for a camera, too, if you wanted—"

"—to take pictures," Sydney finished off the sentence.

"Really?" Oz said, and pulled back as the twins leaned in close to show him. When he looked again through the eyepiece, Caleb and Lucy Bishop were gone.

They spent another half-hour with the telescope. The girls took it to the other side of the loft, where another window looked down over Seabourne itself. It was even possible to see the names of the tankers as they pulled in and out of the docks, kids playing in the street a mile away, dogs in the park where Ellie and Ruff had played football that morning. But Oz was relieved when Sydney eventually said, "Are you hungry? I'm starving."

Downstairs, the sandwiches were mainly pink, too—prawn mayonnaise, salmon, honey roast ham and tuna spread. But they were delicious, and especially so with the pink lemonade. He couldn't believe how neat everything was. After he'd eaten a plateful under the girls' watchful eyes, Oz was beginning to feel a little uncomfortable. Long stretches of silence were a feature of spending time with S and S. They didn't seem to need to speak, and sometimes Oz wondered if they could communicate telepathically. Desperate for something to say, Oz ventured, "Did your mum and dad make you tidy up because of the party?"

"We didn't tidy up. This is how it always is," Savannah said.

In his head, Oz could hear Ruff saying "buzzard."

"So, what about this video game you were going to show me?"

Sydney got up and walked over to a shelf and came back with what looked like a pair of very chunky sunglasses. "It's not really a video game, because there isn't a video or a DVD."

Oz frowned.

"It's called a Spectrum Experience Unit. SPEXIT for short. It's not on sale yet. My dad knows the owner of the company that makes it and they gave us one to try out. Go on, it's amazing."

Oz took the glasses. They were heavier, and the arms slightly thicker, than ordinary sunglasses. They fitted snugly over his ears and once on, the room descended into darkness. All he could see through the lenses were the vague shapes of S and S and outlines of tables and chairs.

"There's a switch and a toggle wheel on the top," Sydney said, and Oz felt his index finger being placed on the right spot. He pressed the button, and instantly everything changed. A 3D image of a pyramid floated in front of him and then a logo for something called JG Telecom, over which a transparent menu appeared. There were three choices—'Wild White Water', 'Bungee Blast' or 'Roller Coaster Reality'. Oz toggled to Wild White Water and pressed the button.

"Good choice," Savannah murmured from somewhere beyond his vision.

Instantly, the faint noise of music from the party below faded and was replaced by the muted rush of running water, with the faint but unmistakable roar of rapids in the background. The room, which up to that point Oz could see plainly around the rim of the glasses, disappeared. And there was the weirdest sensation of floating. Ahead of him was a canyon. In fact, all around him was canyon. Beneath him was a yellow fibreglass hull and he realised that he was in a virtual canoe. Superimposed on the vista ahead, there appeared another transparent menu. Oz toggled to play and pressed the button.

Immediately, Oz felt himself moving forward on the river. Instinctively, he put his hands out for balance and saw that he held a paddle. It even felt like he was holding a paddle.

"Don't worry, it never capsizes," a voice said from somewhere behind him.

Oz was gathering speed as the canyon walls began to slide by. Above, the sun shone in a cloudless sky. Incredibly, when he turned his face upwards he could actually feel its warmth. He put his right hand down to break the surface of the water and felt a cold, silky flow over his skin. Yet when he pulled his hands free and rubbed his thumb and forefinger together, there was no dampness.

The canoe continued to accelerate as a bend in the river loomed ahead. He felt himself pulled along by the current and experimented with his virtual paddle, and quickly saw how he could slow down or turn. Then he was at the bend and the noise of the rapids doubled in volume. He turned the corner and shot forward towards the rushing, boiling water. He dipped and swerved, plummeted and crested. Sometimes he even felt the splash of water on his face, but it was nothing compared with the sheer exhilaration of the adrenaline rush.

Never, in all the games he'd ever tried, had he experienced anything at all like this. It wasn't just the incredible graphics and the noise of the roaring water, it was the fact that it was so lifelike. The glasses cut everything else out and he felt immersed, surrounded by the environment. In short, it seemed…real. He fought the white water, relishing its power, using all his strength to steer away from the treacherous rocks and swirling whirlpools that threatened to suck him down.

Even though a part of him knew that this was a game and nothing else, he was so caught up in it, so totally immersed in its reality, that he gave no thought to stopping. At last, after yet more bends and thrills, a little heads-up display appeared and indicated a two-kilometre mark. The rapids passed and Oz drifted out into flat calm and sat back, exhausted.

"Hello?" said a voice, which he recognised as Savannah's. Oz felt some pressure on the nosepiece of the glasses, and the canyon and the river faded into blackness. And then the glasses were off and he was blinking into the daylight coming in through the windows of S and S's suite.

"Well?" asked a grinning Sydney.

Flabbergasted, Oz couldn't speak for twenty seconds. He was too busy catching his breath. Finally he managed to say, "But I could feel the sun. I could touch the water. It splashed my face…" He put his hand up, but his skin was bone-dry.

"Amazing, aren't they?" Savannah said. "Sydney threw up on the roller coaster."

"I did not," Sydney protested.

"Almost did," taunted her sister.

"But…how?" persisted Oz. "I mean, this is way better than anything I've ever played before."

"You'd have to ask Mr. Gerber." Savannah shrugged. "He's the G in JG Industries."

"And the J," corrected Sydney. "Jack Gerber."

"Hang on, I thought he sold property?"

"He does lots of things. But JG Industries have been working on these SPEXITs for years, or so my dad says."

"But I've never seen these in the shops."

"Not yet. They're being tested—"

"—by us."

"But…" Oz got no further with his questions. Someone was calling his name from downstairs. He went to the landing and looked down. His mother was standing there looking apologetic, while Mr. Fanshaw hovered in the background.

"Oz," said Mrs. Chambers, "can I have a word with you?"

Oz ran down. Mrs. Chambers stood with her back to Mr. Fanshaw and Oz watched as she explained what was going on. "Sorry, Oz. I've got one of my migraines."

The words came out ordinarily enough, but Mrs. Chambers' eyes and eyebrows were doing a dance of their own as they veered in a direction over her right shoulder, where Mr. Fanshaw stood by anxiously. Oz watched as his mum brought her hand up to her throat and feigned strangulation, complete with protruding tongue. It was all Oz could do to stop himself from laughing out loud.

"Oh, no," he said, laying on the concern.

"Do you mind terribly if we leave?"

"It's no trouble if Oscar wants to stay for a while. I could escort him back to number 2," Mr. Fanshaw offered.

Mrs. Chambers' face cracked into a rigor of panic.

"No," Oz said quickly, "sometimes she has difficulty seeing with her migraines. I'd better go with her. Thanks all the same, Mr. Fanshaw."

Oz turned to go back upstairs to say goodbye to S and S, but they were already on the landing peering down, looking like two pink bookends.

"I, uh…"

"Thanks for coming," they said together, then looked once at each other and went back up to their pink suite.

Oz and his mum made it to the pavement after five minutes of profuse well wishes and goodbyes from Theo and Leticia Fanshaw. As they stepped into the road, Mrs. Chambers let out a huge sigh of relief with her back to Number 3. "Sorry, Oz," she explained, "I just could not take another minute of it. Fanshaw kept introducing me to estate agents and solicitors. I suppose it serves me right for bumping into Lorenzo, who has a mouth like the Channel Tunnel. Every single one of the people I spoke to in there had heard that I was thinking about putting Penwurt up for sale."

"And are you?" Oz took his mother's arm and "helped" her across the street.

"No," said Mrs. Chambers, but without as much conviction as Oz would have liked. "Well, I mean, of course I've thought about it. You know how expensive it is to run—"

"Yes, but what about Dad?"

A tiny little thundercloud of anger gathered on Mrs. Chambers' forehead, but then her shoulders slumped. "Oz, I know your dad was enthusiastic about this house, but I just don't see the attraction. I don't know what he saw in the place."

"Maybe if you opened up his study, we might be able to find out." The taboo word was out before Oz had a chance to stop himself. Mrs. Chambers opened her mouth as if to speak, but then shut it and frowned. She reached into her purse for the door key, but hesitated and looked at him earnestly. "Oz, maybe it *is* time we exorcised a few ghosts around here."

"What does that mean?"

"It means that it's a bit silly to keep your dad's study locked like this. You're right; we may well find a little inspiration in there. Lord knows we need some. Go on, I'll get the key and meet you up there in five minutes."

Chapter 6

The Study

Oz didn't need telling twice. He tore upstairs, hardly able to believe what he was hearing. He ran into his bedroom and started changing out of his best clothes, only to remember S and S and their telescope. He went to the window and smiled sweetly up at number 3 before firmly drawing the curtains shut. His phone chirped to indicate a text message from Ellie and he learned that they had drawn their game that morning, two all. He sat on his bed and was on the point of texting her back when his mother, as good as her word, appeared in the doorway.

"Ready?"

Oz was on his feet in an instant, and five seconds later they were outside his dad's study.

"I've warned Caleb that we're going in," Mrs. Chambers said, putting the key into the lock. "There'll be boxes of stuff to go back to the university, unless I'm very much mistaken."

She pushed open the door and for a moment they both stood there in silence. A musty, stale smell hit Oz's nose as he peered into the dimly lit space. It was a corner room, one wall curving outwards as the interior of the bartizan, its one small window looking down onto the drive. Mrs. Chambers went to the window and immediately opened the blinds. Thin, watery afternoon light filtered in to reveal a room crammed with books and a desk laden with the most amazing stuff you could imagine. Even from the doorway, Oz could see bits of arrows, the rusted hilts of daggers, and a bird's skull. To the side of the desk and its office chair was a shabby leather armchair, upon which was a pile of unopened letters and packages. On the wall next to the door was the ancient drop-dial wall clock that had never actually worked, but which his dad had loved. Oz breathed in the dusty atmosphere and smiled.

"Just look at it," said his mother, and let out a deep, theatrical sigh. "Still, no worse than I expected. He couldn't get rid of anything, could Michael the magpie? Well, I don't know if I can face it tonight, that's for sure."

"Can I take some of his stuff?" Oz asked.

"As I said, Caleb has been warned. He seemed just as keen as you were. So don't take anything until you run it past him, and I don't want your room ending up looking like a museum exhibit, okay?"

"No way," Oz said, and earned a long-suffering glance from his mother. "Thanks, Mum," he added, and gave her a hug. A blown-up photo of the three of them on top of a mountain in the rain stared back from the wall above the desk. They both looked at it, and suddenly Mrs. Chambers turned her head away and stifled a sob.

"Mum, we don't have to—"

"Yes…" said Mrs. Chambers in a cracked voice. She began waving her hand in front of her face and shaking her head. "Yes, we do. It has to be done. I'll be okay." She swallowed loudly and, on seeing Oz's troubled expression, forced a wan smile. "I'll be fine. You just go on in and if you find any treasure, we split it fifty-fifty, all right?"

But she wasn't looking at the room anymore. Oz knew that being in this study, his father's private place, meant being just that bit closer to him. And it was obvious that, even after all this time, she couldn't quite face unearthing all those memories. She would, he knew, come back armed with vacuum and dustpan, and it would be her way of dealing with it.

But not now. Not tonight.

When she'd gone, Oz went straight to the desk like a kid on Christmas morning. He picked up small stone Celtic crosses and held Iron Age boar figurines up to the light for inspection. The bird's skull had something painted on its beak in a writing he couldn't understand. He hefted an eight-inch black statue of a kneeling, jackal-headed Anubis, which had 240 BC written in felt pen underneath it, and smiled at a Saxon shield mount with an intertwined serpent motif, which he remembered his dad using as a door stop.

Oz was inspecting a cardboard box at the back of the desk marked "Medieval Arrowheads" when Caleb walked in, grinning broadly.

"How did you manage to convince her?" he asked.

"I didn't. The Fanshaws did," Oz replied, and on seeing Caleb's puzzled expression added, "Long story. Do you think I could keep some of these?" Oz held up a three-inch-long pitted metallic arrowhead.

"Ah, a trefoil. Armour piercing, that one. Probably Viking." Caleb peered into the box. "Don't see why not. Looks like your dad might have been cataloguing them."

"If I take an arrowhead for Ruff and a boar carving for Ellie, and maybe one of each and a Celtic cross for me?"

"Take what you want, Oz. But I wouldn't mind some help with these papers. Some are probably personal."

"Fine," said Oz, delighted with having secured some treasure.

It took an hour to go through his dad's desk, but Oz didn't mind one bit, because in amongst the university documents and paid bills were scattered reminders of shared good times—ticket stubs to the cinema, programmes for football matches and, best of all, photos. Even Caleb laughed at the one of Oz, toothless, on a beach eating an ice cream, most of which seemed to be on his T-shirt.

"Caleb, all this stuff on Dad's desk, are they just things he picked up on his travels?" Oz asked after unearthing a collection of Roman coins.

"Your dad was a Senior Lecturer in Historical Materials, Oz. He was always being given stuff."

"And he could tell if it was real or not?"

"Absolutely."

Oz reached down into the bottom drawer and picked out a wodge of papers. On the top was a file with a name on it that caught his eye.

"Morsman?" Oz read. "I know that name."

"Of course you do," Caleb said. "We talked about him the other day."

"Yeah, I remember. The chap who bought Penwurt. Ruff was on about him the other day, too." Oz picked out the file and read the title properly. "'Daniel Morsman, Charlatan or Visionary,' by Dr. M P Chambers." He looked up at Caleb. "Did my dad write this?"

"He did, indeed. He wrote all sorts of stuff for magazines and journals. Part of his job."

Oz studied the article and frowned. "I know that a visionary is someone who believes in things that eventually come true, like Nelson Mandela. We're doing a bit on South Africa in history at school. But what's a charlatan?"

"Someone who pretends to know a lot about something but really doesn't."

"Cool," Oz said. "We wanted to find stuff out about the orphanage, anyway. Think I could borrow this?"

Caleb frowned and sucked air in through his teeth. "This Morsman stuff is a bit of a tricky subject. There may be something in there that's a bit sensitive. We run everything past the university lawyers before publishing, in case any of us says something that lands us in hot water. Perhaps I'd better hang on to it."

Oz shrugged and put the papers down on the desk.

Caleb had moved across to the pile of correspondence on the armchair. "I think your mum ought to look through these." He picked up a wodge and a large, lumpy padded envelope slid out on to the floor. Oz reached for it and was about to hand it back when he read his own name written on the address label. He stared at it and felt his heart give a sudden leap.

"This is my dad's handwriting. It's got funny stamps on, too, and…" Oz gasped. "It was sent two and half years ago."

"Really?" Caleb said, peering at the date stamp.

But Oz wasn't listening. He took the envelope and ran downstairs. His mother was in the laundry room. She looked a little more flushed than usual, but Oz needed to know.

"I was going to come up and help, but I thought you and Caleb could do a better job," she said, but Oz could sense that she didn't really mean it. "What's that you've got?"

Barely able to contain his excitement, Oz blurted, "It's a parcel addressed to me from Dad."

"Let me see." Mrs. Chambers' face showed a mixture of surprise and mild horror as she looked up to meet Oz's eyes. "You're right."

"So what's it doing in Dad's study?" Oz demanded.

"I honestly don't know," Mrs. Chambers said, but then frowned. "Wait, it must have come just after the accident. It must have got mixed up with his papers. I just stuffed everything to do with his work into that study. I must have just assumed it was for your dad."

Oz read the defeated look of apology in her face and knew that there was no point being stroppy about this. "Never mind. It's turned up now."

"Thanks, Oz, and I am sorry," said Mrs. Chambers, grabbing him in a hug. "Where's it from, anyway?"

"Egypt," Oz said.

"How do you know that?"

"One of these stamps has a picture of the Sphinx on it," Oz said as he disengaged from his mother and hurried back upstairs.

"Aren't you going to open it?" his mother called after him.

"Yeah, but maybe there's more."

But there wasn't. After five minutes frantically searching through the small pile of letters, Oz found nothing more addressed to him. But it didn't matter. One was better than nothing. Grinning excitedly, he ripped the sellotaped envelope open. Inside, wrapped in bright-orange tissue paper, was a small oblong box, six inches long and four inches wide and about three inches deep. It had a brown, mottled colour and was smooth to the touch, except where a date that read "1761" was engraved in the surface. The lid was shut and secured by a copper hinge and clasp.

"A horn trinket box," Caleb remarked admiringly. "Nice present."

"Looks old," Oz said, slightly bemused.

"Mid-eighteenth century, I'd say," Caleb said with a straight face.

"How do you…" Then Oz looked at the date again and knew that he was having his leg pulled. But then a thought struck him. "Wait a minute, 1761? Wasn't that the date of the Bunthorpe Encounter?"

Caleb took the box and examined it carefully. "It was, indeed. Bit of a coincidence, that."

"Yeah," said Oz, "it is, isn't it?" But the tight knot of excitement in his stomach told him that his brain didn't think that at all. After another hour they'd more or less divided everything up into university stuff and Michael Chambers' personal possessions. Oz promised to do some more sorting after school the next day, but then his mother's voice called up to him to say that tea was ready.

* * *

He ate fish fingers, peas, and brown bread, which was up there in his top ten meals to die for. Afterwards, Oz went to the library to try and get some more maths homework done. But he took the box and his dad's old battered laptop with him. He really did try and get his head around more algebra, but Badger Breath's notes might as well have been written in Klingon.

The box, on the other hand, smelled faintly of tobacco and exotic spice and felt solid and wonderfully strange in his hands. It was nice, very nice, but Oz couldn't help wondering why, out of all the things he could have chosen, his father had picked this trinket box as a present. Michael Chambers' study was full of the kind of stuff that Oz would have been delighted to own. So what was so special about this little box? And then there was the article he'd seen on Morsman. Caleb didn't want him to read it, but Oz knew that his dad's laptop had all sorts of stuff on it that no one had ever bothered to erase. He fired it up and typed "Daniel Morsman, Charlatan or Visionary" into the search box. The article took thirty seconds to find and was in a folder labelled "Articles." Oz opened the file and read the first few paragraphs:

> An explorer, intellectual, amateur archaeologist and adventurer, Morsman was the archetypal

Victorian. All the more surprising, therefore, that he devoted the last twelve years of his life to trying to locate the four mysterious artefacts he became convinced he had been destined to find.

Despite years searching for the Obsidian Pebble, the Black Dor, the Ceramic Ring, and the Pearl Pendant that reputedly appeared at the time of the infamous Bunthorpe Encounter, it remains unclear if Morsman ever succeeded in finding even one. His search took him as far as the jungles of the Congo and the deserts of Egypt, all of which he meticulously documented in his journal. But as of yet, this important record remains unaccounted for. Its whereabouts, like the truth surrounding Morsman's bizarre death, remain one of the many mysteries running through this incredible, articulate, intelligent man's life. Yet how could a wealthy, charitable entrepreneur give up everything in the search for a collection of arcane artefacts? Was there more to this quest than the Victorian preoccupation with the supernatural?

There were other files in the same folder, cuttings and notes that were clearly research. One in particular caught his eye. It was labelled "Mysterious Death." In it were a couple of scanned newspaper cuttings from 1941 and an obituary, but underneath his father had typed bullet points.

- Daniel Morsman killed in a German bombing raid on the docks in London during the blitz in 1941.
- Morsman hated London!
- Meant to have been abroad at the time?

He was reading these strange sentences for the third time when Caleb popped his head up into the library.

"How's it going?"

Oz shut the lid of the laptop and smiled. "Not bad. You?"

"Still labelling boxes. What have you got there?"

"Algebra," Oz said, and then added, "Can I ask you something? Why was my dad so interested in Morsman?"

Caleb seemed to hesitate for a long moment, but then walked in and sat in one of the chairs. "Daniel Morsman was a distant relative of your dad's. That's really how this house ended up being his. It all came to light when he started researching the old place's history. I suppose it snowballed from there."

Oz looked around him at the library and the strange symbols, carved into the panels, that Ruff had been so taken with. He couldn't keep the awe and excitement out of his voice as he spoke. "It's this place, isn't it?" he said. "Makes you want to find out about it."

"You sound just like Michael," Caleb said, but he wasn't smiling. "Oz, there's something you need to know. Some people think that Morsman was a bit weird. He believed in things."

"Artefacts like the obsidian pebble?" Oz said.

Caleb's face showed his astonishment. "I should have known you'd find out. Like I said, a lot of people think Morsman was just a crank, but your dad...well, he wasn't so sure. He felt that Morsman was on to something. But your mother..." Caleb hesitated. "Let's just say that Gwen didn't share your dad's enthusiasm."

Caleb hesitated again and looked suddenly very uncomfortable, but Oz pressed him to continue.

"How do you mean?"

"She, uh...she blames your dad's fascination with Morsman for what happened."

"You mean, Dad's accident? But what could Morsman have to do with a car crash?"

"It was research on Morsman that took your father to Egypt instead of him coming straight home from Athens."

"What?"

Caleb sighed. "He went to Egypt on the trail of the artefacts."

"He was actually looking for them?" Oz's jaw dropped open.

Caleb nodded again. "All I'm saying is that your mother is a little…sensitive about all things Morsman. I thought I'd just warn you, that's all."

Oz nodded. They both knew exactly what Caleb meant, but this new information about Egypt was fanning the flames of Oz's conviction. "Do you believe in ghosts?" he asked suddenly.

"Ghosts?" Caleb let out an involuntary laugh. "Why do you ask?"

"Because me and Ruff and Ellie, we heard a ghost on Halloween night in the orphanage."

"Really?"

Oz studied Caleb's face for any sign of derision but didn't find any.

"Really," Oz said. "First floor. We heard footsteps, all of us did. It was coming from one of the schoolrooms. But when we went in there, it was completely empty. Looked like no one had been in there for years."

"No wonder you looked terrified that night."

"We've been trying to work out who or what it might be. We thought maybe it was tied up with the Bunthorpe Encounter. But now, listening to all this about artefacts and Morsman…do you think that the footsteps could have anything to do with—"

"Hey, you two," Mrs. Chambers sang out from the stairwell.

Caleb slitted his eyes and shook his head in warning, and Oz nodded in silent agreement as Mrs. Chambers' head appeared. She took in Oz shuffling papers on the library table. "I thought you were meant to be doing your homework?"

"I am. We were just talking about…algebra."

"Oh well, better leave me out of it." Mrs. Chambers made a face. "I just got off the phone with Lorenzo Heeps. He's agreed to come and pick up most of the boxes of papers that Caleb has sorted. Save us a job, eh?"

Oz glanced questioningly at Caleb, but there was a fixed smile on his face which was unreadable.

* * *

Later, Oz lay in his bed pondering what had been an eventful day. First, there'd been S and S and their fantastic SPEXIT, and then his dad's study and finding the trinket box, not to mention his dad's fascination with Morsman and artefacts. In the darkness, Oz shook his head. Amazing how you could go for years being bored witless, only to have several astonishing things happen in the space of a few hours. His mind was churning. What he should have been doing was worrying about the result of his maths test; instead, he was thinking about just where to start telling Ellie and Ruff about all of this.

He smiled and shut his eyes. So Mum was anti-Morsman… That meant he would have to be extra careful in his digging. Because more digging was what he now had to do. The footsteps and Penwurt and Morsman were all tied together somehow, he was sure of it. And with the added appearance of the trinket box, Oz was totally convinced that his father had reached out to him and sent him a message. Now all he had to do was to work out what it all meant.

* * *

On Monday morning, Oz collared Ellie and Ruff as soon as they got to their desks in room 33.

"You won't believe the things that happened to me yesterday," he said in a conspiratorial whisper. "But the best bit of all was that my mother finally opened up my dad's study, so I got you these." Oz handed over the items he'd taken from his dad's study.

"Wow," Ruff said, handling the trefoil.

"This is really cool. Thanks, Oz," Ellie said, holding up the little carved animal with shining eyes.

"Yours is about two thousand years old," Oz explained to Ellie. "The Viking arrowhead is only a thousand."

"Mine's two thousand years old," Ellie sang a taunting tune to Ruff. "Yours is only a thousand."

Oz grinned. He had loads to tell them. So much, in fact, that he didn't manage it all until lunchtime over baked sausage in onion gravy and mash. By then he'd told them about S and S's telescope and SPEXIT and was on to the trinket box and the Morsman article his dad had written.

"So," said Ruff with his mouth full of sausage, "this bloke Morsman was a little bit mental, then, sounds like."

"Dunno," Oz said. "But he was definitely convinced that these artefact things were to do with Bunthorpe."

Ellie shook her head and frowned. "That's freaky, because I've been reading *A Short History of Seabourne's Ancient Houses* and Morsman wasn't the only one to think that whatever happened at Bunthorpe was weirdly weird."

"What do you mean?" Oz asked.

"Maybe it has nothing to do with it, but there's this chapter in the book about the Seabourne Farriers."

"The whosamawhats?" Ruff said, moving on to his jam rolly-polly with extra custard.

"The Seabourne Farriers. You know, people who shoe horses and stuff?"

"What have horses got to do with anything?" Ruff asked, wiping a drip of custard from his chin.

"Well," Ellie said, dropping her voice to a whisper, "listen to this." She took out a sheet of lined paper covered in her own precise handwriting and smoothed it out on the table so that Oz and Ruff could read it.

"Many years later, William Shoesmith, the pioneering early twentieth-century vet and author, explained in the biography of his ancestor John Shoesmith, the farrier and brother-in-law of Edmund Redmayne (owner of the Bunthorpe barn), how he came into possession of an object of remarkable construction in 1760. Quite apart from being impervious to heat and damage of any kind, he noted its unusual shape—'like that of a shell.' Shoesmith found that, by holding it close to his ear, he claimed to be able to sense an animal's fears and anxieties. Not only sense, but by speaking to the animals immediately calm their fears. By using it in the way described and passing the shell off as an aid to deafness, he was able to calm and soothe any wild beast that was brought to him. Shoesmith and his family became the most successful veterinary business in eighteenth- and nineteenth-century Britain, although his use of the shell remained a well-kept secret. What was also remarkable about the Shoesmiths was their incredible longevity, with John working into his nineties and living to 105, his son Jude living to 104 and his son—William's grandfather Hebert— to 110. Unfortunately, the longevity streak ended with William's brother Charles, who died aged 48 on active service with the cavalry in 1914."

"So what happened to this shell, then?" Oz said.

"Probably lost it, along with all the marbles in his head," Ruff muttered.

Ellie shook her head. "No one really knows. Charles Shoesmith was involved in looking after artillery horses in the First World War. He was killed at the battle of something or other." She consulted her notes. "Umm, Le Cateau in 1914. No one has seen the shell since. But the timing is what's really interesting, isn't it? John Shoesmith came across this shell thingy in 1760 and the Bunthorpe Encounter was a year later."

"So you think they're tied together?" Oz asked.

Ellie shrugged.

"Buzzard," said Ruff. "Shells and artefacts. What does it all mean?"

"It means that Caleb was right when he said Penwurt meant a place where weirdness happens. Something really strange was going on and my dad knew about it," Oz said, thinking furiously. "Oh, and I saw Caleb arguing with Lucy Bishop again, through S and S's telescope."

"You think she has something to do with all this?" Ellie frowned.

"Dunno. But she was in the library the night we heard the footsteps and you have to admit there's something funny about her. You saw how she was when we turned up."

"Stroppy armpit," Ruff said.

"Exactly. And she's always like that. I just have a really bad feeling…"

"Bad feelings?" said a mocking voice behind them. "Overdone it on the fruit and custard, have we, Chambers?"

They swung around. Jenks and Skinner were leering at them.

"Go away," Ellie said.

"What's that you've got, Messenger?" Jenks said as he leaned forward and snatched Ellie's handwritten Shoesmith research up from the desk.

Oz shot her a worried glance, but Ellie was up to it. "English essay on farriers. 'Course, you wouldn't know what they are, since you don't bother doing any homework at all."

Jenks frowned and balled up the paper before throwing it back at her, narrowly missing Ruff's custard.

"Yeah? Well, I wouldn't bother trying to play football anymore if I were you," he retorted.

"Just wait 'til next week," Ruff said.

"Yeah, maybe I'll get a hat trick," Jenks said. Skinner sniggered loudly and they moved away, well pleased with themselves.

The bell went for the end of lunch and as they joined the throng of pupils heading towards afternoon registration, Oz only just had time to hurriedly say, "Get your thinking caps on. I'm sure the answer to all this is staring us right in the face. We've just got to keep working at it."

Chapter 7

Algebra

By the time Oz got back to Penwurt, a chill north wind had blown away the clouds and turned the muggy day to crisp autumn under a clear, pale blue sky. There was now only an hour after he got home before it got dark, and Oz decided to make the most of it before attempting his history homework. As a goalkeeping drill, his dad had taught him how to lay two old mattresses from the garage on the floor and use a wall as his attacker. Oz kicked the ball as hard as he could against the wall and then "saved" the rebound. He did all this in the garden so that, if the ball did get past him, there was grass and shrubbery to act as his backstop.

Practise was hard work, and after forty minutes of stretching and diving, he decided to give it one last blast at full power before calling it a day. But his concentration was waning, and the ball hit a drainpipe and went careening off at an angle towards the south end of the house. Oz watched in disbelief as the ball, caught by the wind, flew almost the whole length of the building, bouncing merrily on a gravel path as it went. Cursing, Oz hurried after it. But just as the pathway petered out and gave way to the small lawn at the very rear of Penwurt, Oz stopped. He could hear voices.

"…nothing you can do about it." Caleb's voice, patient and calm.

"But what if it was? What if we could use it?"

Oz recognised Lucy Bishop's strident tones.

"Yes, but what if it isn't? You'd be showing your hand for nothing," Caleb said.

"But I have to do something," Lucy Bishop said. "I can't just stand back knowing what he's going through…"

Oz heard the anguish in her voice as it died in frustration.

"My advice is to—"

Caleb's voice stopped abruptly as the ball finally rolled over the end of the path and onto the lawn. Oz trotted after it and did his best to be nonchalant.

"Oh, hi," he said as Caleb and Lucy Bishop came into view around the edge of the building.

"What are you doing down here?" Lucy Bishop snapped.

"Uh, I was doing some goalie practise," Oz said, "and the ball just ricocheted off the drainpipe and…"

Lucy Bishop picked the ball up and threw it back over Oz's head the way it had come.

"There. Now you've got it back," she said, her mouth a thin line.

Oz watched as the ball veered towards the main garden and got stuck in the soggy mess of leaves at the edge of a small pond. "Yeah, I can see that," he said drily. "Uh, thanks a lot."

"Sorry, Oz. Private conversation, you know," Caleb said with an apologetic look.

Oz shrugged and went to fetch his ball, all the while wondering why Lucy Bishop was mad at everyone all the time.

The evening got even better at about seven when Oz, trying to get his head around the Battle of Hastings and wondering if the arrow that killed King Harold was anything like the one he'd given to Ruff, heard a car pull in. He went to his bedroom window and looked down to see Lorenzo Heeps emerging from his sleek Jaguar, pausing only to crouch down to check his hair in the side mirror. Oz groaned, but felt a wave of relief on realising that at least no one else had got out from the passenger side and it didn't look like Pheeps was in tow. Five minutes later, he heard voices on the stairs and went out to the landing.

"Ah," said Heeps jovially, "here's the little man himself."

Oz forced his lips into a toothless grin.

"Your mother was telling me how you helped clear the study. Very good of you, Oscar. Of course, some of the university documents will be confidential, so I thought I'd best take everything away and return the private property later." He looked at Mrs. Chambers. "That would be for the best, I think, don't you, Gwen?"

"Well, I suppose…"

"That's okay. I opened all the letters addressed to Dad anyway," Oz stated.

Heeps' eyes narrowed just a smidgen. "Very thorough of you, Oscar."

"I'll give you a hand with the boxes if you like." Oz offered, reasoning that, the quicker it was done, the sooner Heeps would be gone.

For the next thirty minutes, Oz lugged heavy cardboard boxes full of papers and artefacts down to the front door, all the while listening to Heeps banging on about the need for cataloguing and confidentiality.

Finally, the study stood empty and Heeps hovered in the doorway, peering into every corner, satisfying himself that they'd taken every last thing. Suddenly he turned to Oz. "You're sure that there's nothing else of any importance? Nothing that you might have mistakenly held on to?"

"No. I've only got what Dad wanted me to have. I checked it all with Caleb."

"I'm sure you did, but perhaps I ought to double-check, eh?"

"Well, I've given an arrowhead and a boar figurine to Ruff and Ellie, but you can see the ones I kept, if you like?"

"Arrowheads and figurines? No, that will not be necessary." His eyes seemed to bore into Oz's face. "You're certain there was nothing else in here that I should know about?"

Oz thought about that. There were, of course, the trinket box. But it had been in his dad's study by mistake. Heeps would, Oz was sure, have been more than a little bit interested in that. But it was Oz's property. Given to him by his father and delivered by Royal Mail. It had nothing to do with the university. So Oz shook his head and returned Heeps' intense gaze with interest. Finally, Heeps glanced one last time into the room.

"There is, of course, the clock."

"That was my dad's and he bought it after we moved here. Mum will not let you have that," Oz said defiantly.

Heeps scowled, but after a moment of hesitation he finally said, "Splendid. Now, your mother promised me some tea, I do believe."

Oz followed him down to the kitchen and had a glass of milk while Mrs. Chambers poured tea.

"Thirsty work, carrying boxes. Eh, Oscar?" Heeps chuckled as he helped himself to some digestive biscuits. "Anyway, thanks for your assistance. But don't let me keep you from your homework any longer." He glared at Oz expectantly, and on seeing no movement added, "Actually, Oscar, if you wouldn't mind, I'd like a private word with your mother."

Oz still didn't take the hint. He was too busy dunking a biscuit into his milk to really notice Heeps staring at him until he cleared his throat loudly.

"Oh, right, yeah," Oz said, and took his snack back upstairs. But he didn't take it back to his own room. Instead, he made for the toilet on the first floor. Strictly speaking, this was in the part of the house that the tenants occupied, but no one ever used the toilet because there was one in a huge bathroom with a shower next door. Oz hardly ever used this toilet, either, because it was a bit pokey and cold. But it did have one saving grace in a far corner—a metal pipe that ran vertically up from the kitchen below. Once the smokestack from the old kitchen stove, it had a tiny little door secured by a latch two feet off the floor which, his dad had once explained, was used as access to clean the chimney pipe.

But there was no stove in the kitchen anymore. In fact, there was nothing but a square metal canopy which helped carry fumes and smells away from his mum's modern oven. But other things were carried up that pipe, too. Noises, like the beeping alarm of the fridge door being left open, the banging of pots and pans and, when the kitchen was occupied, voices. Oz knelt and undid the latch on the door, tilted his head slightly and leaned in.

"…I have had a chance to talk to a few of the people you met at the Fanshaws'," Heeps was saying, "and I can tell you that Jack is very interested, indeed."

"Jack?" his mother asked.

"Jack Gerber, as in Gerber and Callow. It was their window you were gazing into when I bumped into you and Oscar in town. He sees huge potential in a property of this size. There is a great need for more affordable accommodation in this area."

"Well, that's very interesting, but I haven't had a chance to talk to Oz about this. Not seriously, I mean."

"Well, of course, that is up to you, but I hardly think an eleven-year-old is capable of making a rational decision on such weighty matters. I mean, the upkeep on a place like this must be—"

"Horrendous, yes, it is. But I must discuss it with Oz. That's how we do things. Just hasn't been the right moment. Not yet."

"I see," said Heeps in a tone that said he didn't see at all. "All I can tell you is that Jack would be delighted to deal with you in person. Something he very rarely does, what with having so many expanding interests and being the entrepreneur that he is. However, he is mindful of your, uh…delicate situation. And you know, Gwen, I can't help thinking that if Michael were here, he'd want you to be comfortable and less stressed…"

"Rubbish," said Oz to himself, a little more loudly than he'd meant to.

"Thank you, Lorenzo," Mrs. Chambers said after quite a long pause. "I am grateful for your interest and I know you mean well, but I would still want to discuss all of this with Oz."

"Not at all. And look, if I'm being too much of a bore about this selling business, just tell me to buzz off. But I would so like to see you settled somewhere less… demanding," Heeps said, and Oz knew he'd be beaming at Mrs. Jones with that hundred-watt smile of his at that very moment.

"More tea?" Mrs. Chambers asked.

"No, I mustn't. Phillipa is preparing our supper this evening and I must not be late. Bit of a tyrant in the kitchen, is Phillipa."

"And how is poor Belinda?"

"Delicate. Very delicate. We hope to have her home soon, though, rejuvenated and ready for business." Heeps chuckled.

"Still convalescing at the villa?"

"Yes. Weather's so much warmer in Spain, as you know."

Oz heard the scraping of chairs and Heeps' voice growing ever fainter.

"You know you can pick up the phone at any time, Gwen. I'm here to help in any way I can…"

Oz waited until he heard the front door slam and then went back down to the kitchen.

"I expect you were listening in that pokey toilet, weren't you?" Mrs. Chambers asked accusingly.

"He's a slime bag, Mum."

Mrs. Chambers looked as if she was about to protest, but then said, "He's trying to be helpful, Oz."

"He's trying to get us out of here, more like," Oz corrected her.

"Look, I had nothing to do with that. In fact, it was why I left the party early yesterday. Lorenzo kept introducing me to solicitors and mortgage brokers. He's like a dog with a bone."

Oz nodded. "A smelly old dog."

"Oz," warned Mrs. Chambers.

But Oz was determined to get his point across. "Mum, I know that Dad wouldn't want us to leave here. Heeps is so wrong about that."

"How can you possibly know that?" Mrs. Chambers said as she started taking clothes from the dryer and folding them.

"But I do. I feel it all the time. Like something's going to happen."

"The boiler breaking down again, you mean?"

"No. I mean something special."

Mrs. Chambers stopped what she was doing and looked at Oz. She shook her head, a bemused expression lifting her eyebrows. "Well, there's no denying that you have your dad's optimistic streak running right through you, Oz."

"That's a good thing, isn't it?"

Mrs. Chambers nodded, but Oz wasn't sure if she did it very convincingly. He went back to his room to finish his homework, but got a text from Caleb as he sat down. A minute later, he was running up the stairs to the library.

"Has Heeps taken absolutely everything?" Caleb asked as Oz appeared breathlessly.

"Heeps took heaps. And why didn't you help?"

"I see enough of him at the university," Caleb said heavily.

"By the way, what is it with Lucy Bishop? Why is she so mad at me all the time?"

Caleb shook his head ruefully. "Lucy is a troubled soul, Oz. Her brother…let's just say he's in a bit of trouble and she takes out her frustration on others."

"What kind of trouble?"

"The worst kind. The kind that traps you and never lets you go."

"You mean like drugs?"

"No, not drugs. Not quite…" Caleb paused as if realising that he'd said too much. But then he went on in more measured tones, "Lucy is looking for answers where there really aren't any. Meanwhile, she's doing her degree and I'm trying to help her through all of this as best I can."

Oz nodded. It was an explanation of sorts, although it lacked a little in essential detail. Still, it explained her moods. He turned away but stopped on the top of the stairs.

"Yes?" Caleb said.

"If I get really stuck with my history, can I text you?"

"No problem," said Caleb with the merest little curl at the corner of his mouth.

In the end, Caleb's services were not required, and Oz managed one side of A4 on his own. When he'd finally read through the completed essay and put in the last full stop, he went to his dad's study and threw himself down into the comfy armchair, opened his laptop and found again his dad's article on Morsman. Something had been nagging at Oz's curiosity all day. What was it that had made Morsman want to buy the orphanage? He'd lived there for years as a child, and been to school there. Hadn't he had enough by then? He searched for a passage he'd already read and studied it again.

> Despite being a brilliant entrepreneur, Morsman was essentially a loner. But his wealth did allow him to reach out a helping hand. Indeed, his great friend during his time at Colonel Thompson's orphanage, John Tanner, accompanied him on one of his most dangerous expeditions. Despite warnings from all and sundry, they travelled to France at a time when the Great War began to ravage Europe, on the first of many artefact quests. What exactly took place during that troubled journey is not clear, but on their return Tanner and Morsman parted company, some say not on the best of terms, never to speak again. Indeed, not much is known of Tanner following this split. Morsman, however, spent ever more time and money in remodelling Penwurt, with the addition of the splendid library in the central tower, an excellent example of one of many projects he carried out when not travelling in search of the artefacts...

Oz had the trinket box on the armrest next to him. Though it was just a small space, he'd filled the box with some of the flotsam he'd found in his dad's desk—ticket stubs, folded up photos and some foreign paper money with their inked images of exotic cities and long-forgotten rulers—until there was little room for anything else. The box felt solid and full in his hands as he examined it once again. He ran his fingers over the roughly carved date and the copper hinges and clasp. There was no other adornment apart from a small, inlaid symbol on the under surface which, Oz guessed, was probably a maker's mark. It was barely visible, but Oz picked at it with his nail and saw that it seemed different from the horn around it. Although it looked black at first, Oz cleaned some of the dirt away to reveal bright metal underneath.

Once, Oz's dad had taught him how to clean gunk off furred-up battery terminals in torches with nail varnish remover. He went to his mother's bedroom and found the bottle and a cotton bud and attacked the maker's mark. Years of grime came away with a bit of effort and Oz was able to reveal a pewter-coloured symbol that looked like two mountains over a balance.

It was, like everything else at Penwurt, slightly weird and not at all like the usual stamps on his mum's old bracelets. It made him wonder what secrets this box really had to tell as he ran his fingers over the intricate design. It felt vaguely warm under his finger, and once he could have sworn he saw a faint pulse of light. But after several more goes revealed nothing, he told himself that it had simply been a reflection from the desk lamp.

Oz looked about him at the empty room and felt a wistful pang. Just the desk and his dad's old clock left. It was as if his dad had finally left the place.

Oz got up and walked across to the wall-clock. The face was white and had Roman numerals and blue steel hands. "G. Reading of Coventry" was emblazoned across the middle with the word "Fecit"—which his father had explained was Latin for "made by"—beneath it. It had a glass-fronted rosewood case with a big brass pendulum, and ornately carved scrolls either side of the face. Between the scrolls was an inlaid brass hourglass and more Latin words: "tempus rerum imperator."

For as long as Oz could remember the hands had been at 9.15. It had never worked as a clock, but his dad had said that it was at least a hundred and fifty years old and was a brilliant piece of long-lost British craftsmanship. A sudden shudder rolled through him and he looked around at the empty study again, a mere shell of the treasure-filled room it had been a few days ago. If Heeps could persuade his mother, the whole of Penwurt would go the same way soon.

"Over my dead body," Oz said to no one in particular. He wiped some dust off the clock's glass face and left, shutting his father's study door after him. Back in his bedroom, he put the trinket box next to his laptop on the desk and went downstairs to say goodnight to his mother. Ten minutes later, Oz was in bed. But that night, there was little rest to be had when sleep came. That night, Oz dreamed.

He was on his way to search for a book in the library, except that the library was at the top of an impossibly long spiral staircase. No matter how hard and quickly he climbed, he got no nearer the light that glowed way above him. But beneath him, something stirred—a monstrous Badger Breath Boggs, his head twice normal size, his breath billowing like poisonous black smoke from his grinning mouth. Oz bolted straight through a dream door into a classroom with a blackboard full of hieroglyphics. He could hear Badger Breath approaching and he knew that if he didn't solve the problems on the board something awful was going to happen. The room changed shape; it became long and narrow and the strange symbols on the board were transforming into things with small, pinched faces and black, ugly eyes that began mocking him for not being able to understand them.

But in the midst of the gargoyle-like shapes, something glowed. It was the strange mark he'd seen under the trinket box, and it gleamed with a golden light. Oz reached out to touch it, and instantly the mocking, jeering noises ended and the faces melted and transformed into small, brilliantly coloured floating clouds.

And there was a voice. A calm, pleasant girl's voice that seemed to be telling the clouds what to do in a language Oz didn't understand. But as he watched, the clouds flowed together into an organised rainbow that seemed, all of a sudden, to make perfect, symmetrical, understandable sense. Oz stared at it rapturously, wanting it never to change. But suddenly the rainbow began to shimmer and break up and a noise began to intrude, an incessant buzz, like a trapped wasp. The clouds burst apart into their separate, ugly, oddly shaped parts. Oz wanted the clamour to go away. He wanted the colours to flow again into their beautiful, organised patterns. But the noise was insistent as it dragged him away from the dream and unconsciousness, until finally he opened his eyes, reached out his hand and shut off the alarm.

One glance at its face told Oz that it was morning and time to get up.

* * *

Mrs. Chambers was making sandwiches when Oz arrived in the kitchen.

"Mmm," Oz said, leaning over to see what they were. "Ham and tomato ketchup. Yummy."

"You're a bit chipper this morning," she said.

"Am I?" Oz replied, surprised.

"You don't usually whistle coming down the stairs at quarter to eight in the morning."

"Was I? Whistling, I mean?"

His mother tilted her head at him. He *had* been whistling. In fact, thinking about it, he did feel good but had no real idea why, so he just shrugged and attacked his cereal.

"Oh, what it is to be young," sighed Mrs. Chambers.

Oz just had time to check his email before catching the bus. He fired up his laptop and went to clean his teeth while it loaded. He knew something was different as soon as he walked back into his bedroom with his mouth full of toothpaste foam. Instead of seeing the usual "colliding asteroids" screensaver, his laptop showed something else altogether. On an off-white background, two images slowly rotated on the screen. One was a large symbol, the other a shiny black object with a segmented shape that reminded him of a squat insect.

Intrigued, Oz moved the mouse and tried to shut the page down, but he couldn't. He clicked on the symbol. Immediately, it stopped rotating. He tried to make sense of it. It looked like a weird letter E with the middle arm poking out the back, twice as long as the other two. Oz tilted his head. Could even have been a fork or a trident on its side.

"Oz, if you don't leave now, you'll miss the bus," sang his mother from the bottom of the steps.

Reluctantly, and with one final glance at the two images, Oz grabbed his school bag and ran out of the door, only to remember that he still had a mouth full of dribbling toothpaste. He did a U-turn and spat out the toothpaste into the bathroom sink before tearing out again.

Sitting on the bus to school, he racked his brain, trying to think what could have happened to his laptop. Had it been infected by a virus? Had Ruff, who was a genius when it came to computers, sent him some kind of message? He was still mulling it over as he bumped into Ellie on his way to registration.

"Mega weirdness," he said to her questioning face. But he had no chance of elaborating as he followed Ellie's gaze and saw that Pheeps was making a beeline towards them, her expression set in malign delight.

"My father told me that you're selling that dump of yours at last."

"Did he?" Oz said. "Knows more than me, then."

Pheeps laughed and it was a high, unpleasant noise. "Everyone knows more than you," she spat. "I even know how much you got in your maths test Friday."

"How could you know that?" Ellie said.

Pheeps' eyes sparkled triumphantly. "Badger Breath was marking last lesson Friday afternoon and Daniel Cullen saw the papers. Shame he didn't see yours, Messenger, but it's obvious that maths isn't Chambers' best subject by a long way."

"Get lost," Ellie said.

"Have a nice day," Pheeps said, smiling sweetly.

"I swear, that girl is a witch," said Ellie as Pheeps flounced away.

"She didn't used to be like that," Oz said. "It was only after her mother became ill that she started to—"

"Turn into Little Miss Nightmare? I'm sorry, but I don't buy that as an excuse."

"She was in hospital for over six months," Oz said gravely.

"You reckon? Don't go feeling sorry for her," Ellie said exasperatedly. "Besides, she doesn't really know anything. She's just saying this stuff to wind you up. It's just a sick little game to her."

"Really?" Oz asked, sounding desperate. He hated letting Pheeps get to him, but her mocking had an awful ring of truth to it and he felt his insides twist at the coming lesson. But by then they were at registration, and for once Miss Arkwright was early because she had announcements to make about a forthcoming trip to a pantomime ("Maybe we'll see Badger Breath there," Ruff whispered). As a result they were late for first lesson, where Mrs. Conserdine, a dour Scottish lady who taught science, insisted on her full lesson time.

That left no time to speak about the laptop, since everyone had to rush to second lesson, which was maths. Although he didn't believe everything that Pheeps had said, he felt that there was probably more than a grain of truth in her carping words. Badger Breath handed out the marked papers without a sound and Oz deliberately avoided his gaze. Even so, it came as quite a shock to learn that he'd come next to bottom, beating only Jenks, who had scored a total of seven percent.

At the top of Oz's paper, in a red circle, was a scribbled ten.

Badger Breath stood at the front, a gleam in his small eyes. "Those of you with less than fifty percent will come back here lunchtime to re-sit the exam."

There was a collective groan from nearly a third of the class.

"Will they be the same questions, sir?" someone asked.

"Of course not," Badger Breath rolled his eyes. "And if you get less than fifty percent a second time, you will repeat the exam every day until you succeed in getting more than fifty percent. I suspect it will be a long term with very little lunch for quite a few of you. Now, let us get on with inequalities."

* * *

At break, Ellie and Ruff were full of commiserations.

"I wouldn't have minded, really, except that megaphone Pheeps knows all about it and is broadcasting it all over the school," Oz said glumly.

"Forget about her," Ellie said. "Now, what was it you were trying to tell me before she butted in this morning?"

What with Badger Breath and the test, Oz had almost forgotten about his laptop and the weird images. So he told them as they munched on toast and jam in the refectory. He explained first about the dreams, and then about the black insect image and the funny trident symbol on his screen.

"You haven't sent me anything, have you?" he said to Ruff.

"No way," Ruff replied, frowning.

"Then someone has been tampering with it, because I couldn't get them off my screen," Oz said.

"We need to see them," Ellie said.

Oz thought about the best way to do that all through biology and P.E. But then it was lunchtime and he was back in Badger Breath's class with ten others, waiting for another maths paper. Badger Breath made sure there were empty desks on either side of all the pupils and walked around distributing the papers face-down.

"You have forty-five minutes, starting now," he said when the last paper was delivered. Oz didn't turn his sheet over immediately. Instead, he watched as Badger Breath took out a flask and some foil-wrapped sandwiches and proceeded to lay out his lunch. As he poured out strong-looking, steaming tea, he looked up into Oz's eyes and gave him a knowing and very unpleasant smile.

Oz dropped his gaze and turned over his paper, his heart sinking in his chest.

Ten more questions. Ten more columns of hieroglyphics. He hadn't even attempted any revision since the last test, not that it would have made any difference if he had. Besides, he hadn't known that Badger Breath would spring another test so quickly. Shaking his head, Oz knuckled down.

This time he'd try and get the easier ones attempted first and do his utmost not to get stuck on anything difficult.

Oz chewed the end of his pen in concentration. Unfortunately, the questions were still all algebra and, as usual, confusion crowded in and the letters and the numbers just became a jumble.

But then something really weird happened. Some of the numbers and letters changed colour. On his left, two desks away, Jenks was drawing a missile on his answer sheet, but the figures on his paper looked black, not green and purple and red like those on Oz's. He turned back to his own paper and rubbed his eyes, but the figures stayed coloured, shimmering slightly as he stared at them.

A momentary panic overtook him. Was he losing his mind? But then Oz saw the different coloured numbers and letters rearrange themselves in his head. They floated and melted together just like in his dream. And when they joined, what resulted was a new colour which flowed from his eyes like ghost images onto the paper. And Oz knew just by looking that the new images—which happened to be all in blue—were ending up as the right answer. Quickly, in case the whole thing faded, he scribbled over the blue letters and numbers, barely managing to stifle an excited giggle. His brain was doing algebra! Somehow, a calculator in his head was doing the maths in colour.

He looked at the next question, and then the next, and exactly the same thing happened in each one; coloured numbers and letters floated off the page and melted to form royal-blue answers, with varying shades as the workings out in between. The ten questions took him twenty minutes. He looked up and saw Badger Breath staring at him curiously.

"Sir, I've finished. Can I get some lunch now?"

Badger Breath tried to swallow, but failed as a lump of biscuit went down the wrong way. He coughed and turned an alarming shade of purple. Oz wasn't quite sure whether it was the coughing or simply pure rage at Oz's apparent impertinence that was transforming him into an aubergine, but finally, after wiping his mouth several times with a paper hanky, he got up and strode over to Oz's desk.

"Lunch? You leave here when you've finished and only then, Chambers," he said and managed to pepper Oz with foul-smelling biscuit crumbs at the same time. He picked up the paper with a flourish but held Oz's eyes in a contemptuous glare. "Or are we just giving up, eh?"

"I'm not giving anything up," Oz said, and watched as Boggs scanned his paper. Slowly, the crowing smile slipped from the teacher's face like a greasy egg off a canteen plate.

"But you've finished," Badger Breath said, frowning.

"I just said that. So, can I go now?"

Badger Breath nodded dumbly, his face a dark cloud of confusion. But Oz didn't hang about. He was out of the door in a flash, feeling several pairs of eyes boring a hole in his spine. He had no idea what had just happened, but he didn't really care.

He could do maths.

He could do algebra.

Just wait until he told the others.

Chapter 8

Dr. Mackie's Slip

The first thing Oz did after he got home that afternoon was to look at his laptop again. The images were still there, but with a bit of experimentation, he could now make the images smaller by waving the pointer over the top left-hand corner of the screen. But they never went away altogether. He sent Ruff and Ellie some screenshots of the images. Within twenty minutes, Ellie was Skyping him back online.

"Ruff not around, then?" she asked, and Oz detected the little accusatory tone in her voice.

"He has a paper round most afternoons delivering the evening news."

"Oh, I didn't know that," Ellie frowned.

"Yeah. That's his only pocket money these days, since his dad is working part-time now that Brockets has cut back."

"Is that why his dad was painting chalets over half term?" Ellie asked, frowning.

"Yep."

But they had no chance to discuss this any further as a bleep on the screen brought up Ruff's shaggy-fringed face, and they immediately started discussing the images.

"Wow, these are amazing," Ruff purred.

"I don't know what the E thingy is, but the other thing looks a bit like my grandma's old jewellery," Ellie said. Even via the webcam, Oz could see her eyes glinting with excitement. "This is so cool, Oz."

"Maybe, but the trouble is we can't see how big it really is from the screen," Oz mused.

"Never mind that," Ruff said. "The question is, how the buzzard did these images get on your laptop?"

"All I know is that they weren't there when I went to bed."

"So does that mean that someone sneaked in and installed them while you were asleep?" Ellie asked.

"What, like a screensaver burglar in reverse?"

"Your mother?" offered Ellie half-heartedly.

"No way," Oz said. "She still struggles with emails."

"What about Caleb or Lucy Bishop or that Tim bloke?" Ruff suggested.

"But why? And besides, I would have heard them."

All three of them sat back, befuddled. Finally, they agreed to do some thinking on their own and get back together in an hour or so's time. Oz knew he wouldn't find an answer because he'd been thinking of nothing else since he'd got home. But he was still mulling it over some time later when there was a knock on his bedroom door and his mother called, "Oz, it's me."

He shut his laptop lid and got up to open the door. His mother stood there with Tim, complete with leather tool belt, in tow.

"Tim mentioned to me that some of the radiators on his side of the house were not working properly, so he's offered to check the central heating for us. That's nice of him, isn't it?" Mrs. Chambers was grinning.

"What sort of checking?"

"Bleeding radiators," Tim said.

"They're useless, I know," Oz agreed.

"No," said Tim earnestly, "that's what I'll be doing. Bleeding the radiators to let out trapped air. Makes them less efficient if there's air in them. Can I come in?"

Oz stood aside and watched Tim fit a key to the top of the radiator under his window, whistling jauntily as he did so. Air hissed out, followed by a dribble of water.

"There," said Tim. "Fixed."

Mrs. Chambers grinned and gave Oz a thumbs-up. House maintenance always seemed to make her extremely happy.

"I'll just check the other rooms on this floor, too," Tim said, very businesslike.

"Would you?" Mrs. Chambers simpered. "I'll leave you to it, then, shall I?"

Oz watched as Tim went into his dad's study and heard his mother whisper, "He's worth his weight in gold, that one."

Oz shrugged and went back to his laptop just as a chat signal chimed. He accepted the call, and within seconds Ellie and Ruff were both staring back at him on his split screen.

"Well?" Oz asked.

"Nothing yet," Ruff said.

"I've found something," Ellie said, sounding pleased with herself. "In fact, I know exactly what that thing that looks like an insect is. It's a brooch, and it's from a sale of Victorian jewellery in a shop in Seabourne."

"What?" said Oz, astounded. "But how…?"

"Like I said, it looked like some of my gran's old jewellery. I showed her and she thinks it looks a lot like Bakelite, too."

"Bakelite? Sounds like a sort of bread," Ruff muttered.

"It's a kind of plastic. All the rage when my gran was young, so she says. Anyway, I did a search for Bakelite brooches online, and this advert came up. 'A well-preserved Bakelite dress brooch—with missing metal clip.' The shop is called Garret and Eldred Antiques. They even have a catalogue. I've sent the image to both of you."

Oz opened his email and looked at the image Ellie had scanned. It did look the same, though the quality was poor and it was difficult to be certain.

"You're a genius, Ellie," Oz said.

"Yeah, I know," Ellie said with a dramatic sigh. "I vote we go and look at it on Saturday."

"This is so weird," Ruff said. "I'm sure I've seen that E-shaped thing somewhere, too. Just can't think where."

Oz shrugged. "I only wish I knew what it all meant."

"We'll find out, I know we will," Ellie said.

Oz wished he had her confidence.

There was English homework, but Oz didn't really mind because all he had to do was write a paragraph on Charles Dickens' spooky story about a Signalman who kept getting premonitions. He heard the phone ring downstairs and didn't think twice about it; he was too busy trying to work out what saturnine meant. But when he heard a firm knock on his door a few minutes later, he almost jumped out of his skin.

His mother opened the door and stepped in. She wore a serious, troubled expression. "Oz, I've just got off the phone with the deputy head, Miss Swinson," Mrs. Chambers said.

"The Volcano? What did she want?"

"She rang to tell me that your maths teacher has contacted her. You re-sat your maths test today, didn't you?"

"Yeah," Oz said, intrigued.

"You got one hundred percent."

After long, ticking seconds of shocked silence, Oz got up from the chair, punched the air and let out a whoop and a triumphant, "Yesss!"

Mrs. Chambers looked on, bemused.

"So the Volcano rang to congratulate me?" Oz said finally, after realising that his mother wasn't exactly sharing in his ecstatic display of victory.

"Dare I ask why you call her that?" asked Mrs. Chambers warily.

"'Cos she blows up when you least expect it," Oz stated.

Mrs. Chambers let out an uncertain, "Hmmm," and came and sat on the edge of Oz's bed. "Well, anyway, she said that Mr. Boggs was…uncomfortable with what had happened."

Suddenly, all the elation drained out of Oz like water from a leaky bucket. "Are they trying to say that I cheated?"

"No one has actually come out with it, but yes, I suppose that is what they're saying," Mrs. Chambers said unhappily.

Oz was on his feet in an instant. "That's just rubbish, Mum," he said, feeling his cheeks start to burn. "I don't know how I did it, I just did. And I did revise last week, you know I did, but on Friday it was all muddled, and today…it just wasn't."

"So, no cheating?"

"I swear I did not cheat," Oz said, his voice rising.

"So today, when you re-sat, things just clicked. Is that it?" Mrs. Chambers asked, her eyes boring into Oz's.

"Exactly. Things just clicked…well, more like sort of moved about in colour in my head. But that's what happened. Suddenly I knew what to do."

It was as good an explanation as any, because it was the truth and Oz couldn't think of any other way to say it. Mrs. Chambers held Oz in her steady gaze for a long ten seconds before getting up off the bed and holding him in a hug. "Then that's what I'm going to tell the Volcano when I ring her back. But I've got a feeling they may want to talk to you at school about this as well."

"Great," Oz said, his eyes rolling up towards the ceiling as he let out a sigh.

After his mother left, Oz sat and pondered. He hadn't thought about the maths thing that much, but he could understand that, to Boggs, it must have appeared very strange indeed. Still, that didn't change anything. What had happened, as weird as it was, had happened. He felt his insides tingle with the memory of it. And as his mum always said, you should never look a gift horse in the mouth, even if it is totally bonkers.

He finished off the essay and then went up to the library. He was still utterly convinced that the answers to the footsteps and the weird appearances on the laptop were going to be found somewhere in this room, hidden amidst all the words on these shelves. He paused to look at the ornate carvings of letters and shapes on the panelled walls, all completely illegible to him, and which his dad had said were a mixture of alchemical and astrological symbols.

Oz leaned his forehead against the dark oak and closed his eyes. All was quiet except for the faint moaning of the wind outside and the ticks and pops of the house's ancient plumbing. But then he heard another noise, one which made his heart stutter in his chest. It was faint, but it was enough to make him catch his breath and turn to press his ear against the wood. He strained, barely swallowing for fear of missing it. Then, from somewhere deep below in the bowels of the old orphanage, faint but definite, came once more the echoing footfalls that he and Ruff and Ellie had heard on Halloween. He stayed in the library for another half an hour pressing his ear to the paneling, but heard nothing more.

Finally, Oz looked out of the turret window over the pitched roof and parapets and spindly chimneys of the orphanage. Somewhere beneath that slate and stone was a mystery waiting to be solved. But then doubt reared its gargoyle head. Had he really heard the footsteps that second time? Was it just that he so desperately wanted to believe that this was all tied up with his dad that he was beginning to invent things? He shook his head to rid himself of the nagging voice. There was something in that orphanage. Something strange and intriguing that was begging to be found out. Glancing up, he saw a face in the glass and for a heart-stopping moment was convinced he was looking at a total stranger. But it was only his reflection that stared back at him, and it, too, had no answers to his questions.

* * *

The next morning, Oz and the rest of the students on his bus were late getting to registration because of some failed traffic lights on Rosemount Hill. When he finally made it, Ellie mouthed, "Where have you been?" As he sat down next to her she leaned across and managed to whisper, "I've found something else out," before Miss Arkwright began reminding everyone that the final installment of money for the end of January skiing trip needed to be in by Friday.

"That's you, Dilpak, and you, Sandra, I think."

Both potential skiers nodded while Ruff eyed them wistfully and muttered, "The only time I expect I'll ever go skiing is if Seabourne Hill freezes over and they give out free ski passes to over sixty-fives."

Oz had no chance of finding out what Ellie had to say, because Miss Arkwright was calling his name above the clamour of the mass exodus to first lesson.

"Oscar, can you stay behind for a moment, please?"

Oz had his back to her and made eyes to the ceiling in response to Ellie and Ruff's questioning glances just before he turned around.

"Yes, miss?"

"Miss Swinson wants to see you sometime this morning," she said. "Something about a maths test?"

Oz nodded glumly.

"Didn't you do very well?" she asked.

"Got one hundred percent, miss. Badg…Mr. Boggs thinks it's fishy."

"Really?" said Miss Arkwright, looking surprised. "And is it?"

"No, miss."

"I see. Well, I'm sure it'll be fine," she said, and gave Oz a reassuring smile while her eyes stayed flintily suspicious.

He'd almost forgotten about it by the time it came to third lesson. They were in geography. It was one of Oz's favourite subjects, thanks largely to the teacher, Mr. Gingell. He, unlike Badger Breath, managed to make even the driest subject interesting. Today was no exception as he announced to the class as soon as they arrived, in his best Long John Silver, "Why can't pirates read maps?" He paused expectantly before adding, "Because they think it's too aaarrrd."

The class let out a communal but good-natured groan.

"But they be wrong, mateys. Today we're revising grid referencing and compass points. Divide into groups of three and answer the quiz sheet to find the treasure."

It looked like it was going to be fun, but before the trio could settle in, Mr. Gingell called Oz out to the front. He was quite young as teachers went, knew quite a lot about music and films, and supported Seabourne United. Rumour had it, too, that he and Miss Arkwright were more than just friends, or so Ellie said. He looked apologetic as he spoke in a low voice so that no one else could hear.

"Miss Swinson apparently wants to see you straight away," he said, and on seeing Oz's face fall added, "Don't worry, they'll still be doing this quiz in half an hour. There'll be plenty to do when you come back, arrr."

Oz couldn't help thinking that Mr. Gingell was missing the point a bit as he stifled an inward groan and sent Ruff and Ellie a dejected glance before trudging out into the empty corridors. The Volcano's office was situated in the admin block, where two bespectacled secretaries regarded Oz with humourless expressions. Oz decided that this must be the feeling condemned men got when they walked to the electric chair. Near the main doors he turned into a long, freshly painted corridor.

The Volcano lived two doors down from the headmaster—a tall, constantly grinning man who seemed always to be in a hurry and whom Oz had only seen half a dozen times in the whole of his time at Seabourne County. The same could not be said of the Volcano, whose presence was a constant reminder of the need for "discipline." She was forever bellowing at pupils across hallways, classrooms, fields and yards, unable, it seemed, to speak with anything approaching a normal volume. Instead, she barked orders such as "Pull down that skirt hem, you are not a pelmet," or "Tuck in that shirt, you are not a tramp," or "Pick up that piece of litter, this is not a rubbish tip." In fact, Oz couldn't remember her ever *asking* anyone to do anything. It was always an instruction.

When Oz reached the door with the sign "Miss V Swinson, Senior Mistress" emblazoned upon it, all he could think about was how hard his heart was beating in his chest. It felt as if it might burst through at any moment. But he told himself that he was just being stupid. He hadn't done anything wrong and he had nothing to worry about. Okay, having your wisdom teeth out without anaesthetic was probably a more pleasant way to spend a morning than being interviewed by the Volcano, but so what? Her bark was a hundred times worse than her bite—or so he'd heard. And what was the worst that could happen? As far as he knew, the Volcano had never killed anyone—yet.

Oz knocked three times.

"Come," barked a voice.

Oz opened the door and stepped inside a room that was more like someone's lounge than a school office. There were at least three vases full of flowers, it smelled overpoweringly of roses, and the walls were painted a sickly burnt yellow. Two huge posters of exotic islands covered one wall. Three big grey filing cabinets stood one against another, and in the centre stood an enormous desk with a neat pile of paper on it and three pot plants, one of which was the biggest cactus Oz had ever seen. The Volcano was standing behind her desk, dressed in a voluminous silk blouse and pearls, her coiffed hair poker-stiff. She wore black-rimmed half-glasses perched on a vulture-like nose and her scarlet mouth was compressed into a familiar, disapproving expression.

"Come in, Chambers. You know why I've asked you here this morning, I take it?" The Volcano glared down at him, her eyes half-lidded, her voice accusatory.

Oz shrugged.

"It is at the request of another teacher. An unusual and unpleasant request, which—"

There was another knock on the door and it opened to reveal Badger Breath Boggs. He scowled at Oz and nodded at the Volcano.

"Ah, Douglas. Have a seat."

Badger Breath sat to the side of the desk while Oz continued to stand.

The Volcano leaned forward over the desk. "Mr. Boggs has brought to my attention a very serious allegation—"

"I didn't cheat," Oz said, "if that's what this is about."

The room fell silent. The Volcano's mouth twitched and she shuffled some papers on the desk and thrust one towards Oz.

"This is yours, is it not?"

Oz recognised the first test paper with the ten percent circled at the top right.

"Yes, miss."

The Volcano found a second and handed that to him, as well. "And this?"

Oz read the much smaller one hundred percent written at the top of this second paper. The numbers were written in such a way as to suggest that the hand writing it had pressed very hard into the paper. He saw, too, his own familiar writing beneath.

"Yes, miss."

"Mr. Boggs has brought to my attention the quite startling difference between these results which, you have to admit, are quite remarkable."

Oz shrugged. "I still didn't cheat."

"Rubbish," growled a red-faced Badger Breath, who jerked around in his seat to glare at Oz.

"Douglas," said the Volcano in a silky voice, "I share your suspicions, but I am prepared to give Chambers one chance to explain."

Boggs' jaw muscles started working overtime, but he nodded reluctantly and sat back.

"Now, what we need is to understand how you could do so badly one day and so spectacularly well the next," the Volcano said, peering at Oz, her eyes glinting in challenge.

"I don't know, really. It just sort of clicked."

"Oh, puh-lease," sneered Badger Breath.

"'It just clicked,'" repeated the Volcano. She looked at the papers. "A very spectacular click it must have been, then, to go from ten to one hundred percent, eh?" She glanced at Badger Breath, who smirked. "Had you done any extra revision?" the Volcano snapped, turning back to Oz.

"No, not really. I mean, I did for the first one, but Mr. Boggs didn't warn us about the second one…"

"Did you copy from anyone?"

"The boy sitting next to me was Lee Jenkins. I don't know how much he got second time around."

The Volcano sent Badger Breath a questioning glance and got a mumbled, "Eight percent," in reply.

"I see," said the Volcano quietly. "So you want us to believe that some mysterious brainwave suddenly enabled you to get every single one of these questions right, where two days before you got them all, bar a few pathetic workings out, completely WRONG?"

The last word was roared with such force that it made Oz jump. The Volcano came around to Oz's side of the desk. She wore trousers that were bulging in lots of places and she smelled strongly of a pungent, flowery perfume, which clashed nauseatingly with the rosy air-freshener pervading the room.

"I know all about you and your kind, Chambers," the Volcano snarled. "Single-parent families are the bane of this school and…"

She was interrupted by a knock on the door, which opened to reveal Miss Arkwright, out of breath and flushed in the face.

"Ah, I see you've started already," Miss Arkwright gasped.

"Miss Arkwright," said the Volcano in a syrupy voice, "do join us."

"Thank you," said Miss Arkwright, frowning. "I thought we'd agreed on 11.30 as a start time?"

"Yes," said the Volcano with a smile as genuine as a wax apple, "sorry about that. Had to reschedule. Never mind, you're here now. But Chambers here has no explanation for what happened. We must therefore assume that he did cheat, as it is clearly impossible for him to have been otherwise able to complete this question paper after such an abysmal performance previously. It is my job to consider an appropriate punishment…"

"Did you cheat, Oz?" Miss Arkwright asked.

"No. Like I said, it just clicked that second time," Oz explained.

Badger Breath let out an expulsion of air.

"Well, there is a very simple way to sort all of this out," Miss Arkwright said suddenly.

The Volcano frowned. Badger Breath scowled. Miss Arkwright picked up Oz's ten percent paper. "How many questions did you attempt the first time, Oscar?"

"Three. I got a bit stuck."

"Good. So if I asked you to try the last seven now, could you do them?"

Oz froze. He had no idea if he could or not. Yesterday's test seemed to have happened almost without him doing anything. But he nodded and gulped at the same time.

"Excellent. Here is a fresh piece of paper and a pencil," said Miss Arkwright, clearing a space for Oz on the edge of the desk.

"I hardly think..." began the Volcano, but she was silenced by Miss Arkwright's implacable gaze.

"Surely this is the only way to know if Oz is lying or not?"

The room fell silent as Miss Arkwright's logic sank in.

"Very well," the Volcano said finally with a glance at Badger Breath.

Miss Arkwright turned to Oz and spoke to him. "Now Oz, take your time."

Oz looked at the maths paper, his stomach twisting. The last seven questions, Miss Arkwright had said. First glance revealed Egyptian tomb writing as usual. He knew that the first one was a substitution question and he knew vaguely what needed to be done, it was just that...and then the numbers started changing colour just as they had yesterday. Relief flooded through Oz and he began scribbling furiously. Within ten minutes he'd done all seven. He handed the paper back to Miss Arkwright.

"That was quick," she said, but there was an approving smile at the corners of her mouth as she said it. "Now, if Mr. Boggs could do the marking?"

They all watched as Badger Breath scanned the page. When he spoke, his voice sounded like ice cracking on a lake. "They're all correct."

Miss Arkwright was on her feet immediately. "Right, I think we've detained Oscar for long enough. He needs to get back to lessons."

"I'm not so sure..." spluttered the Volcano.

"There's something fishy going on here," Badger Breath said, and his words emerged through a tightly clenched jaw.

"Apparently it's called 'clicking,' Douglas," said Miss Arkwright as she began ushering Oz out of the door. But even as it closed behind them, Oz could hear Badger Breath's whining complaints persisting. "But he's an idiot. Like all the rest in that set. Probably did this just to make my life a misery."

"I agree totally, Douglas. And Chambers is a prime example of everything that's wrong in this town and in this country. The boy's mother is..."

Miss Arkwright cleared her throat loudly and it drowned out what the Volcano was about to say. At the end of the corridor, Miss Arkwright stopped and turned to Oz. He could see that she was gently fuming, the smile which beamed down on him a bit too toothy and overly bright. "Well done, Oz. And I want you to take no notice of what you just heard. Go back to geography. I just want a quick word with Miss Swinson and Mr. Boggs." Oz watched as she pivoted on her heel and stormed back up the corridor. He didn't wait to hear anymore. He was too relieved to care.

When, an hour later sitting in the refectory, Oz managed to find the time to tell Ellie and Ruff about Badger Breath's accusations, they were appalled. Ellie seemed a little more short-tempered than usual with Ruff, but listened avidly to Oz as he explained.

"That man is such a buzzard gonk," Ruff muttered.

"And the Volcano is such an old witch," Ellie said, frowning.

"Miss Arkwright was brilliant, though," Oz said with feeling.

"But did you really get one hundred percent?" Ellie said, trying not to sound too surprised.

"I know. Don't worry, I can't believe it either." Oz grinned.

"Oz has turned into a maths genius," Ruff said, and clapped him heartily on the back.

"Never mind that now," Oz said, turning to Ellie. "You said you'd found something out."

"I have," Ellie said, dropping her voice low. "Remember I told you I thought it looked like some of my granny's jewellery?"

Oz and Ruff both nodded.

"Well, I showed her a picture and she said it looked like a scarab—"

"A scarab?" Oz asked.

"Yeah. When she was young, lots of jewellery was made to look like Egyptian stuff—"

"Whoa," Ruff said, holding up a hand. "What's a scarab when it's at home?"

"Haven't you come across one of those in *Ancient Tombs 503* for the Xbox?" she sniped. "A scarab is a beetle. The ancient Egyptians wore them as amulets or something and they became popular again in the last century. It was just a fashion thing."

"We are getting to the point soon, are we?" Ruff said, feigning a yawn.

Ellie sent him a blazing look. "A scarab is a beetle, and the old name for a common English beetle is a dor."

"You've lost me," Ruff said.

"What a surprise," Ellie said, sighing heavily. "Watch my lips." She proceeded with exaggerated slowness. "The. Black. Dor. One of Morsman's artefacts?"

"Oh, so you mean dor, not door. Like in when is a door not a door, when it's ajar?" asked Ruff, earning a withering glance from Ellie in the process.

Oz, who happened to be standing next to one of the refectory tables, ignored Ruff, too, but had to sit down on a bench. "So are you saying that those things on my laptop have something to do with Morsman's artefacts?"

"I think that what's on your laptop is everything to do with Morsman's artefacts," Ellie said confidently.

"But why my laptop?"

"Because you're at Penwurt, and something or someone there is trying to send you a message, obviously."

"And you think that this dor thingy is in a shop in Seabourne?"

"Worth a look, surely."

"What are the chances of it really being the one? I mean, come on," Ruff said.

"Shut up, Ruff," Ellie said, nettled. "You're such a doom-merchant. Yes, I do think it's in a shop in Seabourne, and the only way we're going to find out for certain is if you go there this weekend."

"What do you mean, 'you'?" Ruff asked.

"You and Oz. I'm busy."

Oz frowned.

"Oh, come on," Ellie said, flushing a dusky red. "You two don't need me tagging along. I'm just a girl, after all, remember? I mean, you don't want me there being all hysterical and overreacting." She gave Ruff a pointed, icy smile and walked off.

"What was that all about?" Oz asked, shaking his head. "I feel like I've just been slapped in the face just for wearing a pair of trousers."

Ruff was looking very uncomfortable. "Last night at football practice we sort of had an…argument."

"Sort of had an argument? About what?"

"I can't remember now. We were in passing practise and someone texted me, so I just answered it and…"

"You were texting during passing practise?" Oz's incredulity made his voice high and weird-sounding.

"I forgot to turn my phone off, that's all," Ruff said, as if that sort of thing happened all the time. But Oz couldn't ever remember seeing anyone taking a call when Spain played Netherlands in the World Cup final. Ruff, though, hadn't finished. "I did after that. Turn the phone off, I mean. The coach gave me a roasting. Said I needed to prioritize. Think more about the team than myself," he sighed. "But then Ellie started in on me."

"And?"

"And we had an argument about stuff like attitude and wanting to win and I…I may have said that she was overreacting. Like, always overreacting. I mean, what is it with her and wanting to win all the time? I like to win, too, but it isn't everything, is it?'

"It is to Ellie. You do know that she is really good at taekwondo, don't you?'

"Yeah, but…"

"I mean, really good. She's won the last three competitions she's entered."

Ruff was still frowning.

Oz decided that it was time to come clean. "If I tell you something, will you promise not to tell anyone?"

"'Course."

"Some of her coaches think that Ellie might be good enough to be an international; you know, represent her country, eventually."

"An international? Wow." Ruff's eyes blinked rapidly.

"She hasn't told anyone except me. Not her sisters or her mother or father or anyone. But I'm telling you so that you can understand why she is like she is." Oz paused and then added, "Have you met the other Messengers?"

"No," Ruff said, "except for Macy."

"They're great. A good laugh. But there're five of them."

"Five?"

"Macy's the only other one in school."

"Yeah, I know. She's the pretty one that keeps waving at you and blowing kisses, right?"

"Yeah," Oz rolled his eyes. Macy derived great pleasure from teasing Oz and seeing him squirm with embarassament. "The point is that Ellie's right in the middle of that family and sport is her way of being different and standing out."

"Yeah, but…"

"I'm not saying it's right that she wants to kill someone every time she loses at ping-pong, I'm just trying to explain."

"Okay, so now I understand. Sort of."

Oz sighed. "Right, so does that mean you'll apologise? We need Ellie."

"She called me a waste of space. So yeah, I'll apologise, in, like, a hundred buzzard years," he said, and walked off to join the rest of 1C queuing outside the art room.

* * *

Oz spent a miserable hour in art trying to finish off the landscape he was working on. He was so preoccupied he didn't even notice that he'd started to use red paint instead of white for the snow on the mountains. When he did finally twig, he couldn't even be bothered to change it.

He just could not understand what was wrong with Ellie and Ruff. They were both great. It was just that they were so different. He'd hoped that Penwurt and the puzzle of the images might have been enough to make them forget their differences, but it clearly wasn't.

The frosty atmosphere persisted though lunch and Oz, despite desperately wanting to discuss the dor and the other artefacts, decided that now was not the best time. He stayed away from them both and neither one made much effort to come and find him.

He got to room 33 as late as possible after lunch to find Ellie in animated conversation with Sandra Ojo, and Ruff discussing *Death Planet Hub* tactics with Marcus Skyrme. Oz made no effort to break into either conversation and was quite glad when Miss Arkwright flounced in at last. She immediately walked across the room towards a group of girls.

"Ellie, could I have a quick word?" she asked.

Ellie went with Miss Arkwright to the front of the class and an earnest, whispered conversation took place. Oz couldn't hear, but he watched as a range of different expressions flashed across Ellie's face. There was curiosity, followed by mild panic and then, after a moment's thought, nods of enthusiasm. Ellie came back to her seat, but did not acknowledge Oz's nosy glance.

"Right, 1C. I'd like to discuss a little project for Christmas with you all."

Multiple groans emanated from the class.

"No, not that kind of project. It doesn't involve any homework. Now, we were all thrilled by the London Paralympics this year, weren't we?"

Several people said "Yes," out loud.

"Well, I have a close friend who is a doctor—a surgeon, in actual fact. She's been doing some work with limbless children in the poorest regions of Africa. She told me last night that just £30 would buy an artificial limb for one of these children. So I thought that, as a group, it would be a really nice gesture if, instead of sending your friends Christmas cards, you bring in the stamp money so that we can send a charitable donation."

"Will it be one of those blade thingys like in the Paralympics, miss?" asked someone.

"Oh, wow. I want one of those," said Skinner from the back. "They're awesome."

Ellie swiveled around to glare at him.

"What?" Skinner replied, in his usual thick-skinned way. There was no real harm in Skinner, he just had no control over what came out of his mouth.

"There are many, many children who would benefit, but all I'm asking is that we help one," Miss Arkwright continued.

"Why have they lost their limbs, miss?" asked Dilpak.

"Well, some through disease, but mainly it's through violence. My doctor friend has been working around the Great Lakes of West Africa. It's an area ravaged by war. Some children have stepped on buried land mines while out playing, or worse, where there is still conflict, they may have suffered from direct attack."

The class had gone very quiet.

"So, what do we all think?" Miss Arkwright asked brightly.

There was a general buzz of approval from the class. But then Skinner put his hand up.

"Can we write our names on it, miss?"

The back row sniggered.

"No, that will not be necessary, Kieron. But I will write a class letter which we can all sign."

Then Jenks chipped in. "Thing is, miss, my brother says that it's no good giving money and stuff to these people, 'cos they really need to help themselves. I mean, why don't they make their own artifical limbs?"

"Probably because they haven't got the equipment, Lee. I'm sure they would help themselves if they could."

"How do we know they're not going to just melt it down and sell it for scrap?" Jenks persisted.

"Yeah, so that they can buy iPods and stuff," Skinner added.

Several people had turned to look at them.

"Well, you never know," grinned Skinner who was, as usual, enjoying the attention.

Miss Arkwright, looking slightly exasperated and with eyebrows raised, said, "These prosthetics are not made of tin. Besides, I'm sure that this charity ensures that such things do not happen."

"Yeah, but you don't know miss, do you? I think I'll keep my money if it's okay, miss," Jenks said.

But before Miss Arkwright could answer, someone else did.

"What for, Jenks? To buy another rubbish ringtone for your phone?" Ellie had turned almost one hundred eighty degrees in her seat and her sudden outburst took everyone by surprise. "And how can you make jokes about this, Skinner? How can you say you'd *like* an artificial limb?"

"Kieron would be brilliant at Paralympics. In fact, there's a chance he'd get in as he is," Jenks smirked.

The cronies laughed. Skinner grinned uncertainly.

"And anyway, who asked you, Messenger?" Jenks added with a sneer.

Oz could see Ellie's colour rising. Now he knew why Miss Arkwright had spoken to her before she'd mentioned the collection for charity. He suspected that she'd even asked for Ellie's approval. Being sensitive was Miss Arkwright's way. And there was good reason in this instance, since Ellie's little brother Leon had been born with a hand and part of his forearm missing. Not that you'd know that Leon had any problem at all; he was a great football player and almost as fast a sprinter as Ellie. It didn't seem to affect him much, except for the stares he sometimes got.

Yet it was one of the reasons Ellie was so intolerant of people who didn't make the best of what they had. Oz wasn't sure how many of his classmates knew, but with Jenks' malicious skill at baiting people, there was always the nagging doubt that he was yanking Ellie's chain. And Oz knew that she wasn't about to sit there and let him do that.

"You—" she began. But before Ellie could say any more, Jenks went to his shirt pocket and brought out the red-coloured card he had kept for Ellie-type confrontations since their last soccer match. He brandished it in her face, while his own contorted with spiteful glee. There were roars of approval from his cronies.

"Yeah," Skinner said, joining in again, "get off the field, Messeng—"

But he didn't finish. Suddenly, Ruff was on his feet, eyes blazing with some unnamed emotion at the two class wannabbe clowns. When he spoke, his words rang with a fierce anger.

"I can't believe I'm hearing this. What's the cost of a first class stamp? 60p? You have no idea how much that's worth to some of these people."

"Oh, and you do, do you, Adams?" Jenks drawled, waving the red card at Ruff.

"No, I don't. But my brother does. Unlike yours, he's actually been there."

"Oh, yeah?" Jenks mocked, but a little note of doubt had crept into his voice.

"He was a volunteer last summer in Tanzania. The photos he brought back to show me and my mum and dad..." Ruff paused to swallow. It sounded loud in the suddenly silent room. "There's disease and unexploded bombs and mines and kids who even get their legs bitten off by crocodiles because they have to wash in rivers. They have nothing. If we all gave a quid it would mean someone our age or younger might be able to walk for the first time. You're an idiot, Jenks. And an IPOD?" Ruff shifted his blazing glare to Skinner. "Most of these places don't even have electricity. What planet are you from?"

Skinner hesitated and then babbled, "Five-nil," obviously thinking that reminding Ruff of his team's defeat at the hands of the Skullers was a devastating insult. Unfortunately, no one except Ruff had any idea what he was talking about.

There was a moment of total silence as a flummoxed Skinner looked around at his classmates in exasperation. Jenks, meanwhile, appeared so stunned by Ruff's outburst that he couldn't even speak. All he could manage was to frown at Ruff, his mouth working in a way that suggested that whatever it was he wanted to say had got stuck on its journey between his brain and his tongue. But Oz saw, too, that the only pair of eyes more shocked than Jenks' belonged to Ellie, who was watching Ruff in totally bewildered awe.

Miss Arkwright broke the silence by clearing her throat.

"A good point well made, Rufus," she said, smiling at Ruff, who suddenly did an impression of a boiled lobster and sat down quickly. "So, shall we put it to the vote?" Miss Arkwright continued. "Who would like to donate their stamp money?"

Thirty hands, including, much to Jenks' astonishment, Skinner's, shot up.

"I will look forward to your donations on Monday, then," Miss Arkwright said. "And I will get IT to sort out an e-card for us to use, instead of posting one. Thank you, everyone."

* * *

Oz was still thinking about Ruff's outburst when he got home. So much so that he hardly noticed the funny mood his mother was in at teatime, until she dropped a plastic salad bowl for the second time in as many minutes.

"Mum, you all right?"

"Me?" she said, in a high-pitched, flustered sort of voice. "Yes, fine, absolutely. It's just that there's someone calling this evening that I want you to meet."

Oz had just finished a yoghurt and was opening his second. "Oh? Who?"

"An old colleague of your father's. She's just dropping by for a chat."

Oz nodded. People were always dropping by for chats, although there were far fewer now than when his father was alive. Usually that meant that he was expected to say hello, listen to comments on how much he'd grown and how much he looked just like his dad and then, after a few polite minutes, he'd make his escape with homework or football as his pretext. So, when his mother called to him at seven o'clock that evening, he saved the page he'd found on the Internet which explained all about dor beetles and headed down to the living room. There, Mrs. Chambers introduced him to a plump woman with orange-tinted glasses and mousy hair that needed a wash.

"Oz, this is Dr. Mackie."

"Hi," Oz said.

Dr. Mackie was so fat, she had to push herself out of the chair with both hands and not inconsiderable effort. She extended a sausage-fingered hand to Oz.

"Oscar, it's nice to meet you."

Oz took her hand, and it felt cool and a little clammy.

"I can see the resemblance quite plainly," Dr. Mackie said. Her accent was Scottish, but soft and refined. Her clothes all looked a touch too small and her greasy hair was tied back in an untidy ponytail. "And how are things with you, Oscar?"

"Fine," Oz said.

"Good, now we all know each other," fussed Mrs. Chambers, and Oz couldn't help thinking that she still looked a bit flustered. "Why don't you two sit down and I'll fetch some tea."

She left the room and Oz watched Dr. Mackie lever herself heavily back into the chair. "So," she said when she was finally settled, "Gwen tells me you've moved schools this year. How's it going?"

"All right," Oz said.

"Can be difficult, moving up. New challenges. All those new people. It's often quite a stressful time." Dr. Mackie regarded him through her orange glasses with a calm smile. "But Gwen tells me that you have some good friends."

Oz nodded. He did, indeed.

Dr. Mackie leaned forward and several already-stretched seams strained in protest. "Oscar, I ought to explain to you that I am more than just an old friend of your father's. I work in the psychology department. Gwen asked me to come here this evening because she thought you and I ought, perhaps, to have a little chat."

"Psychology?" Oz said.

"You know what that is?"

Oz nodded. "Stuff to do with how your head works."

Dr. Mackie smiled again, and once more Oz was struck by how unreal it was. Maybe it was because he couldn't see her eyes behind the orange tints, but the smile looked as if it could be turned on and off by a switch, while the rest of her face didn't seem to shift at all.

She reached into the bag at her feet and took out a writing pad and a pen. "Gwen told me all about your maths test."

"What about my maths test?" Oz asked, suddenly quite unnerved.

"Well, I know that you were called to see your year master today and that it's clear that you are very capable of doing maths, am I right?"

Oz nodded. For some reason, the saliva in his mouth wouldn't go down his throat.

Dr. Mackie wrote something down and then looked up. "The more interesting question, from my point of view, is why you felt you couldn't do the test the first time around."

"I didn't feel as if I couldn't do it," Oz said heatedly, "I just couldn't. It was like trying to translate Latin."

There was another plastic smile. "You've been through a lot these last few years, Oscar. Losing a parent at such a young age is very traumatic, very upsetting. How old were you when Michael died?"

"Eight and a bit," Oz said, and felt suddenly very irked that this woman was talking to him about his father at all.

"We often do not appreciate fully the effect something like that has on us. It causes very deep scars and we're always left wondering why such a terrible thing could happen. Sometimes, we even think it's our fault."

Oz kept quiet. This was worse than one of Miss Arkwright's "little chats." He even began wondering if they knew one another.

"Have you ever felt like that, Oscar?" Dr. Mackie continued to probe.

"No," said Oz, wondering where all of this was possibly leading.

"Sometimes misplaced guilt can cause the mind to play all sorts of wicked tricks."

Oz frowned. "Are you saying that I couldn't do maths because my dad died?"

Dr. Mackie continued to press home her point in a calm, slightly irritating voice. "Perhaps Mr. Boggs, your maths teacher, reminds you of your father. Perhaps you wanted to punish him for leaving like he did."

This was such a totally mad idea that Oz burst out laughing. "Badger Breath is nothing like my dad."

"I know it may seem like that to you, but under the difficult circumstances of Michael's death—"

"Look, I can explain the maths thing," Oz said quickly. "It's the way Badger—Mr. Boggs—teaches it. It's just taken me a bit longer to understand it, that's all…"

But Dr. Mackie wasn't really listening. She was writing on her pad, talking as she wrote. "Close family members are often very resentful in circumstances like those surrounding your father's death." She looked up and leaned even further forward, her voice dropping low. "I knew Michael very well, and how the insurance company could even begin to suggest that he was suicidal is frankly laughable, but—"

An ice-cold needle pierced Oz's stomach and he jerked upright.

"What did you just say?" he breathed.

The look on Oz's face seemed to have paralysed Mackie. All she could do was return his horrified stare, all pretence at a smile long gone.

"You didn't know, did you?" she said finally, and didn't wait for an answer before adding quickly, "Oscar, listen to me, there is no proof. It was just a question asked at the inquest which the insurance company latched on to—"

"My dad's car crashed," Oz said through gritted teeth. "He died in an accident."

"There's no doubting that, Oscar. And there was no note, but the alcohol…"

Oz's mind was doing cartwheels. The icy needle in his gut kept up an incessant stabbing. This explained everything. It explained why Arkwright was so protective, and it explained Pheeps' sick little games. Oz stood up as a wave of sickness spread over him.

"Oz, sit down, please," begged Dr. Mackie.

But Oz couldn't. The floor was like marshmallow under his feet as he staggered to the hall and yanked the kitchen door open. His mother was arranging biscuits on a plate.

"Oz," she said, startled by something she saw in his face.

"Why didn't you tell me?" Oz said thickly. "All this time you've known, and you didn't tell me."

"Tell you what?" said Mrs. Chambers, but in her eyes Oz could see that she knew very well what he was talking about.

"This stuff about Dad crashing his car on purpose."

"Oz," said his mother, suddenly ashen-faced, "it was the insurance company. They wanted to investigate. They'd do anything to wriggle out of paying—"

Dr. Mackie appeared in the doorway behind Oz. "Gwen, I assumed…"

Oz ignored her, anger driving him on. "But is that what people are saying? That he did it on purpose? Is it?"

"There was a smashed bottle, and whiskey all over the seat next to him," Mrs. Chambers spoke in a kind of trance now, uttering the words, oddly emotionless. "There was some in his stomach, but none in his blood. He wasn't drunk. He must have taken some just before the crash. I couldn't explain it then, and I still can't now, because he hated the stuff. But the insurance company wrote to all his colleagues, asking them if they'd noticed him acting strangely in the weeks before…" She shook her head and whispered desperately, "No one except the insurance company believes he did it on purpose, Oz."

"I bet Heeps does," Oz spat. "I bet he's spread it all over the university."

"Your father's colleagues have been very discreet," protested Dr. Mackie.

"Dr. Heeps' daughter hasn't been," Oz said, his voice getting louder.

Mrs. Chambers stepped towards Oz and held out her arms beseechingly. "I am so sorry you had to find out this way, Oz. But it's something I knew you'd eventually have to deal with."

Oz took a step back. "What does that mean? Are you saying that you think he might have done it?"

"Oh, Oz," Mrs. Chambers said, and started to cry.

Oz rounded on Dr. Mackie. "I didn't pretend to be rubbish at maths to bait Badger Breath, okay?" He looked from the psychologist to his mother again. "I don't care what any insurance company or inquest says. My dad didn't crash that car on purpose. I know he didn't. And anyone who thinks he did needs their heads examined. But not by you!"

He shot Mackie a furiously defiant glare and ran up to his room.

Chapter 9

Garret and Eldred's

Oz locked himself in his bedroom, head throbbing with anger at what he had just heard. He strode blindly from one side of the bedroom to the other, looking at the games and books and the flotsam of his life all around him, but not really seeing any of them. His brain was whirling like an out of control helicopter in a crash descent. Why had his mother or Caleb or someone never told him? Did they think that he was still a child that needed protecting? Didn't they know that it was far, far worse hearing it bandied about casually like Dr. Mackie had just done than hearing it from someone who cared? Didn't they know that other people would have been discussing it, like teachers and all of his dad's colleagues and friends, so that they treated Oz with that awful pity he hated so much?

And Pheeps? His skin crawled when he now thought of Pheeps and the truly horrifying nature of her snide, supercilious sneers. Humiliation and fury fought a battle in his chest and threatened to erupt like a boiling geyser. That she was poison he already knew, but this... His ignorance just made things a hundred times worse and made him suddenly want to roll up into a ball and howl. He groaned, threw himself down onto the bed and buried his head in the pillow, concluding with the utmost certainty that all adults were completely mad. He toyed with ringing Ellie and Ruff, but then began wondering if they had known, too. Known and not said anything in case it upset him.

Some time later, he heard his mother knocking gently on the door and heard it open. She called his name softly, but Oz had his back to her, so he didn't move and pretended to be asleep. He didn't want to speak to her. Not yet. He wanted to get things straight in his head. So he kept very quiet, and after a while she went away.

Oz wasn't sure how long he lay there with his eyes shut, trying to quell the images racing around in his head, but sleep was a long, long way off. The discussion with Dr. Mackie had opened up wounds that had only ever partially healed. The idea that his dad had deliberately crashed the car was just insane. He was as certain of that as he was that the sun would come up tomorrow. But in the dark, small hours, Oz could not help reliving the horror of that night. The tension in his mother's expression as they waited for his dad to arrive home, knowing that he'd left the airport four hours before. The excuses she'd used to pretend that all he'd done was run out of battery on his mobile and stopped at a service station for a bite. The horror he'd read in her face as the blue lights of the police car pulled up outside.

When Oz finally gave up trying to shut his eyes, the luminous dial on his alarm clock read half past midnight. He crept out of his room and tip-toed down one flight. There was a light under his mother's bedroom door. He hesitated, still angry with her for what had happened. He wanted to thrash it out with her, vent his fury, but he remembered the look on her face the night his dad hadn't come home and suddenly he found he simply couldn't do it. He couldn't bear the thought of that look returning. Besides, he argued limply, she was probably asleep by now.

He turned and went back upstairs but bypassed his bedroom and went up to the library. He turned all the lights off and sat in one of the old leather chairs. It was a moonless night and stars sparkled in the velvet sky visible through the glass turret windows. When he was much younger, he'd sat in his dad's lap in this very chair staring at the night sky, waiting for a shooting star to appear. Sometimes they'd sat for hours, but it hadn't mattered that they had never seen one in all the times they tried, because his dad would just talk and Oz would listen with half-lidded eyes until he fell asleep. He'd wake up the next day in his own bed and wonder sleepily how he got there. Oz knew that the man who had spent all those hours with him would never deliberately crash a car into a wall. Accidents happened, and Oz could just about accept that his father had not been indestructible and as much a potential victim of capricious fate as anyone else. But deliberately kill himself?

Never.

But what had all that business about insurance companies been about? He should have asked. Now it would have to wait until morning…unless… He fished out his mobile and sent a single line of text:

In much need of hot chocolate if you are awake.

Twenty seconds later he got a reply.

Just boiling milk. Kitchen in two minutes?

Caleb, of course, knew who Dr. Mackie was, but was visibly shocked to hear about the purpose of her visit.

"Oz, I'm so sorry you had to hear that. You needed to know, but that isn't the way to find out," Caleb said with a look of stark horror. "Dr. Mackie isn't renowned for her tact."

"But why didn't you tell me?"

Caleb shook his head. "Your mother... She loves you to bits, Oz. She just wanted to protect you from all that."

"But she can't, can she? She can't protect me, because she can't make it go away. You knew what Pheeps was on about when I told you the other night, didn't you?"

Caleb sighed and turned off the stove. "I could guess."

"But what did Mum mean about the insurance company?"

Caleb poured the hot milk into mugs and began stirring in the chocolate. "When you get older and have responsibilities like houses and children, you insure your life against horrible things like accidents. That way, if anything happens to you, the insurance company pays out a sum, which can be very large, in order that those left behind are looked after."

"Right," Oz said, accepting a mug, "but Mum said that the insurance company was trying to wriggle out of paying."

"That's generally what insurance companies do. It was a new-ish policy that Michael had taken out after you'd moved in here. He wanted to make sure everything was taken care of, should anything happen. Companies don't pay out on suicide cases in the first two years."

"But he didn't do that to himself. I know he didn't." Oz could hear the faint tremor in his own voice.

"I know that, too, Oz. Michael never stopped talking about you and your mother. A man less likely to want to take his own life, I have never met. But the coroner left an open verdict. That's enough for the insurance company to contest the case. I'm sure they'll pay up eventually, but these things can drag on, and for your mum it's like trying to swim through treacle."

"That's why she wants to get rid of this place, isn't it?" Oz said, suddenly realising what it all meant.

Caleb nodded and Oz frowned, trying to unravel the strands of thought that were knotting in his head.

"Don't judge her too harshly, Oz. She's been through a lot. She depends on the money from us tenants and what she earns doing some copyediting. It isn't much."

He knew that there wasn't much spare money around, but now he understood a lot better why that was. Oz blew over the top of his mug and sipped at his hot chocolate. He felt better instantly. "I just wish there was something I could do to help her understand how brilliant this place is. How amazing it is just to be here."

"You can. Just be you. Have your friends over. Have Halloween parties. Go for a kick about in the park. That's what your dad would have wanted." Caleb's eyes narrowed quizzically. "And now that we've mentioned it, I've been meaning to ask you about football. Do you play for a team now?"

Oz shook his head.

"Why not?"

Oz let the steam from the hot chocolate tickle his nose as he put it to his lips. It was the same question he'd avoided answering whenever Ruff and Ellie asked.

"Your dad told me you were very good," Caleb persisted, regarding Oz over the top of his mug.

"Did he?" Oz said without looking up. Eventually he sighed and explained. "We made a promise."

"A promise?"

"I made Dad promise that, if ever I played for a team, he'd come and watch me."

There was a long moment of ballooning silence before Caleb said, "So playing for a team is breaking that promise."

"He can't keep it, can he?" Oz said bitterly.

"But if you did play, how do you really know he wouldn't be there watching?"

Oz frowned. Caleb was really good at making him consider things that he would never have thought of himself.

"How could he?"

Caleb put his mug down. "Sometimes, keeping someone alive in our hearts can seem like the most difficult thing in the world, Oz. But if we don't, we're in danger of losing the connection that made them so special."

That one made Oz really think. He opened his mouth to argue twice, but shut it again without speaking on both occasions, while Caleb just sat calmly drinking his hot chocolate, his expression unreadable. They continued in silence, each occupied with his own thoughts, sipping at the delicious brown liquid, until Caleb finally said, "Did I tell you about the time your dad and I went to look at the old Celtic settlement in Brittany and stayed at a really weird old hotel?"

Oz shook his head and listened for ten minutes to Caleb's shaggy dog story, smiling at the funny foreign voices he put on, and wincing at the punch line about why they hadn't ordered two eggs for breakfast because "…one egg is usually *un oeuf*."

When he'd finished laughing, Oz put down his empty mug, yawned and said casually, "Thanks for talking to me about this."

"Luckily, I'm something of an insomniac, so it really is no trouble. But I think you should probably try and get some sleep now, and don't worry about what Mackie said."

Oz nodded and got up, remembering something else as he did. "By the way, we think we've found one of Morsman's artefacts."

"Really?" Caleb asked, looking up.

"Yeah. It's called the black dor and it's like this brooch thing that looks a bit like a beetle. Anyway, we'll know for definite tomorrow. At least, Ruff and I will since Ellie's thrown a wobbly."

"One of Morsman's artefacts, you say? Some people think they don't really exist, you know."

Oz thought he could hear a forced element to Caleb's voice. Almost as if he was desperately trying to keep it even.

"Yeah? Well, we won't tell Mum, that's for sure. Anyway, Ellie's really brilliant at stuff like that. Give her a job to do and she doesn't stop until she's done it." Oz rinsed his cup under a tap and thanked Caleb again.

"Any time, you know that."

Oz took the stairs two at a time, his heart all the lighter for having chatted with Caleb. But as he reached the first floor of the east wing, he paused. Someone was crying softly. It was a girl's sob, and it was coming from Lucy Bishop's room. He thought about going back and telling Caleb, but decided it was really none of his business. Besides, another huge yawn almost split his face in two, and at that moment what he needed more than anything was his bed.

* * *

Despite his tiredness, Oz slept only fitfully, tossing and turning throughout the night, his thoughts veering between Pheeps' smug supercilious smile and Dr. Mackie's emotionless delivery of what she'd assumed he, like everyone else, apparently, knew. And there was someone else in his dreams, a grey-eyed girl who kept calling his name, but seemed to disappear whenever Oz looked at her. Judging by the dark smudges under his mother's eyes the next morning, it didn't look like she'd slept very well, either. At least there was no sign of the black dog peeking out from behind the calendar, and for that Oz was thankful. Even so, for a long while breakfast was a silent affair, pierced only by polite requests for milk or toast. Finally, Oz could stand no more of it.

"Mum, I don't care what anyone else says, Dad couldn't have done what they say he did. I just know it," he said in a low voice.

Hollow-eyed, Mrs. Chambers responded in a tremulous voice, "Oh, Oz. I just couldn't bring myself to tell you. I couldn't stand to see you hurt again…" She broke down in a stifled sob.

"I'm eleven now, Mum. I need to know this stuff, especially when other people already do."

Mrs. Chambers grabbed him in a tearful hug. "I'm so sorry about last night," she whispered with her mouth pressed against his head. "I haven't slept a wink."

"It's okay, Mum. Just keep that Dr. Mackie away from me."

"She's banned," Mrs. Chambers said, dabbing her eyes. "I thought she'd be tactful, but she's obviously about as subtle as a mallet."

"A big mallet," Oz said, and was pleased to see his mother smile. "Maybe she did us both a favour though," he went on, "in a weird kind of way."

Mrs. Chambers frowned, but then shrugged. "Maybe." She looked hopefully into Oz's face before adding, "So we're pals again, are we?"

He grinned in reply.

"No more secrets, I promise," said Mrs. Chambers earnestly. Oz nodded, but turned quickly back to his cereal so that his mother couldn't see how uncomfortable her reference to "secrets" made him. After all, he had said nothing to her about the footsteps on Halloween, or of the weird symbols on his laptop, or of Morsman and his artefacts.

"I'm off to the supermarket. Will you and the gang be here for lunch?" said Mrs. Chambers as she cleared away breakfast.

"Doubt it. I'm meeting them in town."

"Anything interesting planned?"

"Not really. Ellie still needs to get something for Macy's birthday, that's all."

"Is she really sixteen in a week's time?" Mrs. Chambers asked incredulously.

Oz nodded. Ellie's big sister was doing her GCSE's this year and the only way she was likely to pass was if the examining board suddenly decided to offer one on "how to make boys chase you," or so Ellie kept saying with exasperation.

Oz planned on catching the ten o'clock bus, so he had time to check his emails before heading out. He'd placed the trinket box on top of the laptop the night before and once again found himself examining it as he waited for the computer to boot up. The maker's mark stood out on the bottom now that he'd cleaned it up, but he gave it a little polish with his thumb anyway, and as he did so, the most extraordinary thing happened. The silver mark glowed under the pressure of his thumb. Not a trick of the light this time, but a definite pulse of yellowish light.

That was nothing compared to what happened inside Oz's head at that same precise moment, though. As clear as day, the image of a girl's face appeared. It was a pleasant, quite pretty face, although when Oz was asked to provide details by Ellie when he tried to explain the dream to her, he found that he couldn't. At least, not with the thorough recall he would have liked. The one thing he did remember was that she had startling grey eyes and dark hair cut short in a bob. He excused his poor memory on the fact that the image lasted just a few seconds before it blinked out. But what he did remember was that the face spoke. And, like a poorly received radio signal, he was only able to pick out a few words.

"Hello, Oscar. I am silly…"

* * *

Oz was late getting to Ballista's. More road works had delayed the bus and the café was packed with thirsty shoppers when he got there. So when he managed to work his way through the crowd, having warned Ruff that he'd be late, he was not at all prepared for what was waiting for him in their favourite alcoved corner.

Ruff was not alone.

"Thought you said you were busy," Oz said, trying to stop the grin that had instantly spread over his lips from breaking out into a laugh.

"Changed my mind," Ellie said.

"Ok," Oz said.

And that was it. Nothing more was said about it. If Oz did wonder if volunteering for charity work or defending your disabled brother had anything to do with improving people's understanding of one another, he kept it all to himself. He wasn't about to press the point or demand explanations. Yet, when Ellie excused herself to go to the loo, he couldn't resist the urge to ask Ruff just one question.

"I did tell you that Ellie's little brother Leon was born with just one hand, didn't I?"

Ruff stared at him in disbelief. "Uh, no. You never said…" his words trailed off as slowly his eyes widened in recollection of the little exchange in room 33 the day before. "Wow. I don't think I'd want to be in Jenks' or Skinner's boots the next time they meet Ellie on a football field."

"You can say that again," laughed Oz.

And when Ellie came back to her seat, Oz couldn't help but sense that something had definitely changed. Both boys were looking at her, Oz with a quiet little smile, and Ruff with renewed interest. But she gave them both identical, trademark, feisty glances and said, "Whatever it is you've been discussing, I do not want to know. Now, can we please get on with why we're here?"

But the smile didn't leave Oz's lips, because he noticed that the faintly amused, indulgent look that had appeared just after her speech had been given to them both. It was the first time that there hadn't been that little smidgen of mistrust in the way she looked at Ruff. He supposed he ought to thank Jenks and Skinner for that, and almost laughed out loud. As candidates for sealing friendships, they were an unlikely pair. But if there was one thing that was going to make Ruff and Ellie friends, it was having common enemies like Jenks and Skinner.

Still with an odd, intangibly warm feeling inside him, Oz launched into telling them about the voices he'd been hearing.

"I know how weird all this sounds, but I'm sure I've heard it somewhere before in my dreams, twice. Once the night before the second maths test, and again last night."

Ellie and Ruff listened in open-mouthed astonishment.

"Whoa, Oz, what are you saying?" Ruff said with furrowed brows. "That this girl is tied up with the trinket box, and she told you how to do maths in your dreams?"

"Told you it sounds mental."

"Maybe not," Ellie said softly, stirring her latte. "I don't mean the maths thing. That's just silly. I mean the trinket box. Maybe she's the missing link. What if she is the ghost, and somehow the trinket box allows her to communicate?"

"So she haunts the trinket box, you mean?" Oz said.

Ellie sat up. "And maybe she's the one that put those images on your laptop, and wants us to find the artefacts?"

"And maybe there's a van outside with lots of men in white coats waiting to take you two away," Ruff said, shaking his head.

"I know how mad it sounds," Oz said, "but it makes a weird kind of sense, too. Look, Caleb said that my dad went to Egypt on the trail of Morsman's artefacts. He sent me the box from there and all this weird stuff has only really started to happen since I found it."

"Except for the footsteps. We heard them before you found the box," Ellie corrected him.

Oz wrinkled his nose in disappointment; he'd forgotten about the footsteps for a moment.

"Well, I've found some stuff out, too," Ruff said, taking a big gulp of hot chocolate, which left him with a cream-coated upper lip. "I was playing some online *Phantom Vamp-busters 3*, and I remembered that if you got to level five you got a password that allowed you to access an online magazine called the *Woolcote Gazette*."

Ellie snorted. "Sounds like a farming magazine."

"And that's where you'd be dead wrong, Miss Know-It-All. The *Woolcote Gazette* is ancient, and it's full of all this really great weird stuff like hauntings and actual alien sightings. It's the bees' buzzard knees, I tell you."

Ellie and Oz exchanged knowing glances.

"Why have I never heard of it, then?" Ellie asked.

"Because they stopped publishing it in 1960-something. But it goes back ages longer than that. Hundreds of years, maybe. Anyway, I got to level seven two nights ago, so I logged on with my free password and searched for Morsman on the *Woolcote* site, and guess what? There was an interview with Morsman's housekeeper in a 1948 edition. Someone was researching Morsman and dug her up like journalists do. She said that the reason he'd spent his whole life searching for the artefacts was because of something he'd found in the orphanage. Something that changed his life."

"So, what was it?" Ellie asked, sitting up excitedly.

"Ummm, it didn't say."

Ellie's shoulders slumped and she threw herself back into the armchair in exasperation. "Fat lot of good that is, then, you total gonk."

"But it proves that there's something there, though, right?" Ruff said before Ellie could protest again. "She also said that his obsession started when he went on an expedition abroad with an old friend called…" He took out a folded-over Post-It note from his pocket. "Uh…Tanner, to find the fifth artefact, which he was really excited about."

"Sugar. A fifth artefact? They must be breeding," Ellie said, spooning up the froth from the bottom of her cup.

"No, wait," Oz said, sitting up. "I read about this Tanner bloke, too." Oz had forgotten until now about Tanner. He'd been mentioned in the Morsman article his dad had written. But he didn't want to steal Ruff's thunder, so he just sat back and listened.

"Everyone thought Morsman was completely barking, because the expedition was to France and they were at war with Germany at the time," Ruff said.

"Was there anything about his death?" Ellie asked.

"That's a bit weird, too. No one understood why Morsman died in London, 'cos he hated the place and hadn't been there for, like, forever. And he was in the docks. I mean, how unlucky is that? To go to a place you've avoided all your life and then get bombed for your trouble." Ruff emptied his cup in a couple of deep gulps.

Oz finally spoke. "We may never find out what happened to him, but I still think we've got a great chance of finding the artefacts, because someone or something is trying to help us. Maybe it's the trinket box or the grey-eyed girl, or maybe it's whoever the footsteps belong to. There is only one way to find out."

They both stared at him.

"Look, my dad was trying to find the artefacts, too, so we've got to keep looking. It would sort of make what happened to him mean more, somehow. And if we found the artefacts, it would be one in the eye for Heeps. I've got a feeling that's why he took everything from my dad's study.

And," he added darkly, "I really would like to see him and Pheeps squirm."

"What has she done now?" Ellie asked warily, sitting up again.

So, after one big, deep breath, Oz told them about what had happened when Dr. Mackie had come to call. And it all poured out, the argument with his mother, the chat with Caleb, everything. Oz couldn't stop it, even though he could feel himself flushing with remembered anger.

"That's awful," Ellie whispered when he'd finished. Oz thought he saw a wetness in her eyes that hadn't been there before.

Oz took another deep breath and sent a couple of darting looks at the two of them before saying, "So neither of you knew, then?"

"Oz, I swear, if I'd have known…" Ellie said, shaking her head, white-faced.

"I'd have told you, mate," Ruff said earnestly.

Oz nodded. That was good enough for him.

"And you think Pheeps has known this all along?" Ruff asked, sitting forward.

"Her father must have."

"Yeah, but—"

"Maybe Arkwright knows something that you don't? 'Careful, you might do yourself an injury? Runs in the family?'" Oz repeated the poisonous phrases Pheeps had hurled at him in a very unflattering, if not altogether inaccurate, impersonation.

"That's disgusting," Ruff said.

"But how can we get back at her?" Ellie asked, fuming.

"Well, like I said, my dad sent me that trinket box for a reason. I think that reason has to do with Morsman and Bunthorpe. If it turns out that my dad had found something…" He let his voice trail off and smiled. "Imagine how that would make Heeps feel."

Ellie and Ruff exchanged tight-lipped glances, then they both looked at Oz and nodded. It made sense.

"So, let's go and find the black dor," Ellie said, pushing back her chair.

"I though you were shopping for something for Macy," Oz said.

"That can wait," Ellie said as she stood up.

"Think we should maybe have lunch first?" Ruff blurted. "I'm starving."

"It's only half-eleven," Oz said.

"Exactly," Ruff replied. "I hate eating late."

* * *

Garret and Eldred Antiques was not in the main part of town. They had to wind their way through a couple of shopping arcades, past the Seabourne International Arena, and walk the length of St Beade's Street to a less familiar area. Here, what once had been a thriving shopping area now had an abandoned, slightly scruffy air. Ruff, who always seemed to know his way about, led them past a shut-up pub and down a dingy side street where every other property had "for sale" signs in the windows, until at last they stood outside a double-fronted shop, where an old-fashioned sign hanging from a brass pole above the door indicated their destination. The grimy shop window was overflowing with dark furniture, bric-a-brac, stuffed animals in glass cages, and books, all coated with thick layers of dust.

"You're sure this is the place?" Oz asked doubtfully.

"Garret and Eldred," Ellie said, pointing to the sign as she pushed open the door.

An old-fashioned brass bell above the door rang as soon as they entered, but once they were in, the large room fell into a dusty, murky silence. Inside, it was even more jumbled than the shop front had suggested. Over in one corner, behind a hurdy-gurdy machine, lurked a taxidermy array with foxes and weasels piled on top of birds and fish. In another, Oz saw a tower of ornately decorated chamber pots, and in between was a minefield of occasional tables, old chairs, wall clocks and bed heads. But that was only as far as Oz could see, because the shop seemed to stretch back for a considerable way.

"Where do we start?" whispered Ellie.

"Perhaps if you indicated what it is, exactly, you are after, I might be of assistance," suggested a voice from the shadows.

Ellie, Ruff and Oz all turned at once. Tucked behind a huge mounted moose head sat a wizened old gentleman, immaculately dressed, with a red spotted bow tie and a pair of half-glasses bridging his nose. He perched on a stool at a small workbench lit by a single desk lamp. Spread out on the bench, on a white cloth, was a bewildering array of tiny cogs and springs and shiny metal cases and glistening pearl dials. The man smiled and stood up stiffly. He wore a clean, navy-blue apron with "Garret and Eldred, Watchmakers and Purveyors of Fine Antiques" emblazoned on the breast. He moved towards them with some difficulty, eyebrows arched in enquiry.

"Uh, well, we're actually looking for a dress clip brooch," Ellie said.

"Well, you've come to the right place, my dear. We have a large assortment. Now let me see, do you have a particular style in mind?" He moved past them and Oz smelled a pleasant waft of after-shave, reminding him of cut grass and heather. They followed him deeper into the shop to a bank of glass cases. The shopkeeper ran a bony finger along the brass mouldings on one of the cases and peered at the faded label stuck to the glass. "Dress clips, yes. Here we are." He looked up. "A gift, is it?"

Ellie and Oz replied at the same time. Unfortunately, Oz said, "No," while Ellie said, "Yes."

Ruff made eyes to the ceiling and said, "Sort of."

"I see," said the shopkeeper, amused. He seemed well-used to muddled shoppers. "Well, there's more than enough choice here. I'm sure you will find something suitable. We have six trays of dress clips in this case." He beamed up at them. "My name is George Eldred, by the way, and I am familiar with where most things are in the shop. Just ask if you need any help."

"We do," Oz said, deciding to take the bull by the horns. "We saw something advertised online—"

"On the interweb?" asked Mr. Eldred. "My nephew has been helping me, you know. Amazing what you can do these days."

"We saw a black scarab brooch."

"We have quite a few of those," said Mr. Eldred knowingly.

"But this one had a missing clip."

"Ah." The shopkeeper held up a finger. "That would be in the imperfect tray." He leaned over very slowly and pulled out a tray from the very bottom of the glass cabinet, while alarming popping sounds emanated from his knees and back. He straightened gingerly, his face a grinning mask of effort, and laid the tray on top of the cabinet. It was completely full of black, scarab-like shapes.

"Do you mind if we look?"

"Help yourselves," said Mr. Eldred.

It took them ten minutes to find it, mainly because everything was covered in dust. But when Ellie held it up and gave it a quick polish, there was no doubt in anyone's mind that it was the exact same item pictured on Oz's laptop. Oz peered at the tiny label attached to it.

"How much?" Ruff asked in a whisper.

"Five pounds," said Oz, pleasantly surprised.

"You can have it for four," said Mr. Eldred magnanimously from the workbench, where he'd gone back to sit.

Ruff, who had seemed a little on edge even before coming into Garret and Eldred's, said, "Right, I saw a secondhand game shop on Gavel Lane. There were some real bargains in the window. I'll meet you outside in about ten, okay?"

"Him and his bloomin' Xbox," Ellie said huffily as Ruff hurried away.

"Mr. Eldred," Oz said as he watched the shopkeeper carefully wrap the dor in some tissue paper, "have you any idea where this came from?"

"I know exactly where it came from. I know where everything in this shop came from. But I need to know who I'm talking to before I divulge that sort of information. Can't be too careful, you know," he said sternly, but his eyes twinkled as he spoke.

"Oz Chambers," Oz said, holding out his hand, "and this is Ellie Messenger."

"Delighted to meet you, Oz and Ellie," said Mr. Eldred. "The curse of working here for sixty years is that I remember every purchase and sale." He held up the scarab brooch. "This came to us from a spinster who had recently inherited a property in Seabourne. The previous owner had been a collector and had not catalogued things very well. I remember going up to the house to evaluate." He looked off into the distance. "Such a lovely property. Her name was Miss Millichamp, and the address was…now, what was it? I can see it now, used to be an orphanage at one time…"

"Penwurt, Number 2 Magnus Street," Oz said in a flat voice. "And the lady was Bessie Millichamp."

"Exactly right," said Mr. Eldred, smiling with delight. "Do you know it, by any chance? Not long ago, I sold a clock to a very nice man who lived there; it was also part of Miss Millichamp's clear-out. I always felt the clock belonged there, myself. Now, what was the man's name?"

"Chambers," said Oz, feeling a knot of excitement tighten in his stomach.

"Chambers, that's it. Nice chap. Very knowledgeable. Is he an acquaintance of yours?"

"Sort of," Oz said truthfully.

"May I ask why it is that you want this particular brooch? Professional interest, you understand. I mean, it is of an unusual design, I'll admit. But we have far nicer ones for the money. And they might even have a clip attached."

"It's exactly the right—"

"Colour," said Ellie quickly. "It'll match her shoes exactly."

"Ah, an accessory. I see," Mr. Eldred's smile was indulgent.

"Did Great Aunt Bessy sell you anything else?" Asked Oz, trying to sound as casual as he could.

"Oh, let me see," Mr. Eldred massaged his chin in concentration. "Of course, we were not the only valuers she contacted, but I think there were a couple of bracelets and four pairs of earrings, some of them really quite nice. One of them pink pearl if I recollect. Then there were a handful of brooches, not valuable, but of some interest to collectors of the unusual, like you two clearly are." His eyes twinkled.

"But you don't remember her selling you a pendant?" Oz persisted.

"A pendant? No, I don't recall anything of that nature, why do you ask?"

The little bell above the door tinkled. Oz looked around to see a man in an overcoat enter the shop. He turned towards the collection of stuffed animals immediately so that Oz didn't see his face.

"My, my, turning into quite the busy afternoon," Mr. Eldred chuckled, his eyes crinkling. "If it's pendants you're after, of course, we have a splendid collection."

"No, it's okay," Oz said quickly. "I was just curious." He was suddenly very conscious of the fact that the person who had come into the shop, who still had his back to them, would be able to hear, quite clearly, everything that was being said.

"Ah, yes, understandably so. Well, there you are." Mr. Eldred handed over the tiny parcel and gave Oz his change.

Outside, Ellie and Oz headed back the way they'd come.

"So this definitely comes from Penwurt. Do you think Morsman found it somewhere?" Ellie asked.

"He must have. Maybe Great Aunt Bessie didn't know what it was. If Morsman died suddenly, perhaps he hadn't had time to sort things out, or leave a will or something. Shame someone came into the shop. I could have asked more questions."

"Let's have a look at it in daylight," Ellie said, pointing at the parcel.

Oz stopped and was about to undo Mr. Eldred's wrapping, when they looked up and were surprised to see Ruff coming back to meet them, walking quickly.

"Shut, was it?" Ellie asked.

Ruff shook his head, making large eyes at them. "You should see that place," he said, with loud and exaggerated delight. "It's brilliant." And then, without moving his mouth, he added in a low voice. "Do not open that parcel. Just shut up and follow me, no questions asked."

He turned and began describing just how brilliant the game shop was again as he hurried up the street. "It's got a copy of *Wolf Ripper 1*. I loved that game."

Three minutes later, they stood in the sparsely stocked shop. It looked run-down and almost about to close.

"Are you completely mad?" said Ellie, looking about her with obvious distaste. "This place is rubbish."

"Just hang on," Ruff said as he positioned himself so that he was half-hidden behind a rack of tacky birthday cards near the window. He picked one up and moved his head so that he could look out into the street through the gap the card left in the stack. When he was happy, he pulled Oz and Ellie around behind him. "Look," he said, pointing out to the almost empty street.

"Lovely," Oz said. "Does that fish and chip shop do curry sauce?"

"Next door to it, you buzzard," hissed Ruff. "The charity shop. Red and black coat."

Oz and Ellie peered through the space in the card rack and as they did, the door to the charity shop opened and a familiar figure emerged and looked up and down before staring directly across to where Oz, Ellie and Ruff were hidden.

Oz gasped. "Lucy Bishop?"

"Almost bumped into her when I left Garret and thingy's," Ruff explained quickly. "She pretended not to see me and veered off. But I've been watching her. She's just hanging about, waiting."

"For us?" Ellie said.

"I'd put a cheese and ham nine-inch baguette on it," Ruff said, ducking back down as Lucy Bishop sent a glance across towards the shop.

"You think she knows we went to Garret and Eldred's?" Oz asked, perturbed.

"Must have seen us go in." Ruff nodded.

"Bet she goes in and asks him what we bought," Ellie said.

"I told you she'd been acting funny around me," Oz said, his mind now racing. "But why is she following us?"

"Obvious, I'd have thought," Ellie said. "She's probably after the artefacts, too."

Oz wanted to scoff at this suggestion, but there didn't seem to be any other fit explanation. "I'll have to hide the trinket box and the dor," he said suddenly. "Soon as we get back to Penwurt."

"Why don't we split up and meet later? Try and throw her off the scent," Ellie suggested.

They stood in the run-down shop discussing their options. It was Oz who finally came up with the plan. He realised that it was likely to be him, more than anyone else, Lucy Bishop would follow. He quickly gave the dor to Ellie and, in hushed tones, explained what he had in mind.

Chapter 10

The Clock

Oz left first. He headed back towards High Street, meandering deliberately around the smaller lanes as he did so. He was sure he saw someone who looked like Lucy Bishop loitering in a chemist shop doorway as he stopped and knelt to tie a shoelace, To make sure he wasn't followed, he decided to kill some time wandering around Waterstone's. There, he went straight to the reference section and looked up Penwurt in *Hidden Haunted Houses of Great Britain*.

At 4.30 he headed for the men's toilet. There'd been no sign of Lucy Bishop in the book shop itself, but it was very big with lots of nooks and crannies to hide in. So Oz waited in the loo for a long ten minutes and then left by the back entrance. He emerged directly into the shopping centre, scooted through two department stores and doubled back along Scott Street to the bus station which, as usual, was heaving with Saturday afternoon shoppers. He made it to the number 6 with five minutes to spare. Panting from the effort, he clambered on and grinned at the sight of Ellie and Ruff sitting right at the back.

"Well, did she follow you?" Ellie wanted to know.

"Definitely," Oz said, wiping the sweat from his brow with the sleeve of his sweatshirt. "But I think I lost her in Waterstone's."

"What do you think she wanted?" Ruff asked.

"Spying, I expect. At least this way we'll get back to Penwurt first and I'll find somewhere safe to hide the dor and the trinket box," Oz declared. "I can think of one or two—"

He got no further as Ellie's elbow met painfully with his ribs and he felt himself being pulled down in his seat.

"Oy," he protested. Ruff, sitting next to him and nearest the window, was also struggling as Ellie yanked at his collar.

"Shut up," Ellie hissed from above them.

Oz felt the pressure ease on his head and looked up at Ellie. She had swivelled in her seat and had her coat hood up to hide her face.

"Ellie, what are you doing?" Oz demanded.

Ellie's eyes flashed warningly. "Shhh," she said, and whispered, "Look who's just got on the bus." The pressure eased a little more so that both he and Ruff could lift their heads a few inches. The bus was almost full and there was now a queue of late passengers on the steps. And there, just about to show the driver her pass, was Lucy Bishop.

Luckily, two very large women had chosen to sit in front of Oz and Ruff, but Ellie was sitting right in the middle on the back seat, in clear view of anyone getting on. But Lucy Bishop, holding a large plastic bag and looking preoccupied and nervous, barely glanced up at the other passengers as she found a seat near the front.

"S'okay," Ruff whispered, "I don't think she saw us."

The bus trundled out towards Seabourne United's football ground; Ellie kept her hood up and half-turned, while Oz and Ruff crouched low in their seats. After a while, Oz realised that Ellie was grinning, her face glowing.

"What's up with you?" he asked.

"Just this. It's exciting. Don't you think?"

"Yeah," Ruff said with his usual deadpan delivery.

"Oh, shut up," Ellie snapped. "If it isn't on a computer screen, nothing ever excites you. This stuff we're doing, it's so mysterious and strange. Can't you feel it? Like it's somehow part of some much bigger adventure."

"Right," Ruff said. "Just like one of my Xbox RPGs. And what usually happens there is that the heroes tootle along thinking everything's okay and stumble blindly into something really buzzard, which ends up trying to disembowel them."

"Really?" Oz said.

"Well, that's what happens in *Zombie Slaughter Sleep Wrecker*, *Ghostripper 2* and *Ghoul Bounty Hunter.*"

Ellie shook her head. "That's only three out of hundreds."

"Oh, and in *Dark Wood Menace 1* and *2.*"

"You've forgotten *Murdering Marauders of Mexico*," Ellie said with a deadpan expression.

"I must have missed that one," Ruff said, but gradually his eyes narrowed and he nodded to himself before adding, "If you are going to crack a joke, could you give us a bit of a warning so it'll give me time to get the flags out?"

Ellie grinned at him.

"Maybe Ruff's right," Oz said thoughtfully. "I mean, I think we need to be really careful. But I think you're onto something, too, Ellie. This thing could be much bigger than we think."

Lucy Bishop stood up abruptly as the bus approached Hockley Row. This was on the other side of People's Park, where Oz, Ellie and Ruff had their Sunday morning kickabout. It meant a long walk around to get to Magnus Street, but they were too curious to worry about that. They hurried off the bus and turned away while Lucy Bishop pulled her coat about her and set off at a brisk walk without a backward glance. It was fully dark by now, and night had brought with it a dank November fog, turning the yellow street lamps into fuzzy orbs. Visibility was dreadful and Oz struggled to see across the street, while on their left the empty space of People's Park stretched away into a grey nothingness.

"Funny place to get off," Ellie said as they waited to follow.

"She's a funny girl," Oz said, setting off briskly.

"What do you think she'll do now?" Ellie asked.

"Dunno," Oz replied. "Report back to whoever it is she's working for, I suppose."

"Of course, it could just be a coincidence."

"No way," Ruff said. "She was tailing us. I'm sure of it."

Occasionally the dark shapes of pedestrians appeared out of the fog, walking in the opposite direction, huddled with collars up against the damp, cold air. Ahead of them, Lucy Bishop hurried along, oblivious, it seemed, of her surroundings. Suddenly Ellie stopped and cocked her head.

"Can you hear that?" she asked.

They paused to listen. The fog dampened the noise of the few cars traveling on the quiet park road, but Ellie wasn't looking towards the street. She had turned her attention to the park itself. At first Oz heard nothing, but then, faintly but definitely, from somewhere in the dark expanse of playing fields, he thought he could hear a faint rustling. It had a rhythmic quality, suggestive of something moving. And moving quickly, at that. In the midst of that rustle was something else, a strange kind of snorting or sniffing, which suddenly stopped.

"What is that?" he asked.

"I have no idea, but it's buzzard and I vote we don't stay to find out," Ruff said, peering into the darknes.

They started walking again, one eye now on the dark fields beyond the edge of their vision. Oz felt Ruff's hand on his arm.

"Look," Ruff said.

Ahead of them, Lucy Bishop had stopped and turned towards the fence. It looked as if she was about to throw something over it, but she hesitated and happened to glance back to where Ellie, Ruff and Oz had, themselves, stopped. They must have been barely visible, but their presence was enough to make Lucy Bishop change her mind. Suddenly, she pulled back and hurried away.

Oz could see no more than ten yards into the park. The only illumination came from the fuzzy yellow sodium streetlights, but in the gaps between the lights the darkness intensified into pools of dense shadow. Oz hurried along towards where Lucy Bishop had stopped, his curiosity aroused, but he was unable to rid his mind of the noise he'd heard, and was desperately trying to imagine what sort of animal might make such a sound. It had to be something large padding across the dry, dead leaves that lay like a carpet on the grass. But what was the cause of that weird snorting? Something that sniffed? That didn't help, since most wild animals depended on scent as much as sight—unless, of course, it was a mole.

"Can't hear it anymore," Ruff said as he walked up to the fence. "Must have gone back towards the trees."

"Think Lucy Bishop heard it, too?" Ellie asked. "Is that why she stopped?"

"Maybe it was just some animal. A fox or a badger or something," Oz suggested.

Ruff nodded and moved close to the fence. "Well, there's nothing there n—UGH." His sentence ended in an involuntary yelp of shock and horror as something loomed out of the darkness on the other side of the fence, just feet away from where he stood. Ruff stumbled back and half-fell. It was just in time, too, as an arm shot through the bars towards him. Oz's shocked gaze shot from Ruff's sprawled form back to the fence, where a face glared at them out of the fog. It was a human face, but distorted and wild. The eyes were black and sunken, the features pinched, yellow teeth bared, the nails at the ends of the dirt-encrusted arms filthy and broken. A low, feral scream erupted from its red mouth and ended in a hissing snarl.

Oz felt the skin contract all over his body. He took two steps back but his eyes never left the fence and the thing crouched behind it. Whoever this had once been, there was nothing left behind those desperate, vicious eyes. A car roared past and the thing pulled back in alarm, and that was when Oz saw something even worse than those yellow teeth. The thing had chosen to clothe itself in a fur coat, dark and matted with filth and leaves, wrapped tightly around a thin body. It had pulled back onto all fours, glaring warily through the bars of the iron fence at Ruff.

But even in the dim and ghostly yellow light of the night, something shimmered around the shape. An aura, little more than a shadow, but that somehow gave substance to the pathetic, stick-thin body covered in a fur coat. It was the shape of a sleek predator, with a long, muscular body and a white-tipped face. Oz shook his head to clear it, and the boy on his haunches came back into focus. Stunned, Oz realised that there was something weirdly familiar about his features, but if he let his mind drift for even one second, the other image, the larger and much more powerful animal image, came back with a vengeance.

"Oz? What..."

He heard his name, but Ellie's voice choked off as the thing lunged again, hurling itself against the bars. Oz dragged his eyes away and grabbed the others.

"Run!" he yelled.

And run they did, pelting along the pavement. To his left, Oz could see the thing moving with them, running on all fours, rump in the air. It should have been ungainly and awkward, since the human form wasn't made for running that way, but when Oz didn't look directly at it, the thing seemed to move with sleek ease, loping along in a ferret-like motion that covered the ground easily. Ruff let out a shout as his foot met with a wonky paving stone and he half-tripped. Oz stopped and turned. The iron bars of the old-fashioned fence had given way to a modern, taller, chain-link variety. Through the mesh, Oz saw that the thing had stopped, too. It was watching them with feral cunning. Suddenly, it turned its eyes up to the gap above the fence.

"It's going to come over the top," Oz shouted.

And even as the words left his mouth, the thing leapt at the fence, scrambling up with unnatural speed. Within seconds it was at the top, swaying slightly, its eyes never leaving Ruff's face as it prepared to leap down. And Ruff could only stare back up at it, his expression one of paralysed fear.

But then there was a new noise behind them on the street. They heard shouts and a canine snarl. Barking madly, a golden yellow shape shot right past them to spring at the fence. Behind, on the end of a long lead, a man followed, half-stumbling, dragged along by the dog's power.

"Whoa, Dusty," said the man, trying his best to haul the dog back. "Bad dog, bad dog." He came to an abrupt halt in front of Oz and Ellie, who were staring at where the thing had been moments before.

"Oh, I'm so awfully sorry. Did he frighten you?" asked the man as he looked into Ruff's chalk-white face.

"No, he didn't," Ruff said shakily. "It wasn't the dog."

They turned to look at the fence. There was nothing there except a very excited Dusty, hackles raised, barking and growling at something unseen in the dark fields beyond.

"Don't know what came over him," the man said in a breathless voice. "He hardly ever barks. Only seen him do this once before, when a mad bull terrier went for him. Bad boy, Dusty." The man jerked the lead and Dusty stopped barking to whine at his master with a flat-eared, shamefaced expression.

"No," said Ellie, "he isn't a bad boy." She went to the dog and ruffled his fur, much to Dusty's tail-wagging delight. "He's a good boy. There was something on the other side of the fence," she explained.

"Oh?" said the man. "What was it?"

Oz sent her a warning glance, and Ellie said, "I…we don't know. But we think it's been following us. Dusty did us a big favour." She knelt down and allowed the dog, which by now had turned from ravening wolf into the friendliest golden retriever you could ever find, to lick her face.

"Shouldn't be anyone in there now," said the man. "Shut the gates at sunset in the winter, they do."

"Probably someone messing about," Ruff said weakly.

The man stared into the grey and black space. "Well, me and Dusty are going straight home after all this excitement. I suggest you do, too. C'mon, boy."

"Oh, we are," said Oz with conviction. "Straight home."

* * *

They ran the final half-mile, and Oz had never been more pleased to see the lights and solid turrets of Penwurt approaching. Mrs. Chambers met them in the hall and regarded them with mild concern.

"Goodness me, just look at the three of you. Why are you so out of breath?"

"Ran home…from…the park," panted Oz.

"Ran? From the state of you it looks like you were being chased by a monster."

No one spoke.

"Right," said Mrs. Chambers, somewhat bemused by their silence, "I've made some pasta with pesto sauce. Are you hungry?"

"Mrs. C, you always know the right thing to say," said Ruff with feeling.

They all felt better after some food, and Oz was keen to get upstairs to properly examine the dor so he declined the offer of second helpings and made eyes to the other two as he hurried to clear away the plates, much to Ruff's obvious disgust. But Ruff's expression changed the minute Oz fired up his laptop and he saw the mysterious screensaver images.

"Buzzard," he said as his eyes lit up like fireworks. "That is so awesome."

Meanwhile, Ellie unwrapped the dress clip and put it carefully down, right in front of the laptop, under the direct glare of a desk lamp. "It's exactly the same," she said, comparing the brooch with the image. Her face was glowing again, partly from the central heating of a drum-tight stomach provided by Mrs. Chambers' excellent tea, and partly with growing excitement.

"So, that just leaves us with working out what the symbol means," Oz said.

"I've seen it before," Ruff said through gritted teeth, "I know I have."

"Let me guess, *Vampire Zombie Bonecrushers 23*?" Ellie muttered.

"No," said Ruff in a less than disdainful way that left Oz wondering if there actually was such a game, "somewhere else." Ruff frowned in concentration. A moment later he sat up and yelled, "The library!" and was out of the door before either Ellie or Oz could react. They followed him up, and a minute later they were both leaning over him as he inspected the library's oak panelling, mumbling to himself as he did.

"There, see?" he said, pointing to the panel at about head height. Oz followed Ruff's finger and recognised the odd-looking trident shape, which had twenty or so other strange symbols all around it.

"My dad said that those symbols are all to do with alchemy and astrology," Oz explained.

"Great, so all we need to do now is work out what they mean," Ruff said, frowning.

"Well, since there are twenty-six of them, the most obvious thing is that they're some sort of alphabet," Ellie said.

"An alphabet," Ruff repeated in wonder. "Of course."

"And your symbol is the third, counting clockwise from the top," she added quickly.

"So it begins with a C. Right, now I need to borrow your laptop." Ruff turned and was off down the stairs again. Ellie and Oz grinned at each other and followed. It was like watching Dusty trying to find a hidden bone.

Three minutes later, Ruff sat back from Oz's laptop, looking smug. "Ellie was right. This"—he pointed to the symbol—"is the alchemical symbol for cinder."

"Cinder?" said Oz with a shake of his head, trying to ignore Ellie punching the air next to him. "Like in bits of burned coal and stuff? But what does it mean? I mean, why would someone put a symbol for a cinder on my laptop?"

"I need to take a closer look," Ruff said.

Ellie and Oz left him to it and took the trinket box back up to the library. Despite Oz pressing the maker's mark thirty or more times, nothing glowed and it felt cold and metallic under his hand.

"Maybe it only works if the moon's full or something," Ellie suggested, taking it from Oz and examining the symbol carefully. But Oz could see that Ellie was not quite her usual self.

"What's the matter?" he asked, although he didn't need three guesses.

"I'm still thinking about the park," she said with a shudder. "What *was* that thing?"

"Dunno," Oz said. "I mean, I know it was a man, but how weird was that get-up? And when you didn't look at him, it looked like something else altogether."

"Yeah." Ellie grimaced. "I saw that, too. His body looked sort of longer and there were markings on his face. It was really weird…"

Oz was quiet for a minute, but then said, "Know what it reminded me of?"

Ellie shook her head, but her troubled eyes revealed that she was in two minds about finding out.

"A polecat. I saw a programme on *National Geographic* last week about them. They're vicious things, and they make this weird sort of noise."

"Like that bloke did," said Ellie with obvious distaste. "Lucky for us Dusty came along."

A head of curly brown hair appeared at the top of the stairs.

"Talking of strange, furry animals," Oz said quietly, causing Ellie to giggle.

"Think I may have got something," said Ruff, striding in. He stared at the two of them suspiciously. "What's up with you?"

"Nothing," Oz said. "Just discussing exotic species."

Ellie put up her hand to stifle another laugh. Ruff frowned, but held out a sheet of paper covered with scribbles. The cinder symbol was there, much larger now. At the ends of each horizontal line Ruff had drawn other symbols, including an N, a funny thing that looked like wonky rugby posts, a weird kind of curly pound symbol and an hourglass.

"What are those?" Ellie asked.

"Those are what are hidden at the blobby ends of your cinder symbol. All I had to do was blow up the image."

"And what do they mean?" Oz asked.

"Well, according to the Alchemy for Pinheads website I found, they're instructions. The N must be number, the funny goalpost thing is the alchemical symbol for pulverise, the pound thingy is the symbol for solving and the hourglass…is an hourglass."

"Meaning?" Ellie asked

Ruff shrugged. "Anyway, I pulverised cinder into c, i, n, d, e and r. Gave them each a number from their position in the alphabet and added them up—"

"Comes to fifty-three," Ellie said, much to Ruff's annoyance.

"Ruff, that's brilliant," Oz said. "Talk about hidden depths."

"Yeah, dark and murky," Ellie muttered.

"Okay. So what does the hourglass mean?" Oz said.

"That, I don't know," Ruff answered.

Oz went very quiet. "I think I do," he said in a low, tremulous voice. "Time, commander of all things."

"You what?" asked Ruff.

"It's my dad's clock," Oz said. "Come on."

* * *

The study was just as empty as Oz had left it, but not quite the same. Oz remembered that Tim had been in there bleeding radiators, which explained why the desk was at a funny angle. Oz stood before it and pointed at the clock on the wall behind.

"And?" said Ruff impatiently.

"There, beneath the pendulum, see it?"

Ellie and Ruff walked up close to the clock. There, inlaid in the scrolls of the rosewood case, was a small hourglass with the words *tempus rerum imperator* engraved beneath it.

"Time, commander of all things," Oz said again.

"Okay, so this clock has an hourglass engraved on it," said Ruff dubiously. "How does that help?"

"Eldred told me today that my dad had bought this clock from him. We know it was from here originally and my dad went back to get it."

"But why?" Ruff said. "Doesn't even work."

"I know," Oz said, trying to concentrate. "But Dad used to say to us that an old boar figurine might be just a mildly interesting blob of metal heavy enough to weigh down the post, but to whoever owned it a thousand years ago, it meant something else altogether. Something really important, and much more than we could ever imagine. He was always on about things having other meanings."

"Yeah, but come on, this is a clock," Ruff said. "Can't be anything else, can it?"

"The hands on this clock have been at a quarter past nine for as long as I can remember," Oz said. "My dad would never wind it. What do you think would happen if the hands were moved around to—"

"Five and three," Ellie said excitedly. "Of course, fifty-three. It makes sense."

"Does it?" Ruff said, peering even closer. "But what has this clock got to do with what's on the laptop? What's it got to do with the black dor?"

"Ruff, I gave up asking questions a long time ago. Let's just do it," Ellie pleaded.

Oz fetched a chair. Standing on it, he reached up and pulled open the glass face. Slowly, he moved the hands around so that the hour hand was on three. When the minute hand reached the twelve position, the clock chimed three times. Oz was so shocked he almost fell off the chair. He had never heard it chime before, and it sounded deep and sonorous and oddly ominous.

He waited until it stopped and slowly moved the hand again until it was on the five. As it reached the digit, something gave a mechanical whirr. Ellie and Ruff exchanged glances and Oz saw out of the corner of his eye that there was a lot of doubt in that glance.

"Let's just wait and see," he said shortly.

The clock continued to whirr, until it finally stopped with a faint, mechanical click. They waited. Nothing happened.

"Maybe if—" Ellie began, but Oz cut her off.

"Let's just hang on another minute," he snarled, more tartly than he'd meant to.

"Yes, but—"

"Ellie, please."

"I only wanted to say that it might help if you twisted the hourglass thingy, that's all," she snapped.

"How can I? It's inlaid…" Oz caught his breath. The brass hourglass symbol wasn't inlaid anymore. In fact, it now proudly stood out of the surrounding wooden casing, and was smooth and solid under Oz's finger. He was standing so close that he must not have seen it pop out. Gently, Oz put his thumb and forefinger around the shape and twisted clockwise. There was a mechanical thunk and the bottom section of the clock, beneath the pendulum, moved forward to reveal a small drawer.

"Wow," Ruff said in wonder.

With trembling fingers, Oz examined the drawer. There was only one thing in it—a folded wodge of very old, battered-looking pieces of paper, which he carefully removed and placed on the desk.

"Better shut the door, Ellie," Ruff whispered out of the corner of his mouth.

Oz waited until Ellie had closed the study door and then, gently and very carefully, unfolded the papers. There were three yellowed and crinkly sheets. The first was filled with a careful copperplate hand.

"What does it say?" Ellie demanded, pushing her head between the two boys' shoulders.

"Looks sort of official. I recognize that name, 'Redmayne,'" Oz said in a whisper.

"He was the bloke who owned the Bunthorpe barn, wasn't he?" Ruff asked.

Oz nodded.

"What does it say?" asked Ellie urgently, pushing her head further forward.

"Okay, okay, we'll have one each," Oz said, handing them out.

"Mine's a will," Ruff said, reading down the list of instructions. "Left his son four horses, two goats and three pigs. Oh, and the stable boy got a butter churn and a milking bucket. Lucky gonk."

"Wow," Ellie said. "This is from John Shoesmith, the farrier, and it's to his brother-in-law, Redmayne."

"What does it say?" Ruff asked.

Ellie was frowning in concentration. "It's some sort of apology. Yes, listen to this…

"It was my firm intention to carry out the instructions of Squire Worthy as delivered through you to me, but, dear Edmund, I confess that I was unable to put one mark of injury on the shell with my hammer, even when delivered with enough force to bend a horseshoe. My furnace left it as cool as marble. What was I to do? The Squire was clear in his purpose. And yet, that moment when by chance I held it to my ear and understood with no shadow of doubt why the injured gelding in the stall before me was lame, left me dumbstruck. I knew instantly that its forelock was bruised and its lameness not due to a nail bind as I had thought. How I knew remains a mystery, yet when the shell was taken from my ear I was as dull and ignorant to the animal's suffering as ever I had been before. To my shame, I confess I kept the shell after assuring you I had destroyed it.

"And yet my conscience has been eased by the success I have brought to our family, and I beg your forgiveness and that of the Squire. Had we known on that day in 1758 when the barn shook so hard and the shell appeared, delivered, it seemed, by some unearthly hand, that it would have brought the Squire such misery, we might have done better to throw it into the river. But now, I must state that such thoughts are far from my mind whenever I use it to ease the suffering of those creatures brought to me..."

Ellie looked up, her face flushed with excitement.

"So this farrier bloke was supposed to destroy the shell," Ruff said.

"But he didn't," Ellie finished Ruff's sentence for him. "He kept it and used it."

But Oz was only half-listening. He stared at the page he held, which had been written in a different hand.

"This looks like it was written by Redmayne himself. Listen to this." Oz proceeded to read the letter out loud to a rapt Ellie and Ruff.

"As this letter may be read after my death, it is my will that the truth be told in regard to the burning of Bunthorpe barn in the year 1761. It is my contention that those responsible did set the fire through spitefulness or fear because they were unable to procure those items which appeared that night under so strange and wonderful a circumstance. Said miscreants, intent on robbery, found nothing to steal, as was my intention. Following the bell ringers' fright, I shut and locked the barn, but returned later to feed the animals. There, in one corner, I found four items which I knew to be not mine and of such strange appearance to be not of usual construction nor pertaining to this area of England. The four objects were an obsidian pebble, a carved black dor, a stone ring and a pendant of oblong design.

"I immediately spoke to my brother in law, John Shoesmith, the farrier who had been with me three years before when we experienced a similar occurrence, this time with the appearance of a black shell. As on that night, we agreed to a similar course of action and set out to deliver the items to Squire Worthy, who has knowledge of such things. Although the shell has proven to be a dread blight on the Squire's family, we felt that he might yet find some good use and succour from their appearance. What was certain was that such items as were found should be protected until such time as the Squire, or others chosen by him, understood their purpose. In so doing we proposed to form, with others, an Obex so as to hinder those Puffers whose dealings and lies have become a blight on our land. It is they who would surely wish to use these four artefacts for their greedy purposes. It is they, I am certain, who were the arsonists that night. Their actions cost me dearly, but I am comforted in the knowledge that they were unable to find that which they were seeking. Squire Worthy took the four items for safekeeping and seemed pleased. It is my fervent hope that the dread and tragic consequences of our discovery of the shell are not repeated. Our duty is to the Squire and his family, and yet…"

Oz turned the page over. There was no more. He examined the roughly torn edges and held them up for the others to see.

"There's a bit missing," Oz said.

"Great," Ruff muttered. "Now let's have it in English."

Oz frowned pensively. "Well, we know what happened in 1761, but something else had already happened three years before, obviously."

"The shell," Ellie said.

"Right, and something happened that made them want to destroy it, but Shoesmith somehow found it helped him be a vet and so he kept it. And then the other artefacts appeared in 1761, and they gave them to Worthy again," Oz said.

"Clear as mud," Ruff muttered.

"But Obex and Puffers? What are they?" Ellie asked.

"Nice little research job for you there, Ellie," Oz said.

"What do you think 'dread and tragic consequences' means?" Ellie mused, but no one had an answer.

Ruff had turned the will over and now gasped once more. "Wow, take a look at this."

On the back of the yellowed paper was a series of numbers, a single row above and columns arranged in groups of four below.

722141158/9229514/181411229267129

1891213/13187922/20152688/9127
228822132422/8122611/8122611/2615614
71813/8122611/59181322/13187922
9127/1891213/8122611/228822132422

"It's another cipher," Ruff said. "The top line is the code, the bottom columns are probably the message."

"That's you sorted for the night, then," Oz said to Ruff.

Ruff didn't laugh. Instead there was a long pause, during which he stared off at the floor intently. Oz could almost see the cogs in his brain whirring. Finally, Ruff said, "There's this site I know for gamers—Cypherspace, it's called. Cheats for games, help with decoding secret codes, that sort of stuff. I'll get on to that."

Ellie threw herself down into a chair. "But what does it all mean?"

Oz stared at his friends, eyes gleaming intently. "It's proof that the artefacts existed, that's what it is. Redmayne confessed to finding them and giving them to Worthy."

"You don't think your dad knew about the letters?" Ruff said.

Oz shook his head. "He bought the clock back from Eldred because he knew it belonged here, but he was always talking about getting it fixed. He just never got round to it. He wouldn't have said that if he knew it was really a safe, would he?"

"So, Morsman found the letters in the orphanage and had the clock turned into a safe to keep them in," Ellie suggested.

"But that doesn't help us explain how the symbols got onto your laptop, does it?" Ruff said bluntly.

When Oz thought about that, it made his head hurt. Ruff was right, of course. They'd been led to this place by the laptop message. And the laptop message had something to do with the trinket box, he was sure of it. He shrugged and said, "No, it doesn't."

"There is, of course, another way to look at this," Ruff said in a small, quiet voice.

"What?" Ellie asked.

"Redmayne goes on about tragic circumstances after discovering the shell, and Shoesmith said they might have done better to throw it in the river. Morsman went looking and died in strange circumstances. And your dad…" He didn't finish the sentence. He didn't need to, because the others knew exactly what he was thinking. But Oz was having none of it.

"Oh, come on, Ruff," Oz snapped. "A curse? That's a bit much, isn't it?"

"What, and finding weird laptop messages and long-lost brooch clips isn't? I know how it sounds," Ruff said, "but have you forgotten what we saw in that park tonight?"

Oz opened his mouth to speak but nothing came out. For once, he was stuck for a reply.

*   *   *

Because Ruff insisted he needed the laptop for his decoding, Oz and Ellie returned to the library once again, looking up the musty old volumes for help on Obex and Puffers.

It didn't take them long to find either. Ellie, searching in an ancient encyclopaedia, let out a groan of distaste as she held up a line drawing of a human brain. "Says here that 'obex' describes that part of the brain that joins the spinal cord to the base of the brain."

"That can't be it," Oz said. He was thumbing through a dusty dictionary. "Wait a minute; it says here, 'can also mean 'to throw in the way of or to hinder.'"

"That makes a lot more sense," Ellie said, looking up. "If Redmayne wanted to throw the Puffers off the track, hindering them might be exactly what he was doing."

"Whoever the Puffers were," Oz said thoughtfully.

They glanced at each other before burying their noses back in the books. What became obvious pretty quickly was that Puffers had nothing to do with wind, as Ellie had suggested, or snakes, which Oz had thrown up because of some vague idea that it might be something to do with puff adders. Eventually, Oz came up with the surprising answer.

"Alchemists?" Ellie said, repeating Oz's triumphant announcement. "Weren't they weirdos trying to be chemists before anyone really knew anything about chemistry?"

"Sort of," Oz said, peering at the book. He looked up. "What do you think of when you think of alchemists, though? I mean, what do you see?"

Ellie cocked her head to think. "Someone in a wizard's hat in a fume-filled old laboratory, with flasks and retorts of different-coloured liquids bubbling everywhere."

"Exactly. You've just described a Puffer," Oz said. "It's what they called the old bellows they used to keep the fires going. You know, those things you squeeze to make air come out of to fan the flames."

"So Puffers are bellows?" Ellie asked.

Oz shook his head. "It's what real alchemists called the fakes. According to this,"—he held up a different but equally moth-eaten book—"true alchemists were a bit like monks. They worked alone, spent years trying to work out the secret of life. You know, philosopher's stone stuff."

"So what were the Puffers, then?"

"Cheats. They were the ones who moved from town to town, fooling people with tricks and fireworks, trying to get people to give them money to turn metal into gold."

"And this Obex was set up to stop the cheats," Ellie said, nodding.

When they told Ruff, he seemed only mildly interested. The code-breaking preoccupied him. "Need the key phrase that unlocks the cipher. Once we get that, I reckon it'll be a piece of cake."

But by half past nine he was no further forward, and Oz suggested they forget about it for the night. Reluctantly, Ruff agreed, but only after Oz said that he was about to make rounds of toast and jam and watch a video.

By eleven, though, the day's events were taking their toll and all three of them traipsed off to bed. Oz lay in his, watching the moonlight paint a crosshatch of silver light on the wall through a chink in the curtains. They knew an awful lot more than they did yesterday, but really, they knew nothing at all about a lot of things. What part did Lucy Bishop have to play in all of this? Who was she working for?

And then there was the thing in the park. Was he just some nutter living on the streets or in the park, or was his appearance part of a mad jigsaw with more parts missing than found?

But what kept Oz awake until well after midnight were the letters in the clock. What did they mean? And why the secret cipher?

The curtains swayed gently in the easterly breeze that had picked up outside, making the moonlight dance on the wall. He looked across at his desk. The laptop was charging, but the trinket box and the dor were hidden away in one of Oz's secret places. After tonight, Oz had decided that he couldn't be too careful.

That night, he didn't dream of the girl with the grey eyes, either.

Chapter 11

Lions vs Skullers

The next morning Oz awoke with a new sense of purpose. Despite Ruff's lack of success with the cipher, they did have lots of pieces of the puzzle and he was sure they were that bit closer to solving the riddle of the ghostly footsteps. He couldn't rid himself of the feeling, either, that the message in the letters would lead him to understanding what had happened to his dad, and to a way of dispelling the filthy rumour of his supposed suicide. Oz had nothing but his own instinct and belief to support this conviction, but at every turn, and with every new bit of information they gathered, it seemed to grow inside him. All they needed now was a bit of luck with Ruff and the cipher.

It was a bright, crisp morning, and though Oz wanted to talk about nothing but yesterday's events, Ruff and Ellie were not in the mood. But then Oz remembered that today was the day of their return match with Jenks' and Skinner's Skullers team, and their preoccupation became instantly understandable. Despite Oz's best efforts to take their minds off the game, all they wanted to do was warm up. So immediately after breakfast Oz went with them for another kickabout.

People's Park was already busy with joggers and dog walkers taking advantage of a rain-free morning. The thing that had loomed out of the dark and foggy emptiness of the night before seemed like nothing more than the vestige of a strange dream. But even a sunny morning could do little to alter Ellie and Ruff's nervous bickering. When a stray shot went zooming off into the distance, arguments flared once again.

"You kicked it, you fetch it," Ellie said, watching as the ball continued to roll off into the distance.

"But you're closest," Ruff argued petulantly.

"It was your rubbish shot!" Ellie yelled.

"I'll get it," Oz said, glad of the chance to get away from their sniping. He knew what this atmosphere was about. Two of the best players in Ellie's and Ruff's team were sick with flu, and another two were doubtful. Their chance of beating the Skullers now was nigh on non-existent.

Oz retrieved the ball, and as he did, something caught his eye, a movement on the edge of the small copse of trees in the very middle of the park. It was hardly even a glimpse, but he could have sworn he'd seen something dark and elongated move back into the woods. He picked up the ball and stared, but there was nothing there anymore. By the time he got back, Ruff was sulking at one end of their makeshift pitch and Ellie was busy moodily plucking at blades of grass at the other. Oz was quite glad when Ruff's dad pulled up in his van. Mr. Adams was a tall, thin man with flyaway hair the same colour as Ruff's and a lopsided grin. He knew an awful lot about football and was unfailingly enthusiastic.

"Hey, Oz," he said as he got out of the van to help Ellie with her backpack. "Been giving them a bit of extra coaching?"

"What's the news on Millie, Dad?" Ruff asked hopefully.

"Millie can't play. It's definitely chicken pox. She looks like a current bun. And Bashir can't make it. He's had to go to Sheffield to his cousin's wedding."

"Sugar," muttered Ellie.

"But that means…" protested Ruff.

"Yes, I know. You'll just have to share goal-keeping duties this week, okay?"

Ruff and Ellie both groaned.

"We've got no chance at all against the Skullers now," Ruff moaned, looking crestfallen.

Ellie gave Oz a half-hearted wave as she got into the van and Ruff clambered in next to his dad. "See you tomorrow, Oz," she muttered. But then, catching sight of the strange look on Oz's face, she added, "What's up with you?"

"Nothing," Oz said mischievously. An idea had sprouted in his head and was rapidly taking hold. "I'm just waiting for your usual question, that's all."

"The one you always say no to?" Ellie said. "What's the point?"

"Maybe one day I'll say yes," Oz said.

"What does that mean?" Ruff said exasperatedly. "Do you want to play or not?"

"Well, since you're short of a goalie, why not?"

There was a long, frozen moment as first Ellie's jaw, quickly followed by both Mr. Adams' and Ruff's, clunked open.

"Really?" Ellie squealed.

"I reckon I could do with the exercise," Oz grinned.

Everyone in the van started talking at once.

"We'll have to register you—"

"The goalie jersey is bright green—"

"Stop standing there like a buzzard—"

Ten seconds later, Oz was bundled into the van and Mr. Adams roared around to Magnus Street.

"I should be back by about half past twelve," Oz said to a flummoxed but smiling Mrs. Chambers as he emptied his kit bag looking for his gloves.

"What's brought all this on?" she asked breathlessly, reaching into the airing cupboard for socks and shorts.

"They need my help," Oz said, shrugging.

* * *

The park where Ellie and Ruff and all the other teams in the league played on Sunday mornings had ten pitches. The team all gathered behind one set of goalposts and listened to Ruff's dad giving instructions. Since it was a mixed league, there had to be a minimum of five girls in each team. Oz knew two of the other girls on his. One was Sandra Ojo, whose voice he'd recognized even before seeing her, and the other was Lottie Barnes. Of the boys, there was Niko, whom he knew, too, but the rest of the players were new to him.

"Now, as you know, we're a bit low on reserves today, but Oz here has stepped in to lend a hand. He'll be playing in goal for us," said Mr. Adams as they gathered at one end of the pitch.

The rest of the team gave Oz half-hearted waves and a few "all rights" and "wotchas," but all in all they looked like a defeated team before they even went on the pitch.

"I know you must be downhearted after last time, but today is a fresh page," said Mr. Adams. "And you never know what's going to happen until you try. I want close marking on their front three; we'll play the ball wide when we can to Ellie on the left and Lottie on the right. They'll take the ball forward and get some crosses in, okay?"

Everyone nodded.

"Right, follow Steve and we'll get warmed up."

Steve, one of the other dads, took the team off to the side and started some warm-up drills. Oz was given a bright-green goalie shirt, which did, indeed, look brand new.

"That's because Bashir doesn't ever do anything to get it dirty," Ruff hissed as Oz commented on its condition.

As he pulled his head through, Oz could see the Skullers all laughing and joking on the far side behind the other goalposts. They wore black and white quartered shirts and looked very confident. Oz was on the point of joining the others for the warm-up when Mr. Adams grabbed him gently by the elbow.

"A quiet word, Oz," he said. "No one is expecting miracles. Just do what you can and, more importantly, enjoy yourself. Their big centre forward is a bit of a donkey, but he is the league's top scorer. He likes to take on goalies—always feints left and takes the ball right. Just remember that. Oh, and thanks for helping out." He gave Oz a clap on the back, smiling broadly.

Oz nodded, trying to quell the butterflies doing loop-de-loops in his stomach, and went to join the others. Ten minutes later, they were running on for the start of the match. Ellie and Ruff had gone very quiet, and Oz had never seen them both so nervous.

"By the way, what are we called again?" Oz yelled to Ruff, who was in midfield.

"Leckwith Lions," Ruff called back. "It's the name of our sponsor." Ruff pointed to the front of his shirt, where the words "Leckwith Building Supplies" were emblazoned across his chest. Oz had one last look around and blew air down into his gloves. The goalmouth was bigger than the ones they played with in school—full size, in fact. But it was the same size as the one he'd drawn on the wall at home, and so he knew its dimensions well enough. It was the Skullers to kick off and, with the ball at his feet in the centre circle, Jenks looked up and for the first time saw who was in goal opposite him. He called to Skinner and pointed at Oz. Then, loud enough for everyone to hear, Jenks called out,

"Hey Skinner, they've got Chambers in goal. They must be desperate."

"Definite hat-trick for you, then, Jenks." Skinner let off a hyena snigger.

The referee blew his whistle for the start of the game. There were twenty-five minute halves in this league, and the first five of Oz's new amateur career were pretty frantic. The Skullers laid the ball back to Jenks, who immediately sent a long, floating shunt up the middle towards Oz as a tester. Oz balanced himself and took the ball cleanly ten yards in front of goal, and was delighted to hear a cheer from the supporters and even more delighted to see the look on Jenks' face as his teammates rounded on him for wasting possession.

Oz ran forward and thumped the ball downfield. After their drubbing a few weeks before, the Lions had clearly done their homework and were close marking the Skullers' attack. Even so, Oz found himself having to catch two crosses and parry one long-distance shot bound for the top right-hand corner of the net, all in the next ten minutes. But through hard work and Oz's skill, the Lions kept the Skullers' forwards at bay for the whole twenty-five minutes.

At halftime Mr. Adams, grinning from ear to ear, gave Oz a segment of orange. "Oz, I had no idea you could play...I mean, I knew you could play, but...where have you been for the last two seasons?"

"Practising," Oz said truthfully.

"Well, keep it up. You're having a stormer."

The second half started much like the first, with Oz tipping a shot over the bar and leaping to cut out a cross meant for the number nine's head, as well as diving low to save a neat shot from the Skullers' left wing, a small but very nippy girl called Natasha Stilson who Oz knew vaguely from his year. She sent Oz a flashing smile as he got up, mud-splattered from the save.

Skinner, who had spent most of the first half niggling away at Ruff by pulling on his shirt and calling him names whenever the ref's back was turned, suddenly began to play very dirty. After one particularly blatant foul, in which Ruff's legs were taken from under him and which earned Skinner a booking, Ellie had had enough. At the next stoppage, she ran back to Oz.

"Next time you boot the ball up-field, send it towards Skinner."

"Okay," Oz said, noting the dangerous glint in Ellie's eye.

The chance came three minutes later, when Oz caught a back header from his fullback and thumped the ball up towards Skinner. It bounced once and Skinner leapt to head it up to his inside right. But just as Skinner jumped, Ellie flew in from her wing and launched herself at the ball. If anyone had any doubts that she was into taekwando, they were pretty certain of it a second later as she connected with the ball in a perfect bicycle kick. Unfortunately for Skinner, she did so two feet away from his head, sending the ball careening towards Skinner's face at full force.

Oz heard the collision, which sounded remarkably like a ten-pound haddock connecting with a wet marble slab, even from where he stood, forty yards away. Skinner did a Titanic, rolling on the floor and clutching at his ear and making a noise like a cross between an injured cat and a bellowing antelope. He didn't stay down for long, however. Five seconds later he was running around the pitch, screeching like a demented owl and clutching the side of his face, where his ear had already swollen to twice its normal size. It took all of Oz's willpower not to roll about on the ground, he was laughing so much. Skinner was mercifully taken off, but not without glowering at Ellie.

When play had resumed, and with no one on the pitch but Oz watching, Ellie stopped on the touchline next to Skinner and did a shadow taekwando move which earned howls of complaint from the Skullers' supporters. But when the ref turned around to look, Ellie was long gone, chasing after the Skullers' fullback, the epitome of innocent enthusiasm.

As the second half wore on, something happened to the Skullers. Their failure to score was causing them a great deal of frustration, and they began blaming each other for simple mistakes. Jenks and the centre forward, especially, seemed not to get on and more than once ended up shouting at each other and calling one another very unpleasant names, until the referee had to intervene and warn them. After Jenks sent one too many long balls skittering over the dead ball line, irritation boiled over in the Skullers' team. The centre forward ran across the pitch and stuck his face belligerently close to Jenks'.

"What the hell was that? I'm not a bleepin' greyhound, you know."

"No, more like a bleepin' snail."

They began pushing and shoving each other, and some of their teammates ran across to separate them. Oz thought about waiting for them to sort themselves out, but then, as he lined up for the goal kick, saw Ruff waving frantically in a big open space on the left midfield. Oz didn't hesitate; he launched a loping pass straight to Ruff, who immediately sprinted forward into the Skullers' half. The altercation between Jenks and the centre forward had pulled two other Skullers' players out of position, and Ruff had seen the gap it had left. Some slick passing got the ball to Ellie, who slipped it between the fullback's legs and got to the goal line. A cross was on, but instead Ellie pulled the ball back to Lottie Barnes, who was unmarked at the edge of the penalty area. Lottie controlled the pass cleverly and shot. The ball dipped low, bounced once and flew over the Skullers' despairing goalie into the back of the net.

One-nil to the Lions.

The team went wild. The spectators on the touchline went wilder. They were hugging each other and shouting, while on the other side of the pitch the Skullers' supporters stood about in shocked silence. Furious, the Skullers coach took Jenks off. He left the thunder-faced centre forward on and ordered his team to go on all-out attack. They flew at the Lions in the last five minutes, but Oz was on a roll. He somehow caught and parried and deflected everything they threw at him.

But there was one more throw of the dice left. With a minute to go to full time, and with the Skullers pushing everyone forward, the Lions' fullback lost his footing and Natasha Stilson broke down the left wing and passed to the centre forward, who had made a run from deep. Suddenly there was no one between the big number nine and the goal, except, of course, Oz, who charged out to challenge. The centre forward was tall and rangy, and came straight at Oz, keeping the ball skilfully at his feet. It looked certain to be one-all. All the Skullers' number nine had to do was beat Oz and slot the ball home, but it was clear that he wasn't going to risk a shot from that far out. The safest way was to dribble the ball in.

Oz, however, had other ideas. He kept coming out, right to the edge of the box, blocking the goal as best he could but keeping his eyes on the ball all the time. Just before he got to Oz, the number nine took the ball left, but Oz, instead of diving, feinted left and went right at exactly the same time as the centre forward drove in that direction. Oz felt the ball hit his stomach and grabbed at it with both hands. A collision was inevitable, and the centre forward's momentum took him right over Oz and sent him sprawling.

There were immediate shouts and appeals for a penalty, but the referee shook his head and the whole of the Skullers team ran after him, protesting, followed by the Lions, who were doing exactly the opposite. What was clear to the referee was that Oz had played the ball, and it was the centre forward's bad luck to have been behind it and to have fallen over the goalkeeper.

Oz had enough sense to stay down on the floor as the ref, who'd had more than enough of the Skullers' followers by now, blew the final whistle. Oz got up, blinking mud from his eyes, and saw a movement behind his goal near some changing rooms. It looked like someone, seeing that Oz was looking and not having expected it, had stepped back behind the edge of the building. That someone had been wearing a very familiar-looking red and black coat, just like Lucy Bishop had worn the day before. Oz wiped his eyes properly with his sleeve, but when he looked again the figure had gone.

There was a noise on the pitch behind him. He turned and saw, to his utter astonishment, that the whole of the Lions team—plus the thirty or so parents and supporters—were all running towards him, telling him that he'd had a brilliant game, cheering and laughing as if they'd just won the FA Cup final. Two seconds later, mothers were kissing him and fathers and brothers were clapping him on the shoulders, while Ellie and Ruff kept saying to their teammates, "Told you so. Told you he was really good." Meanwhile Oz, bemused and mud-covered, basked in and tasted something that he had never tasted before.

Glory.

And with it came a very strange feeling indeed. It took a while for it to sink in, but eventually Oz realised that he had not felt as happy as this for a long, long time. But it was while he waited for Ruff and Ellie afterwards that the best thing of all happened. It was Ruff's turn to collect the flagpoles and Ellie's to sort the shirts, and they were both busy loading the kit into a big van with "Steve's Roofing Services" written on its side, when Oz wandered over to stand next to Ruff's dad's van to wait. He leaned on the bonnet, picking the grass and mud from the bottom of his boots. Mr. Adams joined him and cleared his throat.

"Oz, the way you stood up to that bullying number nine today was…well, it was bloomin' magnificent. It's made my season, it really has." Mr. Adams shook his head. "I didn't know your dad, and I am truly sorry for what happened to him. But I know that, if he'd been here today, he would have been really proud of you. Really proud."

He held out his hand. Oz took it and looked across at the now-empty expanse of pitches and said quietly, "I think he probably was here."

Mr. Adams nodded, sniffed and turned away to stare at a seagull on the goalposts so that Oz had time to wipe the moisture from his eyes. Just as well, because two seconds later Ellie and Ruff appeared, red-faced and grinning.

"I can't wait until tomorrow," Ellie said animatedly. "I can't wait to walk into registration and see Jenks' and Skinner's faces."

"I never thought we'd ever beat them," Ruff said in a voice still resonating with shock.

"Well," said Mr. Adams, "like I said. A bit of self-belief is all you need."

"And Oz," Ellie said.

"And Oz," Mr. Adams agreed, nodding.

"What a brilliant buzzard day," Ruff said.

* * *

They dropped Oz off outside Penwurt, but he didn't get out until they'd finished singing another chorus of "We are the Champions," which Mr. Adams had played half a dozen times on the way back. Tired but content, Oz waved them off and turned to walk through his gate just as the first spots of rain drifted down from the lowering sky. Oz looked up to see clouds moving in quickly from the west. There was a damp and icy wind of change in the air.

The police car was parked unobtrusively at the side of the house, out of view of the road. Oz stopped, frowning as something cold and unpleasant did a somersault in his stomach. Oz didn't like police cars turning up because, in his short and troubled life, he had learned that their occupants were rarely the bearers of good news.

Oz used his key to open the front door and called to his mother from the hall. She emerged from the dining room, looking serious.

"Mum? What's going on? Why are the police here?"

"They're here to see you, Oz," Mrs. Chambers said.

The cold thing in his gut did another unpleasant sloshing manoeuvre. He had no idea why the police wanted to see him, and his mind cast about for possible reasons. Did it have something to do with school and Badger Breath? Could you be arrested for getting one hundred percent on a maths test? His mind buzzing, he only half-heard what his mother was saying, but he managed to tune in when he heard a name he recognised.

"…a break-in at an antique shop. Garard and Aldred, I think they said—"

"Garret and Eldred?" Oz asked, his voice rising.

"Then you do know it?" his mother asked earnestly.

"Yes, but…"

"Come through, Oz. We shouldn't keep them waiting. I'll let them explain."

There were two uniformed police officers sitting in the dining room. They both stood as Oz entered. One was a burly man with a round, lived-in face and not much hair. His name was Sergeant Thomas, and it was he who did the introductions. The other, a petite woman with an unsmiling expression, was a woman police constable called Keller. She held an open notebook in one hand and a pen in the other.

"So," said Sgt Thomas after he'd told Oz who they were, "how did the football go?"

"Good. We won, one-nil," Oz said, turning to watch WPC Keller write something down.

"Good, good," Sgt Thomas continued in a singsong Welsh accent. "Now, I don't want you to be alarmed, or to worry about anything. These are just routine enquiries."

"About what?"

"You know a shop called Garret and Eldred in the old town?"

Oz nodded. "We, that is, my friends and me…we were there yesterday."

Sgt Thomas nodded. "There was a break-in last night. Nasty business. In the course of the robbery, Mr. Eldred was assaulted."

Oz felt all the fun and happiness the morning had brought evaporate in an instant. He sat heavily on the sofa next to his mother. "I was here…all night. Me and my friends—"

Sgt Thomas held up his hand and gave a mirthless smile. Oz couldn't help noticing that Keller's expression didn't change at all as she stared unwaveringly at him.

"You and your friends are not suspects, Oscar. That's not why we're here. As a general rule, we find that robbers don't introduce themselves to their intended victims like you did. No, this robber was after something specific. Wasn't subtle about it, either. Made enough noise to wake Mr. Eldred up. Foolishly, he challenged the man, who then turned on him, poor chap. Luckily someone heard the noise and called us. That time on a Sunday morning we have patrols all over that area, so we got there pretty quick. Could have been much worse. We're here talking to you because we want to try and establish the events of yesterday afternoon. Mr. Eldred was able to give us your address. Now, you went to the shop at about what time?"

Oz could feel his heart beating in his throat like a stuck sweet. A robbery? Who would want to rob a jumbled old curiosity shop like Garret and Eldred's?

"Uh…about three," Oz said, marshalling his thoughts, but finding it difficult to stop thinking about Mr. Eldred. "The shopkeeper, Mr. Eldred, he's all right, isn't he?"

"Badly shaken and bruised. He's in hospital for observation, but he'll be fine," Sgt Thomas reassured him.

"He seemed such a nice bloke," Oz said.

"Why were you at the shop?" asked WPC Keller abruptly. "Not your sort of place, I would have said."

"It isn't. We were looking for something special." Oz sensed his mother's eyes boring into the side of his head, and he dared not look at her for fear they would burn right through his eyes and sear his brain.

"Mr. Eldred said you bought something," Keller barked.

"Yeah, it was a brooch. A dress clip brooch."

Keller frowned. "Funny thing to buy."

Oz gulped. He was very tempted to lie, make something up about Macy, Ellie's sister, always wanting one, but it sounded lame and hollow. He felt his insides knotting. The last thing he'd intended was for his mother to learn about any of this, let alone listen to him explain it all to a stranger.

"My friends and me, we found some old papers in the library here and some stuff belonging to my dad and…" It still sounded weak and pathetic, but at least it was the truth. "Well, we think my dad was looking for something a bit like this brooch."

"Is your dad," said Sgt Thomas, and then corrected himself, "was your dad a collector?"

"Sort of," Oz said, still keeping his eyes away from his mother's face. "He was a lecturer in historical materials. We found a picture of the brooch in an online advert from Garret and Eldred and…"

"I see," smiled Sgt Thomas. "Just a bit of an adventure, was it?"

"Yeah," Oz said, knowing that what he had just said must have sounded pathetic and childish to this big policeman, but oddly glad, because it meant he didn't have to go into all the other stuff. The weird stuff. Maybe this way Mum wouldn't twig, either. He risked a glance at her and had his worst fears confirmed. She looked grey and drawn and very unhappy. She knew, all right.

"Did you happen to notice anyone strange hanging around the area?" Keller went on.

"It's not a very nice area, I know that. But Ruff, my friend, he found a secondhand video game shop, so we went there afterwards."

"But nothing strange or unusual?"

Oz thought about Lucy Bishop and the thing they'd seen in the park, but decided not to say anything. Doubt crowded out all thoughts he had of mentioning them. Polecat sounded like something they'd made up. And though he didn't like Lucy Bishop, he had no right to embroil her in all of this before asking Caleb what he thought was best to do.

"No," Oz said, "we were in and out of there within ten minutes."

Sgt Thomas looked at WPC Keller and nodded. "Right, I think that will be enough for now. Obviously, if you think of anything at all, just let me know. I've given your mum my number at the station." He stood and straightened out his trousers. "You probably won't see us again, but you won't mind answering some more questions if we have any, will you?"

Oz shook his head in agreement, but then asked, "What was he looking for? The robber, I mean?"

"We're not sure. Quite an odd case, in actual fact. Mr. Eldred said that his assailant had sunglasses on and didn't seem to be able to speak at all clearly, but it was dark and Mr. Eldred's sight isn't that good. Thought he heard the attacker asking for a door, so that's not any help."

"Probably just an addict looking for something easy to sell. Half of them are not of this planet at the best of times," Keller said darkly.

Sgt Thomas turned to Mrs. Chambers. "Thanks for the tea."

She nodded tersely in reply.

Oz sat on the sofa alone while his mother saw the police out. He couldn't stop thinking about Mr. Eldred. When he did, it made him feel queasy and sent a trickle of cold sweat down the back of his neck. Oz knew what "door" really meant. It was an easy mistake for Mr. Eldred to have made, because even under normal circumstances door could sound exactly like dor. His mother came back in carrying the kit bag he'd dropped in the hall.

"Sorry, Mum, I'll empty it now." Oz stood.

"No, you will not," she said with quiet fury, her face white. She threw the kit bag down, her hands trembling so much that she had to fold her arms across her midriff. "I want you to sit there and tell me exactly what is going on."

"Mum, honestly, we had nothing to do with any robbery."

"I know that. I mean the other stuff. I want you to tell me why you were looking for a brooch."

Oz could feel his pulse pounding in his head. She knew, and there was no way of wriggling out of it. "Because," said Oz quietly, "because we think it's one of Morsman's artefacts."

For a moment he thought his mother was going to faint. She reached a hand out to steady herself on a chair. She looked as though she'd just seen some dreadful apparition.

"Who," she breathed out the words tremulously, "who put you up to this?"

"No one did," Oz said. "It was Dad's stuff. I found an article he'd written."

"There must be something else," Mrs. Chambers said, shaking her head. "Someone else…"

"Penwurt is in *Secret Haunted Houses of Great Britain*, Mum. It's famous. Dad knew something was going on here. He knew that Morsman…"

"Don't speak that name," Mrs. Chambers snapped. "I swore I'd never say that blasted name again after your father…" Her voice faltered. "You're just like him. Always chasing after shadows."

"Caleb doesn't think it's all shadows…" It slipped out before Oz could stop himself.

Mrs. Chambers' eyes opened wide. "Caleb." She nodded. "I might have known."

She got up and stormed out.

"Mum," Oz called after her, "Mum, wait…"

He clutched the armrest of the sofa until his knuckles turned white. Why was everything so complicated? He felt hot tears sting his eyes and used the back of his hand to wipe them. It was only then he realised that he was still coated in drying mud. He got up and, with a heart like lead, emptied his kit bag, put his filthy shorts, socks and T-shirt into the dirty laundry basket, and trudged up to the bathroom. He turned on the shower and let the water wash the mud away. Feeling clean helped a bit, but as he towelled himself dry he heard raised voices from the library upstairs. He threw on a pair of jeans and a clean T-shirt and ran up bare-footed to see what the commotion was. But he hesitated on the threshold, unable to resist listening.

"I thought I made it clear, Caleb," Mrs. Chambers shouted. "I thought you and I understood one another."

"Gwen," said Caleb calmly, but Oz could hear the strain in his voice, too. "No one has done this deliberately. Michael's work is in the public domain. He wrote several articles on Morsman, as you know."

"He was chasing after those blasted artefacts in Egypt when he should have been at home with us," she said plaintively. "Now the police have been here because some poor man has been attacked, and Oz is tied up in it, and all because of Morsman and his bloody artefacts."

Caleb looked aghast. "I am sorry to hear that, Gwen. But I'm sure Oz—"

"Is just a *child*," yelled Mrs. Chambers. "He doesn't know any better. But I thought you did. I though I'd made myself perfectly clear."

"Wait," Oz said, trotting up the last few steps and announcing his presence. "There is something I didn't tell the police. I think I saw Lucy Bishop following us."

Mrs. Chambers stared at Oz as if he had grown an extra head. "Lucy? What has she got to do with anything?"

"I don't really know, but she always acts really weird around me. We, that is, me, Ellie and Ruff, think that maybe she's been spying. We thought that maybe she'd been after the trinket box."

Mrs. Chambers shook her head in bewilderment. "Why would she want a trinket box?"

"Because we think that maybe it has something to do with the artefacts, too."

He knew it was a mistake as soon as he'd said it.

Mrs. Chambers flushed scarlet and went very calm. She shot Caleb a venomous glare. "Really?" she said to Oz in a strangely controlled voice. "This is the trinket box your father sent you, is it?"

"From Egypt, the last time he was there. I think—"

Oz got no further as his mother cut across him sternly. "Let me see it, please."

"Sure," Oz said a little uncertainly. He hadn't ever seen his mother like this. It looked like something was boiling potently just beneath the surface, and her calm looked paper-thin. "It's downstairs. I'll fetch it…"

"No, go on. I'll follow you."

Oz hurried downstairs to his bedroom. He reasoned that, if he could show his mother the trinket box, she might understand. "Sometimes when I press the mark on the bottom, I think it glows," he said quickly. He retrieved the box from under the bookcase where he'd hidden it and handed it to her. With shaking hands, she took it from Oz and opened it. Carefully, she removed everything that was in it and placed the items on Oz's desk. Then, before Oz really knew what she was doing, she walked across to his bedroom window, opened it and threw the box out with all her strength.

"MUM!" yelled Oz in horror, his hand reaching out in a vain attempt at stopping her. But he was too late. There was a crunch and a couple of woody bounces from down below. "What did you do that for?" he shouted, trying to get past her to look down at the damage.

"Because it's ALL NONSENSE," she shouted through a jaw clenched tightly shut. Oz saw that she was shaking with anger. "Morsman and artefacts and ghosts, all nonsense. DO YOU HEAR?"

Oz clenched his fists and squeezed his eyes shut to fight back the tears that threatened to pour out.

"Things are going to change around here, Oscar. You mark my words. I have tried being lenient with you, tried giving you your own space." Mrs. Chambers shook her head and then said in a low voice, loaded with suppressed emotion, "Ellie and Ruff are not to come around here anymore, do you understand?"

"But they're my fr—"

"DO YOU UNDERSTAND?" she roared.

"Yes," said Oz flatly.

"No Sunday football. No searching for artefacts. No meddling in things that are of no concern to you."

Oz suddenly felt as if his insides were running out of his shoes. No Sunday football? He wanted desperately to tell her how brilliant today had been, but the look on her face told him plainly she wouldn't hear it even if he tried.

"I don't ever want to see a policeman around here asking to speak to you ever again, do you hear?" Mrs. Chambers shook with fury as she spoke.

"Yes." His eyes focussed on the corner of his bed sheet and he kept them there, not wanting to look into his mother's blazing eyes any more.

He waited until she moved and then swivelled his eyes to watch her storm out. When she'd gone he slumped onto the bed, not daring to look out of the window. But it was no good. He made himself sit up and went to the window and peered down. The box lay in shattered pieces on the tarmac below. He wanted to run down and fetch it, but he daren't.

There were more raised voices in the library. It was his mother again, shouting, hysterical almost. He didn't have to creep onto the stairs to hear her. The whole street probably could. And she was ordering Caleb to leave.

Oz spent a miserable afternoon and evening, during which he stayed in his room and only decided on attempting a peanut butter and jam sandwich when he heard his mother go out to her book club meeting. But when he got to the kitchen, he saw something that turned the marrow to lead in his bones. His mother had moved the calendar and the head of the black dog was on show. Suddenly, he wasn't hungry anymore. He sat at the table, his eyes never leaving the fridge door, his mind churning. He knew she was angry, knew she was really upset, but this was worse than bad.

His mind flew effortlessly back to the first anniversary of Michael Chambers' death. His mother had seemed okay up until that morning. Oz had got up and thought she was in bed, made himself a packed lunch for school and gone into her room to say goodbye, only to find her bed empty and no sign of her in the house. He could still remember the dreadful, awful, gut-wrenching panic that had seized him in its trembling grip. He'd gone to the phone and picked it up, had been on the point of dialling 999, reasoning that she'd been taken or had an accident, but then realised that she'd been in her pyjamas the night before, watching TV— or at least staring at the screen while some awful film played itself out in front of her glassy stare, as she sometimes did. He'd put the phone down and tried to think.

Alone in Penwurt, he had waited for his mother to ring or come home. At nine years of age, he had waited and waited. For three long days, he'd waited. He skipped school and caught the bus into town each day and walked, looking for her, wondering if she'd had a sudden loss of memory like he'd seen happen to someone once on TV. But there had been no sign of her and when darkness came, he'd caught the bus home again. On the fourth day he'd become too desperate to put it off any longer, so he'd rung Ellie's mum, who'd made a choking noise on the phone and told him to sit tight.

Gwen Chambers had booked herself into a hotel on the outskirts of Seabourne, which was where Mrs. Messenger had found her, locked in her room, confused and even sadder than before. More than anything, Oz remembered Mrs. Messenger breathlessly making him promise to ring her if anything like that ever happened again and telling him how brave and strong he was and that he'd been right not to phone the police because they'd have come and taken him into care. She told him that Gwen couldn't help herself and that he knew that she loved him, didn't he? He knew that she'd said all that about the police to make absolutely sure he rung her if it ever happened again. But listening to her explaining what could have happened had terrified him more than anything his mother could have said or done. The thought of losing her and Penwurt had given him dark, dreadful nightmares. Still did.

The idea of a sandwich suddenly made him feel sick, and he went back upstairs and tried to rid his brain of that awful memory. He heard his mother come home, heard her go to bed. He tried to heed his own mind's warning to forget about the trinket box and the dor. He knew that it was probably for the best, but he simply couldn't. It was just too important. Losing his father, the trigger for all this sadness, had to mean something, and he was certain that the artefacts held the key.

So, when the hall clock struck two, Oz threw off his bedclothes, put on his dressing gown and slippers, and crept downstairs. He unlatched the back door and fetched the torch from the utility room. It was frosty, the blades of grass on the verge next to the drive glimmering in the thin light of a gibbous moon as he hurried past. Deep shadows covered the spot where Oz had seen the box land. He flicked on a torch.

It was clear that the horn and wood had splintered into half a dozen shards, but he soon had most of them collected. There was a chance that he might be able to glue them all back together into a semblance of the original. The only piece that remained almost intact was the base, but even that had splintered along its length and lay splayed open like a book. Quickly he fitted the damaged pieces together and saw that they weren't, in fact, broken but were easily taken apart and clicked back into position. He unclipped the pieces again and saw that there was a space between the two. An oval, quite regular curved space in which something might well have lain.

Intrigued, Oz shone the torch around, but the dead leaves and bits of twig that the November wind had blown down onto the tarmac drive made hunting for things in this light very difficult, especially since he had no idea of what he was looking for. He was on the point of giving up, because his toes were beginning to go numb in his slippers, when he saw it.

Something dark glistened in the torchlight right at the base of the wall between Penwurt and number 4. Oz hurried over and squatted to inspect it. It wasn't a leaf or a twig or a bit of mud as he'd feared, but something smooth and reflective. So he picked it up and it felt cold in his hand, firm on one side, the other shaped and indented. But on the smooth side, a single silver button sat right at the centre. Squinting, Oz could see that the button had marks on it. Instantly, he realised that the button was what he'd mistaken for the maker's mark on the base of the trinket box. Oz's heart leapt. Despite the cold, and despite all that his mother had said and the punishment that had been meted out to him, Oz somehow knew at that moment that he had probably just found another of Morsman's artefacts. He was certain that what he held in his trembling hand was the obsidian pebble.

Chapter 12

Jack Gerber

The next morning, Oz stayed in his bedroom as long as he could before going down to breakfast. He hoped that his mother had calmed down after a night's sleep, but she had her back to him and didn't turn around immediately as he walked into the kitchen. The calendar still showed the head of a roughly drawn black dog. Oz felt his heart sink in his chest and decided that another apology was probably the best way to start things off.

"Mum," Oz began, "about last night…"

She wheeled around and threw him a withering glance. "I don't want to talk about it. I've made my decision. Live with it."

But her words were unnecessary. Any thought Oz had about trying to get her to change her mind about Sunday football, or Ellie and Ruff, had evaporated with that glance. She looked ragged, her eyes red-rimmed and raw, and he knew she'd been crying. Oz went through the motions of breakfast, the cereal tasting like cardboard, his mind like a clogged drain. He hardly spoke to anyone all the way to school and tried his best to put on as brave a face as he could when he met up with Ellie and Ruff, who were, as expected, in an exuberant mood.

"Look at them," Ruff said gleefully as Oz joined them in registration. Ruff pointed at Jenks and Skinner, who were sitting with their backs to the class, huddled with their cronies, intent on ignoring everything that was going on around them.

"They're pathetic," Ellie said. "In the bus bay, I heard Skinner trying to wriggle out of the fact that we'd beaten them by saying that if you added up the scores from both weeks, they were still four-nil up.

Ruff chuckled and then said loudly, "Read the papers, Skinner. A W is a W."

Skinner, unable to ignore the taunt, spun around in his chair and glared at them, much to Ruff's delight.

But Oz could barely muster a smile.

"What's up with you?" Ellie said, finally noticing Oz's reluctance to join in.

"It's my mum. We had a bit of a bust-up last night," Oz said hollowly.

He started to explain, and had got as far as the police wanting to know what they'd bought, when Miss Arkwright breezed through the door. In a way, Oz was relieved, because he was dreading telling them that they were banned. It was all so unfair; his mother's still-raw wounds over his dad were nothing to do with Ellie or Ruff. Why they had to suffer because of… Oz's melancholic thoughts were interrupted by Miss Arkwright banging on the desk.

"Some important announcements this morning that concern all of you. Mr. Broughton says that the toilet block near the changing rooms is still out of order. Oh, and Marcus, Mr. Broughton also says that he will try and get your football boot down off the roof today. And," she paused dramatically, "the date for the lower school Christmas party has been set for Friday, the 18th of December, at seven. So make sure it's in your diaries."

A buzz of eager conversation skittered across the room, mainly from the girls. Ellie turned to Tracy Roper, who was asking everyone if they knew what they were going to wear yet. But Oz couldn't concentrate on anything. Even first lesson with Badger Breath couldn't take his mind off worrying about what Ellie and Ruff were going to say when they learned that he couldn't play for them anymore.

Maths these days was very different for Oz. Since the second maths test, Oz actually understood what Badger Breath was talking about, even if the way Boggs actually taught the subject seemed boring and rigid. Today was no exception, as he announced to the class at the beginning of the lesson: "End of term exams will be on Monday, the 7th of December. That will give me enough time to mark your papers and return them before the start of the Christmas holidays. Those of you who fail will re-sit at the beginning of January." He smiled unpleasantly. "Give you all enough time to revise over Christmas."

The whole class groaned, but Badger Breath scanned the pupils with the smile fixed on his face like a death's head mask, lingering an extra leering few seconds on Oz.

"Before you ask, the exam will be on everything we will have done this term. Today, we begin transformation and congruent shapes."

Badger Breath had taken to monitoring Oz's behaviour in class very carefully, often picking up his work and studying it. More often than not, he would tut at Oz's workings, but he never actually said anything. Oz had taken to not reacting, simply sitting and staring straight ahead until Badger Breath put his book back on the desk, at which point Oz would simply get on with it.

But today, Badger Breath was merely an irritating fly, barely buzzing at the edge of Oz's awareness. The gut-churning anxiety over what he was going to say to Ellie and Ruff was far more bothersome. It stayed with him throughout the morning and he even forgot the name Madame Chang had given him in French.

"Oz, are you all right?" Ellie asked with a frown of disbelief as he trudged back to his desk after having been made to write "Marcel" ten times on the board, which was Madame Chang's way of ensuring he wouldn't forget it again.

"Fine," he mumbled.

"You're not ill or anything, are you?"

"No," Oz said, but he knew it didn't sound convincing, because he did feel a bit sick. And it was with a stone in his heart that he trudged after the other two to the refectory at break time. Ruff found a seat and began pointing animatedly out of the window, where Jenks and Skinner loitered in a thin drizzle. It was clear that the thought of having to face Ruff's leg-pulling this break was not something they were prepared to contemplate.

"Look at them," Ruff jeered, "like two lost, damp strings of—"

"Stop gloating, Ruff," Ellie said, but it was a half-hearted protest. She was grinning, too, at the sight of the two class jokers having the tables turned upon them.

"But I am the Gloatmaster," Ruff said loudly, standing up and giving Jenks a one-nil gesture with his fingers and sounding like a cheap voiceover merchant. Jenks sent back a very rude gesture with a face purple from suppressed rage, much to Ruff's obvious delight. It was hilarious, but Oz just couldn't bring himself to respond.

"Come on, Oz, the row with your mum couldn't have been that bad, could it?" asked Ruff, seeing the look on Oz's face

But as far as Oz was concerned, it was. He told them exactly what had happened after he'd got back from the match. Ellie and Ruff listened in stunned silence, but their horrified expressions spoke volumes. When he finished with describing how he'd picked up the shattered pieces of the trinket box, he looked up at them, knowing exactly how a guilty man in the dock must feel as he waited for sentencing. Ellie and Ruff exchanged a wordless glance, but it was Ellie who finally whispered in an awed voice, "Sugar. Are you saying that you've actually found the obsidian pebble?"

It was such a totally unforeseen question that Oz could only stare at her and nod. He'd been expecting her to say something about his being banned and no football. But she seemed much more interested in his find.

"That is so cool," she said, grinning.

"Yeah, buzzard," Ruff agreed, his eyes alight.

"But," Oz protested, "didn't you hear the rest of it? I'm grounded and Mum's banned you from coming over."

"That's not going to stop us talking, is it?" Ellie said with a shrug.

"And there's Skype and texting," Ruff added.

"But what about Sunday soccer?" Oz said miserably. "She says I'm not to play."

"League's finished 'til after Christmas now, anyway," Ruff said. "Cup matches. Different teams for that. We usually don't bother." He shrugged and Ellie nodded.

Staring at them as his brain tried to absorb this new information, Oz mumbled weakly, "But I thought…"

"Thought what?" Ellie asked.

"I thought that you would…that the two of you might say…" his voice trailed off.

"Say what, Oz?"

He forced the words out in a rush, eyes averted. "That me letting the Lions down and you not being able to come over… I thought that the two of you might not be bothered to hang about with me anymore."

There was a moment of hanging silence as Ellie and Ruff regarded Oz with crumpled, bewildered faces.

"Are you stark raving bonkers?" Ellie said finally, with a little shake of her head.

"We can still practise football here at school," Ruff reasoned. "And you can still practise goalie stuff at home, can't you?"

"Yeah," Oz admitted grudgingly.

"Why would your mum grounding you make any difference to us?" Ellie said with another shrug. "My mum's always flying off the handle. They get over it."

Oz sat back. It was as if a huge dam of relief had burst inside him, leaving him completely drained. But Ellie wasn't finished.

"The three of us, we're mates, Oz," she said with a slightly cross, quizzical look. "And anyway, we've got two of Morsman's artefacts. Two! We can't give up on that now. I'm doing loads of research on Puffers, and the cipher is driving Ruff mad."

"I'll crack it. You wait," Ruff said, his eyes narrowing.

Oz stared at them both, blinking rapidly. He pushed himself up from where he had hunched forward on the refectory table, utterly flabbergasted. He had dreaded telling them, and yet they seemed to be taking it all in their stride. He beamed at them both and they looked back at him with slightly puzzled, wary looks.

"You have to admit it, Oz," Ruff said as he bit into a pasty, "sometimes you can be a bit weird." But a smile was visible behind the pastry crumbs, while Ellie just kept shaking her head slowly with a "what are you like" look on her face.

"Your mum must have been really ballistic to throw the box out of the window," Ruff said, cheeks bulging.

"Not funny, Ruff," Oz warned him, but he was smiling, himself, now.

"Anything you can do to change her mind?" Ellie asked. "I can usually get around my mum, one way or the other."

"One or two ideas," Oz said happily. He'd had none up to a minute ago, but the others' determination over Morsman was infectious.

Ruff turned back to the window, where Jenks and Skinner, hair plastered to their heads from the drizzle which had suddenly erupted into a downpour, glared in at them venomously. Suddenly, Ruff stood up and began chanting, "One-nil, one-nil, one-nil."

The rest of the school turned to look and, amazingly, took up the chant, too, much to Jenks' and Skinner's horrified disgust. As they slouched away, sending off even more rude gestures than they had before, Oz doubled up in laughter. He giggled all the way through history and got a telling-off from Miss Lenon for finding the name of a fourteenth-century historian called Alanus de Cretyn hysterically funny. Of course, it was made ten times worse by Ruff, who whispered that having a name like that must have been a real bummer for the poor bloke.

* * *

The second half of the Christmas term slid busily by, as the weather turned colder and the days shorter. Oz had never had so much homework to do. The teachers had given up on the honeymoon period of the first half term, and were always on about how much work there was to get through. And what with trying to fit in research about alchemists and goalkeeping practise, Oz found that he was too tired to even dream about the grey-eyed girl anymore. But one morning in early December, Mrs. Chambers sat down at the breakfast table opposite Oz as he spooned cereal into his mouth and proffered a tired smile.

"Oz, I've been thinking. Maybe I've been a bit harsh."

Oz stopped munching and looked up.

"I may have overreacted a little," she added.

The cereal spoon remained halfway between the bowl and Oz's mouth. But Mrs. Chambers was quick to quash Oz's hopes.

"I'm not talking about that Morsman nonsense." She held up a wagging finger. "I don't want hear another mention of that rubbish in this house, is that clear?"

Oz nodded slowly. Mrs. Chambers got up and crossed to the calendar, which she repositioned over the head of the black dog before turning back to sit down opposite Oz.

"But I think that it's a bit unfair of me to ground you for so long. So, and this depends on you making a real effort in your end of term exams, I think that you should go to the school party, and that Ellie and Ruff can come and stay afterwards."

"Really?" Oz said.

"Really."

Oz got up and kissed his mother's forehead. Instantly, her smile became the wide and generous one he was used to seeing. "Mum, we didn't mean for any of this to upset you," Oz said with feeling.

"I know you didn't and I don't blame you entirely. Caleb should have known a lot better than to…" She hesitated, as if saying what she was about to say was suddenly unnecessary. Instead she changed tack. "So, when do your exams start?"

"In a week," Oz said.

Mrs. Chambers nodded sympathetically and began clearing things from the table. "By the way, Lorenzo's calling sometime this week to bring some of your dad's stuff back."

But Oz was only half-listening now. She'd just given him the best news he'd had in days. He couldn't wait to tell Ellie and Ruff. He finished off his cereal and ran upstairs to clean his teeth and check his emails. But his laptop, which had almost run out of battery power just before breakfast and which he'd plugged in to charge, was now stone dead. And there was no light in the bedroom, either. Cursing, Oz yelled down the stairwell, "Mum, electricity's off again."

"Oh, no," Mrs. Chambers groaned. "That's the third time this week. Right, I'm calling Tim."

As Oz did his teeth, he wondered how they'd managed before Tim had moved in. Drains, central heating and now electrics—there wasn't anything he seemed unable to turn his hand to. By the time Oz got back down to the kitchen, Tim was there with his toolbox.

"Thank you so much," Mrs. Chambers was crooning. "The wiring in this old place is ancient, as you know."

"Probably something to do with the fuse box. It's in the basement, isn't it?" Tim said sagely.

"Yes, it is," Mrs. Chambers said. "I have a torch somewhere." She rummaged in the utility room cupboard and emerged with his dad's old rubber-handled work torch. "Tim is going to have a look, see if he can fix it for us once and for all," she said, her eyes gleaming, confirming Oz's conviction that she was halfway around the bend. Why anyone would get so excited about repairing a fuse box was a mystery to him. He watched as his mother led the way down into the basement, which was pretty big and damp and junk-laden.

"Did you do courses in school on house maintenance?" asked Mrs. Chambers, her voice getting dimmer as she descended.

"No. You'll have to thank my dad," Tim answered. "He was always dragging me along to fix things…"

Oz grabbed his bag and headed out of the door. It was a soggy, drizzly day, and the daylight seemed reluctant to make much of an appearance this morning. Oz pulled up the hood of his coat and kept his head down. He'd gone twenty yards when he remembered that he'd left his pencil case upstairs next to the laptop when he'd gone to check his email. The power cut had completely driven it from his mind. He wheeled about and ran back. Inside Penwurt, the kitchen was deserted, but Oz could hear voices drifting up from below. Quickly, he ran upstairs, but just as he reached the landing a door slammed on his left. There was nothing on that side of the stairwell other than Caleb's apartment. Oz backtracked and crossed over. He walked quietly along the short landing and tried Caleb's door. It was locked. Oz shrugged. Maybe he'd misheard. Perhaps the noise that his mother and Tim were making was being carried up to this side.

But he couldn't for the life of him think of anything electrical that might make a noise like a slamming door. He went back to the stairwell and his own bedroom and stopped. The door to his dad's study was open. He was sure it had been closed when he'd gone down to breakfast, because it was always kept closed. His mother's reasoning was that there was no need to attract dust by keeping the door open, but really Oz suspected that she didn't like being reminded of its emptiness.

Intrigued, Oz crept forward and pushed the door fully open. There was still the empty desk and a chair. On the wall, the clock still hung silent and inscrutable, the hands showing nine fifteen. But there was something different. Oz glanced around, and then he saw it. The indentations made by the legs of the desk in the carpet were clearly visible an inch behind where the legs themselves rested. Someone had been in here and moved the desk. But who? His mother and Tim were in the basement. There was no one else in the building except...Lucy Bishop. Quickly, Oz checked the secret drawer in the clock—everything was safe. He ran down to the kitchen and got the key to the study, then ran back up, grabbed his pencil case, locked the study door and dropped the key back off on its hook next to the fridge.

*   *   *

"So you think it was Lucy Bishop snooping, then?" Ruff asked over lunch, after listening to Oz fully recount his morning's discovery.

"Who else could it be?"

"The ghost?" Ellie suggested. "Miss Arkwright did say that poltergeists can move stuff."

"And open and shut doors?" Oz shook his head dubiously.

"What do you think she was looking for?" Ruff asked, spooning apple crumble into his mouth with alarming speed.

"Anything and everything, I expect. She knows we bought the dor from Eldred, don't forget."

Ruff nodded.

"You've got everything safely hidden, have you?" Ellie asked, chewing her lip.

"No one but us three knows about the clock. I can't think of anywhere else that's safer."

And neither could the other two.

Not every day was damp and horrible that December. Occasionally, a proper winter's day would turn up with a sharp morning frost and a clear blue sky, in which the sun tried vainly to warm the air. On these days, Oz would hurry home and make use of the thin afternoon light to practise goalkeeping. It was on one of these bracing days, as Oz hurried back to Penwurt, when he walked through the gates to find two extra cars parked in the driveway. One was a black Rolls Royce with blackened windows. The other was Lorenzo Heeps' Jaguar.

Oz went straight to the kitchen to fetch a glass of milk, and while he was pouring it his mother appeared, looking slightly flushed and a little apologetic.

"Hi, Oz. You're back early."

"No, I'm not," Oz said. "I'm always back at this time."

"Are you?" Mrs. Chambers said airily. "Must have lost track of time. We have guests."

"I saw the cars," Oz said.

"Then you ought to say hello."

"Mum," said Oz, fearing where this was going, "it's not raining and I really need to get outside to practise."

"Don't worry. I just want you to say hello. Just to be polite," Mrs. Chambers added, seeing the look of misery on Oz's face.

Grudgingly, Oz followed his mother into the room where he'd spoken to Dr. Mackie and to the policemen. Heeps sat on the sofa, and it was he who spoke as soon as Oz walked through the door.

"Here's my little man," Heeps said, beaming.

Oz offered a toothless smile in the hope that they wouldn't see his teeth grinding behind his lips.

"Oz, this is Mr. Gerber." His mother waved her hand towards another man sitting in one of the armchairs.

Oz took in a tall, upright figure dressed in a black suit and highly polished shoes. His shirt was white and had a curiously high collar done up tightly with a black tie. Folded on the man's knees was a heavy black coat, with a hat to match. He was very pale, and the contrast between his white skin and his oddly long, swept-back black hair was stark.

But it was the man's face that drew Oz's gaze. It was smooth and taut, except for around the eyes, where a hundred tiny lines spread out from sunken orbs that glittered between dark-rimmed lids that looked as if they'd been deprived of sleep for a long, long time. The face was expressionless and Oz got the strangest feeling he was looking at a waxwork, but those eyes stared back with a dark and calculating intelligence. Gerber stood slowly, like a thin, shadowy insect unfurling itself from a cocoon. He was taller than Heeps as he held out a hand to Oz. It was long and bony and felt cold in Oz's palm.

"How do you do, Oscar?" said Gerber in a voice that was deep and devoid of any accent.

"Fine, thanks," Oz replied, and stood regarding them.

"Lorenzo and Mr. Gerber called for some tea," Mrs. Chambers explained, her expression an unconvincing grimace of a smile.

Oz nodded and gave her a scathing look. He wasn't born yesterday.

An uncomfortable pause opened up and ended only when Mrs. Chambers let out an awkward little laugh and said, "Oz wants to get on with some football practise, don't you, Oz?"

"Yeah. If I can."

"Off you go, then," Heeps said. "Don't let us keep you. We're just talking adult stuff here," he added with a sort of donkey snort as he smoothed his beard with a thumb and finger.

As he hurried away, Oz heard Gerber say in his slow bass voice, "Charming lad."

Oz practised hard, but couldn't concentrate as much as he would have liked to because he kept thinking about how weird Gerber looked. And, more importantly, he kept wondering why he was here at Penwurt at all. Oz had seen a couple of overflowing cardboard boxes in the hall, which meant that Heeps had brought some stuff back. But he didn't need Gerber's help for that.

By half past four, it was getting too dark for Oz to see clearly and he missed a couple of saves. It was no good; he'd have to pack everything away until the weekend. As he replaced the mattresses against the wall in the unused

Rhys A. Jones

garage that had become his storage space, he heard voices and saw a light flick on outside the front porch. It was dark in the garage, the single bulb long since blown, and he knew that no one would see him in this deep shadow.

Heeps and Gerber appeared with Mrs. Chambers behind them. Gerber took a step back to admire the building and Oz heard murmured words like "…magnificent," and "imposing," but despite his straining it was really difficult to hear anything clearly. Passing traffic on the street was loud enough to interfere with Oz's hearing, and it was just about approaching rush hour in Seabourne so cars were annoyingly frequent. From somewhere in the house came the shrill noise of a telephone ringing and Oz saw his mother excuse herself to answer it. He heard the front door close, and then saw Heeps and Gerber exchange some words in low tones.

Straining, he managed to hear only fragments of what was being said. He heard Heeps say, "…bloody stubborn boy," and "…come around eventually," but Gerber's deep, sonorous voice was more difficult to pick up. In a lull of traffic he heard, "…everyone has a price," then a gap and something odd that sounded like, "…Rollins in the manger." They were just isolated snatches which made no real sense at all to Oz. They clearly did to Heeps, though, who broke off and laughed uproariously at what Gerber had just said.

But then movement from the corner of the house caught Oz's eye. Someone was hurrying towards the men. A slight, female figure strode purposefully forward. Lucy Bishop walked straight past a surprised Heeps and went right up to Gerber, who watched her approach without moving. She said something to him and although Oz didn't catch it all, from her tone it sounded urgent and somehow imploring.

"Please…we can't…only you…help him…"

Gerber spoke only once and it was too low for Oz to hear, but the effect it had on Lucy Bishop was to make her body turn rigid before sagging dejectedly. Gerber turned to walk towards the Rolls Royce, but Lucy Bishop put out a hand to grab his coat. Gerber stopped and looked down at the hand. He didn't say anything, but the driver's door of the Rolls Royce opened and Oz saw a figure half-turn as if to get out. Gerber didn't move, but both Lucy Bishop's and Heeps' heads snapped up towards the car. Instantly, Lucy Bishop let go of Gerber's sleeve and took an involuntary step backwards, while Heeps, too, let out a strangled bark of surprise.

Gerber didn't wait any longer. Quickly, he moved towards the car, opened the back door and got in. With that, the figure in the driving seat turned back into the unlit darkness of the car and shut the door with a heavy click. Immediately, the engine purred into life and the car began to glide out onto Magnus Street.

When Oz looked back, Lucy Bishop had disappeared and Heeps was getting into his Jaguar, but Oz saw that he kept glancing about him, as if he was worried that he was being watched. There was nothing smooth about Heeps' leaving, and the big car's tyres squealed as rubber strained for traction against the tarmac.

Oz stood in the deep shadow of the garage, feeling his own pulse beat rapidly in his temples. What had threatened to leave the driver seat of Gerber's Rolls had been more than a simple chauffeur. A shadowy shape had filled the space with the squat, bald-headed driver at its very centre, and that shape had sported dark, folded wings with clawed fingers and a wrinkled, flat-nosed face with huge ears. In the darkness of the garage, recalling it sent a shudder through Oz. He had never seen a six-foot-tall bat before, but suddenly he knew exactly what it might look like.

* * *

Oz told Ellie and Ruff later that night, as they chatted online.

"But what were Gerber and Heeps doing at yours?" Ellie asked.

"Bringing Dad's stuff back, apparently."

"Likely story," Ruff said.

"So if it wasn't a social call, either…?" Ellie left the question hanging.

"Probably looking at a nice property to buy," Oz said grimly.

"But your mum, she—"

"Isn't talking to me about anything anymore," Oz cut across her bitterly. "I reckon she's just ignoring what I think."

"That's buzzard," Ruff said.

"What's worse is that Lucy Bishop is obviously tied up with Gerber, somehow."

"You think she's spying for him?" Ruff asked.

"What else?" Oz said. "But the funny thing is, she was as freaked at seeing that bat bloke in the car as anyone."

"So, what now?" Ruff said.

"Gerber," Oz replied. "We find out as much as we can about him. Try and work out why he wants Penwurt so badly."

Afterwards, Oz went up to the library to finish off an essay on a poem they'd read in class that afternoon, but he took his laptop with him. He'd emailed Caleb to tell him about Lucy Bishop and Gerber, but there'd been no reply. He'd just about given up at ten, as he finished off the essay and began collecting his books for the morning, when he heard the tell-tale tone telling him he had incoming mail. It was from Caleb, and it was a very strange and very short message.

Oz, thanks for keeping me informed. Best we don't do this too often. Be careful, Oz. Be very careful. I suggest you delete this email once you've read it.

He did read it, several times in fact. What did Caleb mean? Be careful of Lucy Bishop, or of Gerber? Oz knew well enough to be careful of Heeps. Or was Caleb talking about something else altogether? He could try ringing him, but Caleb hadn't picked up the last few times he'd tried. Oz suspected that his mum had made Caleb promise not to be in contact.

Frustrated, Oz got up, switched off the light and stared out the turret window at the night sky. He loved being up here when the stars were out, and there were stars tonight, millions of them, twinkling up there in the infinity of space. Oz knew that what he was seeing was light from hundreds of thousand of years ago. The farther away, the longer it took to travel. Chances were that some of those stars didn't even exist in the here and now. It was a mind-boggling thought. The traffic had died and all was quiet on Magnus Street. Somewhere, he heard a dog bark. And, as he moved to pick up his books and go to bed, from deep in the orphanage behind the library wall Oz could swear he heard, faint but unmistakable, the sound of distant footsteps.

Chapter 13

Gloopeck

On the Saturday before the end of term exams started, Oz was in his bedroom grappling with science. But his mind, never keen on being shackled to the revision desk, was having trouble concentrating. Ellie had texted him the night before to say that she'd been picked for the school's under-fourteen hockey team, and would be playing that morning. It was an amazing achievement, given that she'd be going up against girls two years older than she was. Not that Ellie was bothered by any of that; Ellie wasn't scared of anything.

Oz would have gone to support her, but it was an away game against Reghampton in the neighbouring county. So, he'd gritted his teeth and attacked biology, with one eye on the school Christmas party as the prize. Unfortunately, his attack was being repelled at the gate and in the last hour he'd learnt nothing. Not that it had been a complete waste of time; he'd made a paper clip into quite a passable sculpture of a swan, rearranged all the pencils in his desk-tidy in size order, and drawn a dragon biting the head off a knight in the back of his revision scrapbook. And all this despite shoving his laptop under the bed, out of temptation's way.

But he had left his phone on, and suddenly it chirped plaintively, signalling the arrival of a text message. He was surprised to see that it was from Savannah Fanshaw.

Difclty revsng? We cn hlp. Cm ovr.

Normally, Oz would have found a hundred reasons for not even contemplating such an offer, but after an hour and a half of trying to remember what a cell wall did, he was willing to try anything. Surprisingly, he had little difficulty convincing his mother of the merits of a visit to number 3.

"Uh, yeah, Mum, Savannah texted me. They're having a bit of trouble with science revision. I said I'd go over and help them for a bit."

Mrs. Chambers was wrestling with a pile of dirty sheets and an overworked washing machine as Oz explained this. "You're so kind, Oz," she said, looking very harassed. "Lunch will be at one or thereabouts."

The twins came to meet him at the door of number 3, dressed in identical jeans and pink T-shirts.

"As you can see, one of us is wearing a purple wrist band so that you can tell us apart."

Oz smiled nervously as the one with the wristband waved her hand and pointed to herself. "Savannah, as if you didn't know."

Oz hadn't known, actually, but was not going to admit it.

"Come in," said Sydney, and she turned and trotted upstairs. "We've been watching you trying to study."

"Really?" Oz said weakly as he followed. He kept forgetting about their little hobby with the telescope.

"That school biology book you were reading looked awful," Savannah said.

"It is," Oz agreed.

"That's why we texted you. We've got exams next week, too, but we like biology," Sydney explained.

"Even cell biology?" Oz said, not trying to keep the disgust out of his voice. "Chloroplasts and cytoplasm, ugh. It's just so confusing."

"We know," Sydney said.

"That's why we downloaded all the questions asked by science teachers to year sevens in two hundred schools across the country and found the thirty commonest ones," said Savannah with a smile.

Oz followed them up to the attic room, where a pile of papers and white cards lay scattered over the floor between two bean bags. Savannah pointed a finger at a bowl of pink sherbet-filled flying saucers. "Want one?"

Oz did.

"Then we wrote out the answers, like the definition of plant cell and stuff, on cards," Sydney went on.

"And then we play snap with them," added Savannah brightly.

Oz was staring at them, his mouth full of tangy sherbet. He had no idea what they were talking about.

"Try it. First of all, we'll ask you ten biology questions, see how many you get right, okay?" Savannah said.

"We play biology snap for a bit and then we'll test you again. See how you do," Sydney explained breezily.

Oz shrugged. Anything was better than staring at his mind-numbing school textbook.

He got a miserable four out of ten on the test. Sydney then proceeded to deal out thirty index cards to Oz and explained that he needed to look at them carefully, because some of them just differed by a word or part of a sentence. Oz did as he was told, and watched as Sydney took them back and gave them, plus another pile of thirty which were identical, to Savannah to shuffle. Oz had played snap many times before, but this was slightly more difficult. The first few times he got it wrong, and it made him look at the cards much more closely. It took quite a bit of concentration, helped a lot by pink lemonade and sherbet, but after fifteen minutes, Oz was getting a lot better.

"Right," said Savannah, "let's test you again."

"What is an organ?" asked Sydney, holding up a question paper and clutching it to her chest so that Oz couldn't peek.

He resisted, with great difficulty, the urge to say "a big thing with pipes that you hear in church." The truth was he knew that one, anyway. He'd just won a huge pot of twenty cards on that very definition. "Umm, groups of tissues working together," he said, almost automatically.

Sydney beamed.

They asked him another eleven questions and he got them all right.

"That's amazing," Oz said after he got question number twelve on "name of cell that transmits nerve impulses" right, too.

The girls smiled at each other.

"Have you got cards for all of science?" Oz asked hopefully.

Sydney got up and walked to a bookcase. "Energy, gases or friction?"

"We've done all of those," Oz said.

"So, let's play," Savannah said.

At five to one, Oz called his mother and asked if he could stay at number 3 for lunch because things were going so well. By three o'clock, he'd cracked science.

"Of course, you can play on your own," Sydney said as she packed the friction and gases cards away. "You just make two piles of cards and take from each pile in turn. It works just as well—"

"—but it's not as much fun," Savannah added.

Oz had another go on their telescope again, and was pleased to see that they still had the SPEXIT. This time, he chose the Roller Coaster Reality ride. It was even better than

Wild White Water. After three goes Oz sat back, exhausted, even though he'd been nowhere.

"You did say that these were made by JG Industries, didn't you?" he asked, hoping the room was going to stop spinning soon.

"Yes, they are," Sydney said. "And Dad managed to get them to let us keep them for a bit longer."

"Gerber came to my house a few weeks ago," Oz said, unable to hide the distaste in his voice.

"Yeah, we saw him," Savannah said.

"Creepy, isn't he?" added Sydney in hushed tones.

"Mega creepy. But he's nothing compared to his chauffeur." Oz explained to them what he'd seen in the front seat of the Rolls. The girls listened with identical looks of distaste.

"Gerber's been here, too, a couple of times," Sydney said.

"We didn't like him," they said together.

"I thought that he and your dad were friends."

Savannah shook her head. "Dad says it's purely a business arrangement."

"Patent law," explained Sydney.

S and S exchanged conspiratorial looks before Sydney said, "We heard Dad call him a very shady character."

"Why?"

They didn't answer.

"Oh, come on," Oz pleaded. "I need to know what Gerber's really after."

"We know a lot about him," Savannah said.

"A lot," added Sydney, in exactly the same voice.

"Whenever anyone visits, we usually find out more than they want us to know," Savannah said.

"We've bugged the whole of downstairs so we can listen to Mum and Dad talking about us—"

"—whenever we like."

Oz didn't doubt any of this for one second. Surveillance was a pretty strange hobby for eleven-year-olds, but then, S and S were pretty strange girls.

"So tell me, you've seen him up close. What's with his face and hair?"

"He has a birthmark on his neck. A big red one," Sydney explained.

"That's why he wears those funny high collars," added Savannah.

"Really?" Oz said. "But his face...I mean, it's like it's made of plasticene."

There was another exchanged look between the two girls and Sydney giggled. "Mum thinks he has a portrait in the attic."

"A what?" Oz asked.

"You know, like in that book where this man had a painting made of himself and made a wish so that the painting grows old instead of him."

"Oh, right," said Oz vaguely. "So your mum thinks he's weird, too."

Savannah nodded. "Dad just thinks he's had a lot of work done, you know, like plastic surgery."

Oz nodded. The thought had crossed his mind, as well.

"So, why was Gerber at your house?" Sydney asked.

"Heeps brought him. If you really want to know, I think he wants to buy the place."

The look of shock on the girls' faces would have been comical were it not for the fact that it was so disturbingly identical.

"We wouldn't like that," they said in unison.

"We wouldn't want Gerber as a neighbour—" Savannah said quickly.

"—He's not very nice—" said Sydney.

"—He's done things—"

"—Bad things—"

"Once, when Mum and Dad were arguing about Gerber, Dad said that his family used to work for the Germans during the war—"

"Looking after horses for the artillery," Savannah explained.

Somewhere, an annoyingly distant and tantalisingly significant bell rang in Oz's head, but he dared not interrupt the girls. They kept on talking, finishing each other's sentences, almost as if it were one person's thought process.

"Dad said that after the war, Gerber came over here—"

"—and they got into trouble for doing things—"

"—Animal experiments—"

"—Dad says that all the other stuff like the estate agent's business—"

"—it's all just for show, just a way for him to get money—"

"—so that he can do what he really wants to do."

"Which is?" Oz demanded.

"We don't know," Savannah said with disappointment, "but we think it has something to do with animals and the SPEXIT."

Oz glanced across at the glasses with renewed interest, his mind roiling at what a roller coaster ride or white water river rafting had to do with animals.

"So, we don't want him as a neighbour," Sydney said. There was yet another shy but knowing glance between them, and they said in unison, "We prefer you."

Oz hurriedly gulped down some more lemonade. He quickly changed the subject by asking what the moon looked like through the telescope, and shortly afterwards went home with his mind buzzing, not from the satisfaction of having revised all of science, but with the twins' revelations. Was that why Gerber was so interested in Penwurt? Did he see the orphanage as a site where he could do something unpleasant in a quiet neighbourhood, where no one would suspect? But what sort of things were S and S talking about? How were animal experiments tied up with something as brilliant as the SPEXIT?

* * *

When Monday came along, Oz ran everything the twins had said to him about Gerber past Ellie and Ruff, but it still didn't seem to make much sense, something which Ellie, as usual, was quick to point out.

"Animal testing lab?" she said with a withering look. "There are millions of out of the way places you could use, where no one would ever visit. Why pick a house on one of the best streets in town?"

"Yeah, but that's where he's being extra-clever," Ruff said, taking the exact opposite view. "No one would expect him to do anything like that. It's a double bluff."

"Double cobblers, more like," Ellie said.

As for the Gerber family's murky past, it simply reinforced Oz's first impressions of the man. But the truth was, none of them had much appetite or time for Gerber that week because the exams were upon them.

Oz had taken the twins' advice and had made notes of all the important points he had to remember for every subject; he played geography, history, French and science snap whenever he got the chance, both by himself and with Ellie and Ruff at school.

Somehow, they got through the worst of it, until finally they got to the following Wednesday lunchtime and their last exam. They were supposed to go back to normal lessons, but the teachers were all tied up with marking and invigilating the year nine and ten exams, so 1C were left to their own devices. That included reading or, more usually, playing games, so long as they weren't too rowdy. Ellie, Ruff and Oz played hangman and draughts and minesweeper on their phones, while Jenks and Skinner got thrown out for making silly animal noises at the back.

Wednesday afternoon's last lesson was French. But instead of letting them entertain themselves, Madam Chang announced that she had finished marking and proceeded to give them their exam results.

Oz felt his stomach clench. He knew that the school party was at stake here, and he waited nervously for his name to be called out. Even so, it was something of a shock when it eventually came.

"Marcel, très bien, soixante-quinze pour cent."

"How much is that?" hissed Skinner, two seats behind Oz.

Ellie turned and said irritably, "Seventy-five percent," and then added in a French accent for good measure, "imbecile."

Ellie and Ruff did equally well, and as the results kept coming the following day Oz was astounded to learn that he had passed most things, and done pretty well in them, too. Apart from science—in which he had done brilliantly. That evening, his stomach fluttering, he felt at last he could broach the subject of the party over tea with his mother.

"French, seventy-five; English, sixty-eight; geography, seventy-nine; history, seventy…" Oz paused dramatically.

"What did Ellie get?"

Oz stared at her in exasperation. "I don't know. About the same, I think," he said. "Besides, what does it matter what Ellie got?"

"Okay, okay. I was only teasing," said his mother, grinning.

Music, Geography and History were all okay, too, but Mrs. Chambers wasn't going to be hoodwinked.

"So, what about science? You said that was the one you were worrying about."

"Eighty-two percent. Thanks to Sydney and Savannah."

"Well done, Oz," said Mrs. Chambers, her eyes shining.

"So, it's just art and maths to come and art was a doddle. I did this mountain landscape and Mr. Holland said it reminded him of Mordor. It was meant to be Kilimanjaro, but the white paint for the snow on the top looked pants, and I was in a bad mood so I used red instead, and turned it into a volcano."

"I am really proud of you, Oz," Mrs. Chambers beamed.

"So does that mean that I can go to the party, and that Ruff and Ellie can come and stay afterwards?"

"I suppose we should really wait for the maths result," said Mrs. Chambers, but Oz knew she was teasing again.

"Or, I could bet you a pound I'll get over ninety."

"That confident, are we?"

"It was a walk in the park," Oz said, because it had been, since the coloured numbers thing was still happening.

"Okay, a pound it is, but I think that the results so far get you a pass to the party."

"Thanks, Mum," Oz said, getting up from his seat and giving his mother a hug.

"The only thing is that you'll have to let yourself in and get a lift back, because I'm out tomorrow night as well."

"Anywhere nice?" Oz asked, intrigued. His mother rarely went out unless it was to her book club, or occasionally with Ellie's mum for a drink.

"Yes, actually," Mrs. Chambers said, starting to clear the table with a great deal more vim than was necessary. "I'm going to a posh charity do. Jack Gerber has a table and he's asked me to go."

Oz was stunned into a long moment of wide-eyed silence. When he did find his voice he only managed a "But—"

"It's just a charity do, Oz. There'll be lots of people there, Lorenzo and the university crowd. And the Fanshaws, I expect."

"But…"

"You don't mind, do you?" said Mrs. Chambers, stopping her clearing away to peer at Oz challengingly.

"But Gerber is a…," Oz almost said Puffer, but caught himself in time. Instead, he opted for what the Fanshaw secret service had told him. "Sydney and Savannah say he's been in trouble for experimenting on animals and stuff."

"I'm sure that's just a nasty rumour. Lorenzo assures me that Mr. Gerber has lots of fingers in lots of pies, but I doubt that animal testing is one of them. And anyway, I think I deserve a little bit of fun, don't you?"

"Oh, so they're not just trying to butter you up to make you sell them Penwurt, then?" Oz said with feeling.

Mrs. Chambers sighed heavily. "Oh, Oz, we have to start looking at things realistically. We're struggling. Really struggling. Especially now that we've lost Caleb's rent."

"And whose fault is that?" Oz pointed out, feeling the anger rise in him like a red tide.

"Not mine," said Mrs. Chambers icily. "He brought that on himself. He promised me—"

"And you promised me that we would never leave here." Oz was shouting now. He could feel hot tears sting his eyes. "You said, after Dad died, that we'd always have this part of him. We'd always have this place."

Mrs. Chambers stopped clearing away the dishes. She sat opposite Oz like she had a hundred times before, her face suddenly full of pain again, her voice earnest. "I know I did, Oz, and I am really and truly sorry. I thought we could afford it. We should have been able to, but…" She faltered, the words petering out into nothing.

"It's because the insurance people won't pay us, isn't it?" Oz said, the words tumbling out. "Because of what the coroner said about Dad, isn't it? The open verdict thing."

Mrs. Chambers looked up at Oz with a little shake of her head, her brows knitted with incredulity. "Is there anything you don't know?"

"I asked Caleb, since no one else would tell me," Oz muttered darkly. "Mum, I know that Dad couldn't have killed himself, but if we leave here we'll never be able to prove it."

"That's just nonsense, Oz," she said, but she sounded suddenly defeated and tired.

"It's not nonsense, Mum. I believe it, and so should you," Oz pleaded.

But all Mrs. Chambers could do was sadly shake her head as she sat with her eyes closed, fingers trembling slightly as she slowly massaged her temples.

*   *   *

Oz was still fretting over his mother's unbelievable gullibility at school the next day. But there didn't seem to be anything he could do about it, no matter how he approached it. The bet he'd made with her about maths had burrowed to the back of his mind, but when 1C pitched up for third lesson that morning and he saw how everyone fell quiet with nervous anticipation, he, too, felt a sudden pang of anxiety. Badger Breath, in his usual sardonic way, called out everyone's marks but left Oz until last. After everyone else had been named, he summoned Oz to the front and, while he busied himself with some marking, thrust the paper at him without even looking up.

"I don't know how you're doing it, Chambers," he said, in a barely audible whisper, "but rest assured that I will be spending the final two terms of my employment at this institution finding out."

"You're leaving, then, sir?"

"Yes. My blood pressure, already precipitously high, will not stand the infuriation of another academic year with the likes of you, Chambers." He held up the paper and shook it. "Go on, take it." Oz could see the muscles of his jaw working as he spoke.

"Yes, sir. Thank you, sir," Oz said with exaggerated politeness as he took the proffered paper. He stepped away, but then hesitated and turned back to the desk and said, slowly and loudly enough for everyone to hear, "Sorry, sir, but I can't quite read the mark. Does that say ninety-five or ninety-three?"

Heads shot up.

"Five," muttered Badger Breath through clenched teeth.

"So, a ninety-five, then, is it, sir?"

"Yes," snapped Badger Breath, finally looking up and throwing Oz a glare of cold fury.

"Thank you, sir."

Judging from the number of open mouths Oz counted as he walked back to his seat, he was delighted to see that the whole class had heard the exchange. When Oz examined the paper, he saw that the only marks Badger Breath had taken off were for not using a black pen and for bad handwriting. But that didn't matter. A low hum of excitement was audible in the classroom. 1C were celebrating the brilliant news that they only had to put up with Badger Breath for another two terms.

* * *

That evening, as Oz wolfed down a banana sandwich prior to going out, Mrs. Chambers walked in wearing a dress she hadn't touched in a long, long time. She'd also donned long, sparkly earrings and a necklace that he remembered his dad giving to her one birthday not so long ago.

"Well, do I pass muster?" she asked, giving Oz a twirl.

"You look…different," Oz said truthfully, since he wasn't at all used to seeing her dressed like this.

"Okay, I'll take that as a positive, shall I?" She clipped across the flagstones on high heels and wiped a stray strand of hair from Oz's forehead, and then stepped back to consider him, her eyes narrowing. "Don't look too bad yourself, scrubbed up."

"Mum, promise me you won't make any decisions about the house tonight."

"I am just going out for some adult company," she explained calmly. "Is that so bad?"

"No, but I just don't trust Gerber or Heeps," Oz said, desperate to make her understand. "I wouldn't put it past them to get you tiddly and make you sign something."

"Oz, they'd have to get up very early in the morning to catch me out," she said.

But Oz had a funny sinking feeling that she was underestimating Gerber in a big way.

* * *

The school party was being held at the sixth form college, half a mile away from the lower school campus. This meant that, although there were lots of teachers present, including the Volcano, who was on corridor patrol, sixth formers were in charge of the music. In Oz's junior school they'd usually roped in the caretaker as DJ, a man whose musical choice usually consisted of rubbish songs you only ever heard on the radio for a month just before Christmas, followed by sing-along carols. Oz found himself hoping that this party wasn't going to be as bad as those had been. He caught a bus to the college and had barely walked through the big glass and steel entrance when two pairs of hands grabbed him roughly and dragged him into an alcove off the main corridor. Oz struggled and kicked out, and only when he heard Ruff's pleading voice did he ease up.

"Ow, Oz, wait. It's us!"

"Ruff?" Oz extricated himself from the grasping hands and arms, and turned around to see Ruff massaging his shoulder and Niko Piotrowski looking sheepish.

"You didn't have to thump me quite so hard," Ruff complained.

"I didn't know it was you, did I? What's going on, anyway?" Oz smoothed down his ruffled shirt.

"Skinner and Jenks," Ruff growled.

"They have set ambush," Niko explained. "Outside boys' toilets. They have water bombs."

"What's that got to do with me?" Oz asked.

"You're their main target," Ruff added, grimacing from where Oz had landed a good right hook to his shoulder. "Niko heard them plotting. They still hold a big grudge against you for the Skullers losing their unbeaten record."

"Oh," Oz said.

"Jenks and Skinner, they are like rats. Horrible and never far away," Niko said with feeling. "They pick only on smaller and weaker, or when they are more."

"We can't let them get away with it," Ruff said, still rubbing his shoulder, "so we thought we'd intercept you. Didn't know you were going to turn into Mike buzzard Tyson."

"Sorry, mate," Oz said, trying not to laugh. "So, what are we going to do?"

Niko held up a small plastic packet. It was a selection of coloured balloons. "Attack is best form of defence."

Oz grinned. "What's the plan?"

"I found a map of the place next to the office," Ruff said with a glint in his eye. "If we go right here, up the stairs and along the corridor, there's another toilet. We can load up there and then go down the other side, and me and you can sneak up on them from the back."

"We will probably get into trouble…" Niko said.

"And your point is?" Oz said.

Niko grinned.

They followed Ruff up the stairs and along a dim corridor.

"By the way, thanks for warning us about Jenks and Skinner," Oz said to Niko as they hurried along.

"Is okay. I have not had chance to thank you for helping my sister in Ballista's," Niko said, before adding, "She likes you very much."

"Does she?" Oz said airily.

"Now, I get chance to thank Skinner and Jenks in person."

Oz glanced at Niko's defiant expression and said, "Yeah, I think we'd all like that chance."

The upstairs toilet was large, clean and completely empty as they filled their balloons.

"Not too much," Ruff warned them, "otherwise they just become too floppy to throw."

Beneath them, they could hear the bass thump of the music and the dull roar of three hundred excited pupils out for a good time. Ruff put twenty water-primed balloons into three plastic bags and gave one ten-pack to Oz. To Niko he gave a stubby black stick and a smaller cache of five balloons. He held the third bag, which also held five.

"What's that for?" Oz said, glancing at the stick.

"Part of my cunning plan," Ruff said. "Come on, let's go. Got your mobile, Niko?"

Niko held up his phone.

"Text me when you're in position. You make your move on my signal, okay?"

Niko nodded and quickly headed back the way they had come. Ruff led Oz in the opposite direction and down some stairs. At the end of another corridor, they emerged into a room that was full of the aroma of hot dogs and hamburgers and a crowd of milling, hungry pupils.

"Where's Ellie?" yelled Oz, trying to make himself heard over the noise.

"Here somewhere." Ruff scanned the crowd and pointed to a corner where Ellie was deep in conversation with some older girls. "Said she was on a mission," Ruff said, shrugging.

Oz peered at the girls Ellie was with. "Hey, isn't that Katie Sasco?"

"One of Pheeps' Creeps, yeah, you're right," said Ruff.

"What's Ellie doing…" But he never finished. Ruff had grabbed his arm and pulled him through the crowd.

"Come on, we can talk about all that later."

They threaded their way through the sea of faces until they emerged into the relative calm of another corridor. Ruff went right and then left past classrooms and a science lab, until they found another set of stairs and descended quietly. Ruff put down his plastic bag of balloons and his fingers flew over the keys of his phone. A second later, there was a return text message.

"Right, Niko's in position."

"Great," said Oz, "but where are we?"

"If I'm right, the boys' toilets are through those double doors on the right. No one should be coming this way 'cos it doesn't go anywhere except classrooms. Jenks and Skinner will be expecting you from the other direction, so we should be safe."

Oz watched as Ruff moved towards the double doors, opened them a crack, got on his knees and slid his phone through at foot level. Five seconds later, he pulled the phone back and pressed some buttons. A video of the corridor flickered on the screen. There, halfway along, leaning against the wall, was Skinner. At his feet lay a pile of water balloons. Next to him, Jenks paced up and down.

"Ruff, that's just brilliant," Oz said, shaking his head with an admiring smile.

Ruff shrugged. "Old SAS trick from *Desert Commandos 3*. So, are you set?"

Oz nodded. Ruff held the phone to his ear and called Niko. "When you're ready, mate. And remember, leave your phone on." He turned to Oz, said, "Lock and buzzard load," and reached into the bag for a water bomb.

Armed, they listened on Ruff's phone speaker to the weird but unmistakable noise of Niko walking along with his phone switched on. Snatches of giggling were followed by the odd scream and guffaw, and then, after a period of silence, distant but unmistakable, Skinner's sneering tones.

"Well, well. If it isn't Igor. Who said you could come to our party, Igor?"

"Is not your party, Skinner. Is for everyone."

"Yeah? Well, why don't you and your little sister and your cabbage-eating family go back to where you came from?" Jenks' voice this time, cold and hard, with no hint of humour.

"Yeah, go back to Moscow on a mule."

"Moscow is in Russia," Niko said. "And I hate cabbage."

"Whatever," Skinner said.

"Why do you want to live here, anyway? It rains all the time," Jenks said.

"It rains in Poland, too," Niko said.

"Not as much as here. Even rains inside, sometimes. Show him, Skinner."

Ruff shouted, "Now," and they burst through the double doors as the first salvo of water bombs from Skinner hit the broad black canopy of the automatic umbrella Ruff had given Niko, which he'd unfurled an instant before. Ruff and Oz let go a couple of quick throws each, which caught Jenks and Skinner completely by surprise. One lob from Ruff caught Jenks squarely in the chest as he turned, and a peach from Oz met with Skinner's face and left him drenched and gasping like a landed fish. After that, there was no contest. Niko picked them off from the other side and Skinner and Jenks didn't manage to get more than one throw each away before they were cornered, their own bombs forgotten as they huddled, arms over their faces, protesting loudly.

"Not the face! Not the face!" yelled Jenks.

"Three against two. Not fair," Skinner whined, sounding like a spoiled three-year-old, before another direct hit caused the last word to come out as a gurgle.

"But you two against me, that was fair, was it?" Oz said. "Just like you two against Anya was fair, eh?" Even he was surprised by the anger in his voice. He let go another bomb, which splattered into the wall above Skinner, making him flinch.

"That was just a bit of a laugh, Chambers," Jenks protested. It triggered a throw from Niko, which caught Jenks square on the side of the head.

"Not the face, I said." His protests this time were tinged with a hint of a whimper.

"That was for Anya," Niko said, his eyes flinty, "just for bit of laugh."

"These next couple have got paint in them," Ruff announced loudly. "Bit of an experiment with some fluorescent stuff I found in the lab upstairs."

"No," Skinner said, horrified. "This is a new shirt. My mum'll kill me. I'm sorry, okay? I'll say sorry to your sister, too, if you want." He held both hands up towards Niko.

"And Jenks?"

Jenks' face was as black as the interior of Gerber's Rolls Royce. Under his soaked hair, he looked miserable and defeated, but still hesitated over saying the word.

Skinner turned to him, pleading. "Please, Jenks. It was meant to be just us against Chambers." His voice dropped to a whisper. "If it's her you're worried about, she can have my money back. It isn't worth it…"

"Shut up," Jenks hissed, his eyes widening in warning. But it was too late.

"She? Did someone put you up to this?" Ruff asked.

Skinner suddenly looked terrified. Jenks' mouth had become a thin, tight-lipped line.

"Okay, boys," Oz said, seething, "on the count of three. Let them have it."

"NO!" Skinner said. "If I tell you, will you let us go?"

"I'm listening," Oz said.

The words seemed to run over one another as Skinner blurted them out. "It was Pheeps. She said you'd been bad-mouthing her. She gave us a fiver to get you soaked."

Jenks gave Skinner a venomous look and shook his head. But Oz caught a second, surreptitious glance aimed at him, and in that look he saw tortured relief.

"Shall we let them have it, anyway?" Ruff asked.

"Let them go," Oz said.

"What?" spluttered Jenks.

"Go," repeated Oz.

Instantly, Jenks and Skinner pushed themselves away from the wall and ran soggily down the corridor, their hair sopping, Ruff and Niko laughing and lobbing the odd ballon at their heels as they ran. But Oz wasn't laughing.

Pheeps.

He should have known that Jenks and Skinner couldn't have planned something like this on their own. What was the matter with that girl?

Niko and Ruff collected the broken balloon skins and were now walking back slowly, comparing throws.

"You do know that they're both idiotic scum, and what they say is total cobblers, don't you?" Oz said to a beaming Niko.

"We have word for them in Polish. *Glupek*. Means bonehead."

"Right, that's their name from now on. Gloopecks," Ruff said, and all three of them laughed.

"But better word is *przyjaciel*."

"Chee a gel? What does that mean?" Oz asked.

"Friend," Niko said, and held out his hand. Oz and Ruff shook it in turn.

"Right," Ruff said, "we ought to get back. The Volcano's on corridor patrol and I don't want to run into her."

They headed back towards the music, swapping stories of their best Gloopeck-destroying water bomb shots as they went.

While Ruff went in search of food, Oz found the dance floor. He had just finished dancing with Natasha Stilson, who didn't seem at all bothered that Oz had been mainly responsible for the Lions taking the Skullers' unbeaten record, and was on his way to find Ruff when the one thing he had really hoped wouldn't happen, happened. He pushed through a tight throng of nattering girls and half-stumbled over someone's clutch purse before colliding with the one person he had hoped to avoid. As always, she was wearing something that was so different from what everyone else wore that it made you look even if you didn't want to. Oz had a vague idea that her outfit was probably very fashionable and wasn't at all meant to make her look like a fungus, but to his unschooled eye that was exactly what came to mind. With a puffed-out skirt and a straight top, Pheeps looked like an upside-down mushroom.

"Watch where you're going, Chambers," she seethed, recoiling.

"It was an accident," Oz said. He saw the way she quickly scanned him, and registered her twitch of disappointment at seeing him bone dry.

"Really?" An evil glint came into her eye. "Another deliberate accident, maybe? Your family seem to be experts at that."

Oz immediately felt the colour rising in his cheeks. She had the knack of winding him up with very few words. "Look, I don't know what your problem is, but if you're saying that what happened to my dad was deliberate—"

"I don't have to say it," she cut across him like a knife, malevolent eyes glaring. "The coroner said it in a court. He said your father killed himself."

"No, he didn't. They couldn't decide what happened, that's all."

"As good as."

Oz looked at her pretty, malicious face, trying his best to understand why she was like this. "What is it with you? What did my dad do to make you hate us so much?"

"Don't flatter yourself, Chambers. I'd have to care to hate you, and care about you, I most definitely do not—"

"That's not true, though, is it?"

The voice came from behind Oz. He turned to see Ellie pushing through the crowd to stand toe to toe with Pheeps.

"Here she comes," Pheeps sneered. "Chambers' little girlfriend."

"I am not his girlfriend. Never wanted to be. Unlike you, when you were nine."

The smile faltered and withered on Pheeps' face. "Nice try, Messenger, but why don't you just buzz off and mind your own business?"

"I will if you will," Ellie shot back.

"I'll say what I want to say, thanks. Including telling everyone that Chambers' father committed—"

Rhys A. Jones

"So," said Ellie loudly, "you won't mind me telling everyone that your mother wasn't actually in hospital for twelve months, and that she isn't 'recuperating' in Spain at all? She just left because she couldn't stand the people your dad was mixing with, or his whingeing about coming second to Oz's dad all the time, didn't she?"

Pheeps threw a wild glance around to see who was listening and then hissed, "You keep my mother out of this."

"Oz's dad was about to get the job your dad has now, wasn't he?"

"My dad works really hard. It wasn't fair..." Her face, already scarlet, looked suddenly on the verge of tears. "Who told you all this? Who told you?" She reached out a hand and grabbed Ellie's arm.

"I wouldn't do that, if I were you," Oz said calmly. "She does taekwando and stuff."

Pheeps was breathing hard, her mouth a thin, ugly slash. But she let Ellie's arm go.

"We shouldn't be talking about this sort of thing here," Ellie said. "Or in school. It's not a topic for gossip."

"If you breathe one word about my mother..." whispered Pheeps.

"I won't say anything," Ellie said. "But you know what you have to do, don't you?"

"One day, Messenger," Pheeps spat, "you'll regret this big time." With that she sent Oz one final, withering glare, turned on her heel and stormed off like an irate toadstool. Oz watched her go and then turned to Ellie, eyes wide with admiration.

"Where did you get all that from?"

"A friend," said Ellie mysteriously. "Come on, you can buy me a Coke and I'll tell you all about it."

They found Ruff queuing for his third hot dog, got some drinks and retired to a quiet corner, where Oz and

258

Ruff told Ellie about the water fight and listened as Ellie explained where she'd got the dirty on Pheeps.

"She doesn't seem able to keep any of her friends for very long because she's so possessive. Katie Sasco's one of Pheeps' ex-creeps. She plays in the hockey team with me. She's really quite nice, once you get to know her."

"But how did you find all that stuff out about her mother?"

"Pheeps' mother has moved in with her sister. Katie's aunt happens to live three doors away. That was probably why Pheeps wanted Katie as one of her 'best friends,' so she wouldn't spill the beans."

"So they aren't best friends anymore?" ventured Ruff.

"Big bust-up a fortnight ago, because Katie bought a pair of shoes that Pheeps really wanted."

Oz and Ruff exchanged bemused glances.

"I know, pathetic, isn't it? Anyway, Heeps started mixing with Gerber and Pheeps' mum didn't like that at all, or the fact that he was really jealous of your dad's research. And Katie also found one of Pheeps' old diaries and you're in it, Oz." A mischievous grin spread over Ellie's face. "It seems that she did have the hots for you once, and you ignored her."

"Me?" Oz said, flummoxed.

"Admittedly, you were only nine at the time, so girls were probably just yucky." She grinned and then added, under her breath, "Unlike now."

"What that's supposed to mean?" Oz demanded.

"How many times did you just dance with Natasha?" Ellie's grin was bigger than a slice of watermelon.

"She's a nice girl," Oz mumbled.

Ellie nodded. "Unlike Pheeps, who is a nasty bit of work that you snubbed once. And you know what Miss Arkwright says in English about a woman scorned."

"This is bonkers," Oz said.

"Not as bonkers as Katie telling me that Pheeps' dad's study is full of books on you'll never guess what."

"How to be a buzzard gonk?" Ruff volunteered.

"No." Eyes shining, she held their gazes for three long, suspenseful seconds before she finally announced, "Alchemy."

"Wow, that's a bit of a coincidence, isn't it?" Ruff frowned.

Ellie rolled her eyes. "Katie showed me a photo she'd taken of a big blown-up poster on Pheeps' dad's wall. It's a photo of the library panel in Penwurt, Oz. There was all sorts of stuff written over it, but I recognised it straight away."

"How the hell did he get that?" Oz said.

"Lucy Bishop?" Ruff suggested.

"Of course," Oz said. It was so obvious, now that he thought about it.

"But what it means," Ellie went on, "is that our Mr. Heeps is probably a Puffer, too."

Even Ruff stopped eating on hearing this.

"No wonder he took all of my dad's stuff," Oz said, hardly able to believe how stupid he'd been. "He wasn't looking for university property at all. He was looking for Morsman stuff."

"And we know he's big pals with Gerber," Ruff said.

"And Lucy Bishop," Oz muttered.

"I bet they're all in it together." Ellie nodded.

Oz felt something flash through his head. Some little piece of understanding that he knew was important, but which stayed annoyingly out of reach. Frustrated, he tutted and said, "I just wish we knew a bit more about Gerber."

Ellie shook her head. "He's really difficult to research. He's not on Facebook and there's hardly anything on Google. Just boring stuff about his businesses."

"All I found out was that 'gerber' means someone who makes animal hides in German," Ruff mumbled.

"Oh, wowee," Ellie sighed and shook her head sadly.

"Then we're back to finding out what the images on my laptop are all about," Oz muttered.

Ruff, who had happily begun murdering his third mustard and ketchup-laden hot dog, suddenly gagged and ended up depositing a revolting mouthful of chewed sausage and bread in the nearest bin, while Ellie and Oz looked on in disgust.

"Yuck," Ellie said. "That's so gross."

"Sorry, nearly choked on me lightly toasted bun then," Ruff said when he rejoined them, wiping his mouth. "I knew there was something I'd forgotten." He suddenly looked extremely sheepish. "Uh, the code," he muttered. "I think I cracked it this afternoon before I came out."

"What?" yelled Oz and Ellie together.

"I was going to tell you," Ruff said, flinching under their accusatory glares, "but Niko texted me, and then—"

"There was food," said Ellie, shaking her head.

Ruff looked suddenly annoyed. "No, there was Jenks and Skinner about to take out Oz," he said hotly. "I didn't forget, I *prioritized*, remember? And if we hadn't stopped them, they'd have gone after Niko for sure. It should be mates first, shouldn't it?"

Ellie stared at him and Oz wondered if they were going to argue again. But then Ellie nodded and said, "Totally. You're right, it should be mates first. Sorry."

"Exactly," Ruff said, but he sounded more than a bit stunned by Ellie's apology.

"What time is it now?" asked Oz urgently.

Ruff checked his watch. "Just after nine."

"If we hurry, we can get the ten past bus back to my house. Unless you both want to stay here, that is?"

They looked about them at their fellow pupils milling around, squealing and chattering, some of the boys already charging around with their shirts half-ripped, others chasing screaming girls.

"Silly question," Ellie said.

"Very," added Ruff.

Five minutes later, they were running down the street towards the bus stop with a renewed sense of determination.

Chapter 14

Essence, Alum, Soap and Tin

On the bus, they relived the water fight again, much to Ellie's disgust. She was pretty miffed that they hadn't made the effort to find her and made them both promise that, if it ever came to it again, she was not to be left out. Then Ruff began explaining how he'd finally deciphered the coded message.

"At first I thought maybe it was just a simple transposition cipher, but then I wondered if it was polyalphabetic, or even a rotor machine…"

"I didn't know you could speak Hungarian," Ellie said, tilting her head and folding her arms.

"Us codebreakers—"

"Just tell us in English," Ellie said, her eyes flashing dangerously. But Ruff wanted his moment of glory.

"It's all a bit technical," Ruff explained. "Be easier just to show you."

Despite more threats from Ellie, Ruff insisted on keeping his powder dry as the bus deposited them at their stop and they hurried to Magnus Street. It was not an evening for dawdling or outdoor conversation; the temperature was dropping fast. Yet another frost was forecast, and if there were any doubt about that they only had to look at the plumes of water vapour erupting from their mouths like dragon breath as they ran along the deserted streets. Christmas trees, adorned with tinsel and lights, lit up the windows of the houses, and one or two front gardens had Santas and sleighs in lurid displays. But they paid hardly any attention to the neon reindeer and glowing elves as they hurried on.

The wind had dropped and above them the stars glittered in the clear, black night sky. Penwurt was completely dark, the bartizans and spindly chimneys silhouetted against the starlit heavens like dark warning fingers. Noses red from the cold, they went straight to the library and stood around the desk as Ruff finally explained what he'd worked out.

"Wasn't difficult, once I figured out the key," he said, trying to sound nonchalant and failing miserably.

"Which was?" Oz asked.

"Well, that's the thing, I spent ages wondering what word your dad might use as a key. He was almost a professor of history, right? So I was going bananas trying to think of some weird ancient word or saying."

Oz frowned. "But I don't even think my dad knew the letters were in the clock. Like I said, he was always threatening to get the thing fixed so that it would run."

"Exactly." Ruff pointed a confirmatory finger at him. "It was Morsman that found the letters and put them in the clock for safekeeping, right? And it was Morsman that wrote the code on the back as a reminder."

"Why bother? I mean, why not just memorise the message?" Ellie said.

Ruff shook his head. "I reckon it's like having an instruction manual for a new gizmo. You'll probably never read it, but you hang on to it in case you just might have to. He wrote the message down as a back-up, but coded it in case anyone else found it."

"So it was Morsman's keyword you needed," Oz said.

"And what would be easier than something he'd see whenever he reread the letter?" Ruff said teasingly. He was clearly enjoying this.

"Come on, Ruff," Ellie demanded. "Just tell…" She stopped in mid-sentence and her eyes became very large and very round as she whispered, "The clockmaker's message."

"*Tempus Rerum Imperator*," Oz said slowly, seeing it, too, now.

"Exactly." Ruff nodded and fished out a notebook from his backpack. He wrote out *Tempus Rerum Imperator* and then wrote numbers beneath. "So if you substitute the letters for numbers, you can see it's just a simple reverse alphabet cipher. Instead of A being one, Z is one. Look, the sequence of numbers for "tempus" is 722141158, right? So T would be 7 and E, 22. Get it?"

"Hey, Ruff, I'm impressed," Ellie said.

"There's no need to sound so surprised," Ruff retorted, but he grinned as he said it. He flipped over a couple of pages of his book. "So every sequence of numbers spells a word. And, surprise, surprise, they all spell alchemical symbols. I wrote it all down, but I just need to check this off against the symbols on the panels to try and make sense of it." He went to the panel with the wheel of twenty-six symbols and pored over it, consulting his notebook every now and then. Oz and Ellie watched him for a while as he mumbled to himself before Ruff, finally realising that he was being observed, looked up and said tetchily, "I could be a few minutes."

Oz shrugged and turned away. He ran his fingers along the dusty spines of the stacked books on their shelves, peering at their titles.

"What are you looking for?" Ellie whispered, so as not to distract Ruff.

"Dunno, really. Just something the twins said to me. It sounded important at the time, but I couldn't make a connection. And I almost had it again tonight. Something to do with Gerber."

"Was it the fact that he's an ugly gonk?" said Ruff distractedly from across the room.

"Get on with your cipher solving," Ellie snapped.

"Something about Gerber's family firm being involved with the German army in the Second World War," Oz went on, and then turned to Ellie with a little shake of his head. "Why should that be important?"

Ellie started to shrug, but then stopped abruptly. She frowned and her eyes widened. "Hang on," she said, walking along the shelves, searching for a book. "Here it is." She pulled down a black, leather-bound tome and started flicking pages. "Yeah, I knew it."

She looked up at a perplexed Oz and explained, "*A Short History of Seabourne's Ancient Houses*. I borrowed it, remember?"

Oz nodded vaguely

"Remember that stuff I found about Shoesmith the farrier and the shell thingy? I remember reading somewhere...yes, here it is. They worked looking after horses for the British during the First World War. That's a bit of a coincidence, isn't it?"

Oz frowned. "Yeah, but the First World War was, like, thirty years before the second one."

"Still, bit weird, don't you think?"

"Yeah, I suppose there is a bit of a connection, but didn't you say that one of the Shoesmiths was killed in that war?"

"That's right." Ellie scanned the page with her finger until she stopped about halfway down. "Yeah, here it is. At the Battle of Le Cateau in 1914."

"Oh well, it must have been horses that triggered my..." Oz stopped. Something shifted in his brain, like a curtain wafting in the wind to reveal a hidden view. He turned to Ellie, his voice now an excited, harsh whisper. "That's it. That's it!"

"What's it?" Both Ellie and Ruff stared at him, but Oz was running downstairs to his bedroom. He grabbed his laptop and bolted back up to the library.

"Look up gerber," he said as he powered up the laptop.

"I told you, I already have," Ellie said.

"Not Gerber the bloke, 'gerber' the word. There's a German/English dictionary up there somewhere."

Frowning, Ellie started searching the shelves as Oz waited for the laptop to boot up. He found the file he was looking for just as Ellie pulled down a battered book and blew dust off its cover.

"I knew I'd seen it in here somewhere," Oz said, his voice high with excitement. "In 1914, Morsman went on an expedition to France to look for the fifth artefact. Everyone said he was mad because the war was on. But he didn't go alone."

Ellie looked up from the dictionary and read out what she found. "Right, 'gerber, of German origin. Someone who skins animals, a—'"

"Tanner," said Oz before Ellie could finish.

She stared at him in astonishment, brows knitted. "How did you know that?"

"I didn't. But I remembered that the bloke who went with Morsman to France was called John Tanner. You worked it out, Ruff. You told us that gerber means someone who skins animals. Don't you see?"

"No," said Ruff, totally flummoxed.

Ellie's face bore a strange expression of mingled horror and confusion. "Are you seriously trying to tell us that Gerber is John Tanner?"

"It all fits," Oz said, and started pacing up and down the room. "Tanner was Morsman's big mate in the orphanage.

They went to France in 1914 to look for the fifth artefact, but didn't find anything, or at least that's what my dad said in his article. Afterwards, Tanner disappeared."

"But…"

"Don't you see?" Oz exclaimed. Suddenly, it was all so obvious. But the others just gawped at him as if he'd gone bananas. "Shoesmith's shell was the fifth artefact! And I bet Tanner found the thing and took it for himself."

"But what about the Shoesmiths?" Ellie said.

"You said that one brother was killed in action in 1914. Maybe he was already dead when Tanner found him," Oz reasoned.

"Or maybe Tanner had a hand in him dying, too," Ellie said quietly.

The boys stared at her.

"Wait a minute," Ruff said, his voice dripping with disdain. "Morsman was born when, 1880? If Tanner is the same age as him, that would make him a hundred and buzzard thirty. I know he's a repulsive gonk, but…"

Oz's eyes shone. "The twins told me that Mrs. Fanshaw thinks he's some kind of freak. Ellie said he's really difficult to research. Perhaps he doesn't want anyone to know about his past." His voice dropped to a loaded whisper. "What if the artefact somehow keeps him young?"

Ruff's mouth dropped open and Ellie's brows crumpled in disbelief, but then her eyes lit up.

"The Shoesmiths were all renowned for living for, like, ages—over a hundred, many of them—except the bloke who wrote the autobiography."

"But he didn't have the shell by then, did he?" Oz said quickly. "I know how it sounds, but what if it did? What if it was what made the Shoesmiths live longer, and now, somehow, it's having an effect on how Gerber ages? That would make him want the other artefacts, too, wouldn't it?"

"Yeah, but a hundred and thirty?" Ruff said, wrinkling his nose.

"Hold on," Oz said, and quickly fetched the small ladder that fitted onto the bookshelf. He clambered up and reached for the old photograph albums of Penwurt and the orphanage. In date order, starting in 1886, were faded sepia prints of those lucky enough to have found a home under Colonel Thompson's wing. Oz took out the loose print he'd found Halloween night. He found Morsman two in from the end in the front row, a smiling, gap-toothed boy in a loose-fitting, open-neck shirt, with his arm around the head of another, slighter boy.

"This is 1892. Morsman would have been about our age." Oz stared at the second boy. He looked thin and gawky and troubled, his hair tousled and dark, and even with the poor quality of the old sepia print, from the way his head was angled by the headlock Morsman had him in, it was clear that John Tanner had been cursed with a large, dark blemish that covered most of one half of his neck.

"The twins told me that Gerber wears high collars to hide a large birthmark." Oz held out the photograph for Ellie and Ruff to see. When they looked up again, their faces were strained and serious. No one spoke. It all seemed so incredible and yet, somehow, the pieces fitted together perfectly. Oz spoke for all of them when he finally said, "Maybe the coded message has the answer to some of this."

Ruff nodded and turned his attention back to the oak panelling.

"Okay, the letter sequences on the back of Redmayne's letter spell out sixteen words and they're all symbols." Ruff used his finger to point out the symbols as they appeared on his notebook. "Iron, nitre, glass, rot, ummm…essence, soap, soap, alum, tin, and then there's soap, urine, nitre, rot, iron, soap and essence."

"Is that really the symbol for urine?" asked Ellie, making a face.

"Yeah," Ruff said.

"Cool," Ellie said, shaking her head.

"But what does all this mean?" Oz said.

"Maybe we should check the Redmayne letter again?" Ruff suggested. "In case there's something we've missed."

"I'll get it."

Oz ran down the stairs and headed for the study. The first sign he had that anything was amiss was the fact the door didn't look quite right. Not ajar as such, but not quite flush with the frame, either. He noticed a small smattering of shiny dust on the carpet right underneath the lock as he reached for the handle. The door swung open and he saw immediately what had happened. The lock itself lay on the study floor with more fine metal shavings around it. Someone had drilled it out, and that same someone had taken the clock off the wall and laid it on the desk.

Oz stood frozen on the threshold. Nothing else was different about the study, but there was something very different about the clock. The drawer beneath the pendulum lay shattered, the wood splintered and broken. Stomach writhing, he took a step forward into the room, his eyes drawn to the broken clock drawer. It was empty.

"Ellie! Ruff!" he yelled, and heard rapid footfalls as they responded to the urgency in his voice. In a couple of seconds they ran along the landing and through the doorway of the study, where they both froze.

"Oh my God," Ellie said, hand over her mouth.

"Buzzard," spluttered Ruff.

"They've got them all," said Oz dully. "The letters, the dor, the pebble. Everything."

"What should we do?" said Ellie. "Ring the police?"

"And tell them what?" Oz said angrily, not taking his eyes from the broken drawer of his dad's clock.

"That there's been a burglary," Ellie said.

"But has there?" Oz said.

"We'd better check the rest of the house," Ellie whispered urgently, and ran out, yelling, "I'll check downstairs. You two do up here."

But the TV was fine, and so were the CD player and Oz's Xbox and his iPod. All the things that burglars usually burgled remained untouched, and after ten minutes of searching it was clear that nothing else had been disturbed. Not one other thing had been taken.

"But it's still a robbery," Ellie protested as they gathered back in the study. "At least ring your mum."

"And tell her that someone's stolen Morsman's artefacts?" Oz shook his head. "She'd probably get up on the table and do the Macarena." He slapped the desk angrily. "I should have hidden them somewhere else. Somewhere away from Dad's study."

"No good beating yourself up, Oz," Ellie said.

"We've still got the message," Ruff added hopefully.

"I thought you needed the letter," Oz muttered, his words leaden and bitter.

"It was just to double-check," Ruff said. "See if I'd copied everything down right."

Oz looked at his friends. They were desperate to help.

"Come on, Oz," Ellie urged.

Shrugging despondently, his heart iron-heavy and his mind whirling full of self-recriminatory what-ifs, he allowed himself to be led back up to the library. While Ellie and Ruff pored over the coded message, Oz sat in one of the chairs watching them, his appetite for the mystery suddenly gone. If only he'd put the artefacts somewhere really safe, like in the garage with the boxes of old tools. No one would have thought of looking there. Or even in a plastic bag taped to the underside of the lid of the cistern in the unused bathroom. That's what they did in all the films when they wanted to hide something. Oz's mind went round and round in ever-decreasing circles. He hardly noticed how much Ruff and Ellie were concentrating and how they'd pause occasionally to give him a worried glance.

No one spoke for almost ten minutes.

But it was in one of those tense, silent moments that a new sound appeared, faint but definite—the creak of a floorboard twice in quick succession, followed by the dull tattoo of someone, or something, crossing a room.

Footsteps.

Ellie and Ruff paused and Oz sat up. Could it be that their ghost still had the answers to what was going on?

"Hear that?" Ruff whispered.

"It's coming from behind this wall," Oz said, getting up from his chair and putting his ear against the panelling.

"Should we go over there?" Ellie said, but there was doubt in her voice.

"To the orphanage? Tried that, remember?" Oz said, suddenly buoyed by this new twist. "No, the answer's here. In this library, I'm convinced of it. It's here in these books, or the symbols, or something…"

"Maybe we could get a wizard from one of Ruff's Xbox games to cast a spell and reveal it to us," Ellie said drily.

Ruff gave her a long-suffering look. "Very funny."

"Just a suggestion," Ellie said.

"Don't give him any ideas," Oz said.

"Heeps had ideas," Ellie muttered, her face glum. "He'd written them all over the poster I saw on Kate's phone. What does 'orthographic' mean?"

"I dunno," Oz said. "Something to do with printing?"

Ruff's face had gone strangely slack. "Spell," he whispered, his eyes focused on something far away. Oz and Ellie stared at him.

"For crying out loud, I didn't mean it about the wizards. It was just a joke, Ruff," Ellie snapped.

"No, it isn't," Ruff whispered, his eyes burning. "Spell, don't you see? There's a whole section on the Cypherspace page about it."

Oz and Ellie just stared at him.

"I don't mean 'spell' as in jiggery-pokery and wands and stuff. I mean 'spell' as in spelling. That's what orthographic is all about." He pointed towards the wheel of symbols. "I reckon the message spells out an instruction. Look, take the first letter of all of these symbols."

Ellie took a pencil and quickly did as Ruff suggested. "I, n, g, r, e, s, s," she mouthed and scribbled at the same time. Two seconds later, she sat back and announced, "It spells 'ingress at sunrise.'"

"Great," Ruff said, sounding deflated. "I thought it might mean something."

"It does mean *something,* obviously," Ellie said.

Ruff collapsed into an armchair. "Well, if we have to wait until sunrise, we'll need to get some snacks."

But Oz was frowning. He knew this house better than anyone else. "You can see the sunrise through that window." He pointed at one of the huge panes in the turret above.

"And the wall below it has the same pattern of twenty-six symbols as the other one," Ellie said, walking over to it. Behind that same wall was where they'd heard the footsteps moments before.

Ruff got up, walked over to join Ellie and examined the symbols. "They are the same, but they feel different. Look here, see? These faint lines around each one? It's like they were carved on blocks and placed here."

"You mean, like a mosaic?" Ellie said.

"Or a jigsaw," Ruff mused. "Maybe we could prise them out?"

Ruff tried to get his fingernail into one of the faint cracks, but the symbols had been inlaid with great workmanship and the spaces were barely visible. There was no way he could get between them. "I'll probably need some tools," he said.

Ellie nodded and sighed. "Or we wait until the sun comes up."

But Oz was shaking his head. "It can't be that difficult. Morsman built this place. It doesn't make any sense that he set a cipher that could be read for just one small part of the day. We're missing something. It's another puzzle."

"Well, ingress means entry, doesn't it? Entry into what, though?" Ruff pondered.

"A place?" Ellie said. "Like an address?"

"Maybe, or numbers or coordinates to do with sunrise or…oh, I don't know." Ruff shook his head in frustration.

Oz listened to his friends voicing the words that milled about in his own head. Ruff was right. They needed some directions. He looked at the ancient globe atlas standing in the corner, with its compass symbol. He went over and spun the globe, watching the countries roll by beneath his fingers. Watching the sailing ship moving around and the compass rotating into view with each revolution…

"That's it," Oz said so loudly that the other two jumped. "It's a place."

"Like a fish?" Ruff said.

Oz pretended he hadn't heard that. "This library is perfectly aligned on compass points. That wall," he pointed right, "is directly north from the centre of the room. And that one…" he pointed towards where they were standing, "is where the sun comes up."

"The sun rises in the EAST," breathed Ellie.

"Essence, Alum, Soap and Tin," Ruff said, running his fingers over the symbols. "Here's essence." He frowned at the symbol. "Funny, it looks a bit faded and worn compared to the oth…"

He didn't get any further. The slight pressure of his finger had caused the wooden block on which the symbol was carved to move inwards slightly. Ellie caught her breath, and in a second Oz had joined her to watch with barely restrained excitement as Ruff pushed the symbol in as far as he could. It slid in a full inch and stopped. Then he did the same with the alum symbol and the soap symbol. Both slid in the exact same amount and clicked to a stop.

"Oz," said Ruff, his voice a low murmur, "I reckon you should do the last one."

Trembling slightly, Oz put his finger on the tin symbol and pushed. This time, when it stopped moving, there was a faint but definite click, followed by a discernible creak, and the whole six-foot-by-six-foot panel in front of them gaped open an inch on one side.

"Awesome," Oz said.

"I knew it! I knew there'd be something behind these panels," Ruff added triumphantly.

"Ingress," Ellie whispered in awe. "The way in."

Beyond the door was a very narrow passageway, just wide enough for someone to get through sideways. Ruff stuck his head in.

"Wow, looks like they built this inside the walls."

Ellie immediately edged forward, but Oz stopped her.

"Let me get some torches." Oz ran down to his bedroom and found a couple of pen torches which, miraculously, worked. Back in the library, Ellie and Ruff looked as if they'd been arguing.

"What's wrong?" Oz asked.

"Nothing. It's just that…" Ruff began.

Ellie threw him a withering glance and then said, "Ruff thinks we should call someone."

"Well, don't you?" Ruff protested.

"I told you, my mother isn't interested," Oz explained. "She's too busy partying with Heeps and Gerber."

"Yeah, but…" Ruff frowned.

"And Caleb doesn't answer his emails or texts, so who else is there?" Oz demanded.

The other two didn't answer, but both wore slightly troubled expressions. Doubt suddenly clouded Oz's mind, too. Maybe Ruff was right. None of them had any idea what was inside these walls.

But then Ellie shook her head. "Look, we've just found one of Penwurt's big secrets. I mean, it's a hidden passageway, for crying out loud! Come on, where's your sense of adventure?"

Ruff glared at her. "Oh, that's just typical you, isn't it? Just doing stuff without thinking it through." His face had gone bright red. "What if something happens? Guess who'll be blamed for solving the cipher and opening the door…"

But Oz was sold. Having already lost the artefacts, he wasn't about to turn away from this new opportunity to find out who the footsteps belonged to.

"Come on, let's do it," Oz said, and saw Ellie grin delightedly, while Ruff's shoulders slumped. Oz went first, his feet crunching on rough stone, the torch beam picking out the thick curtains of cobwebs that hung off the walls and the roof of the narrow passage. A couple of steps in, he heard footsteps behind him as Ellie and Ruff followed. They inched their way along, and after ten yards or so they came to some steps and descended before turning sharply to find themselves in a wider walkway, this one with wooden floors which creaked ominously as they crept forward. On one side, the rough stone wall remained, but on the other, Oz's hand brushed against a rough texture of interwoven wattle and daub. Here, it was broad enough for them to walk facing forwards.

"How far down do you think those steps were?" whispered Ruff.

"Eight feet, maybe," said Oz.

"So that would have just about taken us to the first floor of the orphanage," said Ellie.

Oz heard an audible gulp from Ruff. "Where we thought we heard the footsteps."

"Not thought, *did* hear them," Oz whispered excitedly. "This floor is the same one as on the other side of that wall." He pointed at the wattle and daub. "We didn't find any sign of footsteps in the room, because whoever they belonged to was outside in this passage all along. Someone knew..." Oz didn't finish his sentence. Ahead of them, close by, a floorboard creaked. They froze.

"If this was an Xbox game, we could pause it and get some hot chocolate," Ruff whispered shakily. "That usually helps."

"Switch off your torch," Ellie said.

"Why?" Oz said.

"Trust me."

Oz did as Ellie asked and saw why immediately. Five yards ahead of them at floor level, a thin, rectangular strip of light suddenly appeared, the exact size and shape of a gap under a door. They crept forward, and then stopped again as they heard something that plucked at their already stretched nerves and sent their imaginations into overdrive. Something howled behind the wall. And it didn't sound like a wolf or a dog; it sounded like nothing any one of them had ever heard before—an unearthly, wailing screech followed by an urgent, tremulous whisper.

"Oz, this is really buzzard," Ruff hissed.

"Come on," Oz said, sounding a great deal braver than he felt. He turned his torch back on and aimed it at the wall above where the light had appeared. The beam picked out a rough wooden frame in the mess of plaster, mud and vegetable matter that the builders had packed between the wooden lattices. An iron ring halfway down the right side of the frame served as a handle for what was obviously a door.

Oz could feel his heart banging against his rib cage. Somehow, he knew that behind this wall lay the answer to the ghostly footsteps. And yet, he sensed that something wasn't right here. All this time, he had harboured the secret hope that the footsteps had something to do with his father. But the noises they now heard were of something wretched, something ill at ease and disturbed.

"Ready?" Oz said, feeling his fingers tremble as he swapped the torch to his left hand. He heard both a "no" and a "yes" as a response. But there was no time for debate. Oz reached for the iron ring, turned it and pushed the door open. What light there was came from a single lantern in the centre of the room. It threw up a watery beam that showed two figures, one standing and holding something beseechingly, the other crouched on its haunches, regarding the standing figure with wild and feral terror.

Oz felt the temperature drop as they entered, but only had seconds to register the fact that it was because the sash window was wide open and freezing night air was pouring in before chaos erupted. The hunched figure jerked its head towards them, and Oz saw a pinched, filthy face and yellow teeth bared in animalistic terror. But his mind also, impossibly, registered the sleek body and banded head of a human-sized polecat shimmering around the matted fur coat the thing wore. It was only a momentary realisation as the creature let out another screech, the noise of a wild animal suddenly cornered.

Oz reached out a hand. "It's okay. We're not here to harm…"

The thing shifted abruptly, and from behind him Oz heard Ellie shout, "Look out, it's going to attack!"

She leapt towards it with her foot outstretched and kicked away the arm it had thrust towards Oz. There was another scream, and before anyone could move it scurried towards the open window and leapt out into the night air.

"God, Ellie," Ruff said in a harsh whisper, "now look what you've done."

"NO!" Another wail, this time from the standing figure. It was a cry full of hopelessness and desperation that pierced Oz's heart. The figure rushed to the window, choking back a sob. It stood for two long seconds, staring out into the night, before turning back to them with an expression of such hate that it appeared almost as inhuman as the wretch that had just leapt out. The eyes that stared up from the gaunt face were a girl's eyes, but they burned with such a terrible, feverish brightness that for a moment Oz couldn't place the features, so distorted were they by anguish and loathing.

But then recognition kicked in. Suddenly, Oz knew why the polecat creature had attacked them as they'd walked home from the park that night. There was no denying that the face they were now looking at and the distorted features of the creature had been molded from the same genetic clay. Oz only had a fleeting second to register all this, because his eyes darted between the hammer that wavered in one of the girl's shaky hands and the smooth dark objects she held in the other—the obsidian pebble and the black dor. Oz felt a pressure at his back and realised that Ruff and Ellie were close behind him, but all he could think of was that insane look in the girl's eyes and the hammer in her hand.

"You!" Lucy Bishop screamed. "This is all your fault."

"What was that thing?" Ruff asked in a very shaky voice from behind Oz's left ear.

"That was her brother," Oz said without turning around.

Lucy Bishop threw back her head and let out an anguished wail.

"What?" said Ellie.

Oz didn't take his eyes off Lucy Bishop as he spoke. "It went for us in the park because it was hungry. She was going to feed it…"

"Not an it!" hissed Lucy Bishop. "Edward, his name is Edward, and you've ruined any chance we had. Blundering, meddling kids."

"What are you talking about?" demanded Ellie.

Lucy Bishop thrust out her hand and the pebble and the dor it contained. "Don't pretend," she spat. "Thought you could hide them, didn't you? But I found them. Go on, deny it. Deny that you were hiding them from me."

"They're Oz's, and you've got no right to steal them," Ellie said, pushing Oz aside to face the distraught girl.

"His?" Lucy Bishop let out a sneering laugh. "These aren't possessions to be bought or sold. They choose their keepers." She kept her eyes on Oz and slowly raised the hammer, pointing it at him. "This is your curse, boy."

Next to him, Oz felt Ruff flinch as he leaned in and whispered, "She's gone stark raving bonkers."

"My dad sent me the pebble," Oz said, wishing Ruff would keep his thoughts to himself.

Lucy Bishop glared at him in utter disdain, but she didn't reply, merely stood with the breath heaving in and out of her chest.

"What's wrong with your brother?" Ellie asked abruptly.

Lucy Bishop's eyes widened and she half-fell backwards, putting her hand out to the wall for support, as if the words had struck her a blow. Glancing back out of the window, she said in a choked voice, "Edward…"

"Is he ill?" Ruff asked.

Lucy Bishop let out a strangled sob, which turned into a derisory laugh as she swung back towards them. "*Ill?* He isn't ill. He's possessed. A demon has him in its clutches. A demon that has twisted his mind. Turned him into a wild creature."

"I'm really sorry," said Oz, "but that doesn't give you the right to steal the pebble for Gerber."

"Yeah, we know you're working for him," Ruff said.

"Gerber," she cackled. "That monster. Never…" She trailed off in a sob.

"Was it you in here the other night?" Ellie asked suddenly. "We heard your footsteps."

The question threw her. "I've never been in this accursed room before."

"But we heard you…" Ruff began.

"What you hear is the house. It feeds on the innocent and the gullible. It's cursed. Like you. Like these abominations." She looked down at the pebble and the dor, her voice now a barely whispered moan of hopelessness. "I tried. I tried to use them to help Edward…" Her breath moved in and out in staccato bursts. "But it's no use."

Her eyes came slowly back up and fixed on Oz. "But somewhere in this house is a place where these things are vulnerable. I have to find it. They must be destroyed before they ruin another life."

"No," Oz yelled, but it was too late. Lucy Bishop fell to her knees and threw the artefacts to the floor. In one smooth movement, the hammer in her other hand fell. Oz saw it plummet, driven by Lucy Bishop's mad strength. But when it hit the pebble, there was no noise except the whoosh of something heavy flying through the air and Lucy Bishop's arm swinging back as if made of rubber.

"Cursed!" she screamed. "Cursed! You see! You see!" Time and again, she brought the hammer down and time and again, there was no smashing noise of splintering metal, just the whoosh of the hammer flying back up as if it were bouncing off a trampoline. After a while she stopped and sat back, sobbing, her sweaty hair over her face like a damp curtain. She looked up again, and this time her expression had moulded into an ugly mask of real hate. "But perhaps

I'm doing this all wrong. Perhaps it isn't the artefacts I need to destroy. Perhaps it's you and this cursed house."

With a banshee wail she flew at Oz, the hammer held high. Oz dived to his right just as her arm came down and the hammer smashed into the door frame. He scrambled forward, half-stumbling and taken off-guard by the ferocity of Lucy Bishop's attack. The torch flew from his hand and rolled over the floor. He turned to see her dark shape coming for him again, brandishing the hammer high above her head.

But then he saw a shadow beside him, and saw it move lithely to stand between him and the deranged young woman. There was a whirl of limbs and an unpleasant-sounding thud as a foot connected with something soft. Oz scrambled for this torch and shone it towards the middle of the room just in time to see Ellie's foot connecting once again in a helicopter whirl with Lucy Bishop's head. It snapped back and Lucy Bishop staggered backwards towards the panelled wall. There was a sickening thud as she connected with the solid wood, and then she slid down like wet wallpaper, the hammer clattering heavily to the floor at her feet.

"Oz, are you okay?" Ellie asked.

Oz got to his feet and wiped dust from his knees. "Yeah, thanks to you."

"Told you she was a ham roll short of a picnic," Ruff said shakily, staring down at the crumpled form of Lucy Bishop. But Oz's attention was elsewhere. He'd gone over to the corner where Lucy Bishop had tried smashing the pebble and the dor. To his utter astonishment, they weren't smashed to smithereens. In fact, they weren't smashed at all.

"Ruff, Ellie, look at this." Oz held out the pebble and the dor for them to see.

"But I saw her pulverise them with the hammer," Ellie said.

"Yeah, but there was no noise, was there?" Ruff said.

"But what does it mean?" Ellie demanded.

"I have no idea," Oz said, shaking his head, "but I think now would be a good time to call someone. Come on."

They went back to the passage and made their way to the gap between the walls. Oz led, but just when he arrived at the top of the steps leading to the library, he heard a voice.

"Hello? Anybody there?"

A head appeared above Oz, squinting into the torchlight.

"Tim? Tim Perkins? Is that you?"

"Heard a funny noise. Seemed to be coming from the library, and then I found this door open and…"

"You won't believe how glad we are to see you," Oz said with relief. "It's Lucy Bishop, she's…"

"Had an accident," Ruff said quickly.

"An accident?" Tim asked, concern clouding his face.

"Yeah. Down here."

Quickly, they backtracked, leading Tim to the room where Lucy Bishop lay. He knelt and felt for a pulse in her neck.

"Is she okay?" asked Ellie anxiously.

"Out cold. But what's all this about?"

Oz, Ellie and Ruff looked at each other and then Oz said, "It's a long story. Lucy stole something from me. We heard a noise and stumbled on this passageway, which led us here."

"We think she's gone a bit weird," Ruff said. "Something to do with her brother."

"What did she steal from you?" Tim asked, looking perplexed.

"Just some old stuff my dad sent me." Oz held out the pebble and the dor for Tim to look at, and his response was refreshingly honest.

"They don't look very valuable."

There was a very pregnant pause before Ellie said, "They're not. They're just historical artefacts."

"Well," Tim said, standing up, "we'll put her in the recovery position, and I vote we get out of here and call an ambulance straight away." He lay Lucy Bishop down on her face and then moved swiftly across the room with the other three in tow. But when he got to the passage, he hesitated. "Oh, one thing. Could you two just check to make sure she hasn't got anything like lighter fluid, or matches? We don't want her waking up and setting fire to the place, do we?"

Oz waited while Ellie and Ruff quickly went back into the room, and Ellie patted Lucy down while Ruff searched the corners.

"No," sang Ruff, "there's nothing here."

"She doesn't have anything on her eith…"

Ellie's voice was suddenly cut off. Tim had shoved Oz hard so that he stumbled forward into the passage, banging his head painfully against the wall. At the same time, Tim followed Oz out and pulled the door shut. Within seconds, he had some thick plastic ties wound around the iron handle and the wooden surround so the door couldn't be opened from the inside. Oz heard the muffled protests from within.

"Oy, let us out," yelled Ellie.

"What do you think you're playing at?" Ruff demanded.

Then Oz found his voice, too. "Tim, what are you doing?"

"Keeping your meddling friends out of the way," he said, and there was something about his voice that made Oz's stomach do a backflip. Suddenly, he was grabbed roughly by the arm and shoved forwards along the passageway.

"Very convenient of you to turn up with the very things I've been scouring this mausoleum for three months for."

"What are you talking about?" Oz said. But all he got in reply was another shove. They were heading in the opposite direction to the one which took them back to the library now, deeper into the orphanage block.

"Your name isn't really Tim, is it?" Oz asked, though he didn't need to. He already knew the answer. Suddenly, it was all blindingly obvious.

"No, it's not. And I'm not a student or a repair man, either."

"Then who are you?" Oz demanded.

"Your worst nightmare. The name's Rollins."

Chapter 15

The Basement

Rollins made Oz go first. He stumbled onwards, his heart sinking abysmally with each step. The walls pressed in on all sides and the air smelled increasingly of damp and decay. There was nowhere to run to even if he'd been able to, and Oz knew that he was in deep, deep trouble.

"Keep going," Rollins whispered, and all pretence at the smarmy politeness Perkins had exuded every time he'd spoken to Mrs. Chambers had disappeared.

"Where are we going?" Oz asked as he shuffled forward.

"At the end of the passage, take a left."

Once again, Oz found himself shuffling sideways, the surfaces rough on his face in front and his jeans behind. They were descending now, the gradient slight but definite.

"Keep moving," Rollins ordered. "At the end are some iron rungs. Climb down."

Oz slowed down as the floor petered out. The light from Rollins' torch was sporadic and shaky. He found the rungs more by touch than sight, but eventually managed to clamber down unsteadily until he hit a stone floor again.

"Go right," Rollins said.

"How do you know about these passages?" Oz asked, moving crablike through the space.

"Cleaning gutters and fixing medieval wiring has its advantages. The inside measurements don't tally with the outside. It's simple maths. I knew these passages were here long before I found them." His voice was dispassionate, and as cold as the stone against Oz's flesh.

"Gerber must be very pleased with you, then," Oz said. Rollins didn't answer.

"I know his real name is Tanner," Oz said, "and that he's after this house and the artefacts."

"I'm not interested in what you think you know. Now move." Fingers jabbed at Oz's shoulders, urging him on.

In the darkness, he shuddered.

They descended another set of rungs, and Oz sensed a change in atmosphere. It was colder and damper, and he felt a moist trickle under his reaching fingers on the wall ahead. He was nudged forward into a small stone chamber guarded by a heavy door. Rollins went to a lever on the wall and pulled it. The door opened with a groaning creak. He stepped forward, flicked on some lights and then turned back to pull Oz in after him. The sudden brightness caused Oz to squint, but after a few seconds recognition dawned, and he realised that they had descended to the orphanage basement.

Oz had been here before. It was just a junk-filled room as far as he was concerned. In his mind's eye he could see the stair up to the kitchen, but it was on the far side. Separating him from the way out was a mass of boxes, discarded furniture and formless shapes covered by dustsheets. But Rollins seemed to sense his thoughts. He pulled out what looked like a flashlight made of yellow plastic, marked with black stripes. He did it expertly, his face expressionless. Oz had the awful feeling that he'd been in this sort of situation before.

"This is an electro-shock baton." Rollins pressed a button and the end of the baton extended eight inches. "A variable voltage stun gun to you. Anything from five thousand to fifty thousand volts at the press of a button. So don't even think about doing anything stupid. Now, just hand over those artefacts."

Oz peered at the thing in Rollins' hands. It didn't look very menacing, but he'd seen videos of people being stunned. It had turned them into screaming, flopping jellyfish and he had absolutely no desire to experience that. He reached into his pocket for the pebble and the dor.

The tiniest flicker of a knowing smile crossed Rollins' face when he saw them.

"Good," he whispered. But this, like all the other words Rollins had spoken, contained no emotion.

Still holding the baton and pointing it at Oz, Rollins began pulling off dustsheets to reveal a bank of equipment the likes of which Oz had never seen before. There were things that looked like computer desktops, black boxes studded with LED lights from which sprouted lots of wires and, on its own on a small desk to one side, a metal bowl, into which most of the thicker wires from the black boxes led.

"Put them in that container and sit down." Rollins indicated the steel bowl. Oz did as he was told and sat on a plastic crate and watched his captor throw switches.

"It was your footsteps we heard on Halloween night, wasn't it?" Oz said.

Rollins said nothing, but Oz took his silence as confirmation of the glaring truth.

Oz was suddenly quite glad that Rollins was busy, so he wouldn't see the disappointment etched on his face as he squeezed his eyes shut so that the hot tears didn't burn too much. All along he'd told himself that the footsteps could not have been ghostly, that such things were simply not possible. Yet a small part of him had harboured a tiny flicker of hope—because this was, after all, Penwurt, the hill where odd things happened. And that sliver of possibility had planted a seed of desperate expectation. If only those footsteps had belonged to one of Miss Arkwright's spirit heralds. Something bringing a message of comfort, a balm for the grief left behind. He hadn't told anyone, but deep in his heart of hearts he'd hoped and wished and believed that the footsteps might belong to Michael Chambers.

Sitting on a crate in the basement, tricked and captured, Oz finally realised how much he'd clung to that hope. He had not dared to tell Ellie and Ruff for fear of their derision which, he now realised, would have been completely justified. He felt stupid and childish for even considering such a thing. Worse, he'd been so wrapped up in his belief, so convinced that his dad had sent him the artefacts and left them clues to Redmayne's and Shoesmith's letters through the symbols on his laptop, that he'd been blinded to what had been going on beneath his very nose.

Suddenly, everything seemed so glaringly obvious. He remembered seeing Tim Perkins coming in covered in cobwebs and dust on Halloween. He hadn't been at a fancy dress party at all; he'd been exploring the orphanage in the secret passages. They'd all been taken in, even Caleb, it seemed. But this was not the way Oz had imagined the story ending, and he was suddenly overwhelmed by a sense of having been cheated. He'd been so stupid, leading his friends into danger, thinking Lucy Bishop was the threat when it was Perkins who had given Heeps pictures of the library wall and Perkins who had been the spy. Lucy Bishop had been as much a victim as he was.

"What's the matter with Lucy?" Oz asked, because he couldn't stand listening to his own thoughts anymore.

"I'm not a doctor," said Rollins as he busied himself checking dials.

"Okay, then, why did she steal the artefacts?"

"Because she knows what they are capable of," Rollins muttered.

Oz glanced at the pebble. It was hard to believe what Rollins was saying. He'd held that thing a hundred times in his hand, and although he knew his dad had been convinced of its significance, apart from seeing the maker's mark glow, there'd been nothing to suggest it was anything valuable.

"So why would Lucy want to destroy it?"

Rollins shook his head. "She's Obex. Meddlers, the lot of them. She thought she could help her brother, but he is far beyond anyone's help."

"What happened to him?"

"A mistake," said Rollins, grimacing as he tightened some screws. "Just an unfortunate experiment that backfired."

"One of Gerber's experiments?"

Rollins turned to look at Oz, and there was just the suggestion of a grudging admiration in his expression before he turned back to his work. "You *have* been busy, haven't you?" he muttered.

"He already has an artefact, doesn't he? The fifth artefact."

Rollins stopped working and once again turned slowly to look at Oz. "Yes, he does. And soon he'll have three when I take him these."

Now that he was in control, Rollins seemed more ready to talk. So Oz pressed him for more. "Did Lucy Bishop's brother work for Gerber?"

Rollins didn't look up from what he was doing this time. He merely said slowly, "Let's just say he was an unwilling volunteer."

"Gerber turned Lucy's brother into something, didn't he?"

"Gerber's had the artefact to work with for years. He's used the best scientists, but all they've done is scratched the surface of its power. Imagine you're a caveman finding a mobile phone. Press enough buttons and it'll make an entertaining noise, but you'd still have no idea of its true capability. Edward Bishop was...unlucky. Gerber's artefact can capture emotion. Let you feel what someone else is feeling when they do something for the first time. Try and imagine what a cheetah feels like when it catches an impala and closes its jaws over the windpipe. There is no regret. It's just pure instinct. Once you've experienced that..."

Rollins' voice trailed off into the cavernous room.

Oz tasted bile at the back of his throat and barely managed to stifle the groan of disgust that threatened. What had they done to Edward Bishop? But then Rollins seemed to come back to himself and spoke again.

"Some people can't handle it very well. Maybe it was the way Bishop's brain was wired, but he didn't come back from his little trip. He ended up believing he was a polecat. And they are vicious predators. Anything gets too close, he wants to tear it to shreds with his bare hands."

"But some of him is still Edward Bishop, isn't it? He knew who Lucy was. And she was feeding him in the park, wasn't she?"

"Was she?" Rollins said, his voice still detached and low. "It wouldn't surprise me."

Oz was thinking about the SPEXIT and of how it made you feel you were actually on a roller coaster or shooting rapids. How would it be if, somehow, it could make you believe you were a rat or a lizard or a polecat instead?

Suddenly there was a hum of power as some of the black boxes lit up. Rollins went over to another shapeless lump covered by a dustsheet. He whipped off the cover to reveal a metal office chair. A cable held in place by black electrician's tape snaked up from the backrest of the chair to an electric light socket.

"Have a seat," Rollins ordered, one eye warily on the wire.

Oz moved across and looked at the contraption suspiciously. "What's this for?"

"Your accident," Rollins explained. "Sit."

Oz frowned, but did as he was told.

Rollins nodded before continuing, his voice cool. "It's really very simple. We've been led up the garden path by people thinking they've found the artefacts before, but this time we've followed the trail from Morsman through your father to you." He nodded towards the pebble. "These things are drawn to certain individuals. They allow themselves to be found only if they want to be. If they are the real thing, we'll know soon enough. Trouble is, they need a lot of power to kickstart them. We don't know why, they just do. But if this works, then I'll have done my job and there'll be just a bit of tidying up to do."

"What does that mean?" Oz asked.

Rollins looked up, his face a blank sheet. "We have to make the stun gun injury look acceptable. Loose cable from the ceiling touches a metal chair in a pool of water into which you have inadvertently walked…"

"There is no water," Oz said, looking down.

Rollins' eyes flickered towards a large plastic container. "There will be. And then fire will engulf the house."

Oz tried to swallow, but his throat was too parched. All he could think about was Ellie and Ruff and Lucy Bishop in that locked room, with smoke pouring in and flames licking at the walls. He shifted uneasily on the cold seat. "But Gerber wants the house. If you burn it down, he won't be happy."

"There'll still be the shell once the fire burns out. That's what's important. Probably pick this place up for a song, then," Rollins said. There must have been something in

Oz's face that made him shrug before adding, "Nothing personal, Oz. This is all just business."

And somehow, that made it all the worse.

Oz realised that he was running out of time. Desperation fought with fear. If he was going to do something about the situation, it needed to be soon. He waited until Rollins turned back to the equipment and took his chance. He bolted up from the chair and ran for the stairs to the kitchen. He was quick, but Rollins' reaction was quicker. Like a striking snake, he stretched forward and pressed the baton to Oz's back.

It was as if someone had hit him with a paralysing sledgehammer. He rose on the balls of his feet and hung there as his muscles seized. His whole body became a juddering block of pain. It lasted only three seconds, but when it ended he fell to the floor, quivering.

"Uh, uh," Rollins said from above him. Oz felt himself being dragged back to the chair and unceremoniously dumped. For several long, agonising seconds, Oz could only sit slumped while his body recovered and the pain ebbed away. All the while Rollins busied himself, twiddling dials so that the machine sent little bolts of blue electricity towards the pebble and the dor as they lay motionless in the metal container. After the fifth attempt, he took them out and, much to Oz's utter astonishment, pressed the smaller dor into the body of the pebble. The dor seemed to melt into the larger artefact, leaving only the slightest bulge. Rollins put the combined unit back into the container and bombarded them with more power. After each attempt he took them out and pressed the maker's mark on the pebble, to no avail. At last, the frustration showed as Rollins' face blotched with anger at each failed attempt.

Oz thought frantically. He didn't want to be hit by that stun wand thing again. He had never experienced so much pain in his life, but on the other hand, he had to do something or in a few minutes, Rollins was going to electrocute him and set fire to Penwurt.

"It works for me," he said thickly. He could taste blood in his mouth from where he'd bitten his tongue from the electric shock.

Rollins glared at him. "What did you say?"

"It works for me when I press the mark. Doesn't for anyone else. It sort of glows when I touch it."

In the silence that followed, Oz heard nothing but his own pulse thrumming in his ears.

"You'd better not be lying," Rollins said eventually, cold eyes fixed on Oz.

"I'm not."

Rollins picked the pebble out of the bowl and, holding the baton an inch away from Oz's chest, he said, "Show me."

The pebble felt warm and familiar in Oz's hand. He turned it over and placed his thumb over the silver mark on the bottom.

"Show me," urged Rollins through gritted teeth, and pressed the baton to Oz's sternum.

Oz thought about what he'd seen Lucy Bishop doing with the hammer. He remembered the way her hand had bounced away, as if she'd been hitting rubber, the way the hammer had left no scratch. Oz took a deep breath, put his thumb on the mark, pressed and at the same time brought the pebble up to hit the baton away.

Several things happened at once. Rollins must have reacted quickly and pressed the baton's trigger, because Oz felt another momentary kick of agonizing pain and he arched backwards in a convulsive thrust. But it didn't last as long as the first time, nor was it as severe. And despite the pain, Oz could see that something had happened to Rollins, too. Just as the stun baton fired, Rollins was catapulted backwards exactly like Lucy Bishop's hammer arm had been. Oz was right; there was something in the pebble that protected it from harm.

There was a tremendous crash as Rollins hit the machines. Sparks flew and smoke immediately started drifting upwards from the overturned black boxes. Oz's convulsion was over in a moment, but his momentum had sent him careening over the back of the chair so that they both toppled backwards. With his muscles like Seabourne County canteen blancmange and unable to protect himself, Oz hit the floor head first with a sickening crunch. A bolt of new pain shot through his skull, but it was what was happening inside it that made him forget the pain in an instant.

From where he was lying and through watering eyes, Oz could still see the room, see Rollins struggling to his feet, tossing aside pieces of equipment as if they were made of cardboard as he tried to get to Oz. But then there was a burst of static and coloured lines, something that sounded like a chime and suddenly, a pretty, grey-eyed face appeared inside Oz's head. It flickered unsteadily, like an old TV, but then the image cleared and he heard a female voice.

"Emergency power low at point-five capacity. Hostile assailant detected. Probability of attack, 95 percent. Would you like me to instigate amnestic deflection?"

Oz blinked his eyes, but the girl remained even as the rest of the room swam. A wave of sickness washed over him, but out of the corner of his eye he could also see Rollins coming, his face distorted with fury, eyes intent on damaging Oz.

"Yeah. Stop him," he ordered.

The last thing Oz remembered of that night was also the strangest thing of all. Rollins lunged towards him with a roar. He took three strides before there was again the sound of something faintly musical in Oz's head. Even Rollins stopped and look around curiously. He looked down even more curiously at the baton in his hand. Then, incredibly, he touched the end of it to his own forearm and pressed the button. The jolt sent him crashing backwards against the basement wall and, like Lucy Bishop having met with Ellie's right foot, Rollins slid, unconscious, to the floor with an expression of bewildered surprise.

Oz tried to get up on to one elbow, but the room spun nauseatingly. The grey-eyed girl was fading and a black wave threatened. He could still see smoke rising from the equipment. He ought to do something, call someone, tell them about Ellie and Ruff and Lucy Bishop before the fire took hold, but he couldn't. He was too weak. Despair engulfed him with the realization that he couldn't help his friends and, worse, that he had failed his mother and father at the last. But then the black wave of unconsciousness finally crashed over him and washed all his pain mercifully away into darkness and oblivion.

* * *

He woke up because he was thirsty. There was no need to, otherwise, because he was actually having quite a nice dream about a water-bomb fight with Jenks and Skinner and finding secret passages with Ellie and Ruff...

"Oz, are you awake?" He heard a familiar voice close by, low and full of concern. "Did I see your eyelids flutter just then?"

He lifted his heavy lids and blinked as the room, strange and white and grey, swam into focus. Daylight flooded in through a large window. There was a slightly sickly smell of disinfectant in the air and he knew instantly that this wasn't Penwurt. His mother's face loomed into view. She leaned over him, a hopeful smile fighting with a quivering lip for dominance.

"Any chance of a drink of water, Mum?" Oz managed to croak before he was completely engulfed in a bone-crushing hug. He thought about protesting, but then, as memory of what had happened in the basement began to creep in, he realised that being alive and thirsty and being hugged by his mother was a pretty good situation to be in, all things considered.

"Oz, I thought that…we thought that you were…" She squeezed him tighter, and Oz heard her sniff. Eventually, she let him go and fetched him a glass of water from a jug on a locker next to his bed.

Oz hoisted himself up onto an elbow, took a swallow from the proffered glass and then remembered with a jolt what had happened before he'd got to the basement. He shot up in the bed and grabbed his mother's arm.

"Ellie and Ruff, Mum. Are they…?"

"They're fine. Both tucked up in bed at home."

Relief surged through him and he let out a huge sigh.

"How long have I been asleep?"

"It's half past seven in the morning, Oz. They weren't sure if you were concussed or if it was just the aftereffects of that thing Perkins used."

Being reminded of the baton and its power sent a sudden shiver dancing up and down his spine. He put the beaker to his lips again and drank greedily, though he couldn't stop the rim from chattering against his teeth. Tepid water from a plastic jug had never, ever tasted so sweet and good.

"It was a stun gun," he said, holding out the beaker for more water. "And his name isn't Perkins, Mum. It's Rollins."

"I know." Mrs. Chambers nodded. "He told the police he couldn't remember who he was, but they have him on file."

Oz noted that her eyes were dark-rimmed and puffy from lack of sleep.

"Did they have it on file that he works for Gerber, too?"

Mrs. Chambers shook her head. "Used to, Oz. He used to work for one of Mr. Gerber's research divisions, but he was sacked six months ago."

"But he was working for Gerber, Mum. He spent all that time with us spying, trying to find out Penwurt's secrets…"

"Now, Oz. You've been through a terrible ordeal. The police are still not sure what Rollins' motives were. There's all sorts of equipment in what's left of the orphanage basement…"

Oz frowned. "What do you mean, what's left?"

"There was quite a bit of fire damage. The orphanage is off-limits until the structural engineers can assess things."

Oz stared at his mother, trying to take in this new information, and the way she'd carefully ignored what he'd said about the artefacts.

"Mum, did Ellie and Ruff tell you what happened? Did they tell you about Lucy Bishop breaking Dad's clock and stealing the artefacts?"

The words made Mrs. Chambers flinch, as if she'd suddenly heard a jarring noise. But she composed her face into a reassuring smile.

"Poor Lucy. She's clearly deranged. They've taken her to a secure unit. She kept on and on about her brother, and her needing to feed him. He was living rough in the park, apparently. They picked him up, too." Mrs. Chambers shook her head sadly. "Mental illness, it's such an awful thing when it happens to someone close to you. Enough to send anyone off the rails, I suppose; we both know that, don't we?" She held his gaze and he nodded slowly.

"I'm not denying that she did break the clock and steal those items you mention, but you see how dangerous all this nonsense is? There's always someone vulnerable out there, willing to believe any old superstitious clap-trap. You should know that better than most, Oz."

Oz knew what she meant, all right, but she was wrong and he couldn't just let this go. "But it isn't clap-trap, Mum! Something happened in the basement; something helped me."

Mrs. Chambers sat down, took Oz's hand in hers and regarded him wearing her most serious face. "The police think that perhaps Lucy Bishop and Rollins were working together. That perhaps they were members of some kind of sect. I'm really sorry for what they did to you. I should have been more vigilant…"

"Mum, none of this is your fault, and Rollins and Lucy Bishop weren't working together…" He faltered as another bit of the jigsaw fell into place. He remembered what he'd heard as he'd stood hiding in the garage watching Heeps and Gerber discussing Penwurt. "Gerber knew Tim was Rollins, Mum. I heard him say his name."

Mrs. Chambers looked suddenly stern. "Oz, you can't go around saying things about Mr. Gerber like that. He's a powerful man, and there's such a thing as slander."

A sudden pang of panic grabbed him. "You didn't sign anything, did you? You didn't sell the place to them?"

A funny little knowing look came over Mrs. Chambers' face. "We did talk about it, but then I said I'd promised you I wouldn't do anything without talking to you first about their very generous offer. Lorenzo still doesn't think I should, but…"

"Tell me you didn't sign anything, Mum," demanded Oz through clenched teeth.

"Calm down. I didn't sign anything, all right? They'd even brought papers, but I was adamant, and then I got the phone call about you and all hell broke loose. By the time I got home, the fire brigade were there and then the police came…" She looked down and gave Oz another wan smile and wiped away a strand of fringe from his forehead. "At least you're okay. And you know what? There is a silver lining. The fire in the basement has melted everything that was in there, so we can say goodbye to those…Morsman thingies once and for all."

Oz's gut plummeted through the floor. "What?" he whispered.

"Amazing, really. Turns out that the basement ceiling is nearly three feet thick. It protected the house above, but it acted like an oven. Everything inside has cooked. Will I miss those old patio chairs or the blue-spotted carpet, I wonder? I don't think so. The insurance will pay for the basement to be redone. So that should make selling the place a lot easier."

Oz knew that his mother was trying to cheer him up, but she was failing miserably. He didn't even protest at her heavy hint about the house being sold, because all he could think about was that the pebble and the dor were gone. Cooked to a carbon crisp in the basement. He flopped back on his pillow, turning his face away so she couldn't see his despair, mind whirling with this new information.

"Oh, Oz," said Mrs. Chambers, misinterpreting the flop as a relapse. "The police are going to want to talk to you at some stage, but not while you're unwell like this. How's your head?"

"Fine," he said, keeping his face to the wall. "But maybe I should go back to sleep. I'm feeling a bit tired."

"Of course, darling." She went and sat in a chair by the window and picked up a book.

Oz closed his eyes. He didn't feel sleepy, but he didn't want to talk anymore. A huge black bubble of bitter disappointment was expanding inside him, threatening to burst at any moment.

The artefacts were gone.

He should have been rejoicing at the fact that he and Ruff and Ellie had survived. But all that was going through his mind were Rollins' words: '*Imagine you're a caveman finding a mobile phone. Press enough buttons and it'll make an entertaining noise, but you'd still have no idea of its true capability.'*

Penwurt was full of secrets. Secrets that Gerber wanted. Oz knew that for certain, now. But what chance did he have of discovering them without the artefacts?

At ten, some doctors came and examined him. They gently pressed the lump on his head and said he'd need the stitches out in a few days. Then they told him that the scan he'd had while he was unconscious showed no damage and, once they'd had a couple of blood tests back, he could go home.

"That's fantastic news," Mrs. Chambers said, beaming. "Right. I'm going to get a coffee and freshen up. I'll be twenty minutes. Will you be okay here?"

"I'll be fine, Mum."

He knew he was being desperately unfair to her, but the truth was that Oz was quite glad to be left alone. He just wanted to wallow in his misery for a while, even though common sense told him it would do no good. The artefacts were gone and there was nothing he could do about it. He was even beginning to wonder if he'd imagined the girl in the basement. After all, he'd had a severe knock on the head and… He looked up. The door had opened a crack and a head appeared, followed quickly by a second, virtually identical one. Two voices whispered, "Are you alone?"

"Savannah? Sydney?" said Oz, sitting bolt upright. "What are you doing here?"

The Fanshaw twins hurried over to Oz's bedside. "We caught the bus in," Savannah said.

"But how did you know I was here?"

"You mean, apart from Magnus Street being full of fire engines and ambulances half the night?" Sydney said.

"Ah," Oz said.

"It was your text message, silly," Savannah explained.

"What text message?" Oz frowned.

"The one you sent us last night. The one that said the basement was on fire and that you needed help—"

"It was us that pulled you out—"

"Although we're not surprised you don't remember anything—"

"You were out cold."

Oz stared at them, knowing his mouth was open but unable to close it.

Sydney took out her phone and showed Oz the message.

Penwurt basement on fire. Need help.

"I don't even remember sending a text," Oz said, frowning.

"Who else could it have been?" Savannah asked.

"Though we admit there's no sender number—" Sydney noted.

"We thought maybe you'd blocked that on your phone," Savannah said.

"I don't think it was me," Oz said.

Sydney gave a dismissive snort. "Then who was it?"

As quickly as possible, Oz told them all about what had happened, from finding the hidden passages and fighting Lucy Bishop, right up until the time the grey-eyed girl had appeared and Rollins had stunned himself into unconsciousness. Being S and S, they accepted it all without question and were only too keen to fill him in on what had happened after that.

"We could see the fire through the telescope—"

"So we sent for the fire brigade—"

"We got you out just as they arrived—"

"There was an awful lot of smoke."

They grinned at him.

"Thanks," Oz said with feeling. "Lucky you were in, otherwise…"

The strange thing was, he didn't feel particularly lucky. Not with the artefacts gone. But it would have been churlish to tell S and S that. After all, they'd just saved his life.

"I sort of owe you both an explanation." He hesitated and then asked, "Did you know that some people think my dad killed himself?"

They shook their heads solemnly, four identical big eyes watching him intently.

Oz nodded, satisfied that they, too, were ignorant. "This is a long, long story and I will tell you all of it when I know the truth. Trouble is, I'm not sure I ever will, now," he added thickly.

"Why won't you ever find out?" Savannah cocked her head.

"Because…" Oz said, fighting back the tears of frustration that threatened, "I wanted to show my mum that Penwurt is special. Show her that my dad was convinced of it and that for him, finding the artefacts would have been like winning the lottery. He would never have wanted to do any harm to himself. He'd have been too excited. And now, with the artefacts gone, there's no chance of anything…"

The twins studied him with a slightly puzzled look.

Oz could only shake his head hopelessly. "Mum said the basement was like an oven. That everything got cooked. Now the pebble and the dor are just black blobs of charred…whatever." It came out as a half-sob. Oz let his head fall and wiped the moisture from his eyes on his pyjama sleeve.

S and S exchanged glances, their eyes large and solemn. Savannah reached into her shoulder bag and pulled out something wrapped in a paper handkerchief. Sydney slowly peeled back the dirty paper to reveal something solid nestling there, something dark and soot-encrusted. She wiped it in the tissue and held it out to Oz.

"Is this what you mean?" they said in unison.

Oz looked down. In Sydney's hand was a black oval pebble with a small bump on its surface that looked very much like the back of a scarab beetle.

Chapter 16

Achmed's

S and S had long gone by the time Mrs. Chambers got back, but Oz was having difficulty hiding his change of mood and the fact that the artefacts were now under his pillow.

"My, you are feeling better, aren't you? What was in that water, I wonder?"

Oz shrugged. "Just looking forward to getting out of here. Did you bring me any clothes, Mum? I don't want to go home in my pyjamas."

"I did, indeed. Clean jeans, T-shirt and a hoody. Standard Oz uniform."

"So, can I change now?"

Mrs. Chambers took the hint and made herself scarce, while Oz changed and quickly tucked the fused pebble and dor into a zipped inside pocket of his sweatshirt. All his blood tests turned out to be normal, and by eleven-thirty Oz and his mother were on their way home.

As they drove through a damp December Seabourne, he borrowed her phone to text Ellie and Ruff and, plucking up as much courage as he could muster, asked, "Mum, can Ellie and Ruff come over later?"

His mother's expression was not encouraging. "I'm not sure that's such a great idea, Oz."

"But we've got loads to talk about. And they'll definitely want to make sure I'm okay," he pleaded, and then added hurriedly, "Not to stay the night or anything."

Mrs. Chambers sighed. "Okay, but it's early to bed for you tonight, with no arguments."

Oz grinned and began texting furiously again.

Penwurt looked none the worse for wear from the front, but an acrid stench hung in the air wherever they went. Oz and his mother took a stroll around the side of the house to inspect the damage. What was left of the basement's charred contents had been dumped outside in a soggy black mess. All the doors to the orphanage were open to let the air in, and the ground level windows had all been blown out. Streaks of black soot smeared the walls and windowsills like blood from a wound.

Seeing it sent a shudder through Oz and he didn't linger; too many what-might-have-been thoughts crowded in. Instead, he went to the warm kitchen, made tea and toast with extra jam and took them up to the library. The panel door was closed and, using Essence, Alum, Soap, and Tin, he opened it up again just to see if it still worked. It did. Inside, the passageway was dark and uninviting and the acrid aroma drifting up from below seemed even stronger, so he suppressed a shiver and shut the panel again quickly. He spent a pleasant hour or two decorating the library with old-school paper chains and cardboard snowmen he'd found in a cupboard, as well as a miniature, nine-inch high, silver tinsel Christmas tree, complete with a glowing star at its apex.

Ellie and Ruff arrived mid-afternoon, but Oz didn't go down to meet them. Instead, he asked Mrs. Chambers to send them straight up to his room and threw himself into bed, feigning sleep. Through a millimetre slit of barely open lids, Oz watched as they tiptoed into his bedroom. He saw them exchange shocked, worried glances, and then he sat bolt upright and yelled "Surprise!" They were so startled that Ellie actually screamed.

"You total armpit, Oz," she said, clutching her hand to her chest. "We were really worried about you."

"And so you should be, letting yourselves be tricked by Rollins like that," Oz tutted behind a wide grin. He was well pleased with his surprise.

"The git tricked you, too, mate," Ruff said.

"You are such a gonk," Ellie said, still not having quite recovered from Oz's prank. She threw a pillow at his head for good measure, but laughed and shook her head as she did so. Oz jumped out of bed, opened the drawn curtains to let in what little afternoon light there was and saw that huge, charcoal-coloured storm clouds were gathering in the west.

Oz looked at his friends and smiled. But the smile he got in return looked a touch forced and uncertain. A little bubble of awkward silence grew as Ellie and Ruff just stood there, looking oddly uncomfortable and glancing at one another.

"What's up with you two?" Oz asked when he could stand it no longer.

Ellie let out a tremulous sigh. "We've been talking and…"

"We just wanted to say sorry," Ruff blurted out.

"Sorry?" Oz stared at them. "Why?"

"Because…" Ellie faltered. "Because if I hadn't just blundered into the passages like I did, or made Lucy Bishop go ape 'cos I kicked her brother when all you were trying to do was make friends with him, maybe none of this would have happened."

"And if I hadn't been so buzzardly convinced that there was treasure to find so that I could get rich," Ruff said, "I wouldn't have been so keen to solve the symbols and…"

"Ruff's right. I am like a cow in a crystal maze," Ellie added miserably. "Oh, Oz, if you'd been hurt or...or..." She trailed off, her lip trembling.

"And I swear, I'm going to give up the Xbox after this," Ruff said, his face pink. "Dad says it's filling my head with so much weirdness that I can't tell what's real and—"

"You're right," Oz said softly, interrupting Ruff. "If it hadn't been for the two of you, I wouldn't have ended up in hospital. But if it hadn't been for you, Ellie, Lucy Bishop would have brained me with a hammer. You saved my life in that room. And if it hadn't been for you, Ruff, we'd never have solved the puzzle, treasure or no treasure, because I know I didn't have a clue. We're in this together. We're a team, aren't we? That's what's important. That's all there is to it."

They were quiet, and for a while all Ellie and Ruff did was study their shoes.

"Think it'll snow?" Ellie asked eventually as she glanced out of the window and dabbed at her eyes.

"Too warm," Oz said.

"Anyway, who cares?" added Ruff. "If Oz doesn't tell us what went on in that basement soon, I'm going to explode. Before you do, though, I don't know if it's just me, but is anyone else starving?"

Ellie made eyes to the ceiling, but they went down to the kitchen anyway, because Ellie's mum had made mini pizzas and a cake in celebration of them all having come through their ordeal relatively unscathed, and Mrs. Chambers had laid them out on the table in readiness. She fussed over the three of them as usual, making sure they had enough of everything as they piled the food onto paper plates.

Oz had watched his mother carefully since they'd come back from the hospital. Perhaps it was just tiredness on her part, but he couldn't help noticing that her hands trembled as she handed out the cutlery, and her smile seemed a little forced. He glanced at the calendar and felt a tiny shiver of relief pass through him. The black dog was completely hidden. But it had been a hard couple of days for his mother as well, he told himself. Maybe what he was seeing was simply a bit of nervous reaction.

Mrs. Chambers issued strict orders that the orphanage was off-limits, but that was an unnecessary warning. None of them wanted to go back there yet. Instead, they took the food and sat in the library's comfy chairs.

"Festive," Ruff said on seeing the Christmassy effort Oz had made.

"Brilliant," Ellie agreed.

They munched pizza and listened in awe as Oz gave them a blow-by-blow account of what happened. When he got to the bit where S and S had revealed the pebble and the dor and produced them with a "ta-da" flourish, even Ruff stopped chewing to gawp in disbelief. Ellie ran her finger over the slight protuberance the dor made in the pebble's smooth surface and shook her head. "I would never have said it fitted there."

"And you say that Rollins was trying to pump it full of electricity?" Ruff asked, his brows knitting.

"That's what it looked like to me," Oz said.

As if on cue, the first distant boom of thunder rolled out over the sky to the west and a few spots of rain spattered against the turret panes.

"So, how did you two get out of that room?" Oz asked finally, feeling like he'd been the only one talking for what seemed like hours.

"Firemen," Ruff said. "But they smashed down the real door, not the secret passage one."

"I expect they'll all be boarded up now," Ellie said wistfully.

"You reckon?" Oz smiled. "All the more reason to explore them again, then, once they repair the basement."

"Buzzard," Ruff said, grinning. "Chuck us a slice of cake, Ellie."

Ellie sighed and handed him another slice. "I don't know why, but I feel really sorry for Lucy Bishop."

"Yeah, know what you mean," Ruff said through chipmunk cheeks. "I generally feel sorry for loonies that come after me with hammers, all the while screaming blue murder."

"Shut up, Ruff. And don't speak with your mouth full, it's disgusting. All I'm saying is that it must be awful knowing your brother has been turned into some sort of a…"

"Polecat. Rollins confirmed it." Oz nodded. "My guess is that Gerber's used fifth artefact technology to find a way of capturing what it's like to be an animal…" He let his words trail off before adding quietly, "Rollins really enjoyed telling me that being a cheetah going in for the kill was the best experience he'd ever had."

"Ugh," Ellie said, making a face.

"Do you think that's what's happened to Gerber's driver?" Ruff asked. "You know, the one you said looked really weird?"

Oz remembered the sight of the chauffeur beginning to unfurl himself from the front seat of the Rolls Royce and let his voice drop to a whisper. "Maybe. I mean, if Edward Bishop thought he was a polecat, why not turn someone into a snake or—"

"A vampire bat," Ruff said, his eyes suddenly very large.

No one said anything for almost a minute. It was Oz who finally spoke.

"When I was in the hospital, all I could think about was Gerber. Let's say he's covered his tracks with fake birth certificates and stuff, and that he's really as old as we think he is. I've seen him up close, remember, and whatever's happened to make him live this long hasn't stopped the ageing process completely, it's just slowed it all down. Just one look at him tells you that."

"So, maybe being close to the artefacts affects the way time passes?" Ellie said.

Ruff was nodding. Drawing on his vast Xbox experience, he said, "In *Reanimator 12*, there are these time bubbles…"

"Ru-uff," Ellie said crossly.

"No, listen," Ruff argued. "All I'm saying is that maybe the artefacts bring a bit of wherever they're from with them. And maybe it rubs off, like…like a sort of dimensional bubble which lets you use up someone else's time and not your own. That's what happens in—"

"*Reanimator 12.* Yeah, we got that bit," Ellie said, but although her words still dripped with sarcasm, she was looking at Oz a lot more pensively now.

"However it works, I bet Gerber's desperate to find a way to make it permanent," Oz said. "That's why he wants the other artefacts so badly."

"And since the artefacts are tied up with Bunthorpe and Penwurt, that's why he wants this place, too," Ellie whispered.

There was another roll of thunder, at which Ruff snapped his head up towards the window. The storm was coming nearer. Rain started hammering on the panes with such ferocity they had to shout to be heard.

"Let's go down and play some Xbox. It's too noisy up here," Ruff suggested.

"Thought you were giving it up," Ellie said, and earned a withering glance in reply.

"First I need to hide this." Oz took out the pebble and the dor and looked around for an appropriate spot.

"Could try the passage," Ruff suggested.

"No," said Ellie. "I know just the place." She fetched the ladder, climbed up the bookcase and took down a heavy, black, leather-bound tome. Inside, a space had been cut out of the pages in the shape of a hip flask.

Oz laughed. "When did you find this?"

"First time we looked for Morsman stuff."

"It's perfect," Oz said. He slipped the artefacts in and read the spine. "*The Victorian Gentleman's Guide to Herbalism*. Don't think we'll forget that one very easily."

In his bedroom, while Ellie and Ruff played Xbox, Oz fired up his laptop and Skyped S and S.

"Just wanted to thank you properly for everything," he said when their faces appeared on the screen.

"We're glad you're home," said S and S together.

Ellie shot Oz a look full of wary incredulousness and, off-camera, mouthed, "Are they for real?"

Ruff groaned as a bear-droid from Pluton 6 imploded on the Xbox screen. "I wish I could get past this Octo-decimator. He gets me every time," he said through gritted teeth.

"Is your friend playing *Death Planet Hub*?" Savannah asked.

"Playing and losing," laughed Oz.

"We know how to beat the Octo-decimator," Sydney said.

"What?" said Ruff, coming around to join Oz in front of his laptop. Half a minute later, Oz looked on, bemused, as Ruff perched the laptop so that the camera was on the Xbox screen and proceeded to take a master class in *Death Planet Hub* from S and S.

"I think I've seen it all now," Ellie muttered, shaking her head in amusement.

The storm was gathering strength with the onset of darkness. Through the window, Oz saw a car's lights pull up on the street outside. A figure huddled inside a coat got out and hurried in through the gate.

"Where are you going?" Ellie asked as Oz rushed out.

"Said I'd meet Caleb in the tenants' kitchen," he said, and didn't stop to explain.

Caleb was sitting at the table when Oz got there, his coat hanging on the chair next to him, a small pool of rain beneath it. His face was unreadable, but his eyes were full of troubled wariness. He didn't get up.

"Oz, I am so sorry for what happened."

"Mum said that, too," Oz said. "Though I can't see how it's your fault or hers."

"I should have known Lucy was heading for trouble. And as for Rollins…" Caleb rubbed the back of his neck in despair. He kept his gaze on the table as he spoke. "I think I owe you a bit of an explanation."

"Yeah, so do I," Oz said.

It earned him a glance from Caleb, but no immediate words.

"Mum thinks Rollins and Lucy Bishop were working together. They weren't, were they?"

Caleb shook his head. "Rollins managed to slip under everyone's radar. But he did know Edward Bishop. He was part of the same research team. He lost his job in disgrace after the experiments, and was trying to get back into Gerber's good books by finding the artefacts."

"So he was working for Gerber."

"Indirectly." Caleb nodded. "But there'll be no proof."

"Lucy Bishop tried to smash the artefacts when we found her. She blames me for what happened to her brother. Why did she do that?"

"There are things about Gerber that not many people know or would understand," Caleb said, looking suddenly awkward.

"Do you mean the fact that he has a fifth artefact and has been experimenting with it ever since he found it or stole it from the Shoesmiths in 1914?"

For the first time that Oz could ever remember, Caleb's mouth fell open in dumbstruck wonder.

"How...?"

"Me, Ellie and Ruff, we make a very good team," Oz said, and allowed himself a small grin at Caleb's surprise.

"So, you know that one of his so-called experiments made Edward Bishop very ill. Lucy was supposed to be protecting you. But in truth, she was trying to find the artefacts to see if they could help her brother. I didn't know he was in the park all this time."

"Is that why she followed us when we went to Garret and Eldred's?"

"She was actually making sure that Gerber's men weren't following you. Unfortunately, it was all proving too much for her. Like her brother, she is very clever, but she's also what some people like to call highly-strung. She must have snapped and stolen the artefacts to try and use them herself. She failed and then turned on them."

"And on me. Lucky Ellie's a blue belt in taekwando."

Caleb said nothing.

"Rollins said something about Lucy. He said she was Obex. Was she?"

Caleb sighed and looked out of the window. He seemed to be weighing things up in his mind. Finally, he turned back and said, "Obex is a society sworn to keep the artefacts from getting into the wrong hands."

"Puffers' hands?"

Caleb let out a mirthless laugh. "You lot ought to work for MI5. Yes, Puffers. Greedy, meddling, ignorant people, like Gerber, who think that the artefacts have been sent for their benefit."

"What do you mean, sent?"

Caleb's eyes held Oz's gaze now. "Some people think that the artefacts aren't from here, Oz. I mean, the here that we live in every second of every day. Some people think that they're from somewhere else."

It was suddenly very quiet in the kitchen as the storm abated momentarily. Oz looked up at the window. The night was impenetrable beyond it.

"You mean, like another planet?" he whispered.

Caleb shrugged. "Planet, existence, universe, who knows? Somewhere different, definitely. But some of us think they're here for a reason. And that reason is not to turn people like Edward Bishop into feral lunatics."

Oz was remembering snatches of conversation between Caleb and Lucy Bishop, and suddenly he looked at his father's friend as if seeing him for the first time.

"You're Obex, too, aren't you?"

"Yes, I am, Oz. And so was my father, and his father, too. We took an oath. As I told you before, our prime concern is for the artefacts. Sometimes that makes our choices… difficult."

Oz didn't quite understand what Caleb meant by that, but he wanted to know more. "Did my dad know?"

"Yes, he did. And I made him some promises."

"What sort of promises?"

"Amongst others, that if the artefacts found their way to you, I'd help protect you." Caleb's eyes fell away. "And I failed in that promise."

But Oz was intrigued. "What do you mean, found their way?"

"Exactly that. It's one of their abiding mysteries. They choose people. Morsman. Your dad. You. None of this is an accident."

"The Puffers, do they know all this?"

"They do."

Oz shivered, but then looked down and shook his head. "You're going to have to explain all this to Mum. Make her listen. She doesn't believe anything I tell her. I know she doesn't want to believe you, either, but something happened in that basement. Something I can't explain yet. But Mum wants to leave here, and I can't, not now."

Caleb shook his head. "Oz, I…"

"You have to," Oz pleaded. "I know this stuff isn't good for her. I can see what it's doing to her already, and I don't want her to be like she was before, but we owe it to Dad to stay here and find out what all this means." There was a long moment of loaded silence in which Oz did not let his gaze fall away from Caleb's face. Finally, Caleb nodded.

"Okay, I'll try," he said. "But I'm not hopeful."

Relieved, Oz led the way up to the second floor and across to the spiral staircase that took them back down to the main kitchen. Mrs. Chambers sat at the table, an empty glass in front of her and a bottle of unopened malt whiskey next to it. She looked up, defiant, as Oz entered.

"Well, if your dad could do it…" she said with a shaky, unconvincing smile.

"Mum?" Oz said in a panicky voice, but then Caleb entered the room behind him.

"What do you want?" she said, her mouth suddenly ugly.

Caleb looked first at the glass and then at Mrs. Chambers. "Gwen, we need to talk."

"After what's just happened here?" Mrs. Chambers demanded.

"*Especially* after what has just happened here."

"What is there to talk about? Rollins is in custody, Lucy Bishop is in hospital. Penwurt is still standing." She raised her glass in mock salute.

Caleb was shaking his head. "This is just the beginning. The Puffers…"

"Puffers? That's another one, is it? Another of those stupid, silly little words like 'artefact' and 'Obex?'"

"If you'd let me explain…"

But Mrs. Chambers was shaking her head. "I don't want to let you explain. Michael was always trying to explain, and look where it got him!" Anger flared and she thumped the empty glass back down onto the table.

"Mum…" Oz started to say, but she silenced him with a look.

"Stop it. I won't have any of this superstitious claptrap in my house. I won't stand for it."

She pushed herself away from the table and walked to the fridge. "You want to know how I'm really feeling, Oz?" She turned to the calendar and ripped it away from the magnets to reveal Oz's childishly ugly drawing in all its glory underneath.

Oz felt all the blood drain from his face.

"There! That's how I'm feeling, okay? The black dog is well and truly out of its kennel. And having him here spouting his rubbish"—she pointed at Caleb—"makes it ten times worse. Can't you see, Oz? It's poison. All of it is pure poison. How many more people are going to get hurt because of some ridiculous made-up nonsense?" Her face suddenly hardened. "Well, I know one thing, it isn't going to be me or mine anymore. As soon as the insurance money is settled for the fire, that's it. I've made up my mind. We're off." She turned her burning eyes on Caleb. "Then you and your Puffers can have this place and everything that's…"

There was a sudden blinding flash of light followed by a clap of thunder that shook the crockery and sent at least one pan crashing to the kitchen floor. The house was plunged into darkness. From somewhere upstairs there was a strange thudding sound. Oz felt his way to the mudroom and groped around for a torch.

"Have we just been hit by lightning?" Oz asked when he got back to the kitchen, pointing the beam first at his mother and then at Caleb.

"I think so. But the turret roof has a conductor," Caleb added in reassuring tones.

"Great," said Mrs. Chambers in a voice that dripped acid, "even the weather has it in for me." She took the torch from Oz and found some candles, which she quickly lit and placed into saucers dotted around the kitchen.

But Caleb wasn't going to let things lie. "Gwen, hasn't what has happened here opened your eyes? There's danger lurking. A real danger that won't go away, even if you move."

"Grow up!" yelled Mrs. Chambers, rounding on him, and in the candlelit room her face looked monstrous, deformed by her anger.

"Oz?" Ruff's voice called to him from upstairs.

Oz took the torch and ran up the stairs. The bedroom was empty when he got there, so he doubled back and went straight to the library. Ellie and Ruff surveyed the room, using their phones as torches to illuminate a floor covered with books.

"Nothing broken," Ellie said. "We just heard this tremendous crash. Must have blown all the books off the shelves."

"Almost blew out the Xbox, too," Ruff said with real concern.

"What's that smell?" Oz asked,

"Ozone," Ruff said. "Lightning makes that."

"Some of these books are still steaming," Ellie said, picking up one that looked more than a bit charred.

"It's hot inside a lightning bolt," Ruff said.

"You don't say," Ellie replied tartly.

After a heavy and awkward little pause, Ruff asked, "Is everything all right with your mum, Oz? We heard shouting…"

"No, it's about as *not* all right as it could be," Oz said, feeling his face burn at the memory of his mother with the whiskey. But then he remembered about the pebble and the dor. "What about *The Victorian Gentleman's Guide to Herbalism*? Have you checked it?"

"Got it. Yeah, all okay." Oz watched as Ellie opened the book and took out the pebble. "Ow, it's really hot. And look, it's glowing." She ran her thumb over the lit-up maker's mark and handed it to Ruff, who did the same.

"Must have had the full force of the strike," Ruff said.

Oz took it from him. It felt like a baked potato in his hand, and the maker's mark was glowing bright yellow, much brighter than he'd ever seen it before. Without really thinking, Oz put his thumb over it. He sensed the change at once. It was like flicking on a switch inside his head. He'd felt it before, in the basement last night, only this time there were no wavy lines or flickering images, just the feeling of a door opening and of something dropping into place. He realised suddenly that it was much lighter in the room than a moment ago.

Oz heard Ellie gasp, quickly followed by a shaky "Wow," from Ruff. Oz spun around and saw what had caused Ruff's surprise. In the centre of the room stood a girl with coffee-coloured skin, short dark hair and grey eyes. She wore a short-sleeved orange tunic and seemed to glow from within, like a TV set.

"Welcome, Oscar Chambers."

Oz couldn't speak. He'd seen the face and heard the voice before, in his head, but this was… He glanced at Ellie and Ruff and stammered, "Ca…can you see her, too?"

Ellie nodded. Ruff swallowed loudly and said tremulously, "Is it a genie?"

The girl turned to Ruff. "I am a Siliconano Osaka-Protocol Holoquantum five fifty point…" Her voice petered out and she looked momentarily confused. "Apologies. Memcore analysis reveals permanent damage has been sustained to manufacturer attribution comms."

Oz had no idea what she was talking about, but he couldn't help noticing that she shimmered slightly and seemed to hover a good two inches off the floor. She was older than them by perhaps four or five years. Her accent was slightly odd, but Oz couldn't put his finger on why.

"Who are you?" Oz asked.

"I am a Siliconano Osaka-Protocol Holoquantum—"

"Soph," Ellie said brightly. "S.O.P.H, Soph. As in Sophie."

Ruff's face cumpled in cringing alarm. He put a hand up to his mouth and whispered to Ellie, "Soph? Are you mad? She's some sort of alien spirit, not a piece of furniture."

"I have no objection to that name," said Soph.

"Do you have anything to do with the pebble?" Ellie asked, throwing Ruff a triumphant grin.

Oz felt a faint tickle in his head, and then the girl said, "You are referring to the base unit, Ellie Messenger. Yes, I am the base unit's avatar."

"How do you know my name?" Ellie said, startled.

"I have accessed your preferred epithet through Oscar's database."

"Ask her to speak English," Ruff hissed.

"I know what she means," Oz said in a whisper. "She's getting your names from me. I can feel her inside my head."

Ruff stared at him as if he'd suddenly turned bright purple.

"So, let's get this straight. You are the pebble? You are the artefact?" Ellie went on.

Oz felt another tickle. "If by artefact and pebble, you are referring to the base unit, then the answer is yes."

"I've seen you before," Oz said, "in my head."

The girl inclined her head. "Limited power has not allowed full manifestation up until this point. The base unit is damaged and the main memsource and cognitive linkage devices are disconnected."

"Does she mean the other two artefacts?" Ruff whispered. "The pendant and the ring?"

This time she answered Ruff directly. "I do, Ruff."

Ruff staggered back against the wall. "Whoa, she knows who I am, too," he quavered.

"The lightning," Oz said. "Of course. It switched the pebble on, somehow."

"Correct," said Soph. "My severely depleted power source has been charged through a recent antimatter positron emission." She tilted her head and smiled. "Otherwise known as lightning."

"Then how come the mark glowed before, if you were so low on power?" Oz asked.

"The base unit is designed to absorb many forms of energy—radio waves, light, heat. Enough to allow hibernating functions such as REM sleep linkage."

"REM sleep linkage?" Ellie asked.

"Does that mean helping me with revision? Maths, for example?" Oz already knew the answer, because somehow it was already inside his head. But he also knew that Ellie and Ruff needed to hear it.

Soph nodded. "A modular sublimsert was all that was required. You were already in possession of the knowledge; a modification of your perception output was all that was necessary."

Ruff was still wide-eyed. He mouthed "SUBLIMSERT?" fearfully to Oz.

Soph answered before Oz could ask. "It is simply a synaptic rerouting and reinforcement programme which runs without the need for consciousness."

"So, in other words, you read my mind while I was asleep, knew what I was struggling with and then pimped my brain for maths?" Oz asked.

"Yes," Soph said, "in other words."

"Told you she was a genie," Ruff whispered unhappily.

"Is it permanent?" Oz asked.

"Of course."

Oz was helpless to prevent a grin from spreading from one ear to the other.

"But where are you from?" Ruff asked, finally addressing Soph directly.

Soph tilted her head slightly and blinked. "That information remains with the memsource."

"I suppose it's no good asking why you're here, then, either, is it?" Ellie asked.

Soph blinked.

"But how come you didn't appear when Ellie or Ruff pressed the mark?" Oz demanded.

"The base unit has a genlock," Soph said. "Access is through a DNA key. You are the only one who matches."

Of all the things she'd said, that was the one that made Oz look for a chair and sit down heavily. "So Caleb is right. The artefacts do find their way to people."

"It has been two hundred and fifty-two years since the key was programmed," Soph said.

Oz's maths brain did the computation. "But the Bunthorpe Encounter was in 1761 and it's 2012 now. I make that two hundred and fifty one years ago."

"That is correct."

"So something happened in 1760," Ellie said.

Soph said nothing.

"Don't tell me. Memsource missing," Ruff said.

"It was you who put the images on Oz's laptop, too, wasn't it? The image of the dor and the cinder symbol?" Ellie said.

"That is correct," Soph said.

"But why?"

"A prime directive."

"So long as we know," Ruff said, looking increasingly perplexed.

"Oz's laptop gave off enough heat for me to absorb energy for single message transfer. The 'dor,' as you describe it, is the base unit power source. Its appearance was a device error message so that the user could rectify if so desired. The symbol, however, was programmed as a primary directive."

"Clear as mud," Ruff said, looking totally lost.

"She means that the dor is her battery. It was flagged up as an error message, just like an 'out of ink' message on a printer when you need to change the cartridge," Oz explained. "But the cinder symbol was something she had to deliver. The message we were meant to get."

Soph looked calmly at him but didn't elaborate.

Oz thought furiously. This was amazing, brain-boggling stuff. Everything everyone had ever said or believed about the artefacts was true, and he was hearing it from the mouth of a mysterious avatar who had no idea where she was from or why she was here. He realised what the Bunthorpe Encounter was all about. If Soph had shown herself to those bell ringers, they would have totally freaked out. As it was, Ruff looked like he was about to throw up. Oz felt himself tingling from head to foot. If only his dad could be here to see this. When he looked up, Soph was watching him intently.

"You are sad, Oz. Would you like to see Michael Chambers?"

The world suddenly tilted on its axis. It was a long moment before he said anything. Ellie and Ruff just stared.

"What did you say?" Oz whispered.

"Basic functions include holotrack recording. Would you like to see the day your father found me?"

Oz heard footsteps in the stairwell and his mother's still-angry voice calling to him.

"Oz, is everything all right up here?"

Rhys A. Jones

But he wasn't listening. He didn't even have to say it. In his mind, Oz thought one word. *Yes.*

He saw his mother and Caleb walk into the library, her face as dark and cold as the passages behind the library wall in the dim light from the candle she held before her. Caleb followed, looking unhappy and strained.

But then something so weird and so unexpected began to happen that Oz forgot the tension between Caleb and his mother. He forgot everything, because, in front of his eyes, the library melted away to reveal another place full of bright daylight. He could still see Ellie and Ruff and Caleb and his mother and the books on the floor, but this new place was all around him, like a film projected on the walls of the library, but in three dimensions.

Oz leaned back in his chair and instinctively shut his eyes before opening them again. The dim library had all but disappeared, but the other place hadn't. It was there as plain as day. He was in a tiny shop crammed full of strange items—jars of all colours and hookahs with elaborate silver stems, urns with sealed stoppers, dried flowers hanging from the ceiling in bunches. The noise of the clattering rain was replaced by the faint clamour of a market in full swing—someone shouting out wares in a strange language, the rattle of carts on hard, dry ground. Rich odours of roses and jasmine filled Oz's nose, and gold filigree danced in elaborate patterns around a door where the globe atlas should have been. An old-fashioned bell rang as a figure pushed the door open. Into the shop stepped a man of average height, with pale blue eyes and dark hair a tad too long for someone of his age.

Oz felt the breath catch in his throat as he watched the man wander in. The face that looked around the shop with unbridled interest was achingly familiar. Oz heard his mother gasp, but she didn't say anything. No one said anything. They were all completely mesmerised by what they were experiencing. It was simply impossible, unfathomable and incredible, yet it was also as if they were actually there, smelling, hearing and seeing this wonderfully exotic place, which looked to be a million miles from Seabourne.

Dr. Michael Chambers crossed the small space between the door and the counter, stopping to examine the ornate urns and bits of armour on display, until a man appeared from the rear of the shop. He was dressed in a brightly coloured striped robe that stretched to his feet, and on his head was a brown fez.

Dr. Chambers smiled. "Good afternoon." He held out his hand. "Michael Chambers. I believe you're expecting me."

The sound of his dad's voice, so clear, so unmistakable, made Oz grasp the arm of his chair as a surging tingle of excitement trilled up his spine. He saw his mother put her hand over her mouth, saw Caleb's incredulous expression, saw Ellie and Ruff gawping like idiots, and he knew that they were all seeing this miracle, too.

In the shop, the man in the long robe shook the offered hand and spoke in a heavy accent.

"Doctor Chambers, welcome to Achmed's. It is my great pleasure to meet you."

"What a fantastic place you have here. Was that a Phoenician Tanit amulet I saw on the way in?"

"It was. We have many things of interest here to a man of your scholarship."

"I can see that." Dr. Chambers looked about him in wonder.

"But that is not why you are here, I think."

Dr. Chambers' face rearranged itself into a wry smile. "No, it isn't. You received my email, I gather?"

"I did. I have been expecting you. As for the item in question, I have it here."

The shopkeeper turned and reached up to a shelf, from which he took a small wooden tray, upon which nestled the obsidian pebble.

Oz had a moment to wonder how it was they were seeing this, when the source of the image—or whatever it was they were experiencing—was surely the pebble itself. If there was a camera somewhere, why wasn't it in the pebble? But there was too much going on in the shop to make him dwell on this conundrum.

Dr. Chambers stared at the pebble and then looked up into the shopkeeper's face. "May I?" he whispered.

The shopkeeper smiled and shrugged. "Of course."

Dr. Chambers took the pebble and held it up to the light. "The craftsmanship, it's incredible. It's like nothing I have ever seen," he said in awe. "And you're sure it's for sale?"

"For sale?" The shopkeeper frowned. "Unfortunately no, it is not for sale."

Dr. Chambers' face clouded. "But I understood—"

The shopkeeper held up his hand. "Doctor Chambers, may I ask that you do one small thing?"

"What?"

"On the underside there is a symbol. See…here…the maker's mark. Please, let your thumb rest on the symbol."

Michael Chambers did as he was asked. "Like this? It feels…goodness…" The symbol glowed a faint yellow beneath his thumb. "Is that supposed to happen?"

The shopkeeper fixed Dr. Chambers with a wide-eyed stare. "It is supposed to happen, but it has never happened in my lifetime."

"What does that mean?"

"It means," said the shopkeeper with a fierce conviction, "that though the pebble is not for sale, it is yours by right."

Dr. Chambers looked up, shocked. "By right? But…"

Again, the shopkeeper held up his hand. "We both know what this really is. Achmed's has existed in this bazaar for centuries. We have sold many exotic and valuable artefacts. But this item…it is not ours to sell. We are merely its keepers. We have been watching over it until its owner claims it."

"Owner?"

"The last time the symbol lit up was almost eighty years ago. Another Englishman. Perhaps you know of whom I speak."

Dr. Chambers nodded. "Daniel Morsman?"

"My great-grandfather was very proud of the day Daniel Morsman came to the shop," the shopkeeper said softly. "Sadly, he was unable to make use of it, and so it was returned to us."

"Well, that is a bit of a coincidence, since I now live in Morsman's house. We were distantly related, you know."

"Here at Achmed's, we do not believe in coincidence. What is meant to be will be."

"Then perhaps the artefacts truly do belong at Penwurt," Dr. Chambers said, and then muttered, "At least, that's what my research is telling me." He hesitated, gathering his thoughts. "I have to ask—have there been other enquirers?"

"Some. But Puffers do not find any answers here." The shopkeeper kept smiling, but there was a grim determination in his eyes.

"Is it safe for me to leave with it? I have a flight out of Cairo tonight."

The shopkeeper tilted his head. "These are difficult times. Airport security might prove, how shall I put it, awkward? Should you wish to take it, I would recommend that we ship it for you. We have a very secure and discreet service, ways in which we can ensure its safe passage."

"I would feel a lot happier." Dr. Chambers took out a card and scribbled on it. "Send it here, and address it to Oscar Chambers."

"Oscar Chambers?" The shopkeeper frowned.

Dr. Chambers nodded. "My son, that well-known collector of historical bric-a-brac and would-be goalie." He let his voice drop to a conspiratorial whisper. "It'll attract even less attention that way."

The shopkeeper smiled and held up both hands. "Wait, wait just a moment." He disappeared behind a beaded curtain and came back with a framed photograph of three smiling children. "These are mine. Yafeu, Sekami, and Rehema."

"They look full of mischief," Dr. Chambers said, beaming. He reached into his wallet and took out a photo of the Chambers family. "My wife, Gwen, and Oz," he said, beaming still.

The shopkeeper smiled admiringly. "They are a credit to you, doctor. It must be difficult to be so far away from them."

"It is. I miss them terribly." Dr. Chambers' face suddenly glowed with warmth.

"Oscar, he has your eyes and his mother's smile."

"He knows how to smile." He grinned at the shopkeeper. "And so does his mother."

"Do they know what awaits them with the arrival of the artefact?" the shopkeeper asked keenly.

"No, not yet. Neither do I, really."

"My heart swells at knowing that you will continue the work." The shopkeeper's voice dropped to a low whisper. "Yet you are aware that, once it leaves here, the others will know, too."

"I'll be careful. You've seen my family. I've a lot to be careful for." Dr. Chambers' face broke into a wry smile. "Although I still haven't worked out how I'm going to explain all this to my wife."

"She does not believe?" asked the shopkeeper.

"Not yet." Dr. Chambers shook his head. "That's the next project."

The two men shook hands and Dr. Chambers turned to leave. He still had the photograph in his hand as he reached the door. He took out his wallet, and just as he was about to replace the photo he hesitated for a second, as if seeing something for the first time; then he smiled and put the snap to his lips and kissed it. The door to the shop opened and the bell rang again. And just as quickly as it had appeared, Achmed's faded into nothingness and they were back in the dimly lit library, the dense darkness pierced only by pools of light from torches held facing the ground.

Chapter 17

Soph

There was another low rumble of thunder, followed by five seconds of breathless silence, until Ellie finally voiced what they were all thinking.

"OH. MY. GOD!"

"Did you just see that…?" Ruff whispered in awe.

But Oz didn't reply. He couldn't find any words to speak. Something huge and warm had burst open inside him and a trembling mixture of grief and elation and wonder overwhelmed him. His father, the Michael Chambers he missed and loved so much, had, incredibly, unbelievably, just spoken from beyond the grave. Tears poured down Oz's cheeks, but he didn't care. Everything that he'd hoped for since he'd heard the ghostly footsteps all those weeks ago had just happened in front of his stunned eyes. He wiped them now, hardly able to contain the urge to climb onto the roof in the rain and shout to the world in triumph. But then he heard a sound in the darkness, a stifled sob followed by rapid footfalls as someone half-stumbled down the stairs. He got up and hurried after.

"Ruff, ask Soph if she can fix the lights," he said, voice wavering as he passed Ruff's silhouette. But no sooner had the words left his lips than the lights blazed on and he heard Ruff whisper, "Now that's really scary."

When Oz got to the landing, the door to his father's study stood ajar. Mrs. Chambers leaned heavily on the desk, peering at the larger, framed version of the photo they'd just seen his father take from his wallet in Achmed's. Oz pushed the door fully open and entered. His mother's face was tear-stained and stricken, her eyes full of pain and confusion.

"Mum," Oz said gently.

"Was that a ghost I just saw?" she whispered, her voice cracked and barely audible.

"Yeah. In a funny sort of way, I think that's exactly what it was."

Mrs. Chambers put her hand to her mouth. The gasp that emerged was tremulous.

"Mum," Oz said, "you've got to listen to me. What we just saw was all because of the artefacts. I kept them, Mum. Dad wanted me to have them. You saw that."

"But it was so real," whispered Mrs. Chambers. "When he kissed the photograph, I…I felt his lips…" Her fingers strayed slowly to her cheek. "It was so…incredibly real."

"You saw it, Mum. We all did. And you saw that Dad sent the pebble back to me for a reason, even if he didn't know what that reason was." Oz hesitated. What he was about to say to his mother was the most difficult thing he had ever said to anyone. "Maybe he sent it back to let us see the truth."

"What do you mean?" She turned from the photo to fix her tortured gaze upon him.

"That was my dad I just saw. The dad I remember. I don't care what anyone says, Mum, that man we just saw would never try to kill himself."

Oz saw the change in his mother's expression as she battled with the truth of it. The fresh agony and grief laid open by the holotrack seemed to be fighting with something else.

"I told them that he never drank anything," she said in another hollow whisper. "One glass of wine sent him to sleep. But there was the whisky bottle on the seat, and in his stomach—"

"Rollins told me that this house has secrets," Oz interrupted her, wanting desperately to ease her pain. "Penwurt and the artefacts and Dad, they're all tied together. And I'm part of it now, we all are. And the only way we're going to find out what those secrets are is if we stay here."

Mrs. Chambers studied Oz's face, her brow furrowed. "I miss him, Oz. So much. And you are so like him." She put out a hand and her shaking fingers touched his cheek. Oz reached up with his own hand and took hold of hers.

"Caleb knows about this stuff, Mum. You have to let him talk to you. You have to listen to what he has to say." Oz looked steadily into her face, willing her to believe him.

She didn't look away, but her eyes were clouded with doubt as she shook her head in bewilderment.

"I don't want the black dog to come out of its cage ever again, Mum," Oz said, and it took a huge effort for him to keep his voice steady. "Please?"

Mrs. Chambers choked back a sob, the fingers of her free hand coming up to somehow try to still the uncontrollable quivering of her lips, while the other squeezed Oz's hand so tightly it felt like his own fingers might break. She tried speaking, but had to swallow her words in convulsive gulps as fresh rivulets of silent tears ran down her mascara-striped face. But finally, she somehow managed to nod and whisper, "I do believe you, Oz. And yes, I will talk to Caleb."

Oz pulled her to him in a fierce hug, and it didn't matter that the study swam as his eyes blurred over again. It didn't matter one bit.

A few minutes later, he went in search of Caleb and eventually found him in the kitchen making tea.

"How is she?" Caleb asked without looking up.

"Having trouble letting what just happened sink in."

"We all are."

"But she wants to speak to you," Oz said.

"Me?" Caleb sounded unconvinced.

"I think she's ready to listen."

Caleb nodded and the ghost of a smile briefly brushed his lips. But as so often was the case with him, Oz sensed that the smile was tinged with bitter sadness. Caleb poured the tea, put down the teapot and motioned to a kitchen chair. "Sit down for a minute, Oz."

Caleb placed a steaming mug of sugary tea in front of Oz and then sat opposite him. It took a moment for his eyes to find Oz's waiting face, and when they eventually did, they seemed sunken and dark-rimmed from too many sleepless nights.

"The artefacts are a poisoned chalice, Oz," Caleb said quietly. "Bad things are coming, and Gerber will stop at nothing to get what he wants. But it doesn't have to be this way. If you like, I can make them disappear again. Hide them for another generation to…"

"No," Oz said firmly. "Soph needs our help. Someone needs to find out why she's here, and I think that it's meant to be me."

"For what it's worth, I think so, too. But it won't be easy." Caleb's words emerged low and full of foreboding.

"I sort of figured that out already. So, I'm probably going to need some help."

Caleb nodded. "Obex are sworn to protect the artefacts, whatever the cost, even if that means doing nothing when action is possible. But I'm beginning to believe that the cost of such devotion is sometimes too high."

He paused, and it was as if there was some inner battle raging behind his deep-set eyes. "I will help you, Oz, but you need to know that maybe I'm not quite the man you think I am."

His eyes slid away again and Oz thought he saw a sudden, haggard regret etched in the historian's exhausted face, as if the weight of a terrible burden pressed down on him.

"You're my dad's friend. Isn't that…" Oz began, but was silenced by Caleb's raised hand. When he looked up again, the regret had been replaced by something else. Something that Oz couldn't quite put a finger on immediately.

"Fate has dealt you a fickle hand, Oz. What happened to your dad was bad enough, but then having to cope with Heeps and his poisonous daughter, and now Rollins…" He shook his head. "I have to take my hat off to you."

"What do you mean?"

"I mean that the right way is not always the easiest. Many would have given up long before now. Left the pebble on that driveway under your window for a magpie to find, or just given in to Rollins. No one would have blamed you for any of that."

Oz blinked rapidly. He wanted to speak, but his tongue seemed welded to the roof of his mouth. But Caleb hadn't finished.

"You've chopped off the head of the Green Knight, Oz. But then, I think you and Sir Gawain have a lot in common. You don't do things the easy way either, do you?" This time the rare smile that crinkled the skin under Caleb's eyes was full-blown and warm. "Where all this leads is anyone's guess and I, for one, don't have a map, but if anyone can handle what's coming, I believe it's you. Oh, and you'd better warn Ruff and Ellie, too, because they're made of the kind of stuff that sticks like glue, whatever happens. Value that, Oz. It's worth more than any amount of money.

"But you know what's impressed me most?" Caleb continued. "It's the way you haven't given up on your dad. You believe in him. You've kept his memory pure in your heart, despite all the gibes and the so-called evidence of ignorant authorities who can only see what's in front of their noses and don't have the gumption to look beyond it. Frankly, I don't think Gerber stands a snowball's chance in hell against you. I'm proud of you, Oz. And I know your dad would have been, too."

Caleb held out his hand and, swallowing the lump that had for some unaccountable reason appeared in his throat, Oz took it.

* * *

While Caleb took tea up to his mother, Oz went back up to the library to find Ellie and Ruff picking up books.

"Where did Soph go?" he asked.

"Disappeared as soon as you left the room," Ruff said.

"Looks like she's only here when you are," Ellie said. "Nothing happens when we press the pebble."

Oz went to the artefact and put his thumb on the mark. Instantly, Soph appeared in the middle of the room.

"Welcome, Oz," she said pleasantly.

"That is so buzzardly awesome," Ruff said in wonder.

"We should ask her questions," Oz said.

"Could I have an Xbox cheat sublimsert thingy?" Ruff said immediately.

Oz and Ellie both made eyes to the ceiling.

"I may be able to help you with your computer games, Ruff," Soph said.

Ruff grinned maniacally and made a fist of triumph, while Oz just shook his head.

"When will you need charging again?" Ellie asked.

"I have sufficient power capacity for twenty years, at this point."

"So, are you a computer?" Oz asked. He could feel the faint tickle in his head again.

"I have computing functions, in that I can interface with technology easily. In addition, I have cognitive linking capability."

"Here we go again," Ruff said.

"That means you can read my mind, too?" Oz asked.

"The link is shared. You have access to my database, but I can also act on your thoughts if they are directed towards me."

"That's so cool," Ellie said, shaking her head. "Send me a text, Oz."

"What, now?"

"Ask Soph to do it. In your head, I mean."

Oz did exactly that. He imagined the message and thought about sending it to Ellie. Two seconds later, her phone beeped. She looked at it and shook her head. "That's, like, so freaky."

"Of course it is," Oz said. "That's because we don't understand it. It's some kind of technology, but so far out of our understanding that it's—"

"Almost like magic," Ellie said quietly.

No one spoke for several moments.

"But what about the hammer thing? Ask her why Lucy Bishop couldn't smash the pebble," Ruff said, the words tumbling over one another in his excitement.

Soph turned her large, calm eyes to Ruff, who immediately frowned. The look of mild terror on his face made Oz giggle.

"The base unit is protected by a tutamenzon field."

"Right," Ruff said, blinking rapidly.

"It extends to whoever holds the base unit," Soph explained. "I will be happy to demonstrate. If Ruff could pick up the unit."

Ruff did.

"And if you, Ellie, could throw something at him," Soph ordered.

"Really?" Ellie said, grinning wickedly and picking up the hefty *Victorian Gentleman's Guide to Herbalism*. "I've always wanted to throw the book at him."

"Hang on a minute," Ruff said. But Ellie needed no further invitation. She lobbed the book hard at Ruff, who was two yards away.

"Oy," he yelled, and ducked as it sailed towards his head. But when the missile was two feet from its target, it slowed to a halt as if the air itself had turned to treacle. It stopped a foot from Ruff's nose and slid gently down to the floor, as did the next book and the next, which Oz threw just for good measure. The look on Ruff's face was priceless.

They asked lots more questions and learned that Soph could 'tradurate' Oz's voice so that when he spoke in English the listener would hear what he said in any other language of his choosing, and vice versa. Then there was Mimtate, where his voice could sound like that of any person he had heard before. And, of course, there was Soph's Panvis holotrack function.

"But, I mean, how can you take a 3D video when the camera, if there is one, is in a tiny base unit the size of a pebble?" Ruff asked, clearly puzzled.

"Reflective omnivision," Soph explained. "Miniscule particles of light are constantly emitted from the base unit, and these are reflected off thousands of surfaces in the immediate environment. These are recaptured and processed constantly. Of course, this is happening at a photonic level while nanoprocessors record sound and olfactory sensation, as well."

Oz looked at Ruff, who was nodding as Soph spoke.

"Did you understand all that, then?" Oz asked.

"No," Ruff said, his eyes glittering, "but it sounds brilliant."

As a further illustration, Soph reran Ruff unnecessarily dodging the books inside the tutamenzon field. She had to show it at least twenty times because the look on Ruff's face was the funniest thing the other two had ever seen, and Ellie kept asking for replays. In the end, Oz had to crawl out of the library on all fours, making a noise like a very sick goat because his stomach ached so much he could neither stand up nor breathe. Too soon, it was time for Ellie and Ruff to go home and, since he was feeling pretty tired from all the excitement of the past two days, Oz didn't object too much.

"We are going to have so much fun with Soph from now on," Ellie said as she put on her coat.

"But we have to help her, too, though. Try and find the other artefacts. I get the feeling that she's a bit lost, somehow," Oz said, trying to stifle a yawn.

"She," Ruff said, "is like some sort of weird, telepathic computer. She can't feel lost."

"But there must be a really good reason why she's here, and we won't know why until we do find the other artefacts. I'm with Oz. We need to do what we can to help her," Ellie said and, as usual, Oz knew that she was right.

They were still in the library, still reliving what they'd been through and planning what to do next, when Mrs. Chambers finally called them down to the hall. There was a new vigour in her voice, a determination that hadn't been there for a long, long time.

"Caleb's going to stay until I get back from running Ellie and Ruff home," Mrs. Chambers said to Oz. She held his chin in her hands, and there was a fire back in her eyes.

"He's also going to try and find us some new lodgers, and he's moving back in tomorrow."

She turned to Ellie and Ruff. "And I think I owe the two of you an apology for banning you. I had no right to do that. Mind you, I think it was as effective as a chocolate teapot, thank goodness."

Oz threw on a coat and watched from the front door as Ellie and Ruff piled into Mrs. Chambers' old banger. The storm had passed over, and above them stars looked down through gaps in the scudding clouds.

"Hey, Oz, no school tomorrow. Fancy a kick about on People's Park after Ballista's?" Ellie called from the back seat.

"It'll be polecat-free," Ruff yelled.

"I'll be there," Oz said, grinning.

As the car pulled out into Magnus Street, Mr. Fanshaw, dressed in an overcoat, slippers and a woolly hat, was putting out the bins. He waved at Mrs. Chambers.

"Sorry to hear about the fire," he yelled above the wind. "Make it a bit more difficult to get rid of the old place, I should think."

"Oh, don't worry about that," Mrs. Chambers shouted back. "We're not going anywhere in a hurry."

"Really?" said Mr. Fanshaw. "But I thought…"

"Byeee," said Mrs. Chambers, and zoomed off, but not before she sent Oz a defiant grin and stuck her right hand out of the driver's side window with her thumb up.

Oz watched them go and then turned back inside. But before he shut the door, he turned once more to face the street, lifted his head, sniffed the air and smiled. In the kitchen, the calendar was back in its place on the fridge door, the black dog well and truly hidden. He pressed the maker's mark on the pebble and Soph appeared in front of him, regarding him with her intelligent grey eyes. He walked to the kitchen window and looked out into the deep blackness of the December night.

"Okay, Dad," he said quietly. "Ready when you are."

Acknowledgements

BRJ for his designs and photographs, CTJ for his interpretation, GMJ for his constructive criticism.

Also available as an ebook • **SPENCER HILL PRESS** • spencerhillpress.com

Finn Finnegan

Darby Karchut

Also available as an ebook • **SPENCER HILL PRESS** • spencerhillpress.com

About the Author

Rhys A Jones was born in 1955 and grew up in a mining village in South Wales with his nose in a book and his head in the clouds. He managed to subdue his imagination long enough to carve out a career in medicine, writing whenever the chance arose.

In 1994, writing as Dylan Jones, he published his first thriller for adults, *Thicker Than Water,* which was subsequently made into a film by the BBC.

A growing desire to move away from adult thrillers and write for children is what currently preoccupies him. *The Obsidian Pebble* is the first book featuring Oscar Chambers and the 'haunted house' he and his mother have inherited. Rhys A Jones has three grown up children and lives in darkest West Wales with his understanding (very) wife.

23216059R00189